Defenseless

Defenseless

Celeste Marsella

A DELL BOOK

DEFENSELESS
A Dell Book / October 2008

Published by
Bantam Dell
A Division of Random House, Inc.
New York, New York

This is a work of fiction. Names, characters, places, and
incidents either are the product of the author's imagination
or are used fictitiously. Any resemblance to actual persons,
living or dead, events, or locales is entirely coincidental.

Dell is a registered trademark of Random House, Inc., and
the colophon is a trademark of Random House, Inc.

ISBN 978-0-440-24466-0

Printed in the United States of America
Published simultaneously in Canada

www.bantamdell.com

10 9 8 7 6 5 4 3 2 1

To my late sister Luisa for being the emotional catalyst to get me started; to my sister Pia for being my indefatigable brainstorming partner; to my brother Gregory for his edgy editing; and for my brother Stacy just for being who he is

CHAPTER ONE

◦◦◦

The Brethren

THE FIRST TIME I WALKED into an autopsy room I tried to convince myself that my sweaty palms were due to the rubber surgical gloves I was required to wear rather than an irrational fear that death could float across the room like an airborne virus and infect me. Five years ago, still in my twenties, I was not yet immune to the disease of death.

The only bodies I'd ever seen had been waked in Italian funeral homes, where the dead had been preserved, prettied, and then gift-packed like keepsake dolls in silk-lined caskets. Death at the morgue was different. Still warm and pulsating, these freshly passé bodies had been scooped off the streets only hours before and dropped, rude and bloody, on stainless steel tables. Back then I still believed in souls, resisting the scientific proposition that after a person's last breath his humanity disappeared into thin air like the smoke trailing a cigarette. So I used to think that if I kept still and silent I could tune into those frequencies used by the transitionally dead to communicate. But before long I was asking myself: What would the recently departed, assuming an afterlife, really want to say to us? *Greetings, Attorney Melone. Telegram from the hereafter: The transition process was a bit messy but death turned out to be no sweat. Really enjoying myself here. Life on earth is just a two-minute test drive for the real thing. See you soon!*

Right. And postcard to follow.

A Manhattan kindergartner could have told me I was fooling myself. I had to face it. If death was communicating, I wasn't on its mailing list. And after a few years of seeing corpses unzipped from plastic bags and sliced open, their innards scooped out and dissected, reality hit. The dead strangers on those metal tables were only shells ready to be cracked open, cleaned out, then either flame-charred or canned for underground storage.

So there I was, nicely calloused, in my fifth year as an assistant attorney general in Rhode Island, when three of my colleagues and I agreed to meet for an après-work dinner at the Red Fez. The Fez was number five on a list of ten "Do Not Visit" establishments that RI assistant attorney generals were forbidden to patronize because of the restaurants' alleged "ties to organized crime." And precisely because of its off-limits status to AAGs, the Fez had briskly evolved into our de facto secret clubhouse. With its Middle Eastern fare and Iranian owners, the Fez must have seemed the perfect underworld hangout for dumb Rhode Island mobsters trying to keep a low profile by avoiding all restaurants with capellini on the menu. The "organized crime" prohibition notwithstanding, my friends and I agreed to meet there at 11 p.m. At that hour midweek we were certain no one in our social or work circles would see us.

The Fez was decorated more or less like Hell—a windowless cave, carpeted, wallpapered, and furnished in deep reds, ominously lit from below by table candles and from above by twenty-five-watt pendant bulbs shrouded in burgundy faux-silk shades that hovered like dire crimson vultures in wait. Our male colleagues at the AG's office—those who were aware of our clandestine Sabbats—not so affectionately referred to the Fez as our "little red whorehouse."

The Fez was quartered in a seedy back alley of downtown Providence, a threatening locale even on a bustling workday. Under a moonless, starless, asphalt black sky I headed over the river walk. Halfway there I saw the girls standing at the corner of Pine Street, ready to cross into the alley. The gang. My brethren. Laurie Stein, Shannon Lynch, Beth Earles, and me, Assistant Attorney General Marianna Melone. Beth ran up to kiss me hello on the cheek, walking me back to Laurie and Shannon, neither of whom bothered to turn around. Working together for the past five years, we had long ago settled into sibling-like familiarity. Our hellos consisted of grunts and a few obscenities as I fell into perfect marching order and we continued down the block.

Gun-shy about advertising our patronage of the shady, off-limits dive, we took a circuitous safari around the back of a closed package store named Hanratty's, where we lined up in front of a badly weather-beaten neon display whose bloodred tubes immediately began taunting us, flickering on and off with a grating buzz.

"A smoke before we go in?" Shannon said, leaning

her six-foot frame against Hanratty's filthy glass window in front of a glowing Budweiser sign. "These insidious no-smoking laws are going to drive me to drugs. At least heroin I can do *inside* the bar."

"As if anyone at the Fez ever stops *us* from smoking," Laurie remarked.

"AAGs," I added. "Membership has its benefits."

Camel filtereds were passed back and forth in the deep brown murk of night, and we smoked them piggishly like floozies on a break. Only Beth, the sole nonlawyer among us, abstained from the nicotine orgy, rattling on about work and whether or not she should chuck the paralegal nonsense and bite the law school bullet.

Laurie counseled Beth. "No-brainer, you little pigeon. With all that research under your belt, you've already forgotten more law than you'll ever need to try a case. You might as well be charming jurors with those baby blues and commanding the same dough as us."

"Forget the money," I sputtered halfway through a particularly ferocious drag. "Being able to tell Piganno off is worth the three years' toil at an accredited law school." I was referring disparagingly to our boss, Attorney General Vincent Piganno. "Until you have a JD after your name"— I tapped ash onto the pavement—"you can only give him the finger *behind* his back."

"Let's eat," Shannon said, tossing her cigarette.

I took a healthy drag of mine and added my butt to hers in the street. We trod half a block farther into the alley and descended the stairs to the Fez, walking straight to the back to set up our usual spot at the bar. Joe, the omnipresent bartender (indeed, he looked as if he never slept), immediately dealt us four sticky coasters and waited, with that embalmed look on his face, for our order.

"Same all around," ordered Shannon, whereupon Joe promptly snapped the tops off four Heinekens and set the bottles onto the soggy coasters.

None of us felt compelled to make idle conversation, or, for that matter, any conversation, especially at eleven o'clock at night after a hard day's work. More often than not I was the one sparking the banter—turning the group's attention to something inanely philosophical, always searching for the deeper meaning of things, trying to get a rise out of my friends, to provoke them or, at the very least, to make them laugh.

"Jurisprudence," I said into the smoke-filled room. "What is it?"

Three pairs of eyes stared into the darkness. The pair shrouded in men's metal Ray-Bans belonged to Shannon. She leaned away from the bar and whipped off the glasses, pointing them at me like a loaded pistol. "Who gives a crap?"

But I forged ahead. "Four educated women in the legal profession, and not one of us has a clue about the meaning of jurisprudence."

Shannon threw the sunglasses down on the bar and narrowed her bloodshot blue eyes. "Lasso your thongs, girls. Saint Mari is going AWOL again."

"Well, does anyone know?" I insisted.

"I do." Beth lectured, "Jurisprudence is the science of positive laws and their relationship to legal ethics. I had to take a course in it for my paralegal degree. It's the set of principles upon which legal rules are based."

"Wow," I said in a flash of crystalline cognizance. "Maybe subconsciously I'm questioning my ethical qualifications to practice law. Come to think of it, maybe the process is completely conscious. All this death and gore we deal with daily could be turning me inside out psycho-logically, slaughtering my soul, as it were."

"Oh, Mari," Beth said. "You just need a vacation."

Shannon retrieved her all-season sunglasses from the bar and hooked them into her terrycloth-short hair, which was bleached to within an inch of its protein-deficient life. She grunted. "Here's the thing, girls. Mari is ill. Her compulsive morgue visits have rotted out her weak mind and her Paxil prescription ran out last week. No one cares what juris*fucking*prudence means, and Mari just *thinks* she cares because she's in drug withdrawal."

"But in fact, Shannon," I said, "I'm not taking antide-pressants; whether or not I should be is another question altogether. And as you very well know, I visit morgues pretrial only so I can fire up the jury's rage quotient—"

"Oh, shut up," Shannon said. "You're a necro-freak with those damn morgue visits of yours. If you aren't on drugs, you should be. Keep the beers coming, Joe," she said to the bartender, who had returned just in time for this specious diatribe of mine regarding the general il-literacy of most lawyers. "On second thought," Shannon said, "get me a double Vox, straight up with olives."

It was shaping up to be a typical night.

An hour later we were all smashed on various forms of alcoholic refreshment, and we hadn't even ordered dinner yet.

"It's your fault. You started the switch from beer to vodka," Beth croaked at Shannon. "We need some food."

At the mention of calories, I reached for Shannon's pack of Camels to assuage a vociferous oral fixation.

Beth looked primly at me, then turned quickly away. She admonished me from behind the fall of her shoulder-length blonde mane. "And you, with the cigarettes. I'm the only clean one here."

"You're becoming an old maid, Beth."

Back her eyes shot, granting each of us a quick zoom-view of their intense violet-blue. "I don't see wedding bands on any of your fingers either."

"Hey, did you hear that one about WASP vitamins?" Shannon said. "Sherry and a Dunhill after each meal."

"Yeah, and Beth never gets drunk because she was suckled on WASP breast milk that has the alcoholic content of a dry martini," cracked Laurie. "Jews, on the other hand, don't drink that much."

"What are you then, *Miss Stein*?" Beth said. "Adopted?"

Laurie huffed a tough laugh as she pulled her hair out from behind her ears to cover the scar running down her right cheek, a souvenir from a defendant who'd smuggled a knife into court in the days before the security system was upgraded. She was sensitive to the five-inch scar only when she was on trial or in public. Back at the office she'd pull her shoulder-length hair into a ponytail and never wear a smidgen of makeup. Secure, she had no interest in plaudits or lipgloss.

The four of us comprised an elite female menagerie at the AG's office. No, we weren't gay—weren't white charmed witches in a sex coven—but we were perhaps as close as you could get to that sort of place without blushing. Though we'd been coming to the Fez for five years, I now looked around the greasy downtown dive as if seeing it for the first time. It was damp. It smelled like a bus station urinal with essence of sweet onion flatulence. The cooks had hairy hands, sweaty chests, and foreheads creased with cystic acne. I loved the place: its relentless drawing of strangers into the fold; that mysterious way its clientele fell into the role of long-lost relatives at a family reunion.

Shannon zeroed in on the bartender with bull's-eye intensity, harnessing her tits. "Okay, Joe, wipe your drool off the bar and score me a couple of olives for this watered-down Popov you're passing off as Vox!"

"I think I'm hanging around with you shiksas too much," Laurie complained. "Next thing you know I'll be sneaking into church to sip wine at communion."

"Amen," said Shannon. She raised her glass for our communal toast.

We drank. We ordered. We ate. We drank more. I wondered silently whether Paxil might not indeed improve my graver moods. And but for a brief follow-on to the continuing disputation between Laurie and Shannon as to which one of them would try in court the double rape/mutilation of three unfortunate twelve-year-old boys, we ate dinner in relative silence. It had been one of those long, dark days where each of us had been buried up to our necks in murder cases and the less aberrant criminally negligent homicides. We were tired, hungry, burnt out.

Shannon was the first to suggest we call it a night. Mouthing an unlit Camel cigarette as if it were an appendage of her latest boyfriend, she signaled to Joe to add up the damage to our cash tab. "I'm going for fresh air and a smoke. I'm beat. I'm toast."

Laurie dropped a fifty on the bar and ambled to the exit. In tacit agreement the rest of us made our cash deposits, rose noisily, and followed her out, sowing in our wake the dissonant smell of various perfumes, the clacking of three pairs of high heels, and a chorus of Vera Wang bangle bracelets.

We trekked down the street in a row, Laurie leading, and Shannon lighting up as soon as she hit the night air. It was now an hour after last call at the downtown bars and accordingly the alley off Pine Street was deserted. Too tired to disobey a traffic light, we waited at the curb of the empty street for the light to change. We watched the light change to red as one car whizzed past us, then as we began to cross, a second vehicle sped into sight, ran the red light, and then deliberately slowed in front of us. Beth backpedaled to the curb and I tensed involuntarily, ready for some youthful Comanche to roll down his window and begin hurling context-appropriate degradation along the lines of which of us would oblige him with the cheapest blow job, when to everyone's surprise the front passenger door swung open and the thunder of an electric guitar from the car's bass speakers boomed and rattled our attention away from the driver. Beth was the first to scream.

I jerked my head in her direction and felt Laurie's arm strike my chest.

"Stop!" Laurie ordered someone. "*Stop!*"

I turned in slow motion back to the car and watched it peel away as a nauseating bundled mass rolled ponderously into the alley.

But I did not really see that car. I could not for the life of me have identified its color or model or provided a single character on its plate. In fact I did not know precisely what I was witnessing yet, nor could I have appended a name to the thing that had galumphed out of the car's cockpit onto the pavement and was now commanding all our attention.

Shannon's reflexes proved the quickest of a paralyzed lot. After a second or two of unbearable tension she clambered into the street and leaned over the dark mass: a human form, flopped over at the waist into a sitting position. A blood-drenched arm lay outstretched in the street as if the thing were trying to hold itself up.

"Bloody. It's still bleeding," Shannon said, appearing amazed at the sound of her own voice. "Whatever it is."

"Out of the way! Shannon, move!" I screamed, my limbs stuck fast to the sidewalk.

It was Laurie who yanked Shannon to safety a blink before the massive black SUV slammed into the bloody mess and sent it hurtling through the air. Released from its dingy blanket, a butter-colored body seemed to float across the street like a leaf before finally belying its weightlessness and smashing halfway through the windshield of a parked car.

CHAPTER TWO

Road Trip

BETH BROKE OUR GLASSY TRANCE. "A body," she breathed.

The rest of us focused our attention across the street where through the shattered windshield of the parked car, the lifeless thing was projecting like a rocket.

Shannon stepped quickly away from the curb. She looked over her shoulder back into the safe haven of the alley. With her mile-long legs, she began striding in that direction.

"Shannon?" I whispered.

"Go," Laurie hissed, pushing me forward from behind. She and Shannon were sharing brain waves. She shook her head violently. "The SUV might spot us."

Taking their cue, Beth and I started walking too, all in single file, rushing while trying not to appear to be doing anything other than going home from a late night out.

It was back in front of Hanratty's Liquors that Laurie spoke up, nodding her head aggressively as if to assure herself of the ethical implications of leaving the scene and evading the soon-to-be-arriving cops. "Shannon's right. Someone from the AG's office will be assigned to this case. And if we're the only witnesses, the state has to hire independent counsel to prosecute it. We'll have to explain what we were doing drunk after midnight in downtown Providence at an off-limits bar. Hey, we didn't really see anything worth reporting anyway. Did we?"

Shannon's glazed eyes were peeled to the distant darkness. Laurie didn't wait for a consensus before delivering her summation.

"I'm going alone to the office to get my car and come back for you. The four of us walking together attracts too much attention." Her head poked up like a feral cat sensing danger. "Listen—*Christ*, I can already hear the sirens—"

"*Go*," Shannon ordered Laurie. "We've got to scram fast."

Laurie pedaled off in her flats, hyperventilating and heroic, looking back once to confirm we were really there and waiting for her, still a team. Shannon was standing up straight, fearless, like always, and pulling her Camels out of her jacket pocket.

Beth, small and shivering, hugged herself and again declined a smoke. "We can't just pretend we didn't see anything."

Shannon puffed hard. "Don't be a baby. We just got shitfaced at a Do Not Visit bar and it's after one in the morning. You know what a defense attorney will do to us on a witness stand?"

"Yeah, but . . ." I stepped in. "Beth might be right this time. If we're not careful, tonight will come back to haunt us—"

Shannon stabbed her cigarette at me. "Why? Because

we saw the body being dumped? What else did we really see?"

"The car," Beth said. "We saw the car speed away. I'm not an AAG. I can't try the case. *I* should give them a statement."

Shannon shook her head, looking at me to explain to Beth why none of us could admit our presence on the scene. At that moment, despite the fact that we were about to get behind the wheels of our cars and drive home, we would have, to the man, flunked Breathalyzer tests, Beth included. And AAG employees entrusted with enforcing the laws of the community aren't permitted to carouse after midnight emptying vodka bottles in off-limits bars in the middle of downtown Providence. Any hypothetical statements we swore out would be discredited, lambasted left and right on the witness stand by even a third-rate defense attorney. Whether or not we ended up losing our jobs, our reputations would still be shredded, composted, and turned into low-grade garden mulch. And for what? Per Laurie's persuasive analysis, we hadn't seen a thing that would help nail the bastard, and coming forward as witnesses might even *help* his case.

"Okay, Beth," I said. "Morally you're right, but I think I'm getting Shannon's gist. Here's the scenario. The cops are going to ask you exactly where you were tonight *and who you were with*. Will you lie to protect us? It's still perjury even though it's only a statement to the cops."

Her eyes narrowed.

"And did you really see the car, Beth? The car that dumped the body? What make was it? Model? Color?"

She thought a second and shook her head, then answered softly, "It was right there in front of us. I should have seen it. The color at least."

"Neither did I," I said. "Or Laurie or Shannon, I'm guessing. We were all too busy staring at the thing being tossed from it. And did anyone see the driver? A face? Male or female?"

I knew the answer, but gave Beth a second of silence to mull it over.

"See?" I plowed ahead. "Nothing we say is going to help. And in fact, AAGs as witnesses could turn the case into such a public fiasco that the perp will find some oily defense lawyer to get him off on a technicality."

Beth shook her head. "But isn't *this* a crime, not saying anything—"

"Less so," Shannon said. "And nothing's gained by coming forward. Evidence-wise, we didn't see much, and there's way too much to lose—including the case. You understand what a *mistrial* is, right?"

Beth neither answered nor nodded in assent. She was unconvinced but had no counterarguments. As luck would have it, I, deep in my homegrown Roman Catholic soul, agreed with Beth. My papist upbringing was taking the form of a wily guilt ghost, a moral hot flash. My instincts were to tell the truth and let the cards fall where they might. But it wasn't only *my* reputation that would get tossed in the dung heap if I came forward and fessed up to the authorities; Laurie, Shannon, and Beth would end up garbage-side too, rotting right behind me on the welfare line. And that responsibility I wouldn't bear alone. So straight into the icy waters of the conspiracy to obstruct justice, I plunged headfirst.

Two more minutes of chilly silence followed before Laurie pulled up to the curb in her antique VW bug. We piled in silently. None of us said a word as we made the thirty-second ride to the AG's lot.

Once alongside my Jeep, Laurie shifted her car into park and spoke over the idling engine.

"There's a dozen cruisers there already," she told us. "Dumbshit Detective O'Rourke was at the body while I was being waved through the intersection at Dorrance Street. I hope he doesn't screw the report up."

Fear over our narrow escape was already inching after us like a creeping oil spill. We slinked into our respective cars and drove home to wait for the morning news.

NEXT DAY, AS SOON as I arrived for work, my boss AG Vince Piganno called me into his office. When I walked through his open doorway, he was on the phone.

"*. . . and you don't have a fucking clue what I have in store for you, you miserable cocksucker!*"

Vince slammed the receiver into its cradle and gave me a rare, juicy smile. "Have a seat."

I was too hopped up on adrenaline to sit. I remained standing while Vince recited the sparse details of the previous night's big news event. A coed from nearby Holton College by the name of Melinda Hastings had been hit by a drunk driver in downtown Providence while she was lying in the middle of a one-way alley, apparently already dead and cocooned in a bloody blanket. The body, faceless and mangled, was found torpedoed through the windshield of a parked car. The bloodied blanket was recovered nearby.

"How in hell do you think that happened?" As if trying to re-create the scene, Vince was staring out his window overlooking South Main Street, a Merit menthol cigarette stuck between the yellowed fingers of his right hand.

I thought to myself, A *girl by the name of Melinda Hastings.*

"Who dumped her there?" he went on insistently. "And how does she end up smashed through a parked car?"

Vince Piganno, or "Pig" as we called him behind his back, was short, stocky, and muscular, a purebred bulldog. He seemed to pant and drool as he fired these routine-sounding questions at me.

"And what I can't figure out is why nobody *sees* a body get dumped."

"It was in an alley after one, Vince."

"Yeah. So it was. Almost one-fifteen to be exact." He stubbed his cigarette out, peering at me with his muddy brown eyes. "What is this anyway?" he barked at me. "Have you already seen the report?"

Here was my moment of truth. Now was the time to come clean, fess up to Vince. The girls would understand. Eventually. Maybe.

"And what is it with you this morning? You look sick. Are you coming down with something?"

"No, no. Nothing, Vince. I'm tired, you know. Kind of weary, that's all."

"Yeah, I think you're *kind of* hu over, looks like to me."

"Vince, can we talk a minute?"

Vince seemed to wince at the premonition of an impending touchy-feely moment. His facial expression and silence had all the indicia of downright terror at the possibility that I might break down in tears, or worse, want to give him a big hug.

"Vince, sometimes things happen you have no control over. An innocent act—like throwing a match into the street and it catches fire on a tossed gum wrapper—and the next thing you know the entire city is up in flames, a conflagration of events that blow up faster than you can control them—"

"Shut up, *Meloni*. I don't have time for your version of Dante's *Inferno*." He lit another Merit with a very pretty sterling lighter. "Clear your calendar. I want you buried in this Holton case up to your neck."

Vince refused to call me Melone with a silent *e*. He'd look at me as if he'd just stepped in fresh dog crap and say, "If you don't pronounce that *e* at the end, Melone sounds like a fucking *Irish* name. You think being Irish is better than Italian? " When Vince said "Melone," he said it with an ending *i*, and punched his voice up a notch, smashing the last voweled syllable in my face like a carnival cream pie.

"But why me? I don't want this case. Give it to Jeff. He's a Holton alumnus."

"Jeff Kendall's as dumb as a doorknob and I don't trust him because he *is* an alum." He leaned over his desk. "And don't you repeat that." Sitting back with the slit eyes of a skeptic, Piganno went on, "And why don't you want it? You're always begging for the high-profile cases. Suddenly you're shy?"

"No, but . . . well . . ."

"I want *you* on this because you're one of my smartest AAGs. You got a lot a class and you don't swear as much as these other assholes. And with that fake Irish name you adopted, Carlyle'll think you're one of *them*. And bringing him down to his bony knees will be sweeter if I do it with an *Italian girl from the Hill*."

Dean Kenneth O. Carlyle, the head honcho at Holton, was Joker to Vince's Batman. Their ongoing feud was a minor subplot in the old Italian-WASP power play in little Rhody. As in a gang war, one of these factions was always trying to corner the market on power in our small state.

"What is it with you and Carlyle? It can't just be that he's ethnophobic."

"*Ethnophobic.* Hah! I like that, Meloni. You're a real stitch." Vince's smile drained from his face. "It's nothing personal. But I just got off the phone with him. The dead kid's folks want a powwow with us. You're going on a road trip to Holton College and I gotta tell you what to pack."

My head began to spin as it always did when Vince was loading his dueling pistol to send me out at sunrise. And he always seemed to pick me for the away games, those times when he needed an emissary from the AG's office to meet with the public. It must be all that *class* he thought I had; I "cleaned up" well. But there was no way I was going over to Holton. No way I was taking this case. There was absolutely no ethical way this scenario could play out without me ending up at the bitter end of the employment line.

"Not me. I can't go there. I'm not prosecuting this case. Why? Why, you ask? Because . . . Because I'll get too emotional over it." I flopped in a chair and breathed deep, got up, and immediately threw myself into another chair. "See, this is the problem, Vince. *I saw this girl get hit by a car and thrown across the street—*"

"I don't want to hear about your troubled childhood. Tell it to the shrinks." As he spoke, he threw papers around his desk in search of something. A pink message slip appeared in his chubby fist. "*Shit.* Here the *fuck* it is." Vince donned a pair of gold-rimmed reading glasses, so smudged I could barely see his eyes through the lenses. "You're gonna meet with the girl's parents . . . and with that no-good-son-of-a-goddamn-bitch-bastard-prick, Dean-fucking-Carlyle."

I winced at his biologically limited vocabulary.

"The bum's office. Holton College. Ten a.m. Be there, or be fired."

"You aren't listening to me, Vince. This girl from Holton. She rolled out of the car like a sack of garbage and then flew through the air like a fly ball into the parked car across the street—"

"Yup, and she's lying on a slab in the morgue, which reminds me, get over there now. O'Rourke's waiting on you for the autopsy. I want the results before Carlyle gets them."

The morgue. Okay. Yes, I could do that. Go to the morgue. Vince unwittingly gave me a brief reprieve from my confessional. I now had an extra twelve hours to see the girls and run my plan by them first: I would give Vince an abridged version of the previous night's events. First thing in the morning I would tell him that I alone saw the Hastings body get dumped. I would take the hit by myself and let the girls rally behind me to keep Vince from firing me. It was the only chance we all had of getting out of this mess in one undivided piece.

Tomorrow. In good Scarlett O'Hara fashion, I'd worry about it tomorrow.

CHAPTER THREE

Morgue 101

FROM VINCE'S OFFICE I went straight to the Rhode Island morgue, where I found not just Detective O'Rourke from the Providence Police Department but the dead girl, whose body lay supine before me in the freezing-cold autopsy room. It was now my job to whip up a soufflé of evidence against an unknown assailant and, to make Vince happy, try to implicate Holton College in a nightmarish murder whose aftermath I had witnessed.

I looked across the room at the mass of bloody flesh on the table and breathed in the familiar scent of refrigerated steel, the feeble odor of pine disinfectant, and the sweet sticky humidity of blood and organs. I went wobbly on my feet, feeling my knees weaken. A trickle of sweat traced its way down the hollow of my chest. I did not want to approach the girl's body but there was no exit for me now, nothing I could do but move forward and do my job.

"You all right?" called out O'Rourke. "You're white as a ghost."

He remained near the door as I marched to the counter where boxes of rubber gloves in assorted sizes were stacked up against the wall. I thrust my hand into the open box marked Medium and extracted two pair. As far as I knew, I was the only prosecutor with this persistent need to touch the bodies of the dead, but we were all required to pull gloves over our hands anyway, not so much for our own protection but to protect the dead from the only thing they had left to give us: evidence.

Draped in the crisp cotton sheeting of a tea party, the high stainless steel table lay smack in the middle of the room under a stark white light. I walked closer. The face of the young woman was pretty much gone—a mere memory now in her parents' minds—but I knew from the chart that she was eighteen, two years older than my little sister Cassie. This thing before me, the tissues and bones constituting the child's remains, was naked and ready for autopsy. Lucky Dack, an investigator from the state medical examiner's office, usually accompanied the bodies from the scene and then undressed them in preparation for the postmortem. But in bona fide murder cases like this one, no one was permitted to touch the corpse until the forensic physicians had done their thing. Some of the best evidence is found on clothing and skin.

Lucky Dack and I had gotten to know each other pretty well over the years. He'd taught me much of what I knew about real death—the kind that hadn't been dressed up in its Sunday best yet. Lucky had evidently left Detective O'Rourke in my care knowing I'd stop O'Rourke from doing anything stupid. By protocol we weren't supposed to be left alone with the bodies. But there was no need to worry about O'Rourke. He wasn't going to budge from the counter he was leaning against. His stomach for death, especially the messy kind, was on a scale with his taste for steak tartare. On that day O'Rourke's presence was required because, as luck would have it, he'd been around the corner at the local Dunkin' Donuts having a gratis Coolata when the body took flight. He'd been right there with us. Barely yards away.

I shot a pair of gloves over to him, aiming at his head, then pulled my own high over the cuffs of my crisp white shirt. I pressed my belly muscles into the table's rolled edge, looking at the young body, still lank in its final stages of leveling off at adulthood. Even though, post-expiration, modesty shouldn't matter, I was embarrassed for her. I wanted to flip a sheet over her nipples, still a live translucent pink, and wanted to cover her pubic area, to protect it now, belatedly, its patch of wiry pubic hair matted down and sticky with fluid. Her head was oddly bloodless: a china doll whose face had cracked and fallen away.

As soon as O'Rourke saw me wince at the shattered mass that had been the girl's face, he addressed me from the distant safety of the counters.

"A drunk in a Cadillac Escalade struck her in that alley off Pine Street. Then the girl's head scored a bull's-eye on the windshield of a neon blue Eclipse. Went through it like a projectile. That's how I found her. Her head inside the windshield, body spread over the hood. Here." He picked up a file from one of the counters, removing several photographs. "Did you see these?"

In the flesh, a few minutes before you.

He held the photos out to me like an overweight kid showing off stolen candy. I walked over and plucked them out of his gloved hand.

In the first picture the girl looked like she'd been trying

to fly. Facedown on the bright blue car hood in her yellow summer dress, her arms and legs spread open like butterfly wings. Her head simply disappeared, plunged into that other, invisible world past the windshield. *Through the looking glass*, the voice in my head said. Time had weirdly slowed for me. I walked back to the steel table as if the empty air had become crystalline-clear water I was wading through. O'Rourke continued his juicy slideshow narrative, and his words took on vivid, preternatural colors in my mind. Maybe I was coming down with something. Or it was a hangover from the night before. Or some different, some new kind of misery . . .

"Look at the shots taken from inside the car. I bet the judge won't let you show those, right? A mush of face on the dashboard. But Piganno'll love it. Your boss hit pay dirt this time."

I flipped through the pictures. Vince grooved on the gory ones. The girl's face was raw hamburger sprinkled with gray brains, sauced with blood. By the time the photographer had shown up to shoot the film, whatever liquids were still inside the kid had drained from her head wounds into the car, pooling on the floor. One of her cornflower blue eyes was hanging from its socket. I came out of my daze to discover I was gritting my teeth. I took three or four enormous breaths and then had what felt like another hot flash.

I placed the snapshots on the autopsy table next to the girl's body and then heard O'Rourke say, "Hi, Doc." I looked up.

A young man in blue surgical scrubs walked in and stepped solemnly to the table. The downtown medical examiners were unfailingly polite, though the younger of them often resented the intrusions of nonmedical personnel.

T. Gannon, MD, his name badge read. He looked like he was in his late twenties and was probably in forensic pathology training at Brown University Medical School. Workmanlike he leaned over the lump of cherry Jell-O and purple Play-Doh that was the girl's face and blew air out of his lips like he'd just broken the record for a three-mile run.

"You guys done with her? The parents want her body transported to the funeral home ASAP, and I'm ready to start."

Murmuring a noncommittal something, I looked closely at her toenails, polished a purplish color my sister Cassie would have favored. Appallingly, I put myself in her parents' place and, struggling against myself, imagined my mother in front of a mutilated Cassie or me. No wailing, no tears, just an icy calm that replaced the portion of my mother's personality already beginning to die with her child. Under my breath I cursed myself for feeling anything at all, for projecting this upending scenario into my own so far straight-up, no-rocks life. I was supposed to be a professional.

Dr. Gannon watched me. "You're Mari Melone, aren't you?"

I nodded.

While I retrieved the Polaroids from the table, he removed the sheet from under her body by rolling her over to her side. "Is something wrong?" he said.

"She's dead. And I've got this out-of-body feeling that I'll be joining her soon."

"Do you always get emotional about your cases? You'll burn out fast that way."

"I'm already charcoaled on this one."

Gannon lifted a scalpel from his table of tools.

"What's this white junk on her pubic hair?" I asked.

"Semen, I'd guess. But nothing's definitive. At least until the labs are processed."

Gannon wouldn't look at me. Lifting a scalpel to the girl's chest, he sank it deeply into her sternum and then smoothly dragged it through skin, fat, and muscle until he had opened the girl right down to her navel.

"That's it for me," the up-to-now vigilant Detective O'Rourke announced softly. He pulled his hands out of his pockets and peeled off his pristine rubber gloves, throwing them into the hazardous waste can by the door. "See you all later. I don't stay for the parts exhibit."

Gannon began an inspection of her organs through her ribs. I waited. I needed to know where the internal injuries were. How she'd been killed. Her whole nightmare might have been a matter of just seconds, but arguing to the jury that this kid was alive and conscious when she was raped and then hit by the SUV . . . Well, I was a prosecutor after all, and I liked an angry jury.

"Torso-wise we've got one punctured lung. I can see that already," the doctor said. "A lot of broken ribs, but very little hemorrhaging. I got a feeling she was already dead when she was dumped and hit."

Yeah, we thought she was too.

After the wave of nausea passed, I asked Gannon about the tremendous amount of blood in the second car. "Where'd that come from if she was already dead?"

"Drained from the open skull. She wouldn't need a beating heart for that. Gravity does the trick."

"So what then? Give me the timeline, Doc."

Gannon gave me a slightly sour look. "I'm waiting on toxicology."

"Will you call me as soon as you know?"

"Why do you show up for these autopsies, Attorney Melone? The other assistant AGs just wait for the report."

"It impassions my trials. You know the old adage. A picture's worth a thousand words. The sight of this poor girl makes me want to vomit. And the jury will see that in my face when I'm talking about her. I like bringing some death with me into the courtroom, but I have to come here and get it from you first."

And then there was that glaring issue of Vince ordering me there so he could one-up Carlyle on the findings.

I pulled off my gloves and dropped them in the medical waste can. "What about you? Do you like cutting up dead bodies?"

Gannon cracked an evil smile. "Less pressure than cutting up a live one. But after five years I'd expect you'd have become rather accustomed to death."

"Never. I still can't believe we just disappear. That we take our last breath and that's it."

"That's what religion's for. Some people feel compelled to believe in an afterlife."

"And you?"

He shook his head. "Science does that to you. Nothing happens without a reason. There are no miracles. Until someone comes around and proves me wrong, I'm not going to church."

"How did you know I've been with the AG five years?"

He resumed his cutting, mucking around in the girl's abdomen. "I asked Lucky about you. He respects you a great deal. Says you're the only one over there with a little class."

"No kidding? *Class.* Men so love that word. And all this time I thought it was my legs Lucky respected."

Young Dr. Gannon kept his blood-covered gloves plunged into the body but paused long enough to crack a smile.

"Call me immediately when the labs and tox reports are back."

"You got it."

As Gannon lifted Melinda's stomach into a dish, I flipped my cell phone open and punched speed dial.

"Yo?" Shannon barked.

"You, Laurie, Beth, my office, fifteen minutes."

CHAPTER FOUR

Purgatory

BY THE TIME I got back to my office Shannon had already made herself at home behind my desk.

"This place is a dump. How do you function?"

"Not well. Listen, before the other two get here, I got a plan about Hastings."

"Don't scare me, Mari."

"I'm going to tell Vince about last night."

Shannon lowered her head and squinted. She was cool under pressure. That's what made her such a great trial lawyer. She could keep her emotions buried, whereas mine were always a bubbling volcano.

"I'll tell him I was alone. Worst-case scenario, he fires me. But maybe I'll get a slight reprimand and of course he'll take me off the Hastings case—"

"Shit." She sat up straight. "He assigned the case to *you*?"

I nodded while Beth and Laurie walked through my open doorway, looking from Shannon to me for an update on what they knew had to be about our most recent transgressions.

"Close the door behind you, Beth," Shannon ordered.

Beth obliged and we all waited for Shannon to break the inevitable silence.

"In a word," she said, "absolutely not, Mari. You will do no such thing. And if you don't understand that, let me put it another way. If you tell Vince about last night, I'll break your fucking legs."

"A simple *no* would have sufficed, Shannon."

"Nothing is simple with you, Mari. I've never known anyone who could blow things as out of proportion as you can. Jesus goddamn Christ . . ."

Finally Beth and Laurie got the gist of our meeting. Neither uttered a crippling word, lest it incite Shannon to physical action. I knew Shannon wasn't finished, so I waited. Shannon was tough as an army sergeant breaking in new recruits, but she would never issue an edict and expect us to blindly follow her command. Mainly because, fear of death notwithstanding, we were, in the final analysis of our friendship, all equals. We expected Shannon to support her case, and we knew she would if we merely kept silent and let her continue.

"Together we have more leverage. What's Vince going to do? Fire his entire senior trial team? He'd be forcing his own downfall. He'd have to resign in disgrace. And *that* he would never do. If and when he finds out about this, he'll rally behind us, you'll see. If only to save his own fat butt, he'll save ours too. But you alone, Mari? He'll fire you to save the office. And it would work. You'd be the goddamn sacrificial lamb. And what's the point of that? We'd all still be lying to him. We'd all still be guilty as hell, including you. We either lie together, or tell the truth together. It's the only way through this."

Beth's eyes had become wider and her breathing heavier as she listened to Shannon and realized I had decided to take the hit alone. I assumed Laurie had already figured it out and was doing mach-speed calculations in her head—the pros and cons of my plan. I had to admit, Shannon was winning this case hands down. Hence our continued silence after she closed her case.

"See what I'm saying, Mari? Do you all get it?"

I nodded again. Beth and Laurie, still speechless, nodded too.

"So, you go do whatever Vince wants you to do, and I swear on my old man's soul, may he rest in peace"—she crossed herself—"if at any time we decide that what we did compromises this case, we'll all go to Vince's office, and we'll tell him together."

Career-wise, Shannon was on the right track with her plan, but ethically she was asking me to stay on our circuitous road to purgatory—and possible disbarment. We remained at static odds, staring at each other until Laurie broke the silence.

"Then may I respectfully suggest," she said, "that we take a more active role in actually realizing what it is that we witnessed and how it might connect evidentially to the murderer."

It took us a minute to change gears from Shannon's fury to Laurie's calm conclusion. During our silence, Laurie cogently continued. "We need to keep on top of what the cops are coming up with and make sure that if we have any blanks to fill, we step in and do it. Maybe we did see something and we don't know we saw it . . ."

"And," Beth added, "we won't know that unless we know exactly what the police are finding out."

"Exactly," Laurie said. "We have to help the cops without letting them—or anyone else—know what we're doing."

Shannon wasn't convinced. "Give me a for instance."

"I can't," Laurie answered. "Because if I could tell you that we know something the cops are missing, it would be time for us to go to Vince. But as you just said, we don't know anything more than they do right now, so let's shut our mouths *and keep our jobs* until we do."

CHAPTER FIVE

Dressed for Success

THE NEXT MORNING I was at Holton College waiting to be ushered into Dean Carlyle's office for my meeting with Melinda Hastings's parents. Though I had no scheduled appearances that day, I was dressed up for court. I was most comfortable in Armani suits with loose trousers. Some days I'd don a bold striped tie and depress the thicker male cops with the possibility I was a cross-dresser. Faking androgyny had proved amusing until I started dating (big mistake) my AG colleague Jeff Kendall (the "freak" Shannon figured didn't even belong in a courtroom and the "doorknob" of Vince's reference). Exactly four and a half minutes into our very first date, while standing in the parking lot of Café Nuovo, and before pulling out his AmEx Preferred Rewards Gold Card for so much as a cheap glass of pinot grigio, Jeff cupped my breasts with both his hands and said, "Hmm . . . yeah . . . nice. These will do."

Because of Jeff's clear preference for sexy females, my

cat was out of its bag, and chatty Jeff cleared up publicly the mystery of my sexual identity once and for all. With respect to emotional subtlety, working with men was a no-win situation. Any AKC-registered female standing upright with two arms, two legs, and one head was a potential object of heterosexual lust. Even after dating kiss-and-tell Jeff, I continued to wear my Marlene Dietrich costumes to work, but a closer look at the hem of my trousers would always reveal a spiked pair of Manolo Blahniks or some equally high-heeled podiatric disaster in the making. For the record, I'm philosophically opposed to high heels. Shoes hiked three inches or more are for sexually insecure women or those under five foot eight who are insecure with authority and need to look men in the eyes. Needless to say, I wore spikes so often that my feet ached only in sneakers.

Outside Carlyle's office on the third floor of Langley Hall, I was holding my hands in my lap while perching uncomfortably on the hard edge of a wooden captain's chair padded with cracked red leather. Flanking me were mahogany tables graced with strategically low-lit brass lamps. The air was thick with an ambiance of stale cigar stubs, oiled leather, and musty oriental rugs. Smoking wasn't allowed in campus buildings unless you were Dean Carlyle with your iron-fisted control over administrative personnel and your full professorship to boot. The upper-crusty dean relished lighting up post-embargo Cuban cigars while sitting around with the other big kahunas at Holton—or so Piganno spun it—tossing admission applications into piles labeled "Admit" and "Reject." (*Ethnic last name? Boom! Right into the trashcan with the butts of those bootlegged Havanas that rat-bastard smokes. . . .*)

The door of the dean's sanctum swung wide and out

wafted cold billows of hermetically sealed air tainted subtly by the odor of a humidor.

Kenneth Oberlin Carlyle materialized wizardlike in the doorway.

"Attorney General Melone." He extended his long white fingers. "Welcome to Holton College. I appreciate your coming in on such short notice."

"*Assistant* AG, Dean Carlyle."

Nodding his acquiescence, he gestured me toward a couch, his eyes firmly fixed on my face. Surprisingly, Carlyle didn't immediately neutron-scan my physique for an appraisal of leg length and breast size. Not even a casual ogling of the bosom, which was odd since he was presumably alive and male, though he looked as zaftig as a dried-out corpse. He was gangly and balding, maybe fifty years old, and really not too bad looking for a dead man.

"Brad and Connie Hastings should be arriving momentarily. I'll go check on them now," he said, abruptly leaving the room.

I glanced around his lair. Spread against the far wall was a work area whose computer, fax machine, and VoIP telephone (laid out like pristine surgical equipment on a long, wraparound mahogany desk) whipped up a high-tech effect that contrasted starkly but quite beautifully with the weathered Bokhara rug covering the floor. A Duncan Phyfe couch that I had no reason to believe wasn't the real thing, plus four matching chairs, occupied the foreground. On the room's opposite flank stood a newish-looking wooden conference table of lighter hue, with about a dozen high-backed, camel-colored leather chairs neatly tucked into it. A single long window was divided into a faux walnut gridwork of small panes intended to echo colonial-era New England, though it instead recalled this one particular state mental hospital in Far Rockaway, Queens, that had once scared the hell out of me during a circuitous taxi cab ride to JFK Airport. . . .

Like a good lawyer I'd done my research. Quietly exclusive, Holton was a private four-year college that had been chartered in 1775 with testamentary funds from Jeremiah Dorr Holton's will. Old J.D. had envisioned a free school where young gentleman could come from far and wide for instruction in all areas of "useful and polite literature." Unlike the overwhelming majority of American colleges, Holton had so far resisted all federal and state pecuniary lures; instead of getting into the big-bucks swing of America's diverse new ethnic society, it had resolved to survive on discreet private funding. And survive it did. Thanks to the eventual institution of tuition, Holton College proved able to exist on the interest generated by its nine-million-dollar endowment. And off the government dole, it could discriminate indiscriminately on the basis of race, religion, sex, or whatever the hell it pleased, all without constitutional interference.

Plus the college had a trump card up its sleeve.

Haughty Holton was, after all, a stepping-stone into a kingdom to which almost everyone secretly aspired. Shooting a brace or two of quail with the English gentry and then having the downstairs maids cook it up for dinner; accepting a knighthood alongside Mick Jagger; changing your name à la Ralph Lauren immediately following his bar mitzvah—didn't everyone in his downtrodden heart of hearts want to be an old-money blue blood?

And thereupon, speaking of the blues, mine had just materialized in the open doorway.

The grieving parents of Melinda Hastings entered

the room followed by a grayish-pallored Carlyle, whose facial features suggested a tightly wound jack-in-the-box. "Please, Brad, Connie, meet Miss Melone from the attorney general's office."

I stood, and Mr. and Mrs. Hastings took turns shaking my hand. Carlyle pulled a couple of extra chairs from his conference table, and the Hastingses sat holding hands across the chair arms.

Carlyle spoke first. "Miss Melone has kindly agreed to meet with us privately. First let me say—and I think I speak for the AG's office as well—we're all very sorry for your loss—"

"Ken," Brad Hastings interrupted him, "let's dispense with the formalities." He turned to me. "I—we—did not authorize this invasion of my daughter's body. This damn autopsy—"

His wife shuddered.

"—I want this entire matter closed. Now. Immediately. I want my poor daughter to rest in peace. Is that clear?"

I hadn't uttered a word. Not that any words were coming to my lips. The more Hastings spoke, the less generous I found myself feeling and indeed the less inclined toward polite conversation, blue-blooded company notwithstanding. I was a bit in shock, to say the least. Hastings looked to Carlyle with surprise and concern, puzzled over how poorly groomed I was for our little meeting.

"Ken?" Hastings sang through gritted teeth. "Is there going to be a problem here?"

"Brad. Miss Melone arrived moments before you did. Let's take a breath and relax."

"*I'm* relaxed," I said. "Or at least I was before I got here. And, coincidently, I've been breathing all day, so why don't you fine people tell me what I'm doing here?"

Mrs. Hastings stood and walked over to sit beside me on the couch. She brushed my hand with hers. It was ice cold. "My daughter is dead. My family is devastated. I want it to end here."

Brad Hastings nodded solemnly.

"Mrs. Hastings," I said, "it isn't my decision whether or not to investigate the black-hearted murder of a young woman. There's a brutal maniac out and about in Providence. The city's decision to proceed with an investigation is out of my hands. It's a matter of the law and of public safety."

The girl's father leaned forward, clasping his large preacherly hands. "Who reviews the preliminary evidence? We assumed you have some authority to review things, to make a determination whether the city goes forward."

I flushed, and then felt a bloodlike metallic taste rise to the back of my palate.

"My authority is to determine whether or not a crime was committed, and what fool wouldn't deduce your daughter was murdered? Beyond that, I have little choice but to prosecute the case to the best of my ability. And I don't understand why you wouldn't want to find and punish the guy who—"

"That's just it. I don't give a damn about *the man responsible*," Sire Hastings shot back. "My daughter is dead. Nothing will bring her back. And I don't want her private life laid out in the street like last night's empty liquor bottles. Can I have your assurance of that?"

"Only, sir, if we end up dealing with an abduction by a stranger. That type of investigation wouldn't involve the victim's background."

"Ohhh," Constance Hastings cried out. Her husband

fixed on Carlyle a long hard stare before standing and shepherding his wife aside.

Carlyle stood too. He looked at me and spoke. "Apparently Miss Hastings had either been raped or been subjected to some very rough sex before death. We got a call from the ME's office shortly before you arrived. We're appealing to you to wrap this matter up quickly and quietly."

I was reeling. Dr. Gannon had released the information without contacting me first? The bloody turncoat— as if he or the ME's office had any say about whom the state might choose to prosecute. I leaned forward and whispered in a rage, "She was murdered and then thrown into the street like trash, and you're saying you don't want to find the person *responsible*?"

Mr. and Mrs. Hastings now sidled forward. No one said a thing.

"Are you all crazy?" I said.

The silence was stunning. I was in some nightmarish dream and no one saw the monster lurking behind the trees except me. I looked at the Hastingses, hoping to appeal to a parent's sense of loss. "How could you care more about privacy than you do about avenging your daughter's murder? This maniac has to be found, has to be brought to justice."

Carlyle looked frantically from me to the parents. "That's enough for now—"

"We aren't finished," I said indignantly.

"We are, Miss Melone. The Hastingses don't wish to discuss anything further," Carlyle said.

How the hell did he know they were done? What was I missing?

Mrs. Hastings twisted away from her husband and sat again in the chair facing me. Her body language suggested she had decided to speak. But she wouldn't look at me. Her words fell into her lap like tears.

"Melinda had some problems. We thought she was dealing with them through the Holton Health Services—"

"And indeed she was," Ken added. "Dr. Becker was counseling her regularly."

"Yes, yes. I'm sure this school did everything possible to help her," Mrs. Hastings continued. She refocused her appeal to me. "Privacy is all we have left, Miss Melone. So please allow us to keep this within our family. For the sake of our other children, I don't want this horrific story splashed over the tabloids. And it is tabloid news, isn't it?"

Of course it was. This was just the sort of nightmare Vince drooled over: A *National Enquirer*–type story about a rich Holton College student brutally murdered . . .

"I'm going to get the autopsy report and lab tests," I said.

Mrs. Hastings began openly crying now.

"Please, Miss Melone," Brad Hastings finally said. "Let this go no further. You must understand our position."

Carlyle hovered over Mrs. Hastings, his hands resting on the back of her chair.

I looked from pale face to pale face, trying to gauge Carlyle's and the Hastingses' real motivations, but I got nothing from this Edvard Munch trio except a slight narrowing of Dean Carlyle's eyes. After a second or two of silence Mrs. Hastings stood and joined her husband and Dean Carlyle. The line in the sand had been drawn and there was no point reaching over it to say goodbye. They gave Carlyle a parting glance, then turned and walked out.

Either the performance hadn't been staged for my benefit, or Carlyle saw that it hadn't worked, because his gentleman act was over. He walked to his desk and sat behind it, refusing to honor me with so much as a have-a-nice-day smile. Instead he commenced a paper shuffle where files were removed from one pile and placed into another.

"Miss Melone," he finally said without looking at me, "we're done here for now."

I stifled a brief shiver and made a quick but gracious exit.

CHAPTER SIX

⸺⁂⸺

You and Me, Babe

I HAD PLANNED TO call the ME about the autopsy results as soon as I returned to my office, but when I straggled into my ten-by-ten cubby I spied a faxed report sitting pretty on my desk. It was printed on ME stationery from T. Gannon, MD.

I dialed him up. A teenage-sounding secretary indicated he was busy, but I held the line, informing the ingenue that if she didn't get him on the phone I was coming over in person. I hit the speakerphone button and began deciphering the doc-speak hieroglyphics in the report.

Melinda Hastings, DOB, DOD . . . yada yada yada. As I'd been present for much of the organ retrieval stuff, I flipped past the routine descriptors and went straight to the lab results. Positive for cocaine, cannabis, and some substance called GHB. The path lab report on the white pubic goo confirmed the presence of semen, which of course could be checked for DNA and then compared to records on file for prior offenders.

I heard Gannon's voice on the speaker and picked up the phone.

"What happened to Melinda Hastings? I've got your report in front of me."

"Myoclonic seizure due to an overdose of GHB, or gamma-hydroxybutyric acid, aggravated by exsanguinations. Simply put, the girl was drugged and then raped and cut up. A quick check on semen DNA is negative in the database."

"Cut up?"

"On autopsy I found blade marks on the facial bones. The subsequent car accident hid the wounds, but he apparently sliced her face up pretty good."

"Good work, Doc. Tell me about GHB."

"It's a date-rape drug you can make in your own kitchen. I think they still use it in Europe as an adjunct to anesthesia. We're starting to use it in the States for narcolepsy. In liquid form it's tasteless and has no odor and no color. Perfect for mixing with a cocktail or strong beer. The girl would have gotten nice and relaxed, like being drunk, and then remembered nothing after she woke up, but of course she didn't wake up because she was drugged unconscious and mutilated. Evidentially it looks like you've got yourself one hell of a dead end, if you'll excuse the unfortunate pun."

"What's a myopic seizure?"

"Myoclonic. *Myo* means muscle and *clonus* means rapidly alternating contraction and relaxation—jerking or twitching—of a muscle. What the layperson would think of as an epileptic fit. There were no defensive wounds on her arms, so she may have been unconscious through the whole bloody episode."

"She was cut while she was alive?"

"Wound condition from the knife cuts, where I could find them on what was left of her skull, suggests some time of clotting or healing. She'd need a beating heart for that."

"Holy Christ."

"Calm down, she was probably unconscious from the GHB overdose."

"Don't tell me to *calm down* like I'm being some blubbering overemotional female. Let's put your face through a meat grinder and see how calm you are."

"Actually, Miss Melone, I'm telling you to calm down for your own sake. Doctor's orders."

"Dr. Gannon, some people are born brittle with no angst receptors. Call me genetically defective, but I'm an empathetic sponge."

"Then I advise you keep yourself well soaked to douse the emotional conflagrations rampant in the jobs we have."

"Let's douse the metaphoric repartee. I just left the girl's parents. They seem to want to keep this whole affair hushed. Is there anything I don't know that you're not telling me?"

"Did you ask your boss? Maybe he knows something neither one of us knows."

"Is that right?"

"*Yeah*, it's right. I've heard he pretty much tries to *run* this town. Vince Piganno thinks he's the mayor of Providence even though he lost the election. He's got his hands in everything."

"Yeah, but he draws the line at internal organs. Hey, one more thing. Why was the autopsy report sent to Dean Carlyle at Holton College?"

"The parents requested the information through him,

which they have every right to do. I gave an oral report over the phone and sent the hard copy to you. Did I do something wrong, Miss Melone? Are you going to *sue* me?"

"I don't chase ambulances, so if you didn't do anything criminal, you're safe from me."

"I'm clean as a whistle, Counselor. I took a course in med school on how to stay out of courtrooms as a defendant, and I got an A-plus."

"Remind me to slap a gold star on your cheek next time I see you."

I hung up and grabbed Gannon's report off my desk and walked down the hall to Vince's office, hoping I could convince the boss to lay off Carlyle and Holton until we had more evidence the college was in any way involved. That we still had no good leads in a brutal murder case was another matter.

Vince's door was open. He was sitting at his desk staring into the blue sky outside his window, and he knew it was me without looking.

"What is it?"

I took a seat in front of his desk. "We've got nothing yet, Vince. The ME thinks the girl was drugged, raped, then cut, died from blood loss and then got thrown in the street already dead. But so far, no likelies—and no criminal connection with the college."

Vince snorted, his whole body jerking. "Fucking great." He looked at me as if he were preparing to throw something.

"So far I see no criminal liability on Holton's part, but that doesn't mean they aren't hiding things after the fact. It's a private institution that we can infiltrate only to a point. Is there anything you can think of in this whole scenario that the school could be covering up?"

Vince zeroed in on the view out his window again, his eyes squinting so tight they were almost closed. "I don't put it past that school to hide evidence if it's tending to point back in their direction. If nothing juicy turns up by the end of the week, get Jeff involved. He's got connections over at that dump."

"You mean 'dumb-as-a-doorknob' Jeff? Anyway, what good would that do? Holton isn't going to give us evidence if it points to one of their own students, no matter how many alumni relatives Jeff has."

Vince nodded slowly as his eyes glossed over and his glance swept from me back to his view of South Main Street. "What happened with the girl's parents?"

"They quite openly told me they wanted the whole thing hushed up. Their daughter's privacy is more important to them than finding her killer."

Vince stood and ambled over to the window, looking up toward the East Side of Providence where Holton College buildings lay scattered and camouflaged amid private homes. It seemed that every year another property was added to its growing estate.

"Privacy, huh?" he said. "What do *you* think they're hiding?"

"The girl had drugs and semen in her. I read between the lines of everything they said, and I think the girl had some ongoing drug problems. Maybe they don't want their names splattered all over the news. It could be that simple."

"Drugs. Carlyle's got something to do with this need for privacy, mark my words." Vince returned to his desk and plopped himself in his leather chair so hard I could hear the air whoosh out of the cushions. "That shindig tonight at Jeff's parents' house? Carlyle'll be there." Vince started idly pushing papers around. "Jeff's parents donated a shitload of money to that new library. It's a social event, so cut out the tough-broad routine with Carlyle. I want you to play sweet and stupid-like—"

"Geez, this sounds like one of my dates—"

"—and maybe you let Carlyle think that you and I aren't quite seeing eye to eye on how to proceed with this case—which shouldn't be too hard for you since I know you aren't going to like this idea—"

I felt a sudden autonomic straightening of my spine. "What is it, Vince?"

"I want him to think you're buyable."

"As in bribes?"

Vince took a hefty breath of stale air relieved by a brief coughing fit. "He's hiding something. He would never have let her parents talk to you unless there's much more they're *not* saying." Vince, the mentor and counselor now, rose from his desk and took a seat in the chair near me. With a crooked index finger, he motioned me to take the adjoining seat. Then he leaned even closer. "But you got to go slow with Carlyle. He's gotta think he's smarter than you, and you've got to let him think *he's* in control. But let him fight a little to make you go with him. Don't go easy—"

"This does sound like one of my dates."

He stood and marched back to his desk. "Stop screwing around, Meloni. I'm serious here."

"Vince, you have no idea just how much I'm not screwing around. I don't even want the damn case, so if you're putting me into your range of fire with Carlyle, I want to know what it is between you two. It can't just be politics."

"I lost the mayoral election because of Carlyle and his

fat-moneyed friends on the East Side. That's it. I swear on my grandkids' souls."

I sank in my chair. "You don't have any kids, Vince."

"Yeah, well, whatever."

"And what if Carlyle's got nothing to hide?"

"Then you can get your ass back here and we'll do everything by the book—*kosher*."

"You mean like *legally*? Like actually waiting for the cops to investigate and find someone for us to prosecute?"

My eyes scanned the ceiling. Maybe I was signaling Vince that I thought he was way off with his plan. Or maybe I was looking for an air vent from which to escape his latest lunacy.

"Don't you roll those eyes at me!"

I squirmed in my chair. "Aw, Vince, we could get in big trouble for this. I could be disbarred for attempted bribe taking. Or more precisely, *extortion*."

"No sweat, Meloni. I'm the one who'd be prosecuting you."

"Right, yeah . . ."

"So you take Carlyle aside. It's your word against his what the conversation was about. And remember, you make Carlyle think you've got the authority to do what he needs done. He's got to think he's dealing with a major player over here."

"Promote me to deputy AG. That would give me the power."

"Jeff's got it. You know that."

"Yup. And how much goes in your political contributions pot when you make Jeff deputy AG without even passing Go?"

As Vince was ignoring my last question, a thought

rolled through his brain like a rogue wave. "But I tell you what," he said. "If you pull this off, maybe I'll work on getting you a raise."

"Can I have that in writing?"

"No."

"You know I'll have to suck up to Jeff to get invited tonight. Socially he and I aren't even on speaking terms. He's a brainless octopus."

"Well, start talking pretty to him. And it serves you right. Next time you decide to date someone, make sure he's worth more than the paper his Dun and Bradstreet's printed on."

"I'll have to tell him about getting to Carlyle tonight."

"Tell Jeff as little as possible. This is between you and me, babe, like that Sonny and Cher song goes."

"It's 'I Got You Babe.'"

"What-the-fuck-ever."

CHAPTER SEVEN

Singing the Blues

JEFF KENDALL HERALDED FROM what most people would consider the right side of the tracks. Schooled at Holton, that small and exclusive college in Providence whose main requirement for admission is social elitism, Jeff completed his "undergraduate work" with a GPA that was in the hole and LSAT numbers that were particularly under par, so upon graduation from Holton he was shipped off to a mediocre law school in Maryland from which he barely graduated. On the other hand, Jeff's dad (Geoffrey Senior) was managing partner at Edwards and Tillinghast, Rhode Island's biggest law firm.

Actually *wooed* from his Suffolk County DA job by the Rhode Island AG's office, Jeff had only recently joined us as an assistant prosecutor on his way to deputy AG. His "interview" for the AAG position was held at the Capital Grille Steakhouse in downtown Providence, and several two-and-a-half-pound baked stuffed lobsters later, Jeff was a *special* assistant attorney general. The appointment and celebration followed the same evening, with Bollinger Special Cuvée and a tart made from local Little Compton gooseberries.

With country-club good looks, molting-soft blue eyes, sandy blond hair always a bit messy, and a face that smiled even at rest, Jeff's ladder of success seemed to have fewer steps than other mortals'. Also, Jeff was a regular stitch, to the point where you found yourself laughing at his burps.

And I fell for the pasteboard prince. In a serious lapse of self-respect, I was flattered into thinking I was special. Yes, I was actually so busy wondering what *he* saw in *me* that I forgot to ask myself exactly what it was that I saw in him.

But after a few sterile dates and one not-so-pristine all-nighter (after being blinded by too much wine), I woke up to the punch line of Jeff's jokes and dumped him. The bloke thought I was kidding at first. Who was *I* to break up with *him*? He thought I was playing hard to get. Suffice it to say, I was dead serious. But Jeff was so cocky he refused to accept being rejected and preferred to assume that, eight weeks later, this fatuous date of ours at his parents' house that evening was the real thing. No matter how much I tried to convince him that I was just doing my job, per Vince's orders, Jeff still thought I had changed my mind and was trying to win him back. I may be gullible when it comes to men, but I try to limit myself to one blunder per man: Jeff Kendall and I were history.

So there I was, fresh from giving their flimsy son the old heave-ho, breaking bread with the Kendalls in their manse on tony Prospect Street.

Mr. and Mrs. Kendall were at the head of a highway-length dining table toasting the new library wing. Jeff was

lolling behind them sipping from a wineglass and sporting a hubris-glazed smile comprised of one part anticipatory sexual satisfaction and two parts alcohol. And though
Jeff was the personification of wealth, good looks, and a
Mayflower heritage, he had about as much chance of getting me in bed that night as an addict bottomed out on
crystal meth.

Presently Mrs. Kendall was crinkling her eyes at me
above a glued-on smile, Mr. Kendall was busy blowing
his own horn, and Carlyle's eyes were boring into mine
like a laser beam. Dinner had ended and I reached for a
glass of Roederer abandoned on the sideboard. I had limited myself to two drinks and this serving was my stealthy
second.

Jeff ushered me toward the back of the room. "Hey,
let's get out of here and catch some jazz at Chan's. New
quartet this weekend. Carlyle's not interested in us
tonight."

"Jeff, a Holton coed is lying on a slab at the morgue
and we're two AAGs. Get real. We are the *only* ones
Carlyle is interested in tonight."

"It's hard to believe you're a lawyer, sweetheart. You're
so naive. Money, money, money. The bottom line. The
period at the end of every sentence. The final frontier.
Tonight Carlyle cares only about his new library and the
money."

"Well, since no one's donating my rent payments, I'd
like to keep my friggin' job. So get me up close and personal with Carlyle tonight or I'll cut off your balls in front
of your parents."

Jeff glanced down at his crotch, then shot me an
eerie sidelong glance. He grabbed the champagne flute
from my hand and placed it back on the sideboard as he

ushered me toward the head of the table. Carlyle moved slightly away from Jeff's father to silently announce our arrival.

Jeff and Carlyle did that pat-on-the-back-handshake thing as Carlyle nodded his head at me. "So nice to see you again, Ms. Melone."

My eyes wouldn't cooperate but I smiled as sweetly as I could. "Dean Carlyle, I hope I didn't offend you this morning. This is such a horrible tragedy for the Hastings family. I didn't make it worse for them, did I?"

Carlyle tilted his head at my subtle about-face.

"Jeff," I said, "would you get me a glass of water?"

"Your champagne is on the buffet."

"I'm driving tonight, Jeff. I shouldn't be drinking."

"Oh, yeah, sure." Jeff rolled his eyes at Carlyle. "I'll be right back."

"The rules have to be followed—at least in public—don't you agree?" I said to Carlyle.

"Absolutely."

"I mean sometimes rules are meant for *other* people, but we all have give the appearance of abiding by them or there would be social chaos—anarchy even." I looked deeply into Carlyle's eyes. "That's why I was so harsh with the Hastingses. I couldn't let it appear that the AG's office would bend to pressure—even from understandably bereft parents. But my heart goes out to them, so I promise you I will do everything I can to keep this matter private and within discreet bounds."

"Even if your boss directs you otherwise?"

"Vince is a great AG, but sometimes he lacks a certain finesse."

"A talent you apparently possess."

"Dean, if there is anything I can do to make this horrid

situation more palatable for the Hastingses—and Holton—please let me know." I took a step closer and leaned toward his ear. In a breathy whisper I said, "And you may call me anytime, office or cell. I'm pretty much a free agent there and it won't be a problem."

I slipped a card into his palm with every number on it except my bra size.

Jeff arrived with my glass of ice water. I ignored him as I backed slowly away from Carlyle.

Jeff took me by the elbow and led me away. "If Vince saw you sucking up like that, he'd fire you on the spot."

"Only if you tell him, Jeff." I kissed him on the cheek and he responded by grabbing my ass.

"Make it worth my while," he said.

He placed my water on a table in the foyer as he skated me through the kitchen toward the back door. "Let's get out of here."

"Shouldn't we say goodnight?"

"They won't miss us. They've all had too much to drink." Jeff suddenly detoured down a circuitous brick passageway off the back hall, leaving me at the top of a steep cement stairway.

"Um, Jeff?" I was peering down into darkness.

"Come on down!" he hollered from below. An echo cradled his hollow voice. "I'm getting a few bottles for Chan's. I can't drink their rotgut wine."

"I'm going home." I took a few steps down. "Jeff?"

Impressed and awed by the cavernous stone cellar, I willed my eyesight to adjust to the thick darkness while Jeff was apparently making his worldly selection among the blended grape varietals. He had disappeared into a smaller room at the bottom of the stairs appropriately fa-çaded with a stone archway. I wondered whether Jeff and his historically wealthy family stored the same things in their basement as we did in mine: my first bike with training wheels that my father couldn't bear to part with, a few odd pieces of broken baby furniture that my mother insisted Cassie and I could make use of when we had our own kids, a rusty old water heater . . .

"Jeff?" I called again, stealing a few more steps into the darkness.

"Come here, Mari. I want to show you something."

"No thanks. I've had all the pleasure I can stand for one evening. I'm leaving."

"Come on. I just want to show you my old man's wine collection."

"I don't know a fig about wine, Jeff, so I can't be impressed."

"I have a 1780 bottle of rum from John Brown's collection. The same shit he traded for slaves."

"It sounds stale."

"Come on, be a sport. My old man lives and dies by this shit."

He locked his fingers around my wrist and pulled me into the musty room. Within seconds his mouth was sucking on my lips like a bottom feeder on the side of an algae-laden fish tank. His hands swept under my shirt and laced up through the band of my bra, and before I could even spit out his slimy saliva, my bra was up around my upper chest and Jeff's mouth was busy at my nipple.

I spit, then pushed him away.

"What's the matter, Mari? You don't like the way I kiss?"

"Was that a kiss? I thought it was drool while you were feeling me up."

He laughed demonically and lunged at me again.

Since being polite was no longer an option, I drew my knee up and knocked him against a wall of wine. Several bottles clanged in their shelving but despite Jeff's overactive sexual thirst not a drop was spilled.

"You fuckhead," I said. "They should have traded *you* to Africa. *Mayflower* my ass."

Jeff straightened his hair. "You have no sense of humor, Marianna."

"You, on the other hand, are a real joke."

While he was formulating his next sentence, I left the cellar and walked straight out to my car. As I was trying to get the key into the lock, I heard Jeff's voice behind me.

"Were you with your usual entourage from the office?"

I ignored him and popped the lock open.

"How long were you there? Did you see it? Hastings's body smash through the windshield of the car?"

My hand trembled on the door handle.

"My buddies and I were at Haven Brothers when we heard the sirens and went outside. You were at the corner backing off into the Pine Street alley. Hastings must have been hit while we were eating wieners all-the-way. Awesome."

"Haven Brothers wieners—awesome is right. I'm still trying to uncover their magic sauce recipe," I said, with as much ennui as I could muster.

He apparently didn't appreciate my humor. Or the fact that he couldn't get a rise out of me.

"Who the fuck do you think you are, Melone? You're a homegrown little Rhody girl who thinks she made it big by going to some second-rate law school. You'll never get one up on me."

"I think maybe I did. Screwing you that one time was about as close to a mercy fuck as I'll ever get. And guess what? You flunked the audition."

But as I was verbally beating Jeff up, my multitasking brain realized that if it had been light enough downtown for Jeff to recognize me the night Hastings was murdered, the killer may have seen me too. Would the killer be able to identify me when he met me at the arraignment? I could just see it now. The tables turned as the murderer pointed to me from the defendant's table. "I know *her*! *She* saw me that night and never told anyone. Obstruction of justice! Withholding evidence! Arrest that woman!"

"Why don't you admit it, Mari? You broke up with me because deep in your heart of hearts you're gay. You and those other dykey friends of yours. And don't tell me Shannon's straight. She fucks *anything* that moves."

"If I'm such a dyke then why are you so pissed that I dumped you? Come to think of it, why'd you ask me out to begin with?"

"I was fooled by your tits."

"Suck on this one," I said. "If you come near me again I'll have you arrested for rape."

"Don't flatter yourself. You're all done."

"With you, finally, I hope."

"With me and a lot more."

I climbed into my trusty Jeep and peeled off through the tunnel of Jeff's hopefully hollow threats. As soon as I was out of view, I called Shannon.

"Jeff saw me on Pine Street," I whispered into my phone. "From outside Haven Brothers."

"Christ almighty! He saw Hastings go down too?" she whispered back.

"No. He was with some of his frat friends when they

heard the sirens. When they came out to see what the fracas was about, Jeff recognized me as I was taking off back into the alley."

"Put that little shit on the phone. I'll break his balls and then slit his carotid if he breathes a word of it."

"He's not with me. I'm alone."

"Then what the hell are you whispering for?" she roared. "I'll call Laurie and Beth. Tomorrow morning, eight sharp, the Dial-up for breakfast."

CHAPTER EIGHT

———◦◦◦———

Green Eggs and Spam

THE DIAL-UP MODEM DINER was a dilapidated coffee shop in another hypogenous alley of downtown Providence. This place catered almost exclusively to regulars. On rare occasions a regular might get an uninoculated friend to tag along if the former offered to pay the medical bills in the likely event of ptomaine poisoning. Otherwise no one still using his birth name would enter alone or willingly. Defense attorneys and judges ate there. Discriminating criminals ate there. Most of the AG prosecutors had informal breakfast meetings there, excepting that handful of Ivy-educated Lord and Lady Fauntleroys who were on a separate career track and would loll into the AG's office circa nine a.m. after eating breakfast at home with their mothers or cooks.

More importantly, the Dial-up was one of the few establishments, like the Fez, whose owners feared reprisals from their choleric, oftentimes armed, patrons if they dared enforce the no-smoking ban.

Shannon and Laurie were sitting alone at a table in the back. Shannon tapped the business end of her unlit Camel against the Formica tabletop. (She had recently weaned herself from the unfiltered model. But bad habits die hard.)

"What's this about Little Gidget Kendall? Is he gonna rat us out?" Shannon would never dignify Jeff by using his given first name.

"He was steaming last night when I rebuffed his latest rape attempt."

Shannon called to our waitress. "Hey! Three javas over here—and a pony of Sambuca."

I lowered my head. "Jesus Christ, Shannon."

Without looking at me, she said, "Okay, what do we do about the Little Prince?"

The waitress approached with our coffees sans Sambuca. "I'll bring Beth a bagel," Laurie said calmly. "Jeff has her locked up in his office, probably taking friggin' shorthand on his lap!"

"Apropos of which," Shannon said, "I've got Bethy applying to some local law schools."

" 'Apropos of which'?" I repeated.

"What, Melone, I can't talk fancy like you once in a while?" said Shannon, throwing her Camel to the table and rifling through her pockets for a match.

Laurie flipped through the menu for effect. "It is too early in the morning for a smoke, Shannon."

"I've been up since five," she fired back. "This is lunch for me." Shannon ran her fingers through her unruly blonde hair and it immediately rebounded, sticking up straighter in the air than ever. "I'm worried about Kendall. I was up all night trying to figure it from every angle. If what we did compromises the case, one way or another we're going to have to come clean. I have no intention of going to my grave with guilt on my conscience. Maybe we should tell Vince before Kendall does."

Laurie looked at me. "Uh-oh, move over, Mari, now Shannon's getting morality. She must have gotten a bum mammogram reading."

The waitress was back at our table.

"Two eggs on hash, wheat toast, and a refill." Shannon held her cup up to the waitress. "And my tits are just fine."

"Glad to hear it," the waitress said.

"Two poached eggs on porcelain," I ordered.

"You want those hard, right?" she asked me.

Shannon answered for me. "We always want them hard."

"Shannon's right, Laur," I said. "Maybe it is time to tell Vince and let him make the call. Maybe after drilling us and realizing we saw nothing worth reporting, he'll just let it go."

"He won't," Laurie said. "If for no other reason than he'll be worried about his own skin. Because don't forget, then Jeff will have all of us under his thumb. Vince will never let Jeff have that power over him. Or anyone else for that matter."

And what Laurie hadn't said was that Vince wasn't a crook at heart. His sensitivity to arrogant people like Carlyle made him morally cognizant of every professional move he made. Privately he used to counsel me that having Italian last names made us vulnerable to the presumption of mob connections. And for precisely that reason, when and if he found out that the girls and I were at the Fez knocking down drinks after hours, we (especially me) were in for some serious repercussions.

"Oink. Oink," Laurie suddenly singsonged through gritted teeth.

Shannon and I twisted round in our seats to see Vince swaggering our way, sporting one of his deliberately disingenuous grins. Come to think of it, I'd never seen a look of unadulterated happiness on Vince's puss. He was either laughing *at* someone, or his face was scarred with its permanent scowl.

"Groan, sigh," said Shannon. "Not a word to him yet," she said to Laurie and me.

Vince was stocky, solid, and physically prepossessing. His big frame and deliberate strides exuded power like a long black limousine idling at a curb. He liked cheap boxed pasta and expensive French wines. He'd been known to covertly decant Chateau Latour into basket-woven Chianti bottles to appear true to his Italian heritage. Vince shopped at Louis Boston, Louie's in Milan, or off the back of Lou's truck in Silver Lake. He wore argyle cashmere socks, a gaudy eighteen-karat gold Rolex watch, and practiced every double standard in the book. Vince had many faces, but no one saw the one in his mirror before he went to bed at night.

And there he was, looming and in our faces. His corpulent belly, vested in a stylish, handmade charcoal gray suit, was pushing so heavily against the table edge that its spindly legs squawked a few inches along the floor.

"Well, well, well, if it isn't the female half of the Brady Bunch."

Shannon had found a match and was lighting up that Camel with no protest this time from either Laurie or me. Vince, it was clear, had no interest in fencing with Shannon. It was me he'd come to see.

"So, Meloni, Jeff told me about last night. You and Carlyle cozying up."

"Jeff was too busy admiring himself in the mirror to see anything that happened last night. What else did he say?"

Shannon kicked me under the table while Vince was dragging over a chair that had been minding its business at a table across the aisle. No sooner had he plunged his wrecking ball of a body into the chair than our waitress came by and placed a cup of coffee in front of him. He took a Merit menthol out of a shirt pocket and lit it with Shannon's matches. His nails were clean and shiny from a new manicure and the stones in his gold cuff links were black onyx as he pointed his finger at me. "You're high profile with this Holton murder, Meloni. Everything you do now is under a microscope. Don't screw up on me."

Then he suddenly tacked: "They found the Hastings car parked down by the river at Fox Point. Looks like she was cut up in her own car, dumped from it, and he abandoned it there. Cops are going over it now with a fine-tooth comb. Problem is, most of those rich brats are slobs because they had to leave their maids home, so finding anything probative in her car is going to be like finding a toothpick at the Johnston Landfill. I'll need DNA from every kid on campus to make a match."

"Hey," Laurie said, "what about the blanket? Anything from forensics yet?"

Vince nodded broadly. "Best news of the day. It was from Holton student health services. But again, it had a couple of thousand hairs on it—all from different sources. I guess they don't believe in doing laundry over there." He looked directly at me. "That blanket's our arrow pointing right to the school."

He checked the time on his big shiny watch. "Meloni, wipe all that egg off your face and get back to the office. And no more drinking until this case is over, especially at the seedy joints."

Shannon barked a hard laugh. Laurie sat up from a heretofore slouch. And I choked on my coffee.

Vince stubbed his unsmoked cigarette out in the ashtray. Then he looked directly at me again as he lifted Shannon's matches from the table. "What's this?" He pretended to study the matchbook cover. "The Fez? Is that what this says?"

"I got it from a defendant in lockup," lied Shannon.

"You're all pushing my envelope," he said. He kicked his chair back and stood, rattling the table settings. "Just remember, I can *fire* the lot of you." He lumbered away.

"He's never said the F word before," whispered Laurie. "Do you think Jeff told him already?"

"Nah," said Shannon. "We'd have been fired *and* fucked before he even sat down. The question is, do we show that little prick Jeff our soft underbelly and beg him not to tell Vince? Or do we just leave it be and see what happens?"

I knew the answer clear as rain: Tell Vince ASAP. Lay out our vulnerabilities on direct to save ourselves from a fatal cross-exam wherein we'd be serving time for obstruction of justice while the freaking murderer went free after a mistrial.

But instead I said, "Let's tuck in our shirts and wait a bit."

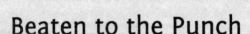

CHAPTER NINE

Beaten to the Punch

BACK AT THE OFFICE, with a renewed feeling of resolve I flipped open the Hastings file, ready to call the detective assigned to the case and go over the evidence with him piece by piece. I picked up my phone and began dialing the station when Vince's face appeared in my doorway like the Ghost of Christmas Future.

"My office. Now," he said without looking in my eyes.

I replaced the receiver gently as Vince marched away. Like a soldier ready for inspection, I grabbed my blazer and followed Vince to his office down the hall.

When I arrived he was already sitting at his desk looking down at a closed file folder.

"Sit," he said.

I eased myself into one of the four burgundy leather chairs flanking his eight-foot desk and fingered the brass upholstery tacks as Vince took his time getting to the point. This make-them-sweat routine was not Vince's style. He usually got right to the punch, literally and figuratively, when he was laying on bad news. And this tête-à-tête, I knew, was not a convivial hi-how-are-you visit.

"I liked you, Meloni. I really did."

I instantly noted his use of the past tense.

"I thought you could be one of my stars, because you had something the others lacked. A certain . . ."

"Flair? Style?" I was smiling. Vince wasn't.

"But I should have known when you silenced that *e* on your last name you thought you were too good for us here at the AG's office."

"Vince —?"

"Shut up and let me finish." He took a deep breath but he still wouldn't look me in the eyes. If I were a defendant and he were my jury, I'd be looking at serious jail time.

"Jeff just left here. Where were you the night Hastings was murdered?"

There was no point in lying. People like Jeff Kendall don't get rejected by someone like me without serving up a healthy dollop of hot revenge.

"All right. Okay." I breathed deep, relieved that I could finally confess to Vince, but scared as hell because I knew I should have told him sooner.

"I saw Hastings get dumped. A second later the SUV slams into the body and it flies across the street into the parked car. It was dark and happened so fast that I couldn't even tell you what color the car was."

"What the fuck were you thinking!" He exploded. "Why didn't you call the cops? Or me? Or even your girlfriends? Christ almighty, even the paralegal Beth would have advised you not to run. But what do you do? You go home and hope no one finds out."

He didn't know about the girls.

"And where were they anyway? You're never without your panty crew."

"I don't answer for anyone but myself."

"Is that so? Then you're all fired."

"Wait a goddamn minute—" I sprang from my chair, fed by the fury I was feeling for Jeff Kendall. "We can get through this, Vince. We can."

He waited in silence while I tried to figure out how to dirty the truth with another lie.

"I worked late. I was hungry and didn't feel like going home to eat alone, so I went to the Fez. There aren't too many other places with their kitchens open after eleven. I had a quick bite and was on my way back to my car at the lot when Hastings happened. I got scared. I was actually trying to protect this office—and the case. And I swear, if I had seen anything the cops could use to find the guy, I never would have run. I've been over it a million times in my head—Christ, I've been having nightmares about it—I didn't see a damn thing that could help the case. Nothing!"

"So it was late and you were hungry and you picked the Fez to eat at. Haven Brothers trailer is open till two, but . . . oh, wait . . . Haven Brothers doesn't have a liquor license and you probably needed to satisfy your four-drink-a-night habit too, right?"

"Well . . . that was the other reason I didn't stick around . . . I'd had a few drinks . . ."

Vince stood, kicking his chair out from behind him. "You are really pushing my buttons, Meloni."

He was quiet for a minute. Then he asked, "What happened with Carlyle last night?"

Was he changing gears? Could I actually get past this without much flak?

"I did what you wanted. I gave him my numbers and told him to call me. I think he got the idea I'd help him out any way I could. He was pretty nice actually."

"So he bought it? That you'd betray me for him?"

"I think so, Vince. But then I thought Jeff Kendall liked me, and he betrayed me, so I'm a lousy judge of character, aren't I?"

"Jeff didn't betray you. He showed me more loyalty than you did by running from the scene of a crime." He began pacing behind his desk. "I want you to take some time off, Meloni. I'm putting you on unpaid leave."

Vince wasn't much of a kidder, but I gave it a shot anyway. "Vince, that's not even funny."

His pacing stopped. Slowly he lowered himself into his chair and then refused to look at me as he spoke softly. "When's the last time you knew me to be a comedian?"

"Unpaid leave until when?"

Vince leaned back in his chair calmly. Much too calmly.

"Indefinitely. I've got to think this thing through."

"Come on, Vince."

He bolted up straight, angry that I was even trying to put up a defense.

"An Italian girl from good solid parents who give you a home and a good education, and what do you do? You spit in their faces and try to Anglicize your name by dropping the last vowel. I should have known you'd spit in my face one day too. It's all about loyalty and respect. And you have no respect for me because you respect wet dicks like Carlyle and Jeff Kendall."

"Spit in your face? No respect? You *told* me to play nice with Carlyle. I did what you wanted."

"Too well, I think. I'm done for now. You can leave."

"Vince, this is my job we're talking about. My career!"

"You want some career advice? Go talk to *nice guy* Carlyle. Maybe the dean can give you some career advice. And while you're at it, maybe he can tell you who killed the Hastings girl."

"What's this about? It can't just be about Hastings and a few drinks at the Fez. I don't believe this."

Vince shot up from his chair and threw a volume of the Rhode Island General Laws across the room, just missing me by a thin page. "You left the scene of a crime—a murder! And even after you knew Jeff saw you, you *still* didn't come straight to me. You put the integrity of this entire office in jeopardy. Now get out of here. And on your way out, send Shannon in. She's getting the Hastings case."

It took a few seconds to unfreeze and move but when I finally trod out of Vince's office he was asking his secretary to call Shannon in. I headed her off at the pass.

"Jeff told him. Admit nothing. I swore I was alone. No point in all of us taking the hit. He suspended me without pay."

Shannon started to laugh until she saw the sick look on my face. Then she twirled to the wall and slammed her fist hard against it. "Oh fuck, Mari. Fuck!"

"I'll tell Laurie and Beth. Then I'm going to see Jeff. We've got to make sure he shuts his mouth about the rest of you."

I made a pit stop with Laurie and Beth and then went to Jeff's office.

Uncharacteristically, he was in early. Jeff didn't usually saunter in until ten unless he had the rare court appearance. Perhaps he had set his alarm early that morning to have his chat with Vince and then witness my subsequent hanging.

He was hunched over his desk reading the *New England Law Journal*.

"Good morning, Jeff. Are you still trying to nail down that fine distinction between murder one and jaywalking?"

He looked up, expressionless, and then went back to his paper. "What do you want?"

I stared at this man, trying to recognize something familiar in him. After all, hadn't we been lovers? Then I realized that I didn't like myself when I was around Jeff Kendall. He made me question my own worth.

"Jeff, tell me. What's it like to be an asshole? Because I've always aspired to be one but I could never master it as well as you."

He sat back and laughed. "Years of inbreeding," he said. "Sensitivity becomes a recessive gene and then you drown the softhearted ones at birth." He was still smiling. "I had an obligation to inform my boss about one of the cases this office is prosecuting. Anything else, Counselor?"

"And you knew he might fire me over this? You knew and yet you still told him without coming to me first."

With the emotional intensity of dry ice, Jeff didn't raise a cool eyebrow. "He fired you? Actually I'm surprised he went that far. He's always had a certain *familial* affection for you."

"I'm suspended without pay. And for the record, the others were not with me. Do you understand what I'm saying?"

"Marianna, I didn't really see anyone else. Vince can call them in and ask them whatever he wants. I did what I had to do, and I'm done with the whole affair. And with you."

WHEN I RETURNED to my office Shannon was sitting with her long legs hiked up on my desk. At my arrival she whipped her legs down and waited for my opening statement.

"Jeff doesn't care about the rest of you. It's only me he wanted to screw. So I guess you're safe for now."

"Okay. Don't do a thing. Let me talk to Vince when he calms down." She tousled her spiked head. "I can't believe he really did it. Shit, shit, shit on a stick."

"I just had breakfast. You're making me a little nauseous."

"Go home and watch a few thousand episodes of *CSI*. I'll knead him around a bit and maybe he'll soften and rise to the occasion like a man instead of collapsing under pressure like a goddamn wet noodle."

I flopped into my chair. "I really feel sick."

"You've got a few moguls to ski right now, that's all. While I work on the Hastings case, I'll be working on Vince too. Don't worry, sweetie, everything will be fine. I promise."

"Shannon, when you start sounding all sweet and so-licitous like Beth, I know I'm in for the giant slalom."

CHAPTER TEN

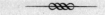

Wonder Bread

I HAVE TO ADMIT, I'd thought my suspension was one of Vince's torture tactics, a temporary ruse to teach me a lesson, but after two weeks with no pay, he was still holding his ground. He still hadn't outright fired me, but he wouldn't let me back either. I was beginning to think Vince was hoping I'd quit and save him the bad press of public explanations (and severance pay).

By the fifteenth day of my unpaid leave, my anxiety and agitation had quelled into something akin to post-traumatic stress, whereby I'd returned to the safety of the nest and was hiding out at my parents' house to continue my wait for his call.

It was a Saturday morning, and I arrived at their humble home armed with treats from the neighborhood bakery. My mother's kitchen smelled, as it always did, of dinner the night before. My father, an Atwells Avenue cobbler, had made his American version of Pasta Putanesca: Bumblebee Chunk Light Tuna dropped into a saucepan of bubbling, garlicky tomato sauce. In anticipation of my visit, my parents had left a note on the refrigerator door informing me that they had left early that morning to attend Cassie's soccer game. They would all be home by noon.

Strange how it always felt safe in my parents' house, so unlike my own apartment. Maybe it was my perennially empty refrigerator, which even during flush times held a jar of instant coffee, Post Grape-Nuts cereal, and a quart of lactose-free skim milk purchased mainly because of its long shelf life. My linen closet was always jam-packed with cleaning items, all unopened or used only once. I bought cleaning supplies the way other people bought the latest workout equipment: It looked great on display and I'd definitely start using it *tomorrow*.

Some would say my reluctance to open a can of Ajax and my loss of appetite in the face of any dish *I* cooked was a rebellion against my mother's obsessive sterilization of our childhood home and her fervent love of cooking. But it wasn't that at all. As a perfectionist, I just wanted to leave cooking and cleaning to professionals like my mother. Tearing her away from a dirty stack of dishes was like pulling a five-year-old off a carousel in the middle of a ride.

Under her sink my mother kept her well-used bottles of Clorox, Windex, and Comet Cleanser. Shredded cleaning rags salvaged from my father's stock of old T-shirts were doused and drained in a plastic bucket, brimful with witches' brews specially mixed for various household surfaces. In her cooking my mother used only fresh herbs from her garden and farm vegetables in season. Even in the frost of winter she grew parsley and oregano indoors.

Nestled among the clay pots of my mother's windowsill

greenhouse was my father's dented metal cup from "the old country," his precious Rome. Dad never referred to himself as Italian. Not because he was embarrassed at being Italian, but because he was prouder of being Roman.

I had just kicked off my shoes and opened the morning paper when through the kitchen window I saw my father carefully guiding his midnight-blue Oldsmobile up the narrow driveway alongside the house, a beaded crucifix swaying from the rearview mirror. I pulled open the back door to greet them.

My mother angled herself out of the passenger side of the giant Olds wearing polyester pants that rode several inches above the top of her nylon ankle stockings. She wore flat loafers—a discount-mart copy of J. P. Tod's driving shoes—and the vinyl handbag she carried was covered in C's, ambitiously aspiring to both Coach and Coco Chanel. The discounted originals I had bought her were wrapped in tissue on the top shelf of her closet, saved for special occasions.

My sister Cassie swung open the rear car door. Her head was white-wired to earbuds that were hidden in a rebellious mess of brown curls corralled with an elastic band and falling in a heavy ponytail to her waist. Cassie resembled my father's side of the family, wavy-haired and olive-skinned, whereas I, in contrast, was more my mother: northern Italian with pale skin and hazel eyes, my hair a light brown artificially sun-streaked to a golden blonde.

"MA! YOU GOT THE DONUTS?" Like an Italian fishmonger's wife's, Cassie's voice now shattered the air, her impregnable expression telling me the iPod attached to her hip was cranked to the max.

"Cassandra!" my mother shushed as she circled around the car. "Take those things out of your ears! You'll be deaf by thirty."

Cassie (as we had been ordered on pain of death to call her) splayed her fingers over her hip and made a fake show of spinning down the volume. From her midriff-baring blouse Cassie's belly button protruded as insouciantly as a baby's. Her exposed navel was so "cool" she didn't give a damn about sucking it in to flatten her soft, round belly. Defiance made her more American. She swore that one day she would legally change her name to Sara or Brooke or Elizabeth or, possibly, something even whiter, totally devoid of vowels. Since poor Cassie quailed at the idea of being seen in public with her old-fashioned, Medicare-aged parents, letting them attend her soccer game today was a selfless gesture.

"Why did I have to come home?" Cassie whined as her car door slammed shut.

I took another step through the open doorway so they would notice me. My father spoke up first.

"Marianna! How is my little *bambina* today?"

I shook my head and smiled. I was two inches taller than he, and he hadn't called me *bambina* in years. Only my mother still referred to her daughters as her little babies. I held the door ajar for my parents and they wiped their feet too many times on the outside mat before entering. Cassie, bolting indoors in front of them with her head down, had missed the mat completely.

"What's the deal?" Cassie earnestly complained to me, underscoring her sacrifice. "Why are you here again?" She threw her duffel bag behind the door.

"I'm temporarily unemployed and an outcast among

my friends and legal colleagues. With any luck my boss will just fire me and not report me to the Bar Disciplinary Committee where I will be immediately stripped of my license to practice law *anywhere*."

My father leaned over the kitchen table and dropped the box of donuts in the middle.

I sighed as I put a teapot on the stove and rotated the knob to high. I'd brought along two special treats— espresso from the upscale market Venda's, on Atwells Avenue, and a dozen almond biscotti perfectly flavored for dark roast coffees and espressos. My parents could remain true to their ethnic heritage in America if they wanted, but I'd be damned if they couldn't be a little classy about it and stop boiling Maxwell House coffee in a saucepan.

I mixed the black powdery grind with the boiling water and then filtered it directly into our cups until the sludge settled to the bottom of the filter. I briefly daydreamed about how it might taste with a soft, honey-glazed Dunkin' Donut. Then I quickly popped a piece of sugarless gum in my mouth from my private stash in the kitchen drawer.

"Do we have any Coke?" Cassie asked. She pulled the door of the refrigerator open and banged things around until she located the milk. "I guess I'll have milk. Why don't you get a new job and tell your boss to pound sand?"

"Or get married," my father suggested.

Cassie rolled her eyes as she sat at the kitchen table next to my father and pored over the donut box, rummaging until she found a chocolate-filled donut with sprinkles from which she took a bite before setting it down on the bare table next to the carton of milk.

"A glass," my mother said to her.

"The carton's almost empty." She took an aggressive swig, the milk splashing over the front of her face and onto the floor. She choked and as she stood my mother patted her briskly on the back. I slipped the plate of biscotti onto the enameled yellow table, placing it next to the box of donuts under which my mother had already, with a bit of domestic sleight-of-hand, slid a lace paper doily. My mother went on speaking to me as she patted Cassie's back. "Maybe you *should* get a cleaner job, Marianna. Not with the criminals all the time."

Cassie stuffed the rest of her donut into her mouth. "Does your boyfriend know you were actually fired from your job?" she spit at me through a mouthful of dough.

My father pounded his fist on the table. "Cassie, your sister and that Irishman were just friends."

"Jeff wasn't Irish, Dad. And we haven't been friends for months."

"Your problems started when you turned your back on your own blood. You don't want to be Italian anymore?"

"Alfeo," my mother said, "have your coffee." She pushed the sacrificial box of donuts under his nose and poured the black mud into his cup. My father noticed the biscotti and lifted one up to his nose. "What is this? Stale already?"

"They are supposed to be hard like that. It's one of those fancy cookies you dip in the coffee." My mother took the biscotti from his hand and creased back the cover of the donut box so it would stay open.

My father mumbled discontentedly as he pushed the donuts away, laying his thick hands flat on the kitchen table. Though my father never bit his fingernails, they looked bloody and gnawed to the quick because the leather tanning oils he worked with stained the cracks of his dry skin and ragged nails. He polished each pair of shoes after it had been reheeled or resoled. It was a special touch that kept customers coming to his shop from miles away. I was never able to walk into his shop without cringing from the smell, wishing my father's hands were soft and white. I looked down at my own fingers and noticed my new French manicure, the polish already chipping.

"Right, Marianna?" Cassie woke me out of my reverie. She was tapping away on her newest handheld techno-contraption. Somehow she'd found a way to use it to study for her SATs.

"What?"

"I don't need to study. You'll get me into your old college."

"You'll need at least an 1800 to get into Boston College—or a trust fund initially endowed by slave traders so you can add a new library wing."

"I don't need college."

"Cassie, you are the most unadulterated, cocky little brat I've ever known. Get your gutter-low scores up on those SATs, otherwise the only place you're headed is the take-out window at Burger King."

My cell phone rang and Cassie grabbed it from the table. After saying "yup" a few times she held it out to me. "It's some man with a fussy accent."

I spit my chewed wad of diet Dentyne into the trash under the sink and took the phone.

The "accent" was Dean Kenneth Carlyle's stodgy Brahmin speech pattern. He said he'd called my office and, after learning I was on leave, had tried my cell.

"I'd like to meet with you again, Miss Melone."

"AAG Shannon Lynch has the Hastings case. You'll want to talk with her now."

"Yes, I know. But it's *you* I want to see. Monday morning at nine?"

CHAPTER ELEVEN

The Summons

AT EXACTLY 8:52 MONDAY morning, still on unpaid leave, I was picking away at a fresh manicure outside Dean Carlyle's office when his secretary appeared from the end of a long hall. She looked like a pigeon as she made her way toward me, head down, pecking at seeds. Not wanting to seem too curious, I kept my own birdbrain lowered too, posturing that I was lost in important thoughts. Her thick-soled Mary Janes made a swooshing sound as she dragged her heavy, support-hosed feet over the burgundy oriental runner, worn to the threads as a proud testament to the age of this venerable institution. At the last believable moment I raised my eyes and resisted the urge to shout *Boo*.

Her lips opened to display a mouthful of crooked yellow teeth as she looked at me with a sour smile. Was that expression of hers really as arrogant and astonishingly Fellini-esque as it looked? Did it convey a pathetic pleasure in being Carlyle's gatekeeper? Was I having a nervous breakdown?

"Good morning again, Miss Melone. I'm so sorry for the wait. Dean Carlyle will see you now. Please follow me."

In contrast to the plump body sucked in firmly by her high-necked wool suit, her voice was elegant, resonating with a clubby tone of private enclaves, special privileges, and secret passwords.

She ushered me into Carlyle's office. He was beaming while standing tall and erect beside his desk. Today he reminded me of one of the news anchormen on the BBC cable channel out of Boston and, just a bit, of the gynecologist who'd laparoscopically plucked that ovarian cyst out of me. I decided I was feeling a little stressed.

"Had you noticed our extensive renovations?" he began, fluttering his airborne hand, which I was tracking like it was an encephalitis-bearing mosquito.

"This entire floor, for instance, though gutted to the studs, was essentially retained," he went on, "as were most of our antiques, some of which date back to the school's inception almost two hundred years ago. We've made certain to incorporate them in every office, so that each office is pretty much identical in style and no single functionary has the appearance of seniority. Something everyone learns here is that we're a team. One for all and all for one. The Musketeers. It may sound hokey but conceptually it's critical for us. Teamwork and dedication. It's a mantra here at Holton."

I would have made Vince proud had I stood up right then and told Carlyle to shove his tortoiseshell reading glasses down his throat. Or, perhaps, just shoved them down there myself. (And then maybe I could watch Carlyle don duck-hunting attire, throw me in the air, shoot me, and hand me over to his cook for supper.) I fought these impulses, still hoping in the back of my soggy brain that somewhere in this lecture would be some juicy information I could take to Vince and get back to work.

"Sit, please," Carlyle said, motioning to the couch. "Okay, let's see. Why did I ask you here?"

He waited for me to sit. Then, pulling those atrocious tortoiseshells down from the top of his head, he readied to pronounce his hefty agenda.

"Mr. Piganno wants the police to begin an investigation of our students. Did you know that?"

"I'm no longer privy to what our AG wants, Dean. As you know, I'm on leave."

Carlyle continued. "Would you mind if I asked the details of that . . . ah . . . suspension? Did he perhaps learn of our brief chat at the Kendalls' dinner party?"

"I'd rather not discuss it, Dean."

He nodded. "Mr. Piganno doesn't like this school and everything it stands for. He resents our tax-free status. He doesn't understand the value of what we do here. He's trying to indict the entire school over the unfortunate death of one of our students. Crime in this part of the state is rampant. The *Journal* is rife with stories of street gangs in the area. It's absurd to assume that Melinda Hastings met foul play at the hands of another Holton student."

"Street gangs." I nodded. "From my experience they drag girls into allies, beat them senseless, rape them, and then leave them there for the morning trash pickup. Not exactly this killer's MO. The murderer might not *necessarily* be another person of Miss Hastings's *social standing*, if you will, but let's not forget her body was found with a bloody Holton blanket."

"But do you agree that descending on our grounds with a sweeping investigation of all our students is over-broad? Vince Piganno would have DNA collected from every male on campus if he could."

"I assume the police are questioning some of her closer friends and associates and trying to narrow it down."

Carlyle pulled a chair in front of me and sat, rubbing his bony hands on his skinny knees. "Can I be honest with you, Miss Melone? I'm afraid. Afraid of a public investigation of this school that will permanently tarnish our reputation."

"I can understand your fears, Dean Carlyle, but—"

"Please call me Ken." He leaned toward me like a father ready to tell his young child a family secret. "I don't know, Marianna. May I call you Marianna?" He shook his head. "Is there a real need to publicize the investigation? This entire matter *could* be kept private? Am I right?"

Sure he was right. But there was this little problem of Vince Piganno and privacy being one of his least favorite things.

"Sometimes publicity is a handy tool in arriving at the facts, sir. People come forward who otherwise wouldn't when they read the ongoing coverage in the paper or on the six o'clock news. But I agree that a certain amount of privacy or dignity is owed to the deceased's family as long as you aren't using it to cover something up."

"I agree. I agree." Carlyle stood from his chair. "I like the way you think, Marianna. And this is actually why I called you here today." He stood abruptly and beamed at me with a full mouth of gray teeth. "I have a *proposal* for you. . . ."

From behind it, he nudged his chair closer to me and sat facing me again.

"Since that day we met with the Hastingses, I've been thinking about you. You have a flair about you, a certain style. Tough but fair, strong but with a gentle spin."

He was making me sound like a Maytag washer.

"Have you ever considered changing your employment situation?"

"To what? I'm a lawyer."

"Of course, but there are other areas in which to practice those skills outside a courtroom. Hmm? Here, for instance."

"You're insulting my intelligence, Dean Carlyle. I told you I no longer have control of the Hastings case. There's nothing I can do for you at the AG's."

"Now you're insulting *my* intelligence. This has nothing to do with Melinda Hastings." He popped up from his chair again and took a few steps away from me. "Let me try to explain. I know a little bit about you, Marianna Melone. For four years you worked during the day and at night attended Suffolk Law and made law review? Correct?"

I sat still and listened.

"Initiative and perseverance. I like that. And you've been employed as a prosecutor since you graduated?"

"I've been with the AG for five years, yes."

He crossed the room slowly, lifted a piece of paper from his desk and held the paper in the clawlike clasp of his long fingers. Despite in all likelihood having memorized the thing, he was making a show of slowly rereading it now.

His glasses kept sliding down his nose.

"Went to Classical High."

Again, I was silent as he read.

"Graduated with honors from Boston College. You made the dean's list every semester."

"I take education very seriously."

"Yet you didn't apply to a better law school?"

"I couldn't afford a better law school. I had to work during the day to pay for tuition."

As I listened to Carlyle talk about me, I realized that his translucent skin marked him more as a sixty- than fifty-year-old. His knees were sharp under loose-cut flannel pants. His shoulders were a narrow hanger for his boxy suit and button-down white shirt, all of which seemed not so much clothing as a uniform for properly bred gentlemen. It galled me to begin noticing something comfortably attractive in this man's patrician authority and dated, conservative dress. I wanted to believe he saw some special worth in me. I wanted him to like me. Was Vince right? Did "wet dicks" like Ken Carlyle and Jeff Kendall impress me?

"What is this all about, Dean Carlyle? Is that my resume you're reading from?"

He shook his head dismissively. "Just some notes." Carlyle held up his hand, then returned to his chair across from me, leaned forward, and folded his hands. "From time to time we encounter minor problems here on campus, with a student or two. Small indiscretions. Too much coddling at home can produce . . . the occasional bad egg."

He paused. I blinked, and he smiled at me.

"But obviously nothing resembling what you've seen as a . . . ah . . . prosecutor." He smiled again. "As far as I know, we've admitted no serial killers." He broke into a broader smile. He looked genuinely happy. A regular Steve Martin.

Then his face got all craggy again. "And this, Miss Melone, is where you would come in. Indeed, some of these student indiscretions have the potential to border on—appearance-wise at least—the outer fringes of criminality." He let the sentence sink in. "I need someone who knows the law, can intervene promptly and forestall any inadvertent disasters with whatever means are at one's disposal, and God knows, in the unlikely event that—"

"That there's an arrest?"

"Perhaps. And again, I am not referring to the Hastings matter. You would have absolutely nothing to do with that case if you came on board."

His eyes were focused with crystalline clarity on mine. What was he really saying? That the position required, above all, a good sense of prosecutorial discretion and great personal sensitivity, given that these college kids and their families were the hoi polloi. Was I being sounded out re my willingness to use my connections to smother potential criminal charges against the students? Did Carlyle think I had the power to talk the AG's office out of anything? Especially now, having been excommunicated. Vince would enjoy nothing better than blowing Holton up, with my head as the fuse, and then using the vacant hallowed grounds as a bocce court.

But I had a vague sense that somewhere in this mire of conflicting worlds—Carlyle's and Piganno's—there was a solution for my present job predicament. Perhaps the cobblestoned path back to the AG's office was littered with fallen petals of Holton ivy. There was no doubt that somewhere within Holton's impenetrable walls lay some secrets to Melinda Hastings's untimely death. Maybe if I

gathered rich bouquets of evidence and delivered them
to Vince, he'd soften and let me through the back door
to my dingy minuscule office with the rusty metal desk
under the cracked ceiling fixture. . . .

Confronted with my poker-faced silence, Carlyle
continued, lecturing me as if I were a child being taught
how to cross a street.

"Marianna, someone like you understands the importance of confidentiality. A school of this caliber can't
have its linens aired in public. The alumni don't like it.
The families of our students don't like it. I need someone
like you to keep this place in shape morally. In short, I
need you on my side."

I kept my mouth shut, since I was pretty certain I was
being offered a job, not because of my sterling academic
and professional history, but because I had done such a
stellar job of convincing him, that night at Jeff's parents'
house, that I was crooked to *just* the right degree.

His abdomen caved in slightly as he caught his breath.
He exhaled slowly, took another more normal breath, and
then continued.

"You haven't said a word. Tell me what you're thinking."

"Well, let me sum this up, Dean. You want me to su-
pervise and discipline a pack of silver-spoon brats who
screwed around in high school and aren't used to opening books or taking notes, yet they want to graduate from
a prestigious college, but could never get into or out of
one without Holton's special kind of leniency. Now then,
are you sure you want me to work here?"

Surprisingly, he chuckled in response, but then his
face went suddenly blank, as if he had experienced a
small electric shock.

"Assistant Dean of Student Ethics. I was going to

wait until the fall semester to institute the position, but after learning of your recent employment difficulties, I decided to launch it without delay and offer it to you. You'd have the critical role of enforcing our standards and keeping everybody happy in the process. . . ."

Carlyle stood and walked to the window. His office sat above a quarter acre of lush New England lawn leading up to the building's black wrought-iron gates. Lining the walkway like palace guards were twenty-foot-tall Bradford pear trees, austere in their winter bareness. The trees thrust hundreds of gray spiny branches into the sky like tall rifles held to attention.

Carlyle spoke to the window. "None of what you hear or see at Holton must ever go beyond our walls. Especially this discussion of ours today. The press is never far from our gates, and they do not see those gates as hallowed, Marianna. Reporters sniff the ground like stray dogs for scraps of gossip on those students of ours who come from political families, or those students with celebrity parents. . . . You understand."

"Dean Carlyle." I breathed deeply. "I do understand what your concerns are. It's so important to have a strong value system in any organization. To keep the machine running smoothly . . ."

I went on and on, barely cognizant of the slippery babble flowing from my lips designed to soothe Carlyle's deepest fears of negative publicity, incipient indiscretions, and rotten eggs. But as I spoke to him I was thinking only of how to use Carlyle's fears to the advantage of the AG's office and, concomitantly, of mine.

Carlyle turned and looked into my urgent hazel eyes with one of the most heartwarmingly paternal and crinkly grins I had ever seen. "Consider this an interim position until you find something more suitable. Of course this means you would have to officially resign from the AG's office. Maybe you'll be pleasantly surprised and actually enjoy it here."

I looked up at Dean Carlyle and rose from the couch. He walked to me from the window, took my hand and shook it vigorously. "And did I mention the generous salary?" He smiled as his glance at last fell to my shirt, where my cleavage was showing ever so modestly at the second opened button of my blue oxford shirt.

CHAPTER TWELVE

———— ✤ ————

Juicy Fruit

I SPENT A QUIET two days holed up in my bedroom, where old Pooh Bear and I did some heartfelt soul-searching. As much as I wanted to hike my salary into the triple digits, I knew Holton wasn't the right place for me. I felt safer with my AG cohorts and assorted criminal types. And the truth be known, I felt like I belonged there. I loved being a prosecutor—with my three dearest sisters-in-crime.

We all loved our work, the four of us, and we were the luckiest of friends. Each of us was a separate gear and yet together we meshed like the happy transmission of a bright yellow Miata. I knew what made Shannon race to the finish line. I knew what connected her to Beth, and Laurie, and me, different as we all were. And I knew what ultimately distilled all our differences into that single something that made us similar: the ultimate car chase. That adrenaline rush of catching the bad guys.

No one gets rich nailing criminals for the bureaucracy. You don't see Harvard Law grads under the employ of the state except as a stepping-stone to their already-mapped-out political callings. A career prosecutor is to a lawyer what a secondhand consignment shop is to Sotheby's. We loved what we did and money was beside the point. Shannon, Beth, Laurie, and I enjoyed locking up criminals. It was rotgut lawyering, but absolutely heady. We were frustrated cowboys killing outlaws without guns. And Shannon's proclivity was special; she had a touch of evil in her. Beyond Clint Eastwood and his Dirty Harry, Shannon was the dirtiest harry of them all. She was our group's Arnold Schwarzenegger. The Terminator.

After each of my trials I would wait, wide-eyed and sweaty, while the jury deliberated. "Guilty as charged," came the foreman's pronouncement, and it was like drinking an iced Gatorade after a two-day marathon in ninety-degree heat. Forty-eight hours after the sheriffs dragged the defendant away in handcuffs, I'd be champing at the bit for my next case. I needed my work. I craved it like a drug. I had been doing what I loved with three women who were likewise addicted. Even Beth, a paralegal who never made it into a courtroom, got a rush backing us up with her rabid research when an issue of law needed briefing. No one knew her way around a law library like Beth. What chip on her shoulder did Shannon bear that had led her to the AG's office? And Laurie? And me? I couldn't pretend to know. But putting criminals behind bars gave us all a purpose and made us feel better about ourselves.

Made me feel better. Until some psychotic murderer ending up killing my beloved AG career—along with the unfortunate Melinda Hastings.

And I knew that accepting a position at Holton would

mean forever burning my AG bridge behind me. But two days later, financial reality hit hard and Vince wouldn't even take my calls, so I sent Secretary of State Laurie Stein to his office to deliver my latest appeal: Take me back after some reasonable period of exile or I was officially resigning and accepting a job *elsewhere*. I advised Laurie to postpone telling him about Carlyle's offer. (Telling Vince I was taking a job with his nemesis Carlyle would have sounded too much like blackmail, and, like most powerful men, Vince never responded favorably to threats.)

Within fifteen minutes Laurie called me with his response.

"After I told him, he stared out the window for five extra-long minutes, then he said, 'Send her my best wishes and tell her to come clean out her office.' That's all he said. Without so much as one obscenity."

"He's not even mad at me anymore. That's bad."

"He was weird, like when he's really serious, you know, when all the bravado is gone."

"Right. Okay then. Thanks, Laur. I'll be in touch."

Laurie had started to speak, but I hung up on her so she wouldn't hear the crack in my throat. I dried my eyes and assumed my classiest phone voice to accept Dean Carlyle's offer of employment pending my formal resignation from the AG's.

After hanging up with me, Laurie must have hand-delivered her report back to Shannon, who forthwith called a private meeting to discuss my suicidal tendencies and the special talent I had for shooting myself in the foot, jumping the gun, cutting off my nose to spite my face, etc., etc. . . .

I got to the Biltmore Hotel bar at about twelve-thirty. Shannon, Laurie, and Beth were already there. Methinks they had a pre-meeting meeting.

Laurie was staring at me as if I were a puddle of spilled Ebola virus; Beth slowly lifted her bottle of Coors Light to her frosted pink lips, looked at me guiltily, then set the beer back down without taking a sip; and Shannon was clacking her five-inch spiked heel against the side of the bar. Shannon constituted a major flaw in my women-and-spike-heels philosophy. She was well over five eight and was about as sexually insecure as Mae West, yet she wore Catwoman heels as often as I did. Only once did I ask her why. "Because I like the way they sound," she said, "like a horse on pavement. And men are scared shitless of them."

At the moment, I was a bit afraid of them myself.

Shannon, on the other hand, was afraid of nothing. She had the temperament as well as the haircut of a West Highland terrier: if something moved too fast she'd put her nose to the ground, shake her head, and then promptly rip the unsuspecting thing to shreds before eating it.

"Hey," I said before any of them had uttered a word. "You should all be happy for me. I can now wear my Jimmy Choos to work without worrying that someone will steal them off my feet for street value." I looked around for a stifled smile, hoping to fend off poison darts with a fistful of humor. But their chilly silence continued painfully.

The filth at the AG's office, I considered, *could* be rubbing off on me. My collegial language had become the patois of the gutter. Ugly obscenities preceded my every noun. What good were my weekly French manicures and Blahnik stilettos when I was rubbing shoulders with drug addicts and cops sporting shag mustaches yellowed with nicotine? With a new job at world-revered Holton, couldn't I punch my whole life up a level? Couldn't I, so to speak, shake the gold dust of myself out of the muddy sluice pan of mass humanity and buy passage into society's elite echelons?

Beth interrupted my lofty ruminations. "Laurie," she said, "tell Mari she can't leave. Especially now."

Now? As in *now that we are all coconspirators in an obstruction-of-justice rap?*

"Beth," I answered, "this has nothing to do with *that*. I needed a job and maybe this could be a big break for me. It's an impressive position. Assistant dean at a place like Holton. Not to mention the huge salary increase. And maybe, just maybe, I can find out some dirt on the Hastings murder. Who knows? And I would think you'd all be happy for me. At least I landed on my feet."

Laurie shook her head and looked at me with her super-steady brown eyes. Her hoarse, serrated knife-edge of a voice always made her seem tougher than she really was. "I'd be worrying more about my head than my feet if I were you. If you're going to work at that country club for educated morons, you're going to need Paxil, Valium, and a weekly dose of antiseizure meds—"

"What do *I* think about this new job?" I asked rhetorically. And then I answered myself. "Well, Carlyle *is* tough. Now that I think of it, he had a tricky way of leaving much about himself and Holton vague, provisional, unsaid, and then he wrapped it all under the protective covering of his *privacy* speech."

Shannon was hunched over the bar, her eyes blindly focused on a day-old newspaper. "Jesus," she said. "You're already talking like one of them."

"Yeah," Laurie said. "You actually do sound disturbed to me. What the hell does that mean?"

Nurse Beth rushed to my rescue. "It means," Beth explained, "that you have to read between the lines of what he's saying and you won't find out the truth about anything that goes on there until you officially become one of them. Isn't that what you mean, Mari?"

Shannon punched Beth on the shoulder. "Of course *you* would support them, you stringy WASP. Mari should take you along as her interpreter. You speak fart like they do."

"I'm going to miss you terribly," Beth said. "These two will torture me without you around."

"Enough of this country music sentiment," Laurie said. "Is it the money? You let Carlyle pimp you for a pay increase?"

"How much compensation *is* Holton offering you?" Beth asked. "If you don't mind my asking."

"Double what I'm making now."

"Only part of which is salary." Laurie snorted. "The rest? Hush money."

Shannon slid out of her shoes and, swami-like, yanked both feet into her lap, all the while still perched on her bar stool. If she'd had underwear on, it would have been peeking out now between her legs. Suffice it to say, it wasn't.

"Listen. We're going to find out who did Hastings and then rally to get you back at the AG's where you belong. Those are *our* two jobs and the sooner we get to them, the sooner you come home."

"Vince'll never hire me back. Especially after I take the Holton job. And I *need* a job *now*."

No one said a word until the bartender returned,

whereupon we ordered cheeseburgers and fries all around for old times' sake. Laurie held up her drink to me. "You know we won't leave you blowing in the wind. Right, girls?"

Laurie and Beth raised their glasses and clicked mine.

Shannon raised her own glass and toasted the air. "To cheeseburgers, hard liquor, and cigarettes, forever."

"And to lung cancer," Beth stage-whispered.

"And to fat asses if we all keep eating and drinking like this," I said.

"Come off it, Mari," Shannon said. "At least you have fat in the right places. I have the derriere of a juvenile giraffe and most of the guys at the office have bigger tits than I do."

Shannon was the sole one of us who ate her burger, complete with roll and French fries. Despite never dieting, she was as lean as a panting greyhound.

"Mari, I'm not even going to bother with Shannon, but why are *you* smoking so much?" Beth said.

"So I won't eat the burger."

"It's a diet," Laurie explained. "If she's smoking she can't chew. I'm on that diet too. Except I do filtered low-tar. But hey, heroin, methadone, all the same thing."

"Well, has anyone ever heard of gum?" Beth suggested. She picked up her bag and peered inside. "I think I have some fruit gum in here somewhere . . ."

We all watched as Beth searched for the salvation of our lost souls and burnt-out lungs in the bottom of her Vera Bradley bucket tote. "Chewing gum doesn't cause cancer," she lectured. "And smoking is out of style."

I stubbed out my Camel. "So is Juicy Fruit after the age of five."

Returning to her burger and taking a vociferous bite, Laurie said, "Still. Something in this whole scenario is out of sync. You and Vince together are like a black comedy routine. I can't believe he's letting you go."

"You ask me," Shannon said, "I think she broke his heart."

"Does Mr. Piganno have a heart?" asked Beth, quite seriously.

Laurie said, "I think you'd better be careful is all. Carlyle's need to protect the school against the AG's firepower seems obvious. And, P.S., Vince knows about the job already."

"How?" I said. "Besides Carlyle, you three are the only ones who know."

Beth abandoned her gum quest and hooked her bag to the back of her bar stool. "My guess would be Jeff," she said. "Don't forget the alumni connection."

Shannon jawed an unlit cigarette. "And I'll tell you what's really scary. Vince is quiet as hell about it." She looked at Laurie and Beth for confirmation. "Not screaming like you'd expect, right? What's up with that?"

"Perhaps, like us, he's worried about her," Beth suggested. "Did anyone consider the possibility that if the killer is preying on Holton students, Mari is going into the slaughterhouse without a gun?"

"I have a gun," I said.

But I didn't seriously think I'd ever need to use it. And did I think Vince was worried about me? Nah. I understood Vince better than the rest of them due to our similar genetic makeup.

"This Holton job offer kicked Vince over the edge and he's angry as hell. But screw him. He never should have dumped me by the wayside. I wouldn't go back now even if he begged me."

But that was my pride talking. Truthfully, I wasn't even as tough as little Dorothy lost in Oz. I'd rushed headlong into the throes of Holton—the complete opposite direction of where I really wanted to be, which was on a yellow brick road back home to the AG's office where I belonged.

CHAPTER THIRTEEN

Jeepers

HOLTON COLLEGE WAS NESTLED haphazardly among the large stucco and brick houses of wealthy Providence East Siders. Over the years many East Side homes, some of them historic, had been deeded to the college on fund drives or simply purchased on the open market for use as departmental offices, faculty domiciles, and student dorms. Holton's Ivy League aspirations were a complement to the smallest state in the country, and striving to assume a position alongside colleges like Brown University and the Rhode Island School of Design, Holton was helping give Rhode Island a national presence. But the flip side to the shiny coin was the college's ongoing removal of prime residential property from the Providence tax rolls, which stuck in the craw of the city's middle class and provided Vince endless hours of scatological material. A variation on one old maxim was a Piganno favorite: "The filthy rich get richer and the shitty poor pay their taxes for them."

It was early February, a month after the start of spring
semester and twelve days after I had "cleaned out" my old
AG office and skulked away with a shoebox full of broken
pens, unsharpened pencils, a few used legal pads, and my
proverbial toothbrush. I had never been one for trinkets,
or long goodbyes.

I pulled up to the high iron gates at the front entrance
of Holton's administrative campus. All was disquietingly
quiet as I drove through in my dented ten-year-old Jeep,
the one I had paid "one large" for, in crisp twenties, to
Mickie DeMedici in the back room of North Providence
Auto Body.

Mickie D was a friend of my father's from the Hill.
He said he'd picked the Jeep up at a South Attleboro car
auction in "as is" condition from the new husband of an
old girlfriend. "Legit," he said. "All legal."

"Please, Mickie." I coughed, stuffing my spent cigarette into an empty Coke can on his desk. "Save your fairy
tales for the local cops when *they* question you."

Well, for my own peace of mind I did make Mickie
swear on his grandchildren's eternal souls that this particular vehicle was as pure as the driven snow. You should
have seen him, his face flushing, begging me in his pid-
gin English, laced with low-class Italianisms, not to make
him utter his grandkids' names in this godforsaken room
where so many questionable deals had gone down. But
wouldn't you know, as soon as I whipped out those fresh
twenties, Mickie was saying "Marie, Little Anthony, and
Salvatore" faster than a kid reciting his Christmas list,
faster than a crack-addict stoolie, faster than—

Whatever.

So, with my possibly purloined Jeep, through Holton's
hallowed gates I drove for my first day of work as an

assistant dean. No sooner was I past the wrought-iron portals than a man in formal uniform stepped outside and slowly approached my car. With a twirl of his index finger, he asked me to roll down my window.

"I'm Marianna Melone. It's my first day here."

Focusing on his clipboard, he checked something off. When he lifted his head a broad smile had transformed his features and—voilà—I got saluted.

"Oh yes, ma'am. You can park over there today . . ."

Three empty spaces beckoned, each annotated by a small white sign imprinted with a gentle admonition, *Visitors Only.*

"But in the future you'll have to find street parking. And I can tell you this, the cops around here are very generous with their tickets. I've seen them, watches at the ready, waiting to tag someone for being thirty seconds past the meter."

"Thanks for the tip."

I pulled my Jeep next to an immaculate black Lexus and hurried up the granite steps to a set of heavily carved wooden doors. Massive brass knockers in the form of lion heads stared angrily at me. One of the great doors yielded to a shove and then groaned open, and I proceeded to another modest flight of well-worn marble steps and two more portals, of black enamel this time, fitted on the top half with heavy beveled glass. Before I could reach for the brass push-plate a petite woman with a coal black pixie haircut pulled the double doors wide open from the inside.

"*Bonjour,* Miss Melone? I am Rita, your secretary."

Her accent was still unidentifiable. "Are you French?" I asked.

She smiled as she guided me down the hallway toward my office. "Oh no. I'm from Venezuela, but I love to speak different languages. It makes me feel international. Someday I will travel the world."

"Have you been here long?"

"Hah! I was here when they broke the ribbon, as they say. I don't look centuries old, no?" Rita stopped and held her hands together as she faced me. "You hear the story about the husband and wife who always were cheating on each other? The wife thinks her maid is on her side and tells her everything. The husband is sleeping with the maid but knows nothing about what the wife is doing. The maid makes both of them think they are so smart for keeping their secrets from the other spouse. I am like the maid. To keep the house in order, I must know everything."

Rita continued her march toward my office, a quarter the size of Carlyle's but identically equipped, minus a conference table. A threadbare and presumably antique oriental rug branded my space into the Holton "club." At the AG's I'd been accustomed to hiding my expensive accessories in a locked desk drawer, so now, from sheer force of habit, I dropped my small leather bag into an empty bottom drawer and slammed it tightly closed. (Of course, given that Bottega Veneta comes discreetly unblemished by logos or initials, only a fellow fanatic would have been able to identify my bag's upper-bracket pedigree.)

"Leave your things here and follow me. Dean Carlyle will meet you in the conference room upstairs for the senior administrative staff meeting."

"Senior staff meeting?" I said. "Already?"

"*Ja, mein Fräulein*," she said, nodding. "Every Monday

morning the assistant deans report to Dean Carlyle on
what has been happening in their respective departments.
Issues are discussed and problems are resolved." She motioned for me to follow her and drew me close to her side
as she whispered, "But it is only Dean Carlyle that you
need to hear. Come now."

Rita arched dark eyebrows as she walked out of my
office toward a spiral staircase. As we ascended together
I gazed upward at an immense crystal chandelier suspended from the ceiling. After passing several offices, one
of which I recognized as Carlyle's, we arrived at the walnut door of an attached conference room.

Rita pulled it open, patted me on the back, and gently pushed me in.

"Marianna, welcome aboard!"

The dean was standing just inside the entrance. The
room was so brightly lit I squinted and then frowned and
then smiled. And then squinted again. Behind Carlyle
was a peanut gallery of grinning, eager faces.

"How are things going so far? Are you finding your
way around?" Without waiting for an answer, he turned
on his heels. "This is our senior management team."

The room's gorgeously polished, rectangular mahogany table looked like a bigger, taller version of the
table dominating Carlyle's office. Arrayed precisely down
this table's center were three crystal pitchers of ice water.
Each seating position featured a clean legal pad, a newly
sharpened pencil, and a matching crystal water goblet
resting upside down on its own linen cocktail napkin. I
was moving on up in the world. The dean looked around
the room before giving an eyebrow-nod to a woman standing alone by one of the windows. This stocky five-foot
blonde with a short bob, who had no qualms about giving

me a quick but intense once-over, now swung her arms wide and took several long manly strides toward us. She was built low to the ground, as my father would say—her legs were unusually short for her body.

"Assistant Dean of Operations," Carlyle crisply declared as she stood before us.

"Byron Eckert, Reese House, 1998," she said dryly.

"Long name," I quipped. But still no smile, not even the hint of one. From either one of them.

"Byron was All-Conference in women's soccer," he said. "Weren't you, Byron?"

I wouldn't have been surprised if he'd patted her on the shoulders at this point and mussed her hair a little, like a proud father. But he didn't. He simply stood by, hands at his side, in perfect military control.

"Yes, sir," Byron answered.

"Byron oversees financial operations. She's the money person. Sort of our COO." Carlyle made serial eye contact around the room, shaking his head. "Finances are an unfortunate but essential fact of life. Isn't that right, Byron?"

"It's how we survive," she said flatly, looking straight at me. She opened her mouth as if readying to say more, but Carlyle was already moving on to his next introduction. One by one the rest of his handpicked staff presented themselves to me with not a vowel-suffixed surname in the bunch.

"Mitsy," Carlyle called out to an older, taller woman whom Byron had been chatting up when I entered. This slender salt-and-pepper brunette had remained near the window, listening intently and smiling cautiously. "Come meet Marianna Melone."

The woman wore an elegant tweed suit and low-heeled

shoes. Carlyle began speaking of her as if she weren't present. "Dr. Mitsy Becker is a registered nurse with a Ph.D. in psychology. She's our Assistant Dean of Student Health Services. You two may want to get to know each other better when you have some time. After all, sometimes all a student needs is a little talking to. I hate to call it counseling, but I don't think Mitsy would approve of an alternative characterization of her function here. Would you, Mitsy?"

"That would be my word, yes."

Mitsy extended her hand. Her smile reached out to me and seemed genuine, and there was a stylish and comfortable something in her eyes, as if she were unafraid to let me focus in on them, plumb their depths.

"I'm happy to meet you," I said, shaking her hand.

She served me a second helping of her beaming smile, and I thought she might be the only one of this crew who would share her knowledge with me. Then she took her seat at the long table and waited out the elaborate verbal and physical curtsies of the remaining introductions, watching me all the while with a look not only of humane solicitousness, it seemed, but, just maybe, motherly concern.

"Tripp, come on over and meet Marianna," Carlyle barked, this time to a young man seated by himself at the table.

A feature of the dean's welcoming ritual seemed to be that no one stepped forward until summoned by name.

Tripp hoisted himself up and sauntered over. About thirty years of age he seemed like a young Carlyle clone, a preppy of the absolutely intolerable variety. Boy's standard haircut, flannel shirt, polished wingtips, the works. Plus the whole supercilious attitude, to a damning and

stereotypical T. If the boss hadn't been present, and if
Shannon or Laurie had been around to cheer me on, I'd
be having myself a field day chewing this Tripp up and
spitting him out. *Hiya, Tripp. Did I get that right? Tripp,
is it? Cool name. Family name or was it shortened? I had a
first cousin, Chip, named after his father, Jock. As in "chip
off the old Jock." Poor Chippy's dead now, though. Terrible
shooting accident with my gay uncle, Doogie.*

Tripp shoved his hand at me. "Tripp Hoven, Angus,
1996. Admissions. Pleasure!" he chirped. His immacu-
lately manicured fingers slipped in and out of my hand
like silk.

Carlyle rocked back and forth on his heels, watching
the pair of us as if we were dogs he'd just crated together.
Would we get along? Who would assume the dominant
position? As long as no one peed on me I'd let them drink
from my bowl. My determination to do my job and appear a team player outweighed my instinctive reaction to
mock Tripp's horn-rimmed glasses that screamed *genteel*
and *old school* so loudly I verged on asking him whether
the whole getup was a joke. But none of it was a joke.
It was so the opposite of a joke. I'd learned at least that
much from my old friend Jeff Kendall.

"Tripp here's in charge of new applications and the
admissions process overall. You, Marianna, get into gear
after that. Ideally, Tripp does his job so well that you have
nothing to do."

Carlyle focused on another young man who, lolling
in a chair, had looked to be scrutinizing Tripp's introduction as if we were bugs on a slide. I had never met such
intense people. "Chad? Come on over, please."

Carlyle turned to me. "Chad Fletcher is the Assistant
Dean of Career Services. Pretty self-explanatory, yes?"

He looked at me, then at Chad. "Chad networks our students with other alums." The elegantly dry dean suddenly smiled, alerting us to the pending utterance of some elegantly dried-up witticism. "Sort of like a fancy employment service for family members only. Right, Chad?"

"That's what we like to accomplish whenever possible," he said.

"All right, then," Carlyle said, clapping his hands once. "Let's get started, folks."

The dean made a body count as the group settled into their seats. Abruptly his face turned lime-sour. "Tripp, what time do you have?"

"My watch reads 9:05. But it could be fast, sir."

"Chad," he said. "How about you?"

"Me? Oh, yes sir, I have five past nine too, sir. Yes. Oops, 9:06 now." Even as Chad curved his mealy mouth into a half smile he remained oddly wide-eyed. Chad seemed to be one of those people who literally couldn't give you the right time of day without a dress rehearsal in full costume. Everything by the script.

Suddenly, in a breathtaking burst of aggression, Byron yanked her chair out from the table so forcefully it clattered against the edge, riveting everyone's attention, if not waking the dead. "It's almost ten past nine, sir. He's late." She plopped into her seat angrily.

"Well. Let's get started then."

At last, down Carlyle sat, the rest of the groupies dropping to their own chairs like gassed flies. The dean turned to his pigeon-toed executive assistant, seated primly and quietly to his left. "Make a note, Joan, it's ten past nine and McCoy's not here."

Suddenly, as though on cue, both conference doors exploded open.

There, on the threshold, framed by the misty Montana light of my imagination, stood a man very close to six feet in height, clad in a suit that looked a week overdue for dry cleaning. Everything in his expression feigned seriousness except the stereo twinkle in a pair of deep blue eyes.

He straddled the double doorway, both his hands still cupping the brass knobs. "Sorry, boss," he said. "Battery's dead on my Timex."

"Sit down, Mike." Carlyle still hadn't looked at him.

He collared a seat from a corner of the room and eased it in next to mine. "Be still my heart," he whispered, winking at me.

In closer proximity his aftershave was a mix of citrus and musk. The stone in his pinky ring was emerald green.

"All right, then," Carlyle pronounced. "Now that *everyone* is here we can begin."

The dean's opening oration was about the nine-hundred-pound gorilla in the room, or, more precisely, the body on the morgue slab.

"Melinda Hastings—a recapitulation for our new member. Most of you are aware of the press release I issued the morning after she . . . her body was discovered. Holton publicly expressed our condolences to the family regarding the unfortunate incident, etc., etc. Holton's *official* position, and as far as I know the *still* current position of law enforcement authorities"—Carlyle looked at me either for verification or as a dare to contradict him—"is that she was murdered by some local thug with no connection to this school. I don't think I'm being coarse if I propose that we continue to move beyond that tragedy. Her family wants nothing more than to put it behind them, and I agree with them. For Melinda's sake and for the sake of this institution, I think we should respect the Hastingses' mourning process and let the *state* do its work."

Why did I get the feeling he was talking directly to me?

He waited barely a minute before he not only *moved on* but sped away from the Hastings murder (much like the "thug" who'd dumped her body in the middle of downtown Providence). I decided to keep my mouth shut (and keep my day-old job) by not mentioning that pesky little evidentiary item of the Holton blanket in which Melinda was coddled when she was dropped from the *local Providence thug's* car.

After a few seconds of satisfactory silence, Carlyle gazed off into the far horizon. Then suddenly he shifted into high gear and dug into the business at hand. He was like the coach of the favored team, telling us that as proven winners we had to keep the students' spirits lifted and their aspirations high, murder notwithstanding. For about twenty minutes he pep-talked us.

"As you know, each year we are absolutely inundated with applications. Tripp, how many did we have to select from last spring?" All eyeballs transited Trippward. Tripp eagerly cleared his throat.

"Around twenty thousand applications for five hundred spots, sir. That translates into forty applicants per opening."

"All right, then."

Many more numbers, ratios, and equations followed, the attending staff taking close note. Everyone except McCoy. Cryptic phrases like "added value" and "bandwidth" took swift and awesome flight across the room. I had been a practicing lawyer for five years but was still mightily impressed by everyone's smooth articulation. Words were pronounced slowly and deliberately. Each humble syllable, lowly consonant, and meek vowel was sounded out for all it was worth. Damn. This was worlds away from what I was used to, either as a prosecutor or as a girl from the Hill where "cheese pizza and two small Cokes" was about as heady as the conversations got, and where most sentences were shot out at point-blank range, articles severed here and verbs blown away there, and all the gaping holes plugged by obscenities—

"To cut to the chase," Carlyle went on, "we are this year once again engaged in a very selective and competitive process . . ."

Of course, Carlyle had made this speech a half million times, not only to his administrative staff but to financial donors and anyone else who would listen—including the students. Still, the people arrayed around me were all mesmerized smiles and audible gasps, as if the pap he was spewing were iambs from a recently unearthed folio of Shakespeare. Like actors in some perennial theatrical run, they'd continue to feign awe at this monologue over and over again until *Same Time Next Year.*

Prompted by Carlyle, Chad now harangued us with the details of Holton's sterling record in postgraduate job and academic placements. As if Carlyle and everyone else didn't already know the numbers.

Byron, while verbally mute, watched the goings-on with kinetic intensity. Her eyes darted from face to face, and she gnawed at her bottom lip like a reformed chain-smoker who was too well bred to chew gum in public.

Interestingly, Mitsy wasn't queried for information,

nor did she volunteer any. Did Carlyle maintain some special reservoir of respect for her? Or was it simply that in age she was Carlyle's peer?

McCoy too said nothing, never picked up a pencil, and was never questioned. Thirty minutes into the second hour, the Hulk yawned, stretching backward in his seat as far as he could without flipping.

Just as Carlyle's words ebbed to a close, McCoy bolted upright in his seat.

Carlyle noisily slid his chair back as if readying to stand. No one else budged. Carlyle tilted his head back and sharply caught his breath, as if he'd spied a tarantula on the ceiling.

"Mike," he said to McCoy without looking at him. "The cafeteria matter. Are you on top of that?"

"Yup."

Carlyle swallowed, rather loudly. "Could you elaborate?"

"Rita has the report. The facts are all there. I don't do the wrist-slapping."

There was a teensy-weensy narrowing of Carlyle's eyes. "Your brevity never ceases to amaze me, Mike."

Carlyle's eyes shifted ominously to me.

"I especially invited Mr. McCoy to attend our staff meeting this morning."

Carlyle looked McCoy head-on for the first time.

"Thank you for interrupting your busy day, Mike. I've scheduled a one-on-one meeting today between you and Miss Melone here." To me, Carlyle said, "Marianna, this is our Chief of Security, Mike McCoy." Then back to McCoy, "Marianna is our new Assistant Dean of Student Ethics. Faculty lounge at eleven-thirty, Mike.

Give Marianna an overview but make it thorough. She needs to get a quick read on all our open matters." He dropped his chin. "Among *other things* there's the Cummings problem. We need it dealt with prudently but tactfully. It's volatile."

Turning his attention to me, Dean Carlyle went on. "Mike gets most of the initial complaints. It's you he'll pass them on to for processing."

I looked at McCoy for polite corroboration. He gave it to me—with a wink.

McCoy's clumsy audacity certainly took me aback, and yet the others in the room were unmoved. My mouth dropped.

Thing is, there are glances and there are winks. And there are simple winks and *suggestive* winks—like the one McCoy gave me. Criminal ventures. When men wink at me that way, my autonomic response is to punch them in the offending eye. I now resisted this urge, though just barely. Actually I was getting the distinct impression not a soul present would have minded if I'd laid the fool flat out on the conference room floor.

Carlyle began to wrap things up. "Please be prepared to present your departmental updates to the group next week. Same time, same place. And I remind you all again, the Hastings matter is to be broached tactfully, if at all, and *never* with any non-Holton affiliates."

The dean paused and then looked in my direction. Given that no one could rise from the table until cued by Carlyle, the staff watched him like hawks. The fan in the heating system kicked on and in that instant I became acutely aware again of how unnaturally bright the conference room and its occupants were; the glare of freshly buffed lemon oil on impervious oak. The AG's office now came to mind as counterpoint. Our weekly case updates: dim lights filtering through heavy cigarette smoke . . . rancid alcohol on the breaths of attorneys, perps, and cops alike at the nine a.m. court arraignments . . . bodies slumped wearily in folding chairs of hard dirt-hued plastic . . .

At last Carlyle stood. "Once again, my admonition: Out of respect for the family, mum on the Hastings matter," he declared.

Pencils hit the table as if the dean had pronounced "Time's up" at the end of an exam.

Carlyle flapped his fingers in the air in that odd, distrait way of his and then glided swiftly out, a politician making his exit, shooing away questions. With the exception of McCoy, his sycophantic fan club popped up from their seats and followed their master out the conference room door. Only Byron was still in her chair, staring at us and still sharpening her teeth on that bottom lip. Her attitude suggested either instant freeze-dried resentment of me or an understandably long-smoldering antipathy toward McCoy. Frankly, it puzzled me that someone as apparently unpolished as this McCoy was at a place like Holton. Unlike me he wasn't even trying to fake gentility. Really the bloke seemed too secure to even give a fig. But that didn't explain how McCoy got hired in the first place. Maybe the same way I did: Carlyle thought he was *bendable* or at least a little bent.

"What time do you have?" McCoy asked me.

My man's oversized steel watch was rolled around on my wrist, its face turned toward the floor. As I was still smarting over his dirty wink, I now refused to give McCoy the right time of day and left my watch facing the floor.

Unfazed, he took my wrist and turned the watch in his direction. His grip was firm but soft, as if he were cupping a broken-winged bird that was weakly struggling to get away.

"Eleven o'clock," he announced. "I'm hungry."

CHAPTER FOURTEEN

Pommes Frites

MCCOY BOLTED FOR THE conference room exit. I followed. Over his square bulky shoulder he said loudly, "You been to the faculty lounge yet?"

"No. Is it in this building?"

"No, but we'll walk. Fresh air does you good."

He cavalierly held a succession of doors open for me as we made our way out of Langley Hall. Gently touching my back, he guided me outside and down the stone stairs. The guard who'd greeted me earlier that morning saluted McCoy with a good-ole-boy grin, and a grounds-keeper cleaning sidewalks tipped his hat cheerfully as we walked by.

"It's just up there." McCoy was pointing toward a four-story Victorian mansion, gunmetal gray with a pale yellow trim.

"Have you been here long?" I asked. "Everyone and his gardener seem to know you."

"People are the best source of information. Some guys read books. I talk."

McCoy's beat-cop walkie-talkie had been bleating during our walk. Its raucous precinct-style soundtrack startled me with homesickness for the AG's office. I wandered into a daydream. I should have been on my lunch break right now with the AG girls, waiting on a blue-cheese burger whose side of greasy fries I would gaze at with deep longing while smoking one of Shannon's nutritious cigarettes.

But instead, I was climbing a spiral flight of sun-dappled stairs, past a modest, glass-encased selection of books authored by prominent faculty. No aromatic cheeseburger, no crispy hot fries, no wise-ass girls. At the stairway's summit was a dark wood vestibule cocooned in oak and red leather. Small circular reading tables with ceramic inlays were carefully set with complimentary copies of the *Providence Journal*, the *Wall Street Journal*, and the *New York Times*, each paper pinioned on thin wooden spines and fanned with geometric exactness. What would it have been like, I wondered, to grow up in a house like this? Would I have missed all that blue shag carpeting and those Naugahyde La-Z-Boys my parents were so fond of?

"It's impressive at first," mind-reading McCoy said, gliding into the faculty lounge at his breathtaking clip. "But you'll get immune to the fancy window dressing." He ushered me into the main dining room. "Good thing Carlyle made us reservations in advance. I can't get a hamburger in this joint without preordering. I hope you like roast duck and salmon. Christ, they put peas in the spaghetti here."

"Something tells me you're an ex-cop."

We were standing at a banquet table. The cavernous room was soundproofed by palace-sized oriental
rugs the color of day-old blood. Linen-shrouded tables
glittered with silver tureens and ornate platters. A small
Vietnamese woman in a starched white uniform was re-
arranging utensils and scattering fresh linen napkins to
cover drips on the tablecloth. Her charcoal-black hair
was tied in a tight bun.

"How'd you guess I was a cop? My cheap suit?"

"You talk like one."

I felt like saying he looked like one, smelled like one,
and ate like one, but I didn't know him well enough yet.

He lowered his head to speak to the small, yellow-
skinned woman. "Mae, you have my burger and fries
ready?" She grinned shyly and disappeared into the back.
"And what does a cop sound like?"

"You don't waste words. No small talk. You know—
just the facts, ma'am."

He smiled but didn't laugh. His teeth were white and
straight. Just as we reached the register at the end of the
long buffet, Mae returned with McCoy's food and a second uniformed waiter appeared, offering to ferry my tray
to a table. I let out a small groan, realizing I'd left my
handbag at Langley. "Damn, I forgot my bag."

McCoy chuckled, narrowing his eyes at me. "You
young broads are always looking for a free meal. I'll pay
this time, but you know, this means you have to sleep
with me after lunch."

As I handed the waiter my tray I apologized for forget-
ting my wallet and asked if I could return and pay later.

"Oh, no, ma'am. We don't take cash in the faculty

dining room. You'll see a charge next month on your personal account."

With a helping hand from the waiter, we set our trays down at a table with a view. The outlook from the dining room's bank of six-foot-tall windows was stupendous: Providence in panorama, the large white dome of the statehouse rising on a solitary hill in the majestic distance.

"So," McCoy said, cutting short my scenic reverie, "Carlyle wooed you over to our side?" He layered spirals of catsup on his cheeseburger and French fries. "AG's office for five years, right?"

"Five years, yes. Had we met while I was there?"

"No. I'd remember. You don't exactly melt into the woodwork."

"I assume that's a compliment?"

"Only if you like my taste in women."

"So," I said, cutting him short, "you were a cop. You're too young to be retired, no?"

"Hmm, gorgeous, funny, and smart too?"

I didn't respond because frankly I was tiring of his flirtatious repartee. I just stared at him, one corner of my mouth turning down sourly.

McCoy sat up straighter. "Smart like a shark, I guess. I retired early with a disability pension. I took a shot in the shoulder. Okay?"

I shrugged. "I guess so."

"Now let's talk Holton business. If you and I are doing our jobs right, nothing here gets to the local cops, let alone the AG's office. And if things ever spiral out of control, I still have a buddy or two on the force."

"I'd say Melinda Hastings is about as out of control as you can get."

"That's different. I'm talking about campus horseplay, not sicko axe murderers."

"And what makes you so sure the murderer wasn't a student?"

McCoy guffawed out loud. "You are so damn cute."

"McCoy, let me advise you. Calling me *cute* is right up there on my gag meter with winking."

He sat up even stiffer. His pupils looked a little enlarged. "Christ, you're a volatile girl. We're trying to have lunch, aren't we? Now where were we?"

"We were talking about your naiveté."

He dropped the French fry he was holding and sat back in his chair. "Meals with you are going to be a real blast, I can see." Retrieving his fry, he continued, "Carlyle wants the school to maintain a low profile. He's a fly-low-under-the-radar type. The Hastings thing threw him for a real loop. Before that, most of the stuff we saw here was petty—peeing on the sidewalks, a few loud parties, public drinking, a little weed. Now Carlyle wants to play it super safe. You know, no news is good news? He's bucking for president of the college when Hatchett—the current president—retires this spring."

McCoy resumed eating, shoving half his burger into his mouth and trying to talk and chew at the same time. Somehow he got the words out without opening his mouth too wide, though he still managed to gross me out. "All we gotta do till then is keep things status quo, which isn't going to be as easy after Hastings."

I made a mental note to tell Shannon about McCoy's ongoing friendships with the guys in blue. I doubted the AG's office knew the cops were pulling Ken Carlyle's chestnuts out of the fire with assists from Mike McCoy.

"So I take the report and do the investigating and then you go head-to-head with the students and families and massage the plea bargain and penalty phase. But don't get too puffed up with power, sweetheart. Carlyle's strings get pulled by the mega-money interests and the old blue bloods, and your strings get pulled by Carlyle. Someone has to be the middleman, the fixer."

"The fixer? So I'm here to clean up messes? Carlyle actually told you that?"

"More like Teflon. With you here, the cops and AG's office might not scrape too deep into our muck. But stick with me and you should be safe."

"Let's talk muck."

"I told you. Small stuff. Beer, weed, and a wayward panty every now and then. But after Hastings, even the little crap is gonna get blown out of proportion."

"And why exactly should I trust *you*?"

"Do you have a stupid house designation and date after your name?"

"No."

"Well, neither do I." He stuffed a handful of over-catsupped French fries into his mouth. "And neither does the rest of the help. But everyone else in this room *does*."

I smashed boiled egg into my lettuce with my fork. "Keep going."

"First-year students get assigned to a dormitory. Except here at Holton it's called a house. They can live off campus after the first year, but they keep their house designations forever. It's like a military rank. They introduce themselves for the rest of their natural-born lives with names, house designations, and the year they graduated. It's a variation on a general Ivy League theme. This is an exclusive club. Once you graduate you're a lifer. That's why you should trust me. 'Cause neither of us is part of the club."

"The lower classes should stick together and rise up against the infidels?" I popped a cherry tomato into my mouth and considered squirting it over him between my two front teeth.

"Come on. Tell me you don't want to get old with yellow crooked teeth and a head of wild gray hair around a prune-wrinkled face, wave martinis in your hand and treat everyone liked hired help, and get away with it because your ancestors were criminals let out of prison in England and herded like sheep onto a boat called the *Mayflower* and then deported to America?"

I laughed.

"You see what I mean? The jealousy's inescapable, and it's just the luck of the draw."

"Your point. I surrender."

"So, you ready for your first case?"

"I think you're my first case."

"Quit horsing around."

"Okay, okay. Is this the volatile-but-must-be-handled-discreetly matter Carlyle was talking about?"

"Lisa Cummings. She's stealing food from the student cafeteria. She's been at it for weeks. The staff has seen her."

"Maybe the girl's hungry and doesn't have the bread for the bread."

"Unlikely. Unless she's eating low-cal cash. Skinny as a beanpole. Maybe the family trust fund dried up and she isn't getting her allowance. Or she's snorting it all up her nose. In any event I got another complaint yesterday. The report's already on your desk."

"We just climbed the vice ladder from beer and weed to *cocaine*."

He wiped his mouth on his still-unfolded linen napkin. "You just read the report and then we'll talk again." He pushed the remaining half of his cheeseburger to the middle of the table. "I'd rather have half a cheeseburger than a whole veggie burger."

"I'm still trying to convince myself I like salads."

"Yeah, I like salads too—with Stilton blue dressing and a porterhouse steak on the side. And a bottle of Taupenot-Merme Gevrey-Chambertin. You want coffee? I'm getting a refill."

I nodded. "Nice accent. You're kind of a mysterious man, Mike."

Sauntering away, he clapped his walkie-talkie to his ear and managed a conversation while herding two cups of coffee back our way from the buffet table. He yanked four creams and a few packets of sugar out of his pocket and tossed them on the table. "I forgot to ask how you like it."

"You got a call?"

Still standing, he leaned over me. "My wife. Her private investigator wants to know who the cute young thing is I'm having lunch with."

"Yeah. So I guess this is as good as it gets. Let's go back to those cheap burgundies."

"How old are you? Twenty-five?" He sat.

"Thirty-two. I'll be thirty-three in the spring."

"You look younger."

"It's my baby fat."

"You see fat. I see curves." He gently smiled out of one side of his mouth.

"Come on. Was that call about a student?"

"Wasn't about a student. The red carpet's getting

rolled out for some VIPs. Alumni and donors. A dinner at the president's house tonight. Money. Big money. Do you mind if I shirk my gentlemanly duties and leave you here?" He took a last gulp of his coffee, rattling the cup in its saucer. "You can find your way back?"

I nodded.

McCoy craned his head backward until he was looking up at the ceiling like someone searching for birds in the chandeliers. At last he cracked his neck—it sounded like a hardwood log being split by lightning—and then he groaned in pleasure, or in pain, or a combo, scrunching his eyes up like Spanky of the Little Rascals.

"You need a chiropractor, McCoy, or a better sex life."

His eyes twinkled. "Tell me about it." He patted me on the hand, looked at his trusty Timex, and rose from the table. "Late. I've got to go. See you soon."

"What time is it, anyway?" I asked.

"Twelve thirty-three." He winked again and I let it go.

He was a third of the way across the vast hall when he turned back to me and yelled out cheerily, "And that man's suit you're wearing? Doesn't fool me for a second!"

CHAPTER FIFTEEN

———— ∞∞∞ ————

Guardian Angels

I RETURNED TO MY office to find the envelope McCoy had promised me, a manila nine-by-twelve neatly marked "Confidential" and placed squarely on my desk. When had he dropped it off? The few minutes he'd been late for the staff meeting when his takes-a-licking-and-keeps-on-ticking Timex had been on the averred blink? I had to wonder whether McCoy wasn't far more efficient than he pretended to be, his nonchalant and poky demeanor a charming act designed to throw people off guard.

I was about ready to tear the seal when I noticed a young man in his early twenties standing in my open doorway. Head tilted, he was staring at me with half-lowered lids. His fashionably short auburn hair and his clean-shaven face argued against his cracked leather flight jacket that looked like an antique from World War II. The cuffs of his baggy chinos puddled over laceless white sneakers. Slung over his shoulder was the kind of black nylon bag postmen use.

His eyes aimed so intensely at me that I was too curious to look away.

Was he the twenty-first-century Messiah incarnate? Was I receiving a dispatch from Melinda Hastings's murderer? Had Vince sent a hit man?

He finally spoke. "Hi there, I'm Elliot Orenstein, editor of the *Veritas*, the school newspaper."

"Oh." I took a lungful of air and then blew it out. "You make a good reporter," I said. "You have a clever way of making yourself urgent."

He looked at the empty chair in front of me. "Right. Can we talk for a minute?"

"I'm a little overwhelmed right now."

"I'll only take a minute or two. I'm not a big talker."

I tucked McCoy's manila folder into my top drawer. "Sit."

After removing a small pad from under the mysterious black flap, he dropped his laden bag on the floor. Pen poised, he looked up at me, his head rising before his eyes met mine.

"Herr Carlyle sent me. I'm on a special mission to make you look like the new Holton savior."

"Ah."

"I'll follow you around. We'll talk. I'll watch you. You tell me about yourself. You get the idea?"

"Yeah, but the stuff I do is confidential. It won't work here."

"I don't read your files and I don't attend meetings. What you did as a prosecutor, how you apply a prosecutor's experience here — Carlyle wants all that granola. But actually we're all curious as to why you were hired in the first place."

"We?" My insecurities were rearing their egotistical

heads. Did these kids think I wasn't qualified for a stint at this brain freeze? But I'd be damned if I'd let him put me on the defensive. It was a position I didn't want to get comfortable in my first day on the job.

"The students," he explained. "I mean does Carlyle even want to find out who killed Melinda Hastings? Or does he just want it smoke-screened until it fades into ancient history?"

I sat forward in my chair. He may have just placed the first paver in my road back to the AG's office. "You think it was a fellow student?"

He shook his head. "This is a small school. Everyone knows everyone else. I can't imagine how a Holton student could kill someone and think he could get away with it."

I sat back and retrieved the manila folder from my drawer, signaling my dismissal of Elliot. "Well, I squirm at questions. It's a learned behavior but necessary for an AAG. So I won't be a good subject for an in-depth interview."

"So give me some pabulum to keep Carlyle happy— and my job secure. Come on. You've got to have balls . . . oh, sorry, *the intestinal fortitude* for a place like this or you'll get eaten alive. Believe me, I know firsthand."

"Do I detect a dollop of bitterness?"

"Emotions are a waste of time. Hey, maybe I can even ease your transition. Assimilation isn't easy in this fortress." He whipped his backpack over his shoulder and stood. "Anyway, think about it. You'll get me some brownie points with Carlyle, and my colleagues at the paper are clamoring for your interview. Do you mind if I come by again tomorrow at about this time?"

He aimed those eyes at me again, waiting for an answer.

Simple and straightforward, he didn't sugarcoat his motives. I respected the kid's honesty.

"I don't know what my schedule is yet. This is my first *hour* on the job."

"I'll stop by. If you're here, you're here."

Without further ado, he walked out of my office. I sighed and flipped open McCoy's top-secret package. The enclosure was comprised of three brief documents: an incident report signed by McCoy himself, including a note on his interview with the suspect; a statement from the cafeteria manager, Robert M. Miller; and an invoice on the letterhead of Holton's food services, itemizing the values of the allegedly pickpocketed edibles.

I rushed through the coma-inducing background details. The perp, a sophomore named Lisa Cummings, lived on campus in Halsey House. McCoy's narrative was composed in a highly personalized shorthand. Though his writing was choppy and clean like his speech (McCoy wouldn't know an adjective if one jumped up and bit him on the nose), it featured definite upgrades in grammar and diction. And as was the case face-to-face (N.B. that Côte de Nuits burgundy), his tough-guy routine didn't quite play out in print. He hit several tongue-in-cheek notes which would have gotten him fired on the spot at the AG's:

SEPTEMBER 20, 2:45 P.M. *Met with student, Lisa Cummings, in my office in room B347 at Langley Hall. She shredded a tissue and asked me to hurry because she was late for a meeting. I read her the statement of Bob Miller, cafeteria manager. When I was done, she denied stealing and claimed Bob*

*Miller had been mistaken. She asked what proof
we had other than Miller's word. I enumerated
eyewitness reports from food-service employees.
She appeared to begin crying, though I saw no
actual tears. She continued to deny the thefts. Ms.
Cummings alleged that Miller "has a thing" for
her and that her rejections might be causing him
to retaliate with these lies and accusations. Ms.
Cummings kept staring at her watch and fidget-
ing. She told me to stop looking at her "that way"
so I begged her pardon and asked her to excuse my
squinting as it was a habit and I was also having
a migraine. She suggested I was torturing her and
then inquired as to my age. I suggested that she
make an appointment with Assistant Dean Becker.
Ms. Cummings refused and then asked to be excused. I excused Ms. Cummings at 3:15 p.m.*

Rita, returning from lunch, popped her head in my
office.

"My first case," I told her, sighing and indicating the
paperwork strewn over my desk like mismatched puzzle
pieces. "Double murder-suicide with rat poison."

"Ooh la la, Miss Melone. Don't joke like that after
Miss Hastings, yes? Seriously though, you have looked up
the Cummings girl's rap sheet and mug shot?" she said.

"Rap sheet? Mug shot? Now *you're* joking."

"You haven't heard of them before? No? The police
use rap sheets—"

"Rita, why do our *students* have rap sheets?"

"*Pardon, mademoiselle.* I call them that. They are just
general background information, plus curricula vitae on

first-degree relatives, and, for the students who are so-called legacies, any important information about their alumni relatives, whether they are on our annual donor list, etc., etc. Nothing *really* personal *there. Savez-vous?*"

Rita's glinting, wide-open eyes made me suspect there were super-private student files the college kept in parallel to the routine records. The use of dual folders, a practice not unknown in the private sector and in covert branches of government, would possess obvious utility for a fancy uptight institution like Holton. Rita now took several minutes showing me how to access the school's local area network and pinpoint each kid's administrative and academic file on my office Mac.

"And where can I find the cafeteria manager?" I asked her.

"His office is behind the cafeteria kitchen. But, *mein liebchen*, he is neither here nor there! I think Mike McCoy is the one who will have the eyes for you."

"I get the feeling Mike McCoy's eyes are all over the place. Maybe they should stay on his wife."

"Wife? No, no. Mike isn't married. But you are right, Miss Melone. If he didn't have wandering eyes perhaps he wouldn't be divorced."

"That's weird. Divorced men rarely joke about being married."

Rita threw her hands up and shook her head. "That man has more mysteries than the Father, Son, and Holy Spirit. Maybe he is playing games with you. Sometimes men tell women they are married and it makes them more attractive. No?"

"In Doris Day/Rock Hudson movies only, Rita."

I clicked on the link entitled "Lisa Cummings–Halsey House–2008." The "rap sheet" data was comprised of

SAT scores, a picture and fingerprint of each student, and alumni information. The cafeteria bandit, Lisa Reed Cummings, turned out to be a flaxen-haired, well-heeled girl from New York. Almost a beauty and no dummy academically, at least until recently. Nothing suggested this young girl was short on either cash or a proper, well-scented, pillows-fluffed upbringing.

"Thanks, Rita. I think I can take it from here."

"*Oui, mademoiselle*, I won't be far."

Rita twirled into her exit and I began reading.

Lisa Cummings, Halsey House, 2008
(no partner listed)
929 Park Avenue
New York, NY 10028

PARENTS/GUARDIAN:
Margaret B. Cummings, mother (father deceased)

FAMILY ALUMNI/AE:
Charles Cummings, Halsey House, 1958
(father—deceased)
Chester Cummings, Halsey House, 2004 (brother)
Kent Cummings, Halsey House, 1932
(grandfather—deceased)
James Cummings, Halsey House, 1954 (uncle)

HIGH SCHOOL:
Chapin School for Girls, 2004

No infractions came up on her administrative sheet. Academically, her GPA had fallen from a 3.5 to a 2.7 as of the previous spring semester. Lisa Cummings was a C-plus student with an A-list background. Rita had told me that most personal information was stripped out of the network versions of the student files (sensibly so, since modern colleges were lousy with brainy young techies fluent in hacking abilities). I sent Ms. Cummings an e-mail requesting a meeting at ten the next morning. She was stealing like a third-world refugee, which seemed nonsensical. I had to sit back a moment and wonder: Was this perhaps some kind of rigged test case? Was Carlyle going to pop up out of a Trojan horse?

I took the opportunity to do some online snooping, and scrolled through and past the C's, until I got to the H's, where Melinda Hastings's name should have been. It apparently had already been deleted from the student roster. I checked every available Holton database for any mention of her, or anything else of murder-related relevance, until, at about half past three, I heard the familiar sound of a police scanner/walkie-talkie in the hallway and my girlish heart quickened. I walked to the wall mirror in my office—next to the door—and pretended to be brushing my hair. Mike McCoy was speaking with Rita at her desk. I struggled to make out their words but then McCoy's scanner got louder and I hustled breathlessly back to my chair, composing myself for a knock that never came. McCoy and his walkie-talkie faded away down the hall.

I leaned back in my chair wistfully. Or maybe I was getting bored. Boredom was not something I was familiar or comfortable with, so I got on the wire to the AG's office to see if the girls would meet me after work for a quick dinner. I was missing them already and eating alone seemed distinctly depressing.

It was Laurie who grabbed the phone. "Forget it. Too busy. And Shannon's on trial. You could try Beth, but the poor girl's fingers are bleeding from all the trial motions we've got her doing. I *hate* giving her typing to do. We've got to work on the law school route for her."

"Yeah, know what you mean. But, Laur, I've got trouble to a much greater degree than a JD right now."

"We're multitasking over here, Mari. Stay calm. They got that cool gym over there. It's one of your perks, so you should check it out. Pig claims it never should have passed zoning."

"When in hell did Piganno tell you this?"

"Today. We bombarded his office this morning to try to talk some sense into him but he just started lashing out at us. He's been tearing into everyone's hide all day. I actually think he misses you. The man's going to have a heart attack he's so steamed. And Shannon keeps shoveling coal into his fire, so the Pig should be dead and on a spit by Easter and then we'll get the new AG to hire you back."

"Cut him a break, Laurie."

"What's this I hear? Spare the Pig? The same guy who keeps telling us to keep an eye on you?"

"You're freaking me out. He wants you to spy on me?"

"Fuck if I know what's in his mucked-up brain. I just smile at him and bob my head. Shannon, on the other hand, has been towering over him and ranting in gutter slang. I don't think even she knows what she's saying half the time."

"Any new threats from Jeff?"

"Quiet as the mouse that he is. The cops haven't come up with much new on Hastings either. So far, we're still clean. Well, except for you . . ."

"I'll call you if I get any scoops re Hastings from this end."

"Hey, wait, what about the drug in her? GHB. No tie-in with that to Holton? Check it out campus-wise."

"Laurie, Vince isn't going to get a warrant to comb the entire campus based on GHB use. It's as easy to come by as hootch. Lots of oversexed bad little boys use that drug."

"Go take a cold shower. See you soon."

With little else to do on my first day of this cushy job, I closed up shop early and headed for the famed Holton gymnasium to pedal and sweat the demons away. As I walked toward the monstrously ugly orange steel building, I pondered to its gnawing depths the question of whether Vince Piganno would ever be ready for the call in which I would offer up my firstborn to him for a chance to come home. Every now and then, when I was growing up, my father, apropos of really nothing, would screw up his face and tilt his head at me and say, "Marianna, watch out for the Sicilians. They're known for their grudges."

On to the treadmill.

CHAPTER SIXTEEN

Bathing Suits Required

THE GYM WAS A fat ugly duck of a building, squatting amid a flock of elegant brick Georgians whose owners, God bless them, had objected strongly and loudly to the groundbreaking. The interior was another story. This high-tech gymnasium was fairy-tale lavish. White marble and Roman columns were visible through fifteen-foot glass front doors. Beams of midday sunlight cascading from the domed glass ceiling turned the highly polished marble floor a brilliant, dazzling white. Over at the dreamy equipment counter, hundreds and hundreds of fluffy white towels were stacked in flawless columns against the wall, a sort of white-cloud backdrop for the most amazing array of exercise accoutrements and athletic footwear I had ever seen.

"May I see your ID, please?"

About a foot above the Carrera marble counter perched a shiny pair of hard white breasts covered just barely to the nipple in a tight, white cotton muscle shirt.

A human being was also attached. What she *really* looked like was some six-foot super-specimen of a genetically engineered species from a gorgeous planet in a victorious galaxy far, far away.

"Hello, Miss Melone," she read from my ID. "I'm Denise. Your first time here?"

Her voice—straight out of one of those Japanese bishoujo games my sister and her friends liked to play—was as beautiful as it was artificial. Her oversized white teeth peeked out from behind contoured Bobbi-Browned lips.

I nodded, ashamed to go up against the high-tenored silkiness of her voice. My voice was deeper, rough around the edges, a type of street jive learned after so many years of communicating with derelicts and criminal defense attorneys. My words sliced like a machete through thick vegetation, while Denise's trailed sentences like wisps of smoke.

She pushed a towel and locker key across the counter toward me.

"The entrance to the gym is through the women's locker room right over there. Have a nice workout. If you need anything, let me know."

Soft, thirsty, dove gray carpeting—probably replaced every six months—and immaculate white walls greeted me on the far side of the door. Every mirror was equipped with its own box of tissues, chrome receptacle, and hair dryer. On the counters were sleek trays filled with individual bottles of shampoo, soap, and tampons. Most of the mirrored stations were occupied by slender young bodies attired in either skimpy bikini underwear or thongs. Some of the girls were naked. They were all chatting over the hum of hair dryers, breasts bouncing freely as they alternately lifted and lowered their arms to fluff up hair or flip a brush.

These girls had probably been weaned on grilled chicken, asparagus, and dry white wine. Under a microscope their DNA was linear and sleek like a high-speed Acela train gliding through life on a cushion of air. And then there were . . . well, *my* genes . . . curved and sultry, meandering down a circuitous road that would take me only as far as age forty-five before they conked out and insisted I cut back on carbs before they'd take me home again.

Thinking such psychotic little thoughts, I found a locker and opened my trusty duffel bag—the one I stored in the trunk of my Jeep in the off chance I was suddenly inspired to exercise. I donned my musty sneakers, gym shorts, and an old T-shirt of my dad's and had almost made it to the exercise room when a Jacuzzi the size of a Boca Raton swimming pool slowed me down. None of the six naked women in it was talking. Nipples of varying shades and in some cases alarming sizes looked to be afloat right at the surface of the rippling water. The attached women relaxed with their heads thrown back against the tiles. Directly above was a large sign that read BATHING SUITS REQUIRED IN THE WHIRLPOOL.

I jaunted up the stairs.

The weight room itself was sterile, white, and unadorned, crammed with Nautiluses, treadmills, Stairmasters, and stationary bikes. A station of free weights against the far wall, its dumbbells and barbells neatly stacked, looked like a torture contraption. All the bodies in the room were lean and tightly spandexed, with the exception of—

McCoy's.

In the corner lifting weights, he was shirtless, tattooed, and thickly muscled. Rivers of sweat coursed down dense dark chest hair. There was no reason for me to look away. He was in an exercise-induced spell.

I mounted a bike and began to pedal. Within seconds a voice snuck up behind me.

"I've never seen you in the gym before. You must be a first-year."

I glanced back at two young men, both about twenty, and then faced forward again and continued pedaling as I answered. "I'm not a student."

"You work here?" The one who'd spoken to me had walked up to the side of the bike close enough that I could hear his breathing, still rapid from exercise or swimming. His wet, blond hair was slicked back.

"They shouldn't hire babes. I mean how are we supposed to defer to authority when the authority looks like you?"

"Why don't you two boys go take a cold shower?"

He laughed.

"Come on, Cory," his friend said.

Piqued by my rudeness, Blondie wasn't going away easily. "What office do you work in? Maybe you could type papers for me after hours."

In front of my bike now, he placed his hands on the bars, his face inches from mine. I blanched inwardly at his naked sexual aggression. As if my pedaling were driving me closer to him, I stopped and sat up, racking my brain for some pithy feminist ammunition to spit into that smooth little mug of his, when Mike McCoy appeared, as if he'd rappelled in by helicopter.

"Hey, Cory. I see you've met Miss Melone, the new Assistant Dean of Student Ethics."

McCoy and the brat exchanged gorilla stares. McCoy wouldn't budge an inch. After no more than a second's hesitation Cory leaned toward McCoy and they shook hands. Smart boy.

"Mike. Thanks for saving the day. I was on the verge of becoming this woman's slave for life. Or making her mine. But—Student Ethics—that *would* look untoward, wouldn't it? Like a prisoner currying favor with the warden."

"There you go, Cory." Mike turned to me. "Young Sherman here is the president of the Reese House membership, Marianna," he said.

"How wonderful."

Sherman thrust his cold hand at me, taking hold of mine in a firm grasp. I read the words that were embroidered in a small crest on his T-shirt: Reese House, 2008. Holton.

"We've met before," he said to me. "That Danish film at the Avon Cinema. You were in front of me in line. I never forget the rear view of a beautiful woman. Are you a dancer?"

"You really should practice your pickup lines."

"Pickup? That's presumptuous of you, *ma'am*. I was merely complimenting you."

I got down off the bike, grabbing the towel I'd slung over its handlebars. "I've had enough of you, buddy." My voice had gone uncontrollably low and raspy. "I am the Assistant Dean of—"

McCoy stepped in front of me. "All right, kids. Enough fun. No rumbles in the gym."

Sherman lowered his head in a respectful bow. "You're overly sensitive, Ms. Melone."

"Let's go, Cory," said his friend, who had the bright gray eyes of a wolf pup. The friend's tone was plaintive, not demanding. He held his hand out to me, tentatively and solicitously. "I'm Rod Lipton."

I shook his clammy hand reluctantly. He smiled at me, but the grin lasted an agonizing moment too long. Lipton was taller, lankier than his friend. He was obviously used to playing the peacemaker, the good cop to Sherman's bad, the one who took the punches so Cory could walk away with no bruises and a preserved ego. Everyone should have a friend like Lipton, I thought.

"You're spunky for a California girl." Cory still wasn't going to lay off.

Lipton let go of my hand. "No, no," Lipton interrupted, "she's from around here. Come on, Cory, let's go."

I looked at Lipton. "How do you know where I'm from?"

"I heard it somewhere. It's a small school. You're from the AG's office, right?"

Sherman jumped back in. "AG, huh? Are you here because of Melinda? A bit of bad luck for the old girl, I'd say."

"Bad luck is when you slip in a pothole," I said, muzzling the fouler retorts stomping through my brain. This wasn't the AG's office, where a "fuck you" would have been more than enough response to bullshit.

"No," he had the audacity to answer back, "that's just stupidity for not looking where you're going. But maybe you're right, Melinda was a clumsy kind of girl now that I think of it."

The two young men walked off—Cory and Rod—talking and laughing in the muted tones of an inside joke.

"Sherman's a smooth operator," McCoy said once they were out of earshot.

"Smooth? I should have punched him in the face."

"He may have punched you right back. He's a spoiled Hollywood horror with a bad temper. He wields a lot of power with the students and the administration. His family has the connections *and* the money to make trouble."

"I was a prosecutor. I can handle him," I said, getting back on the bike.

"Hmm. Maybe you could handle *me* a little too, while you're at it."

McCoy stayed to my rear, but I could feel his smile on me. He was the type who scattered lines to women like seeds onto a patch of ground, waiting to see what he could harvest.

I kept pedaling in silence. Any response from me would sound like some silly line too, but I was beginning to feel that I couldn't help myself. Everything about this McCoy character seemed geared to suck me into a trashy but deliriously yummy B-grade romantic comedy. That he probably used this charming brand of assault on every woman he met didn't matter. It was a pretty damn delectable assault. Maybe my weakness was due to a desperate need for a sentimental journey down Lovers' Lane after dating, dumping, and then being double-crossed by Jeff Kendall.

Or—perish the thought—I was actually falling for a dumb ex-cop.

"I think I can handle both you and Sherman," I said.

McCoy came around the front of the bike. The look on his face brought my pedaling to a halt. "You watch out for Sherman," he repeated. "At the AG's you were only dealing with scum. Guys like him, you have to handle like molten lead—he can burn you."

A few seconds passed and I realized he was frowning, squinting at me.

"Getting a migraine?" I said.

His grimace took a half turn upward before rising into a sunny smile. I got a tingle looking at his gleaming white teeth through the frame of his opened lips. He tugged at both ends of the towel looped around my neck, drawing my face within inches of his.

What was he doing? In the middle of the school gym surrounded by students. My first day of work and I was going to be fired for fraternizing with a coworker I hardly knew. I felt a twang of panic but I kept looking him in the eyes, not moving a muscle.

He nodded his approval—I hadn't bridled—and then, as if taunting me, he abruptly let go of the towel, flourishing it in the air like Zorro.

"You're a real jerk," I said.

He nodded again, then backed away from me. "Got some work to do. See you soon, gorgeous."

I watched him saunter toward the exit, wiping his hairy armpits with his towel. Yuck. What *exactly* was I finding attractive in this guy?

Pondering that, I pedaled until five-thirty, walked the treadmill until six, and was out of the shower by six-ten. While I was drying myself I heard someone come into the women's bathroom and close the door to one of the toilet stalls. Passing the stall on my way out, I peeked down and saw a pair of pink crocodile shoes facing the wall. I waited at the sink, running the faucet, and after a few more moments heard the familiar sound of several long steady inhalations.

Yes, I had done a little cocaine in my not-too-distant youth.

I left the bathroom to avoid having to confront her, but then immediately felt guilty for leaving. I was, after all, now a sort of legal counselor to these students. I found my locker and dressed quickly, but minutes later when I got back to the shower room the crocodile-shoe girl was gone. I grabbed my backpack from the locker, slamming it shut, and ran out the main entrance of the gym, where I bumped smack into—

"Hey, Byron! Did you see a girl with pink crocodile shoes just leave here?"

"Real or embossed?" she droned sarcastically.

Ignoring her, I peered down the four-way intersection at Wheeler and Butler where, once again, I saw nothing. I dropped my shoulders, feeling all my weight settle down on my heels.

"What's your problem, Melone?" she said, backing a foot or so away.

"Problem?" Realizing then that Byron and I were just not meant to be soul sisters, I looked back at the gym and changed the subject. "I just had a great workout. Beautiful gym."

"Dean Carlyle's baby," she said, looking over my shoulder at it. "We worked incredibly hard on that project."

"I know. I heard the zoning was a real bitch."

"Zoning? No. The approvals flew right through the board. I'm talking about the capital expenditure. It took us five years to get the funding and we were still a million short. Ken stepped in and saved the day with some incredible last-minute donations. He's a whiz at generating capital."

"I probably misunderstood about the zoning."

"No, I don't think you did." She took a step closer. "That's probably the outsider gossip. Don't bullshit me, Melone. You get your priorities straight and we'll both get along. Okay?"

Because she was dead-on—my priorities weren't exactly crystal clear—I was as speechless as a child who had just wet her pants. But I pulled up my britches and went for another shot. "Have we met in a past life? You just met me yet your hatred for me seems to have a long history."

With that, she moved right up in my face. "I think you're a fraud. You're an insecure, prissy little broad with your fuck-me stilettos. And why are you here in the first place? Ken must have had a good reason for saving you from the unemployment line, but for the life of me I can't figure it out."

"Seems my employment history is an open book around here, huh?"

She actually chuckled, deep and throaty. "Your employment history, and the fact that you're a lousy lay. There might be one thing you and I agree on. Jeff Kendall's a shit. He screws you front and back before you know which side is up."

I smashed my rising temper underfoot like a glowing cigarette while Byron turned toward the gym laughing like an oil baron at a fossil-fuel-burning furnace in an ice storm.

What Jeff's history was with Byron Eckert I couldn't begin to imagine, but it was comforting to know she hated him as much as I did. If I never got a solo chance to pay Jeff back for putting me in this position, maybe someday Byron and I could use him as the rope in a heated game of tug-of-war. I'd even let her win.

———∞∞∞———

CHAPTER SEVENTEEN

Candy from a Baby

DAY TWO, 8:35 A.M. Five minutes late, I rushed across the street toward Langley. Wind rustled the trees and the clouds in the sky hung low and dark. A squirrel darted across my path. The door to the building had been propped open with an old-fashioned, thick wooden shim, and a few autumn leaves had scurried into the front marble corridor. The building was overheated and the interior air was darkly perfumed and stale. Secretaries, sipping coffee and huddling, wisecracked a litany of mild grievances as I walked by their offices toward my own.

Rita seemed to be Langley's only non-cantankerous secretary that morning. She was standing by the door of my office with a crisp smile and a hot cup of coffee. "*Guten Morgen, mein Fräulein*," she said. "Your ten o'clock appointment is early. I have her in my office. Should I ask her to return later?"

"No, I'm here. Send her in." I took the coffee. "You're as good as a dream, Rita."

Seconds after I'd settled into my desk I glanced up at a stick figure standing solemnly in my doorway.

"Hi, I'm Lisa Cummings. I have an appointment at ten. May I come in now?"

One of her hands seemed to be grasping the wall. A short pink raincoat with a Burberry print lining hung loosely from her shoulders. She was a gaunt, pale slip of a girl.

"Come on in."

Lisa shuffled to my desk and stopped, awaiting further orders.

"Close the door and have a seat," I said.

Back to the door she went, pushing it closed with both palms like it was made of heavy iron. She dragged her feet oddly as she slogged back to me, but I kept my eyes on her face. She sat and plucked a ball of used tissues out of her pocket, holding the wad in her hands like a beloved baby blanket.

I put on my prosecutor's face and leaned forward in my chair.

She wrapped an errant lock of hair behind her ear and paused, looking at me blankly. She knew why she was there. She would either deny everything, or admit the theft and offer an excuse. That was the drill at the AG's and I didn't figure on human nature proving too different here. But I wanted her to talk first. She sniffed and dabbed her nose a few times with the ball of tissues and then kept massaging it with her thumbs. I saw no tears but I slid my own box of tissues toward her anyway. She shook her head and her thin blonde hair moved in clumps, as if she hadn't showered in days. The lock pinned behind her ear fell free, veiling one of her eyes.

"Are you having financial problems?" I finally asked.

She shook her head and began rocking back and forth like a hysterical child. With both hands she held the tissue to her nose. Her skin was a transparent gray.

Time to buck the suspect up.

"Okay, Lisa. Do you want to tell me what's going on?"

She shrugged her shoulders and hazarded a glance at me. "I don't know why I do it." She clenched the tissues in her hand.

I paused, then began again. "How are things going in school? Your grades?"

She shrugged her bony shoulders again. "All right, I guess."

"Are you missing classes?"

She focused keenly on my eyes. "You talked with my professors?"

"No."

"I've got the notes from the classes I missed."

"Good. All right, then. Would you like to talk to Dr. Becker?"

"I already do—once a week. But I don't need a psychologist. I just need to . . . um . . . just get back to classes. I missed a couple of tests, I think."

"Lisa, I can't say you have psychological issues, but you are coming across to me this morning as very scattered, very unfocused—"

"I'm immature," she said straight-faced. "That's what my therapist in New York said."

"Oh. Okay. Well then, help me out here. What should we do about this stealing?"

Down bobbed that floppy head of hers. Her shoulders heaved silently as she exhaled. She said nothing for a few seconds, but neither did she move a muscle to get up and leave.

"I told Mr. McCoy I would pay for the food."

Hmm. Simple confession with *no* excuse. Why was I surprised? "Are you sure you told Mr. McCoy about reimbursing the cafeteria? It wasn't mentioned in his report."

"Ask *him* why he left it out. He probably left a lot of stuff out."

"What else did he omit, Lisa?"

She shrugged and shook her head, as if it weren't worth the effort to defend herself.

"Well, reimbursement is not quite the issue at this juncture. Where I came from at the AG's office, people are prosecuted by the state for stealing. It's a criminal violation."

Her eyes went feral and wide. I expected her to start screaming bloody murder, but instead she gulped miserably for air and doubled over in airplane-disaster posture, clutching her knees.

Without straightening up she began addressing me in a low baritone, her eyes pinned to the floor. "The school wouldn't prosecute someone like me. Would they?"

My guess was no. But I wasn't telling Lisa that a group which included Dean Carlyle, Mike McCoy, and probably countless others were wedded to the unalloyed truth: *Have bucks will travel.*

"Whether or not the school brings criminal charges is irrelevant. You can't keep stealing. Can we at least agree on that?"

She sat up as if I'd astonished her with simple logic. "Okay." At which point she reached into the back pocket of her jeans and unfolded a thin packet of cash, peeled off a single bill, and placed it on my desk. Neither of us moved. "Is a hundred enough?" she asked softly.

Maybe she wasn't so naive after all. I shook my head slowly and slid the money back her way. As I was looking at her, my stomach flip-flopped as if *I* were going to cry. "No, Lisa . . ." My voice cracked, so I stopped talking.

Lisa picked up the bill and bunched it together with the shredded Kleenex in her fist. She was absolutely oblivious to my clemency. "Sometimes I forget to bring money with me. I'm not used to needing cash."

"Is that how it's been taken care of in the past? Shoplift stuff and your father pays the tab later?"

Disregarding me, she rose listlessly from the chair and emptied her pocket of mangled tissues in a wastebasket by my desk. I wondered if that hundred-dollar bill had become part of the trash. "My father's dead." She turned back to me. "How did you know about that? Bergdorf's had to sign a confidentiality agreement. It was supposed to be a secret except for my family and the lawyers."

"Bergdorf's? You stole from Bergdorf Goodman?"

She settled herself down in the same chair while reaching for my box of Kleenex. She sniffled richly and sneezed. The wings of her nose were a translucent crimson-pink and her eyes were rimed with redness. "I'm sorry, Miss Melone. Maybe I'm not making myself clear. This has nothing to do with money."

"All right, Lisa. Maybe Dr. Becker can help you sort through this. But I want you to write a letter of apology and reimburse the cafeteria manager. Also, go do some community service. Just thirty hours—anywhere you want. Bring some proof back to me when it's complete. Then this whole thing will be over, and no one will ever know it happened."

"Community service? Where's that?"

"There are local soup kitchens. And the Salvation Army is always looking for volunteers to help out in the store. Anything you want."

"Yeah, sure," she sang in the key of sarcasm. She turned her wrist to read the thin gold watch. "I've got to go."

"Class, I hope?"

She shook her head. "I'm meeting someone." She looked up at me. *"Cory Sherman."*

She had said his name as if on a dare. I kept silent— didn't jump at the bait.

"At least Cory doesn't try to *help* me. I don't want anyone's help. You should all leave me alone. Just leave me alone."

"When you stop stealing, perhaps we will. But until then, I, for one, will not leave you alone. I'd rather help you stop than punish you, but that's up to you."

Of course I realized I was one of those do-gooders she chafed at, but why beat a dead horse. Lisa was the kind of fragile looney-tune whose behavior begged for the help that she consistently refused. I waited for her to say more so that I could feel I'd accomplished more than reciting the Ten Commandments to a deaf person. But Lisa was done, and she slowly pulled herself up to go.

My first case at Holton. Child's play compared to the D.A.'s office. A voluntary confession without breaking a sweat. But as I watched her dragging herself to my door I realized Holton's special salve of leniency had already rubbed off on me. I was a quick study. If Vince had heard me telling a confessed unrepentant larcenist to write a letter of apology for repeated acts of theft, he would have thrown me in a jail cell next to the thieving bum and instructed Shannon to swallow the key.

The heels of Lisa's shoes caught in the carpeting as she dragged her feet to the door. Not until her hand touched the knob did I finally give in, looking down at the pale pink crocodile pumps.

I bolted up from my chair. "Lisa, wait!"

When she turned to look at me, her expression was dazed as if the mere act of turning made her dizzy.

"I heard you at the gym yesterday. In the bathroom."

"I wasn't at the gym yesterday."

"I saw those shoes. They're hard to miss."

"I don't know what you saw, but you're wrong." She waited a few beats. "Can I go now?"

My phone light began blinking. "I can easily verify whether you signed in at the gym yesterday."

She snorted and swung the door open, then disappeared down the hall.

Rita must have seen Lisa amble by her door. My intercom buzzed. "Miss Melone? Your boss is on the line. Your *old* boss."

I waited a few seconds, screwed my courage to the sticking post, as Lady Macbeth would advise, and picked up.

"You got anything to say to me?" Vince snapped.

"Can I come home now?"

"Hey, this is your dime. You got something or not?"

"My dime? I didn't make this call."

"Lynch told me you were on the line for me. You girls playing games?"

I waited for the sound of distant gunfire as Vince took practice shots at me from across town, but I couldn't even hear him breathing.

"No games. I just want to come back."

"Dig up some dirt over there and hand it to me on

a silver platter and then maybe I'll let you back here *to shine my fucking shoes.*"

"After I shine your shoes, can I have my job back?"

"You can work your way *up*, you know, through the ranks, so to speak."

"You know, Vince, now that I'm on the outside I can see that your asshole status is really well deserved."

"Nice talk. That blue-blood Holton patina is really rubbing off on you, huh?"

"Screw you, Vince."

I waited for the red-hot comeback. But he just hung up. I hit the new-line button and dialed back. Vince's secretary picked up. "He won't take your call, Miss Melone. Sorry."

"Get Shannon on the line."

An eternity of seconds later, Shannon picked up. "Hey, Mari."

"Vince just called me. Says you told him I was on the line for him."

"Ah, I just thought if I got you two back to the negotiation table you might work this little lovers' spat out."

"Call me crazy, Shannon, but I think he may be putting a contract out on my sorry life."

"Anger is a good thing. Means there's still some love there. What do you got for me? Anything?"

"Kids strung out on cocaine. Nothing murderous as yet. How about you?"

"That blanket Hastings was wrapped in—from the health services over there? We got a court order to unseal the health records. And get this one. Holton is claiming they don't keep *written* records. What kind of bullshit is that?"

"Keep me posted."

I replaced the receiver in its cradle gently so as not to further break my cracked emotional state, but I almost fell apart when I looked up to see Elliot Orenstein standing in my open doorway again and watching me.

"Eavesdrop much?"

"Your door was open."

"Shucks, and no bug screen either."

He smiled sourly. "Touché, Miss Melone."

"What can I do for you, Elliot?"

"I'm back for my interview. Ready to vent yet?"

"No, and you shouldn't be hanging around my office. I told you, confidential stuff going on here."

"I know. I just saw Lisa Cummings leave here. She's flunking out of a class we're in. Absent half the time and cruising for a crash."

"Close my door."

He spoke while turning and pushing my door shut with his unlaced sneaker. "I scored a perfect 2400 on my SATs. I was hoping to get an education, but there's nothing here worth learning. So I end up tutoring rich brats whose last honest educational effort was their sixth-grade spelling bee. No one gives a crap about grades here."

"Stop whining. That means less competition for you. So you'll graduate with a 4.0 and go on to a Harvard Ph.D. without even refilling your Mont Blanc."

He tilted his head. "Good point," he said, then flopped into the chair Lisa had just vacated. "But I use Bics. You gonna spill, or what?"

"Okay, Elliot, rule number one if we're going to be pen pals. No names. I can't be talking personal about the students with you."

"Works for me. Anyway, it's *you* I want to talk about."

"I don't think I like you."

His head jerked the slightest inch, but his comeback belied hurt feelings. "Get in line, Miss Melone. What makes you think I care who likes me and who doesn't?"

"No one lives in a social vacuum."

The kid swung his messenger bag over his shoulder and got up to leave. "Well, just for the record, I don't think I like you either."

"You little brat—"

He broke out into a raucous laugh like I was Jackie Mason in the Catskills. "I knew I'd eventually get a rise out of you. Want to talk now?"

"Yeah, I want to talk. I want to talk about GHB and who's using on campus."

"GHB, huh?" He sat and dropped the bag to the floor. "What's in it for me if I tell you?"

"Um . . . let me think . . . An interview?"

He nodded, smiling, and took his pad and pen back out. "Riverside Park Apartments. Cory Sherman and his gang."

"That was easy."

"Have you met Cory? He's something of Carlyle's pet."

"I met him."

"If you're like most women, you found him irresistible. Him and his sidekicks."

"Rod Lipton?"

"He's one of them. It's not much of a mystery why this administration puts up with their depraved behavior. Money is the school mascot. Sherman's uncle is—"

"Yes, I know."

"You'll find a drugstore in their apartment on the river. But Carlyle just looks the other way."

"Does the head of security know?" I asked, referring, of course, to Mike McCoy.

"McCoy gets his orders from Carlyle. He's the one who always bails them out."

"Are you sure you aren't just averse to authority figures?"

"You're an authority figure and you're affable—but maybe that's because you're amazingly naive for a seasoned trial lawyer."

"Naive? Watch out, Elliot, or I'll break your Bics."

He sighed like I was some thickheaded child. "Mike McCoy is a puppet."

"He seems like a straight shooter to me. Of course I'm on tenure-track to unemployment by discussing any of this with you."

"Carlyle won't fire you. You're his façade of morality— his Swiss bank account. As soon as he finds your strings you'll be dancing like a marionette, just like the others."

"Your cynicism matches my naiveté point for point, I'd say."

"You'll see I'm right. But I like you anyway. You're guileless but you're not stupid. You'll learn the ropes around here pretty fast, I think." And with that, he whipped his black bag across his shoulders and stood. "You see? I'm getting an interview out of you and you haven't even consented to it yet."

CHAPTER EIGHTEEN

Life and Its Alternative

I WAS FINALLY BEGINNING to accept the fact that I was never again going to see the inside of 150 South Main Street unless I committed murder myself. But daily routine, like emotional balance, kept my soul grounded, as the New Age flunkies would say.

I'd finally nailed the trick of finding the same parking space near Langley Hall every morning, getting my coffee and raisin-bran muffin down at the student bistro with Elliot, who was, in his own arrogant yet endearing way, becoming a loyal sidekick, and then heading to my minuscule office to open the hottest, latest, fresh-from-the-oven files on spoiled little ne'er-do-wells. Elliot was actually more helpful to me than any of the administration in wading through the sterile waters of Holton. He was smarter than most of them, and enjoyed making sure I knew it.

Most of my cases were easily resolved via negotiations so simple I could have done them in my sleep. The process was pretty much analogous to plea-bargaining with criminal defendants. When there was hard-core proof of cheating, I made the student agree to retake an exam. If a student whined about an unfair teacher, I'd schmooze with the partisan professor and then mollify the young scholar with optimistic promises of change. Sometimes these things just required an intermediary to improve diplomatic relations between professor and student, and I'd play the obliging middleman, preferring to douse as many fires as I could. Many cases boiled down to personality conflicts and students who expected teachers to be extensions of their parents—parents who had spoiled them silly and let them get away with murder at home as long as it was kept in the family. I was surprisingly good at the job. On some days I actually felt like an ace.

More surprising, though, was that Ken Carlyle didn't want to know much about what went on in my office unless a "special student" was involved. In the twisted lingo of Holton's administrative insiders, "special student" denoted not a kid in need of remedial help, physical concessions to disabilities, or financial aid, but one whose parents' summary annual donations to the school exceeded a certain amount of money (which figure was kept as closely guarded as the formula for Classic Coke). When a "special" student's name arose at a staff meeting, Carlyle would dramatically slow down the conversation, signaling to one and all that our staff meeting had, temporarily, segued onto hallowed ground.

All in all, I thought I was actually cooking with fire, until one Monday morning, the beginning of my fourth week at Holton, when living hell broke loose.

Early to the office at seven-thirty, I was in an upbeat mood, and as I jaunted briskly to the front gates of

Langley I took an emotional inventory of my petty existence at that sparkling moment in space and time: The Hastings murder investigation had lost some wind and Carlyle seemed to have retreated from the warpath; Mike and I were in an exciting flirtation stage still free of any messy physical componentry; Vince had not yet sent a hit man after me; and, once again, I had scored my excellent parking space. Life was good.

The icy air burned my cheeks, making me tuck my face into my coat lapels, so I didn't see Mike McCoy's grim face until he was close enough to grab me by my sleeve. "Where's your car?"

"Oh, hey. My car? I just found a museum-quality parking space and no way I'm losing it for a make-out session." I smiled at him, but he obviously wasn't in the mood for coquetry.

"Let's go."

He was pushing me out of the gates toward the street. "Are you crazy? I'm still in the probationary period and there's a staff meeting this morning." I pulled his arm off my sleeve. "Stop it. What's wrong?"

As if distracted by something, he looked away from me.

"The staff meeting is canceled. Let's go get your car." He wouldn't look at me.

"All right, but if I get a ticket, you're going to have those buddies of yours at the station pull it out of the system."

I couldn't seem to get a smile out of him.

"Mike? What is going on?"

"I'll tell you in the car," he said, and arm in arm we hustled through the cold toward my Jeep, where he jumped into the driver's seat and inched out of my tight parking space.

"Is this a date?" I joked.

He blew air out of his pursed lips in a faint whistle. "There's been another murder. Another student."

I kept my eyes on the road, a childish and eternally hopeful part of me waiting for Mike's low barreling laughter: *Just kidding, babe,* or something like that. But I knew, there in that car with him, that something serious was going down. But I didn't *really* know he wasn't joking until he said, "Same MO."

"Where are we going, Mike?"

"Lisa Cummings is dead."

Something deep down in my throat constricted with a squeak and I groaned out loud, grabbing the wheel from him in a stranglehold. Mike fought the wheel away from me as the Jeep began swerving toward the curb. "Stop it!" he ordered. "Let go. Now!" He pulled the wheel to the right and slowed to a stop as he guided my car off the roadway.

"I saw her at the gym. She was doing cocaine. I should have called Mitsy. Maybe they could have hospitalized her. I'm a lawyer, not a fucking psychiatrist!"

"Get a hold of yourself. This has nothing to do with her cocaine use," he said.

"How do you know? Melinda Hastings had drugs in her too. Maybe this all has something to do with drugs."

"Cocaine and date-rape drugs are two entirely different substances. I don't think Hastings or Cummings voluntarily ingested GHB to get high."

"What happened exactly, and when?"

"Last night. Lisa's body was found at a private boathouse

at the foot of Grotto Ave. The owner noticed the door half open from his upstairs window and went down to investigate. She was lying in a dinghy next to the guy's twenty-foot sailboat."

"The owner?"

Mike pushed the gear in drive and pulled away from the curb.

"The poor schmuck threw up outside before he went back to the main house and called the cops. He lives there alone with his wife. Their only daughter left for college in the fall."

We drove across Blackstone Boulevard into the East Side's hidden enclave of ten-thousand-square-foot McMansions. Mike pulled up to a multitiered redbrick chateau looming on a hill and overlooking the Providence River, the inlet separating the East Side of Providence from East Providence, the town.

We walked to the back of the property and saw, about a hundred yards down the lawn near the river, a lone boathouse, toward which Mike began to descend and I followed. I was reminded of an old and crucial lesson that day: Never get cocky, because even for an old pro like me, death always had encores.

A forensic team had already removed the small rowboat from the boathouse and laid it out on the lawn. We stopped and watched from a safe distance as the medics lifted Lisa's sodden body out and onto a white sheet in which she was then mummy-wrapped. The limp thing was hoisted by its ends into a black body bag and zipped shut. As I crept closer, Mike slowed up and hung back, his eyes closed to a squint. Either he was giving me some private space to react to the human gore I was approaching, or he wasn't the big tough guy he pretended to be.

Globs of curdled red matter floated in a red puddle in the boat's hull. One of the medics stooped over the small mess with a hand shovel in one hand and an evidence bag in another, looking for anything that might belong to the killer, like a fleck of lint or a strand of hair. He shook his head and a couple of the other ME investigators covered the boat over in clear plastic while they waited for the tow truck that would remove it for more extensive testing.

Mike stepped up and tapped my shoulder in temporary farewell and then walked over to a couple of cops hanging back by their curbed cruisers at the street. Two techs lifted the body bag onto a stretcher and began rolling it toward the ME retrieval truck parked on the road above.

I recognized Lucky Dack as he exited the small boathouse structure. Lucky was so coal black he looked purple in certain lights, and was six four and impossible to miss. They called him Lucky because he'd won a state lottery, netting himself a yearly hundred grand for the next two and a half decades. Despite the windfall Lucky hadn't quit his job at the morgue, and never would. To say he loved his work would have been a keenly accurate statement.

He walked over to me. It had rained the night before and a brackish wind was slapping my hair around my face. "Lucky," I said softly.

"Hey, Miz Melone. Didn't think I was gonna have the pleasure of seeing you again so soon." He stepped back and nodded his head. "Another one of those college kids, huh?" He looked me sharp in the eye, making his own eyes sparkle, and held his hand over his chest. "I was heartbroken, you know, when they told me you . . . left the AG's. I must admit I was shocked."

My simple shrug communicated volumes.

"Sure, sure," he said. "You can explain another time." He glanced down at the ground, pursing his thick lips.

"What happened here, Lucky?"

While Mike helped two cops unwind yellow tape to cordon off the sidewalk and street, Lucky walked me to the medical examiner's wagon as we talked.

"I'm thinking she was killed or drugged somewhere else. Not enough struggle here. But he cut her up while she was in that boat." He shook his head. "She was a pretty girl." He raised his eyebrows. "Poor sweet thing. Her face was sliced up like a breakfast melon." Then he leaned over and whispered to me. "And she was wearing a pretty little dress and panties. Brassiere. Kind with lots of hooks and straps. You know how I love that stuff."

Word around the medical examiner's office was that Lucky liked his women cold.

Lucky had a way of laughing with his head. It was a soundless laugh refined over the course of his twenty-year employment at the city morgue, where so much of what Lucky found amusing didn't deserve raucous laughter. In his line of work he understood that there is no conversational etiquette in death. He managed completely one-sided conversations in which he did all the talking to an unwilling audience of the deceased's relatives. Lucky fully expected these semiparalyzed silences while the concept of death congealed in the hearts of the survivors and became a thing able to be stacked in their mental attics like a box full of memories.

The back doors of the ME wagon slammed shut.

The press was now all over the place. A lone plain-clothes detective was conversing with Mike and the cops, and for a brief moment Mike caught my eye as I finished up with Lucky and said my goodbyes. As soon as we parted company, Mike rushed over, though he said nothing. We walked back to my car in silence and he opened the passenger's side door for me. "Wait. Let me sign off with these guys"—he nodded in the direction of the police cars—"and then I'll drive you back."

He slammed the Jeep's door shut and sprinted back to the police, who had left the vicinity of their cruisers and, apparently feeling freer now, were lounging around the scene proper. The truck carrying Lisa's body was backing out of the driveway. Reporters were venturing toward the cops. Though the latter were no longer needed on the scene, they lingered. Cops are press-hounds and another Holton student death was a tremendous story.

Feeling a bit light-headed, I rolled down the car windows and breathed in the sharp iodinated air. I watched from the chilly silence of my front windshield as the various players renewed old friendships around the bloody grounds, chumming it up while the camera crews shot the entire incongruous scene through their wide-angle lenses.

"Marianna."

I turned sharply to my side window to see Ken Carlyle's face staring at me.

"Dean Carlyle."

Mike was suddenly behind him. "Hey, Ken, what's going down?"

Carlyle did a half turn in his direction. "Holton's reputation, I assume, if these murders continue. I hope you're on top of damage control." Then Carlyle spoke to Mike as if I weren't present. "And why is Marianna here?"

"I wanted her to see it. She should know what she's dealing with."

I stuck my head partially out the window. "Um, excuse me." They both turned to me. "I understand why you might be concerned for my welfare—from what I'm seeing, women aren't safe on their own campus—but I can take care of myself. Thanks."

Mike gave me a nod and then abruptly walked around the front of the car, got in the driver's seat, and turned the engine. I rolled up my window as Carlyle backed onto the lawn to watch us drive away.

"What was that all about?" I asked.

"Two bulls locking horns. He wants me to use my magic wand to stop the psychopath who's goring coeds and strewing their entrails in a path to Holton's door."

And with that the wind seemed to go out of my sails. The color of the morning light seemed to subtly change, as if the whole universe were infused with doom. I opened the window. "I think I'm going to be sick, Mike."

He pulled over and stopped. "Lower your head between your knees."

I didn't move, so he pushed my head down and held it there. "Take a few slow, long breaths."

As I inhaled and exhaled, dizzy with nausea, Mike's fingers massaged my skull as if he were a mentalist or a chiropractor. Or a shampoo girl. Then, as if reading my mind, he suddenly pulled his hand away. "You feel better?"

I lifted my head slowly and turned to him. His big, wolflike eyes frightened me. Their pupils seemed pinned open.

"What's wrong, Mike?"

"Nothing," he said, coming out of his trance and squinting a bit as if he were in pain. The slow breath he blew through pursed lips created the faintest breeze in my hair. "I just never thought nausea could be sexy."

Mike dropped me at Langley with a promise to deliver my keys back later. I secluded myself in my office, where I slipped one of my quick-dissolving migraine remedies under my tongue and then waited for my computer to boot up. I was typing a quick e-mail to Shannon when my phone line lit up and I answered it without waiting for Rita.

"Hey, sweetie," Shannon said in a breathy whisper. "Another fucking murder over there and Vince is bleeding from his fangs."

I could picture Vince sticking another pin in my voodoo doll.

". . . so is this an unbelievable coincidence or what? You find yourself a nice, quiet little job and put all the blood, guts, and grime of the AG's behind you, and, hello? Holton students start dying like grounded sea turtles! Are you an unlucky bastard, or what?"

"I don't think it was a coincidence, Shannon."

"Meaning?"

"Maybe Carlyle expected this. Maybe he knew the murders would continue. That's why he wanted me here. There's a kid I've been talking to—a student. He thinks Carlyle wanted me as a cover. What's there to cover here—besides these murders—that the other assistant deans weren't already handling?"

"You're getting employment counseling from a snot-nosed kid?"

"I know. I shouldn't be talking to the students. Carlyle wanted him to write about my shiny new position in the school paper—some propaganda about me being an ex-prosecutor and coming here to clean house—but he seems more interested in playing Sherlock Holmes. The kid's like a bloodhound, and I think he's trustworthy."

" 'Trustworthy student' is an oxymoron. And how would Carlyle *know* the murders would continue unless *he* were the killer or an accessory?"

"Don't be ridiculous."

"I'm not, sweetkins. I'm just pointing out how ridiculous *you're* sounding."

"After Cummings is processed, I want you to make me copies of the autopsy, lab, and toxicologies. Everything you've got. And don't even breathe an objection. You owe me. I took the hit for all of us."

"Your wish is my command."

CHAPTER NINETEEN

Babel

OTHER THAN HAVING MY keys dropped off to me by messenger, Mike disappeared for the rest of that murderous day. I waited until the next morning and then sniffed out his office in the basement of Langley by following the stale odor of moldy limes—a.k.a. his aftershave. I found him sitting quietly at his desk reading the *Providence Journal* with the lights off.

"Hey, babe," Mike said without looking up. He flung the paper on the floor and extracted a tiny pad from his breast pocket. "I was just getting ready to ring you up. New case. We're having a problem with this girl, a sophomore. Let's see now." He flipped forward a few pages in his pad.

Exhaling audibly, I flopped into a chair. "Hah. Just like that, eh? This place doesn't skip a damn beat."

Mike tucked his pad back in the shirt pocket, stood, and pushed his door shut. He returned to his seat, leaned over the vacant lot of his desk, and looked me square in the eyes. "Not even an eighth note of a beat, and if you're smart, you'll keep your foot tapping to the rhythm."

"There's a serial killer doing Holton coeds and we're discussing the next *disciplinary case*?"

McCoy shifted in his chair like he suddenly needed a fresh dab of Preparation H. "Do you have a death wish or something? We have to *look* as if we're taking care of daily business around here or Carlyle will boot us both out." He was practically lying across the top of his desk now, close enough to grab me by the throat. "So before you start spouting your mouth all over the place about a serial killer on the loose, let's wait a day or two and see what the evidence drags in so it won't look like *we're* doing the investigation. *Comprende*?" He bolted upright and pulled his damn pad out again. "Now, can we get back to *this* case before the staff meeting?" He looked at his watch. " 'Cause you've got to be there in approximately fifty-two minutes."

I cocked an eyebrow at him. Another tough nut in the party-mix bowl of my life.

He winked, and then smiled at me. He waited until I smiled back at him. I smiled back at him. Because the only thing worse than giving in is continuing to fight a lost cause. And fighting with slippery and charming Mike McCoy, I was beginning to realize, was always going to be like catching the wind.

He riffled through the pages of his notepad. "Okay then . . . Mila Nazir. A Pakistani princess, literally and figuratively. A real pip of a girl. Took an exam with cheat notes written on her upper thighs. When the teacher caught her and asked to see the notes, she screamed assault and kicked him in the b—, ah . . . crotch area."

"Wonderful," I said. "In a school where students beat professors, a few murders must seem pretty humdrum."

"Whatever you do with Nazir, clear it with the boss first, huh?" He popped up out of his chair, scratching his backside. "Now, you've gotta go, but remember, I'm never far if you need me—no matter *what* you have in mind."

As miffed as I was over our earlier impasse, Mike's smile still made me go a little soft in the knees. I rose slowly from my seat, not wanting it to appear that I was following his command, and as I was crossing his threshold, he said, "When are we having lunch again? I'm *so* hungry." I didn't bother with a reply.

Back upstairs at my office I found Rita standing in my doorway. She wished me a good morning in Swahili and then zipped dryly through a list of potential calamities.

"There is a girl in my office going through many tissues. She will not tell me her name but I believe it is Emily Barton, and although I am not a psychiatrist I think she may be hysterical. You have two calls from the attorney general's office, but these are your social friends, am I right? Miss Eckert was here just to see if you were in, but I think she did not really need to speak with you although she looked angry. But she always looks angry. Shall I continue?"

"Give me five minutes and send the crier in."

Rita tapped her watch face. "Staff meeting in thirty minutes."

I returned the call to the AG's and asked for either Laurie or Shannon. Vince got on the line.

"I'm giving you the heads-up. Carlyle scheduled a press conference tomorrow and I'm coming. Carlyle knows nothing about my showing up, so don't tell him. Understand?"

"Why're you telling me?"

"Meloni, do you think for one minute Carlyle hired you for your talent? He hired you to get to me. Your resume in his in-box was like manna from heaven. He must have chuckled at his good fortune."

"I never sent him a resume."

"You tell me why he suddenly needed you in his stable. To get to me, that's why."

"You are an egocentric paranoid, Vince. As if Holton *fabricated* an administrative position and put me in it, *just to get to you*. Do you hear yourself?"

"You know nothing about that place and the shit that goes on there. Nothing. Trust me on this one and don't let Carlyle sucker you in."

"Fine," I said as we slammed phones down simultaneously.

I composed myself from Vince's call, and in the remaining minute or two before Rita sent in the crying student, I pulled up Emily Barton's rap sheet. Not surprisingly, her background was similar to Melinda's and Lisa's, and, for that matter, Jeff Kendall's: Money and several Holton alumni flowered their family trees.

Emily had graduated from Pomfret School with a shockingly low GPA of 2.5. Considering Pomfret's "extra-year postgraduate study program," I was surprised they'd even graduated her with her class. Must have been the embossed Crane wrapper she was delivered in at birth.

There was a soft knock at my door. I took a deep breath and re-sported my jacket. "Come in," I said.

There stood a model-thin girl about five five with a light bronzed skin tone. Her mahogany-hued hair fell like a glossy waterfall around her shoulders, and, like my sister Cassie, she could probably have swept the floor with her thick natural eyelashes. She wore no makeup.

"I have to talk to someone," she said. "And I apologize. I don't have an appointment."

"Come on in."

The girl sat without further formalities, and as soon as I returned from closing the door after her, she broke out in a barrage of tears. She was actually choking before I had the sense to interrupt her. But at Holton I could never be sure whether student emotion was real or the ingenious performance of a very clever kid.

"I'm so sorry," the girl said. "But I'm having a hard time with all this."

"This?"

"I think I was raped and no one at this school seems to care."

"You think?"

"I know I was drugged, and when I woke up, my panties were gone . . . and I sort of knew I'd had sex . . ."

"I'm sorry," I broke in. "Are you Emily Barton? My secretary seems to have recognized you."

She nodded. "Dr. Becker told me to come see you. She said this would be confidential, right?"

"Of course."

"The night before last, some students from Reese House were at an off-campus party and this guy I dated a few times followed me outside as I was walking back to my dorm through Patterson Park. I pushed him away. And then he yelled at me. 'You stupid bitch,' he said. 'Who do you think you are?' " She began crying again. "I'm scared."

"And you were drugged at this party?"

She shrugged. "I'm not sure. I'd had a beer with Lisa before I got there."

"Lisa Cummings? Where was that?"

"Her apartment. We were studying for a psych exam. She told me about the cafeteria incident that Mike made such a big deal over."

"Mike?"

"McCoy. Head of security." She tilted her head at me, anticipating my next question. "He likes the students to call him by his first name."

"What time was that—that you were with Lisa?"

"Around eight. She said she was tired of studying, but she was getting fidgety. I think she wanted to do some coke. I left. We were supposed to meet back up at a party— I didn't want to go alone—but she never showed—"

"Where was the party? Riverside Park Apartments, wasn't it?"

She hung her head and sniffled again. "I'm not saying any names—"

"Who's the guy, Emily? Who's the guy who followed you out of the party?"

"I can't say. It'll get worse if I do."

"If you don't give me his name there's nothing I can do."

"Talk to him privately? If I make a formal complaint against him . . . I'm afraid of him. If he's angry enough, he might hurt me. And everyone will say I enticed him, brought this all on myself."

Yes, it's difficult to be as beautiful as Emily and not be the subject of "unwanted advances." I looked at her shapely legs stretched out in front of her from under a denim miniskirt, the taupe leather ankle boots with a two-inch princess heel, her flesh-colored skintight sweater and chocolate leather cropped jacket. As a prosecutor, how many times had I heard from rape defendants: *The bitch was asking for it.*

"Emily, girls are getting murdered at this school and you've got some important information that we should make public."

"You're so wrong. This guy is no murderer—"

I pounded my fist on my desk and screeched, "What do you know about murderers? Mommies have chopped limbs off their newborn infants, so stop telling me how to do my job and tell me his goddamn name so I can stop him!"

At my outburst, Emily popped from her chair and Rita tornadoed through the door, missing Emily by a hair. "Babel is falling?" she said, trying to lighten the mood.

Emily looked at me. Flickers of contempt were drying her tearstained eyes. Screaming at her was the wrong tactic. It had pushed her farther away. I was a thick-skinned prosecutor used to dealing with slippery witnesses, guilty defendants, and lying defense attorneys, and I was treating Emily like a defendant—degrade and assault, put her on the defensive so she'd talk.

I stood from my chair. "I'm sorry. I didn't mean to raise my voice." But without another word she walked around Rita and out the door.

Rita waited a few calming seconds before announcing to me that I was late for Monday morning's rescheduled staff meeting. She sagely suggested I cool my heels and get my general marching orders from Carlyle regarding the Emily Barton matter (orders which I'd have to follow since I seemed to have few other options).

I gathered my notes on the previous week's student miscreants and headed to the conference room twenty minutes late.

CHAPTER TWENTY

———— ⪦⪧ ————

Locked and Cocky

CARLYLE WAS SITTING AT the head of the conference table with Byron to his left, Tripp Hoven and his evil twin Chad to his right. Mitsy's smile was the sole welcome as I pulled out a chair and took my seat. After maybe a millisecond's glance at me, all the players retargeted Ken, their tongues visible as if he were doling out communion wafers.

"Marianna, before you arrived this morning we were making our way around the table with departmental updates. Byron was giving us a quick rundown on our newest pledges."

Was I hearing this right? A student had been murdered the day before and we were opening the meeting with *the newest pledges*?

Byron made a big show of flipping her notebook closed. "Do I really have to repeat it, sir?" She beamed at Ken like a friendly chow begging for her bowl.

"Not necessary," Ken said. "Marianna"—he cleared his throat—"how are you doing? Anything to report?"

I cleared my own throat and swallowed hard. My hands trembled a bit as I opened my pad and ran down my list of perpetrators and moral degenerates—one plagiarist, one drunk and disorderly, and a miserable cheating bastard (on some multiple-choice quiz in an elective health-care class). All in all, a calm week in the general population at the Holton Correctional Institution, except of course for the recent butchering of Lisa Cummings. Ken displayed little interest in my harangue, so I had to assume the families of my ne'er-do-wells were penny-pinching, underendowed coupon clippers.

Or just perhaps Ken *was* preoccupied with those two bodies bleeding on his doorstep.

"Ken," I said, "I met with Emily Barton this morning. She claims she was date-raped by another student."

Ken sat up. "Did she give you a name?"

"Not yet."

"Then we'll wait and see what happens. May I remind you, Marianna, you aren't supposed to be digging up dirt. I'd prefer that you throw some on the already burning fires around here."

The rest of his team bobbed their heads up and down like epileptics.

"We should forget a student who claims she was drugged and raped? Lisa Cummings was raped and murdered Sunday night. A month ago she was weaving around my office like a drunken sailor and it wasn't from booze. Melinda Hastings was also raped and murdered and she had cocaine and GHB in her blood. Do we not suspect a connection between these rapes, murders, and drugs—"

Carlyle popped out of his chair. "I will have no more talk of *drugs* in this school. Do all of you hear me?" He looked around the table.

Byron smirked. Chad and Tripp avoided his stare like brain-damaged genetic twins. Mitsy remained drawn and stone-faced.

Then he refocused on me. "Marianna, prior to your late arrival this morning, we spoke briefly of this newest tragedy and again I stressed the importance of minimizing the damage this is having on the school. Let's remember this incident was also *off-campus*. Miss Cummings was found without so much as a piece of lint on her connecting her to this school—"

"That conclusion may be a bit premature—"

"*Miss* Melone, I'd like to go over this with you in more detail, so please meet me in my office after this meeting."

I calmly closed my legal pad and nudged it gently forward on the table with my fingertips. Ken turned his head to Mitsy and then, with the lethargy of a tortoise, turned it back to me. Either he was stretching a very sore neck, or looking to vent emotional steam en route to his final words to me:

"And, henceforth, we will abstain from any reference to drug use," he said, his voice purring threateningly like an idling chainsaw.

I raised an imaginary hand. "You mean like put our collective heads in the sand and hope that no more bodies show up buried there?"

"*What did you say?*"

I admired the way Carlyle controlled his rages. There was little doubt he wanted to strangle me. His right eye twitched in two-second intervals. I thought of how Vince Piganno would have deported himself after one of my particularly sarcastic attacks. Vince would have thrown a pencil at me, or a legal pad, or a fifteen-pound marble

paperweight, or whatever alternative missiles were within
arm's reach. We assistant AGs all expected such outbursts
from him. Par for the course. Comes with the territory.
Were complaints ever lodged against the boss? No freaking way. The word from fallen comrades on the outside
(of which I was now one) was that the results were a dis-
honorable discharge, a paltry two-week severance check,
and a lifetime enemy of an impugned and pugnacious
Pig.

And here was Ken Carlyle, whose face was registering
only the slightest flush.

"Ken," I said, "how exactly should I deal with students
in trouble? Ignore them? I should have done more for
Lisa. Maybe just being in a drugged and weakened state
made her more vulnerable to a murderer. I feel guilty
about Lisa."

Oh brother, had I gone out on a shaky limb. Trying
the emotional tack with Carlyle, and exposing honesty
to these anemic vampires, was like hooking up a Kohler
faucet to my carotid artery.

And I'd uttered the dirty D word again.

Carlyle's eyes were protruding ever so slightly from
their sockets when Mitsy's warm, soft voice deflected his
attention. "Marianna, you've been with us too short a
time to be feeling responsible for any of this. And please
bear in mind, Melinda Hastings was murdered before
you began work here."

Ken's eyes had retreated, so I took advantage of his
stone-cold silence to introduce my next topic. "Fine then.
Another disciplinary matter. Mila Nazir. She's *physically*
abusing the professors. I'd like to give her a warning and
require her to write a letter of apology. If that's not too
harsh a reprimand?"

Closed eyes and a deep breath punctuated Ken's continued silence. I assumed he was mentally counting to ten.

"Mila . . . Nazir," he repeated. "Yes, we've had some problems with her in the past." He nodded paternally. "She's a bit spoiled, to say the least, but I'm not sure her behavior is socially unacceptable in Pakistan due to her social rank. We do have to be sensitive to that fact."

"We do? Because I'm not really sure why. I mean, if we wanted to perform clitorectomies on women in America, would it be *okay* because it's socially acceptable in Muslim Africa?"

"A letter of apology sounds minimally painful, Ken," Mitsy piped up again. "I agree with Mari. The girl really should refrain from that kind of behavior here. I understand she actually kicked her professor in the—"

"Stop," Ken said sharply. Then he deigned to look at me. "I want you to merely explain to her—nicely—that she will have to *temporarily* adjust her attitude as long as she is visiting this country. We don't want to offend her by letting her think the mores in her own country are . . . less appropriate than those of the United States. Are you understanding me, Marianna?"

What was beginning to worry me was that I really *was* beginning to understand him, or at least the way his mind worked: deny and delete. And then I wondered, if I was so easily able to understand Vince Piganno and Ken Carlyle in the same instant, who exactly was I?

Ken pushed his chair back. "It's ten forty-five. Is there anything else before we adjourn?" After a mere second or two of silence he stood, said, "My office, Marianna. Ten minutes," and turned abruptly out of the room.

Chad and Tripp immediately began conversing in

hushed tones. Byron joined forces with them, undoubt-edly just to irk me. Mitsy's routine was to arrive and leave by herself, displaying zero interest in lingering with the group. Today was no different. She was the first to walk out the door after Carlyle.

I pushed my chair back from the table, rising slowly, stalling. They stalled too. Working with this bunch was like being back in grade school. No sooner was I over the threshold than I heard the laughter and snickers as I headed to the principal's office.

CHAPTER TWENTY-ONE

Censored

I BEGAN THE SHORT trek down the hall to the warden's office, and there, at the end of the hall, was Elliot Orenstein with his back to me. I walked briskly past Ken's office, then pulled Elliot aside.

"What?" He pivoted, regarding me like we were old friends and he was in a bad mood.

I looked around like a fleeing felon. "Come with me."

Elliot followed, remaining a step behind as I navigated the corridor, down the stairs, to my office.

I poked my head in at Rita as I passed her door. "If Carlyle calls, tell him I'm on my way."

I waved Elliot by me. "Get in it quick."

He stalled in my doorway, waiting for me to pass him. "It is a shame you hide yourself in men's clothes," he said, looking at my Ralph Lauren two-button pinstripe suit. "You look really good. So many older women get fat."

"Come in and shut the door, Elliot."

He dutifully followed as I spun into my chair and

swiped my desk clean, shoving everything into the top drawer. I wasted no time getting to my point. "Okay. So what do you know about the latest death?"

He sighed deeply and settled himself into his usual chair facing my desk. He dropped his book bag to the floor and looked up at me. "Miss Melone, I am not Inspector Clouseau. I'm sure I know nothing more than you."

"I'm late for an appointment with the dean. So hurry up and answer me."

He eyed me suspiciously. Possibly assessing my emotional stability?

"Do you want something from me?"

"Information. Any student buzz about Lisa's death?"

"They just found her. What could I possibly know that you don't?"

I fixed my stare. As a lawyer I knew how even a facial expression can be culled for incriminating information. I refused to respond, because even in my answer, if he were smart enough, he would detect hints of information I wasn't sure I wanted to disclose yet.

Elliot broke into a satisfied smile. "I think your prosecutor antennae are up. I'm guessing you haven't left your AG job behind you that easily."

He continued, "You went to the Cummings murder scene because your instincts directed you there. Humans may be higher up on the evolutionary rung, but we're all still animals at a base level. You sniffed something out, and you wanted to be there."

"It wasn't voluntary. I was escorted there. And how do you know I was there?"

"They kept us behind the tape. Bug-eyed students wondering which one of us would be next."

"I'm sure only the females were pondering that

question. Now, you've got one more minute to tell me if you know anything or I'm off to my appointment. *And I'll never talk to you again.*"

"About murder, I don't know anything. But—and it's common knowledge around here—Lisa was a drug addict. That's what I know. But I doubt that had anything to do with her murder, otherwise half the students on this campus would be dead."

Employment preservation should have been my prime concern, especially since I was batting 0 for 1 in the job department. I should have ended our conversation posthaste. But my prosecutor's instinct—yes, I was descending the evolutionary ladder—kept me rapt in Elliot's words for whatever information I could cull.

"Are you sure 'addict' is the right word? Are we talking needles?"

He smiled benevolently as if I were asking him the address of Santa's workshop. "Heroin, you mean? I don't know exactly. Melinda Hastings and Lisa Cummings—they both would have given up anything for their next line of white powder."

I watched the lights blink on my phone.

"And now they're both dead." He pulled his chair closer to my desk and leaned in. "And I think you're enjoying it. Playing sleuth to murder instead of issuing demerits over stolen bagels—"

"That's sick!"

Rita knocked on my door and cracked it open. "Dean Carlyle awaits."

I nodded to her, and then she palmed a pink message slip in front of me. In lovely Rita's curlicued script it read: *Kartabar 12:00, Mike.*

"Be there or be square, as the children say," giggled

hypersexual, lovelorn Rita, who gave Elliot a quick smile, then softly shut the door.

Elliot spoke again as soon as Rita left. "Maybe these deaths are part of an elaborate drug ring going bad. Maybe Carlyle's a part of it."

"I guess you're free to make fun of me now, since I invited you here."

"It's more like I was brought in on house arrest."

"Yeah, except this office is *my* jail, not yours, so scoot and thanks for the info."

"Sure. Just remember, Carlyle's smarter than you."

He lifted his book bag from the floor while I scurried around in my brain for the obvious argument against Carlyle's being so smart that he hired *me*, a prosecutor, to keep campus drug use under wraps, but I couldn't think of anything clever to say. "If Carlyle knows about student drug use, why *did* he hire me? That doesn't seem so smart to me."

Elliot squared his jaw and leaned forward again. "Maybe he thought he could turn you against the AG's office by getting you fired—"

"How did you know I was fired?"

He laughed. "Well, I wasn't sure . . . until now."

There was no graceful way out of that blunder, so I remained silent and let him continue.

"Rumors. Small school, remember? So back to my theory, Carlyle makes sure your boss knows he's offered you a job, then your boss *fires* you and Carlyle takes you into his fold. And I bet he's paying—he's probably paying you really big bucks to work here. Am I right? Much more than you were making as a civil servant, I bet."

"That's not quite the timeline of events."

"Okay then, second case scenario, Carlyle's going to

get you so inextricably bound in the school's shady practices that you in effect become a coconspirator and you have to keep quiet. Or, least likely, the trustees forced him to hire you as independent counsel to protect Holton from the legal ramifications of student murders."

"What do drugs have to do with the murders? What's the motive?"

"Motives are tricky things. You have to get inside people's heads. But on the more mundane side, maybe the girls needed to be silenced so they wouldn't expose Carlyle."

"Wait, so now Carlyle killed the girls?" I laughed.

Elliot considered me. He let me laugh at him. And if I expected a scathing retort from him, I was disappointed.

"You know what, Miss Melone? I like you. There's a gullibility about you that makes you attractive even though you're a blood-sucking lawyer and part of this warped administration. So I'm going to help you out." He sat silently a couple of seconds while I allowed him his patronizing moment of self-aggrandizement. "Does Carlyle want you to find out who's responsible? Think about that."

Frankly, I didn't think Carlyle cared about the murders except for their obvious financial repercussions to the school. He just wanted it all to stop. But I wasn't going to admit that to a student—even one as smart as Elliot, who'd probably come to the same conclusion long before me.

"I'm sure Dean Carlyle would like to know who's murdering Holton students. I think he hopes it's not one of the student body. Bad press and all that, right? And just for your information, I was *not* hired as independent counsel. I am who I am, and that's all that I am, I'm—"

"Popeye the sailor man," he finished. "I was weaned on old cartoons." He stood to leave. "I think we make a good team."

I must have been seeing Elliot and thinking Mike McCoy, because I let a wink slip from my right eye.

As Elliot trailed off down the hall, I grabbed my bag and headed upstairs to the wastelands of Dean Carlyle's office, where I found him emptying his crystal ashtray into the trash under his desk. The office was musty with fresh cigar smoke. He banished the bowl to a small table by the door and, after returning to his desk and sitting, looked directly into my eyes and spoke.

"Mila Nazir will be dealt with, for now, as I instructed at the staff meeting."

"I'm pretty good with English, so I understood that order the first time, *sir*."

He placed his open palms softly down on his desk. Looking at his fingers, he said, "I don't know why you insist on being ornery, Marianna. You have a good future here. Why are you sabotaging it?"

"I'm used to the simple tenets of right and wrong. Holton, I guess, is big business. I would have had a hard time working for Enron too."

He took a deep breath and looked me in the eyes again. "Holton is not Enron. We do not *steal* money or *cook books*. But in some regards, you are correct. Without endowments we would not survive. And some of us, who have made Holton our lives, feel that this school is performing an important educational function. Under my helm, Holton is becoming a top college contender—"

I noted he gave President Hatchett no credit for Holton's steady rise into the major leagues of secondary educational institutions.

"—survival and growth is our prime concern. Obviously, if one cannot breathe, hunger is secondary. Donations are Holton's oxygen. So try to overcome your hunger for simple morality. Remember, Marianna, real life doesn't come in black and white."

"At the AG's it does."

"Can you adapt?"

I pondered that question while Carlyle remained at his desk, maintaining his position of authority. Today we weren't equals. He continued his lecture.

"I told you I needed someone who knew the law, who could forestall potential brushes with the police on campus. Now, what do I mean by that? Do I mean that you should cover up murders? Of course not. On the other hand, if there's a rowdy party, students drink too much and disturb East Side residents with something like public urination, should there be an arrest? Should it be front-page news? In short, Marianna, is something like public urination *black* or is it *white* in your *personal* penal code?"

I nodded my head. "You want me to philosophically switch teams."

"Exactly. From an AG's point of view, public urination and murder are both criminal offenses. Both black. But from your *new* perspective—as a Holton employee— public drinking, loud parties, and the mild criminal sequelae should be *gray*."

"That's a defense perspective."

Ken tilted his head. "Right again."

"Why me? You already had McCoy in place."

"Not for the most recent events. Murder is black in any penal code. I need *you* and the wisdom of a seasoned prosecutor to make the distinctions between murder and all else that goes on here that appears in shades of gray."

The word "whitewash" came immediately to mind, but I stifled the word before it burped indecorously from my mouth.

Carlyle tucked his chin tightly to his chest. "Now, the next question is, are you able to do the job I hired you for?"

It was about the same time I began questioning the existence of God and Santa Claus that I realized life is merely a series of events related only by their chronology. This moment in Carlyle's office was just such an event: a blip in time wherein I was unemployed from the AG's office and insolvent. So I had no choice. I either played Carlyle's shady game of black and white or I was out in the dark with no flashlight.

I looked at my watch. It was ten past noon. McCoy would be waiting for me at Kartabar, a cold beer pressed to his warm lips.

"I'll do my best, Ken."

I left Carlyle and went straight to my Jeep, puckered up in the rearview mirror, and prepared to pry some information from typically tight-lipped Mike McCoy.

CHAPTER TWENTY-TWO

———◊◊◊———

Santorini

MIKE'S SHOULDER WAS BRUSHING mine as we sat in a semi-circular leather banquette at an eclectic cozy restaurant named Kartabar that was warmed in dark woods, hides, and rust-colored walls. I inhaled Mike's half-dreamy, half-comical smell—citrus and musk—and let his odor mingle in my head with the cooking aromas of cardamom and almonds. He had chosen a dark table in the back, well away from the windows, where he sat with a beer in his hand. Pulsating Greek music was playing at a perfect midrange level in the background, just loud enough to summon up a white-sanded isle in a turquoise blue sea but not so loud that we couldn't luxuriate in the prettier lagoon of our own hushed voices. Mike's lame excuse for sitting next to me on the banquette instead of the chair across was so that we could talk without screaming across the table, but the tiny table was barely two feet in diameter, the music was lilting softly in the background, there

was no one sitting on either side of us, and Mike was full
of lovely crap.

Despite my urge to sail into a stuporous pipe-dream
fantasy and embark on a hallucinogenic vacation to
Santorini with Mike McCoy in tow, I tied a safe slipknot
to reality and tried to reel in some new information about
the Hastings-Cummings murders via general carping
about Holton.

"Emily Barton was date-raped by another student and
this morning Carlyle said we should *wait and see what
happens*. Does everything get swept under the shags in
that place, or what?"

Mike let me vent. He smiled during my rampage,
then followed with his devil's-advocate routine, mollify-
ing me while trying to make me see the potential other
side of the story. A shortcoming of my legal background,
I held my position like a dog with its bone. During the
eight or so years he'd been at Holton, Mike had molted
some of his rigid cop skin and had softened into more of
a team player.

"You'd be surprised what some of these kids will do
to stay in school and graduate. When I brought Melinda
Hastings in on an exam-cheating scam, she threatened to
accuse me of sexual harassment if I didn't bottom-drawer
the complaint. You know, babe, it's possible the Barton
girl might be lying just to cover up her bad grades."

Mike was calling me "babe" all the time now. Was
the name reserved only for me? I reluctantly admit I
had begun to like it. I always wanted to be a babe, and
in this little college-town restaurant, I could be a closet
blonde without the AG girls ever knowing. Letting a man
call me "babe" would weaken our united front and be a

betrayal of our code of female superiority—a creed we held on to despite all prevailing evidence to the contrary. We all firmly believed that, in general, women were smarter than men, but so what? A damn lot of good a brain is when the quickest way to a man's heart is through his pants. When's the last time a man tried to guess my IQ while I was leaning over in a scoop-necked T-shirt?

Mike broke my reverie. "These kids can be a hoot. One girl pretended her mother was dying of cancer to explain her bad grades. The girl was going to weekly counseling with Becker and fabricated the surgery, chemotherapy, and finally some new alternative treatments they were trying on her dying mom as the last-ditch effort to save her life. Turns out mommy was at their winter home in Palm Beach. Unbelievable, huh?"

"How did you find her out?"

"Oh, Jesus, best part of the story! It's the kid's birthday, and the mother comes up for a surprise visit."

"No way!"

"Yup. Tanned, blonde, and healthy as a young mare. The closest she'd been to a doctor was her plastic surgeon. You having another one of those salads or you going to eat some real food today?" He motioned for the waitress.

"I'll have the chicken salad in grape leaves," I said to the waitress, who appeared to be barely past the age of majority.

"Whoa! Chicken wrapped in leaves? Don't go crazy on me now."

Before I could answer him, he was already cooing at the waitress. "Now, I know what you're thinking," he said to her. "But don't be jealous. I've got enough love for both of you."

"Swell," I said. At any minute I expected him to call

her "babe," and I could feel the arrow strike my heart as
my hand slipped off the life raft and I sank into the ocean
with the rest of the fish in the sea.

Our waitress held both her hands in her apron pockets like guns in a holster as she cocked her weary head to
the side. "Mike, do you want something or not?"

"Burger, fries, and another Corona, hold the lime,"
he said.

"We don't have burgers, McCoy. You know that."
Then, without another breath, she just walked away.

"Where's she going?"

"She loves me," he said. "They'll fix me something
in the kitchen that I'll eat. This is the first time I've ever
been here with a broad—I mean girl—woman, whatever.
She must be mad. You know how possessive the young
ones can be. But don't worry. I'm yours for the asking."

"What happened to your wife? Did she get tired of
your wandering eyes?"

"Eyes can't commit adultery."

"Yours can."

"Don't start giving me compliments or I'll be eating
you for lunch."

"Wife, Mike?"

"She dumped me three years ago to marry her high
school sweetheart. So I'm all yours."

Time to change the subject. "I had a private meeting
with Carlyle today and frankly I'm still flummoxed as to
why he hired me."

"Private meeting, huh? I wondered why your skirt was
extra short today."

"I'm wearing pants."

"Oh, then it must be my fertile imagination."

I tried to give him a punch to the shoulder the way I'd

seen Shannon do so many times, but it didn't quite come out the same. He grabbed my hand before it even made contact and then he held it until I tugged it gently away.

Mike gave up and downed the last of his Corona. "Carlyle thought you'd be easier to tame. He's always been a bad judge of character."

"Point well taken. He hired you."

"Feeble retort, Marianna. I expect more from you."

"In what way, Mike?"

"Can I start by holding your hand again?"

"Why?"

"Because then we'll be well on our way to second base."

"I'm not playing ball with you."

He laughed and leaned in close. Someone came into the restaurant and a blast of icy wind slashed through the overheated air. The waitress plopped a second beer on the table in front of him. Mike took a hefty swig.

"Anyway, this date-rape thing—you gotta ask yourself why a girl like Emily Barton is going to those parties over at Sherman's."

"You know about this already?"

His eyes closed. "Emily Barton went to Mitsy. Mitsy told me. Anyway, Sherman hosts some fancy shindigs— expensive champagne, designer drugs, and hoi polloi guests. Everyone wants to be on Sherman's guest list."

"So she deserves it?"

"All I'm saying is that Sherman and his crew are predatory wolves. Women should stay away from them or they'll get eaten."

"Or murdered?"

"Slow down—"

"Come on, Mike, why couldn't there be a connection?"

He shrugged. "I've staked that place out many a night. But it's goddamn private property, so I can't bust in."

"Melinda and Lisa were drugged. Emily too."

"No argument there. But without more, how do you connect the dots?"

"Well . . . I'm thinking maybe my tack with Sherman has been a bit off course. What's that old line about bees and honey? Maybe I should just open up my jar of honey and see what I can attract."

Mike's face bloomed into the sunniest smile I'd seen yet. "You, my dear, are a very scary woman. Too smart and too pretty for any man to survive the initial attack."

I followed that line with the most coy, girlish smile I could muster. Beth would have been proud of me. Laurie would have rolled her eyes. And Shannon would have broken my nose.

Mike's smile morphed into a grin. "And you've got one contagious smile," he said.

The waitress brought Mike sliced chicken in a pita loaf with tomatoes and mayonnaise. I daresay neither of us had any interest in the kind of nourishment found in chicken sandwiches but we ate anyway while Mike asked me about my home and family. I gave him a pencil sketch of the last ten years of my life. I wasn't so sure I wanted him to know me that well, mainly because I didn't know *him*. Maybe I could trust him as far as Holton was concerned—but about my personal life, I remained mute.

Mike snagged the check and stuffed some bills into it so fast I didn't have a chance to object. He walked me down Thayer Street, where my car was parked. The meter had expired. Mike grabbed the orange parking ticket from my windshield and put it in his pocket without letting me see it. "I'll take care of it."

"No. I'll pay it."

He laughed. "Who said I was going to pay? Give me your keys."

I handed him my keys in the blind assumption that he intended to drive back with me. He opened the driver's door and told me to get in and open the window. Again, starry-eyed, I obeyed. Then he dangled my keys through the window. I took them and started the car as he leaned his arms on the roof and stuck his head down through the open window, slipping me a Holton business card with his cell number on it. "I'm gonna make this violation go away. It'll be our secret." He winked and slapped the roof. Added to my growing body of feminist perfidy, I'd surreptitiously begun yielding to his winks like sweet Judas kisses. What a traitor I was!

"And" — he popped his head back in — "you be careful with Sherman and his gang. Remember what I told you that first day at the gym."

I smiled at him, only half-listening to the words coming from his lips, inches from mine. When he'd finished talking, I didn't respond, but neither did I turn my head away. He came closer, and I met him until his lips grazed mine, and for a few brief seconds we seemed to agree that the softer brushing of our lips against the other's was not merely the prelude to a kiss, but a sensation unto itself that should be savored and drawn out. I was oblivious to time passing, so I can't say for how long we continued to explore the softness of the other's mouth, but when he could no longer hold off, he reached his arm behind my head and pulled me into him. We kissed until I couldn't breathe, and then, without warning, he pulled himself away and stood outside my window, wiping his wet mouth on the back of his hand. I was surprised that he wasn't smiling. He merely slapped the roof again—no wink this time—and sauntered away.

I watched him march down Thayer Street. His car was nowhere in sight and I wondered where he was going. I turned the key in the ignition of my tattered Jeep, ready to follow him to the ends of the earth.

CHAPTER TWENTY-THREE

—∞∞∞—

Jaded

THE TOXIC EXHAUST FUMES that wafted up through the Jeep's perforated floorboard knocked me to my senses. I made a swift turn off Thayer Street toward Langley and ten minutes later I was hanging my jacket on the back of my desk chair.

Within seconds Rita appeared in my doorway holding a mug of steaming liquid. "You are back early?"

"I am?"

"From your *rendezvous* with Mike?"

"We had lunch, Rita."

"Pity."

Rita then announced that in my absence an impromptu press conference was convening even as we kibitzed. "Dean Carlyle called for your presence, but I told him you might be unavailable, otherwise indisposed, out to lunch, etc., etc." She gave her pixied head a few shakes. "Well, I could only assume . . . I mean, Mike has never taken a girl *just* to lunch. . . . Did he pay the check?"

"Yes, but he was still stiffed when I came right back to the office."

"*Stiff.* Ooh la la. You are so clever, Miss Melone."

"Press conference, Rita. Where?"

"President Hatchett's house. *Pronto.*"

I EXITED LANGLEY by its back door and followed a narrow wooded walkway to the rear gates of Haddon Hall, the president's house. Brick archways bejeweled with wrought-iron chandeliers lined the path to the limestone mansion. News trucks and police cars were taxied up along a circular driveway. Security guards and campus police dotted a two-hundred-yard radius. The static of walkie-talkies came and went in the crisp afternoon air.

I heard the echo of my skinny heels on the granite steps as I made my way to the entrance. Before I had a chance to lift the heavy brass knocker and send it crashing into the black enamel door, Saint Peter's gates swung open and Ogden, President Hatchett's creepy caretaker, met me.

"Welcome," intoned Ogden the invertebrate, whose jellied spine was crooked and whose pockmarked skin was set off nicely by oily hair. He attempted a natural smile but his gimpy left eye and stunted gray teeth gave all his expressions the same Transylvanian gleam. I flashed my ID while Ogden asthmatically pushed the door closed behind me before a camera-laden battalion marched up the steps.

I walked to the main dining room, where a catatonic group of Holton staff shuffled around. A low-lit chandelier and a pair of ostentatious silver candelabra, each holding a dozen candles, made the crystal table settings sparkle. The long dining table was covered in a brocade tablecloth that matched the deep burgundies of the room's wall-to-wall oriental rugs. Newer iterations covered original rugs that had probably aged in situ into pricy antiques. Nothing gold, gilt-edged, or brass was anywhere in sight. And then—and Beth would have been proud of me—I realized the house looked opulen and not gaudy precisely because of this absence of gold d brass, and because instead there was everywhere the cool quietude of silver, pewter, and glass.

While I was looking around for Vince, Ken caught sight of me. He and a white-haired gentleman with a full, soft jaw and skin the color of dough kept up their chatter though their eyes remained glued on me.

Ken met me halfway. "President Hatchett, this is Marianna Melone. Our Assistant Dean of Student Ethics."

We shook hands as Ken described my previous career at the AG's office.

"A former prosecutor. That is, she brought criminals to justice for the state. I'd say it's a bit of good fortune to have her on our side now. Agreed, President Hatchett?"

Hatchett's thick gray brows almost met in a deep frown. "Yes, yes," he said in a luxurious baritone.

The president looked past me at a sudden commotion. There at the front door stood Oily Ogden and a vicious-looking Vince Piganno. Ken snapped to attention and tapped on the microphone a few times. The room grew even quieter.

"Welcome, friends," Ken Carlyle said. "Thank you all for coming. The president and I would like to welcome you. President Hatchett has invited you into his home to offer a few brief words on the recent unfortunate events that have occurred in the Providence area involving two of our students. Without further ado, President Hatchett."

Carlyle stepped back, motioning Hatchett forward.

"Welcome," the great Hatchett began. "Let me get right to the point. Because protection of our students is our primary concern now, we have increased the number of private security personnel on campus and have brought in a few good men from our own Providence police force to maintain a constant presence on the campus grounds—"

"Thanks to some friendly persuasion from the attorney general's office." Somewhere in the throng, Vince had nabbed a WJAR microphone.

"Well, well," the cheerful Hatchett went on as if he had just spotted the intruder, "Attorney General Piganno, come on up and assure these worried parents that we have everything in control."

Vince surrendered his microphone, offered his parting smile to his press fan club, and glided to the makeshift podium at the dining room table.

Flesh to flesh, Vince and Carlyle exchanged handshakes, then Hatchett had his turn.

I held my ground amid the heavily artilleried press group and remained in the front as Vince delivered his first words.

"Dean Carlyle is quite on point when he says that our main interest should be and is the protection of the student body and the uninterrupted completion of the educational process each student has begun and is entitled to. Until this *maniac*"—Carlyle winced at Vince's emotionally charged characterization—"is caught, you should all rest assured that we are acting in concert to find the *animal* who has committed these egregious crimes against two of your students. And rest assured that no stone will be left unturned in uncovering his identity *even if it means finding one of Holton's own liable.*"

There was an audible gasp in the audience. Ken gritted his teeth before trying to nudge Vince out of the way. But he was no match for the bullish Vince, so Carlyle boomed his voice across the room without the assistance of electronic amplification.

"But let me make it very clear that absolutely no such evidence exists suggesting that the perpetrator has any connection whatsoever with this school."

Hands shot up in the audience. Before Carlyle could end the press conference, a question rang through the air.

"Is there any truth to the rumors that someone from your student body *is* indeed under investigation, Dean Carlyle? That a sexual predator may be enrolled here?"

"None whatsoever. Thank you all," Carlyle said. "And thank you all again for coming." He turned abruptly away from the crowd.

"I want you in my office now," he hissed at me as he walked away, herding Hatchett with him.

Vince stood by, registering my reaction to Carlyle's order. "You'd better go. Your master is calling."

"You said this was scheduled for tomorrow," I whispered.

"Your boss tried to hoodwink me by moving it up to today, but I was ready, because people like Carlyle are predictable."

"Are you happy?" I said to Vince. "This is what you wanted."

"Don't act like a lover scorned, for Christ's sake," he spit at me. "And don't ever let emotion get in the fucking way of business."

Words of wisdom from a man who hadn't let emotion get in his way of firing me. Vince had liked me. I knew that. But he'd still severed the cord because he thought it was what he had to do.

I left and wove down the front steps of Haddon Hall. Seeing Vince had made me homesick. I wanted to go to the nearest bar and drown my sorrows, but I put on my emotional blinders, and went straight to Carlyle's office for the second time that day.

CHAPTER TWENTY-FOUR

Too Much Ado about Nothing

"YOU KNEW PIGANNO WOULD be there?" Carlyle fired at me.

To protect Vince maybe I would have lied to Carlyle, but as it turned out, the surprise timing of the press conference made my answer mostly honest.

"Seeing Vince Piganno today was as much a surprise to me as you, Ken. But Vince always does the unexpected. He's unpredictable. That's why he's so good at what he does."

"I'll accept that answer for now. But I want some damage control here. I've already conferred with our PR people about a press release that will be shot to all the major networks and newspapers. The PR people will be in touch with you. The gist of our position is that there is no evidence of Holton involvement except that damn blanket. The police have been combing this campus for over a month and have found nothing. As far as Holton is concerned we have been exonerated from culpability. Are you with me so far, Marianna?"

"That's not quite true though, is it?" I said calmly as Carlyle held his breath, looking almost afraid to blink. I continued, "The blanket was from Health Services, where both Melinda and Lisa were patients—seeing Dr. Becker, I believe. Maybe the killer was being seen there too. No other way to get that blanket, right, except there? Maybe we should comb through those records."

The ones that don't exist.

Carlyle's jaw was undulating, but he'd still not uttered a word.

"And weren't Melinda and Lisa being seen because of their drug use? I know you don't like that word—'drugs'— but I can't think of a better one to describe *cocaine—*"

"That's enough." He broke his stare and turned toward his desk. "Yes, they may have been seen at Health Services for one reason or another. Let's say, for a headache, or the flu—"

"No, Ken. Did you forget I met Melinda Hastings's parents? Both you and they admitted that Melinda had been seeing Mitsy for *counseling* at Health Services. And Lisa herself told me she was seeing Dr. Becker weekly. You don't get counseled for the flu."

"That blanket was probably in Miss Hastings's car when she was abducted, and that's all there is to that. I understand I'm not as experienced as you in matters of evidence, but one blanket does not constitute a connection between these murders and Health Services. Does it? So *you*, Marianna, will make a quotable statement in a press release saying that the AG tactics are only so much hysteria. That the police investigation is now focusing *outside* our campus. Relay, somehow, that your old boss likes to make scenes. Much ado about nothing, etc., etc. Do you understand? And coming from you, a former

AAG—and one who knows Piganno pretty well—that will have quite a compelling effect."

"Is that what this is about? Why you hired me? Pit me against Vince Piganno and the AG's office?"

"I'm not interested in your personal relationship with your old boss. This is business I'm doing here. I'm asking you to disseminate the truth. And the truth is there is no reason to believe these murders are Holton-related except insofar as the victims happen to be two Holton students."

I nodded. Why argue? Argument is emotion. My old boss had taught me well.

BACK IN MY office I put Rita on Elliot's tail, who, might I say, was not so easy to find. He lived alone, as most of the students did in this exclusive school, and didn't answer in his dorm room or at class. Rita sent him an e-mail and two hours later he materialized at my office door.

"Elliot, I want you to publish a story about these murders. Any angle you want. Just make sure you stress that no Holton students or faculty have been implicated and how you think it's unfair that the AG made the statement at the press conference a few hours ago. I assume you heard it?"

"I was there, yes. But Carlyle's already pissed that I never wrote the story *he* wanted me to write about you."

"Remember that speech you gave me about having intestinal fortitude in a place like this? Well, get some and stop quivering, because after you write the first story I want you to print another one. But I need your blood promise that you will not double-cross me regarding how you got this information."

"Sure. Whatever. But why are you suddenly trusting me?"

"Quite simply because Carlyle gave me an idea and

I'm running with it, but you have to *pretend* you're a *real* reporter and refuse to name your sources even under threat of a lengthy prison term."

"Prison might be more interesting than this place. Anyway, I enjoy doing things for you. You're the only real person I've met here."

Of course, I thought, because I'm the only one who doesn't belong here. With the possible exception of Mike, but Mike seemed a lone ranger who didn't quite fit in anywhere.

"For now," I continued, "say the information is from unnamed sources. A female student is preparing to claim date rape by another student. Say that you're outraged that the male student's reputation is apparently more important than sexual assault and personal safety. Yada yada yada. You understand?"

He stared out the window as I spoke. "You want me to publish a story in the school paper saying that Emily Barton is being ignored because this other student has more clout with the administration than she does because his family donates megabucks to this school every year. Is that about the gist of it?"

I shot Elliot a sidelong glance. "Exactly where do you get your info?"

"I told you it's a small school. How do you think the reporter at the press conference knew enough to ask about a sexual predator in our midst?"

"Remind me never to let you read my diary. Anyway, write the story—leave all names out for now. Print a special edition if you need to. I want it out ASAP."

I couldn't wait to see Carlyle pee in his pants when he read it. Ah, the power of the press, especially bad press. I'd learned more things from Vince than I knew.

Elliot silently packed up and left with what I discerned was a slight smile spreading across his self-righteous mug.

As the day inched forward I realized I was missing the girls like caffeine withdrawal. I'd come to depend on the sounding boards of Laurie, Shannon, and Beth. Here I thought our drinking sprees were just a way to relax, to blow off the steam of overheated courtrooms and hot tempers, when in fact we'd actually been helping each other figure things out. Whether it was one of our daily trial tactic dilemmas or the latest abdominal cramp that *could be ovarian cancer,* we each brought our troubles to the table (or the bar in our case) and hashed them out.

I got a cup of caffeine for my ever-threatening migraine and headed back upstairs to my office. Lo and behold, as soon as I negotiated the last turn of the hallway, I stumbled upon Rita whispering "Mademoiselle?" as she pressed an ear against my closed office door. So intently was she listening for my answer from within that she was unaware I was approaching from behind.

Rita cracked open my door and padded like a cat into the office. I followed on her heels.

"Oh, Rita?" I sang.

She jumped around, stifling a scream. "You frightened me."

"You seem a bit on edge."

She retreated to my doorway, muttering haltingly as if she were angry with herself. "Well, yes, everyone is. Students dying . . . such violence . . . it's not right. Not right at all."

"Are you looking for me?"

She looked around my office and then focused her view to the empty hall beyond. "Too quiet here. I was looking for . . . just some company. . . ."

She whimpered something else as she walked out of my office and down the hall to hers and I picked up my phone to call my friends and arrange a fun-and-frolic at Nick and Tony's on the Hill for a slice, a shot, and a schmooze—just like old times.

CHAPTER TWENTY-FIVE

Good Night, Gracie

NICK AND TONY'S GOURMET Pizza on Atwells Avenue was a hangout for all the local colleges (and for younger high school kids who wanted to hang with the bigger fish). Although we were all in our thirties and well over the college-age hill, the girls and I were always more comfortable in places where the décor was unsophisticated and the food fried.

The girls were bringing me Lisa Cummings's autopsy reports to add to my file on Hastings that I had photocopied from the AG's before I left. Emily Barton's sexual harassment complaint would be my newest addition to *their* case file. And my senses were telling me all these events had an ominous coherence.

I arrived early and sat at the bar. Booths lined the windows and a pinball machine and a coin-operated video war game flanked the restrooms. Red-checked tablecloths had recently been Americanized with paper placemats to save money on cleaning. Worn-out Frank Sinatra CDs droned in the background. Frank, the Chairman of the Board, Old Blue Eyes. He was as close as Nick and Tony could get to American music without feeling like traitors to the homeland. Not that I minded. With Frank crooning in the background, it took a beer and a half to get me all wound up in some blue romantic mood, even in a greasy joint with sticky plastic menus.

"*Salute*, Nick. *Salute*, Tony," I called out to the two brothers who worked behind the U-shaped bar.

Tony waved as his brother Nick walked out from behind the pizza oven. Nick's hair fell in damp curls around the yellowed collar of a white chef's jacket bloodied with tomato sauce.

"*Salute*, Marianna. Long time, no? You forget your old neighborhood now you're a big-shot lawyer?"

Nick and Tony had come to America as kids. After years of working in coffee shops and restaurants, they'd bought their own pizza parlor. Tossing pizzas. Selling beer. Never aspiring to more, they'd taken the quick route to a buck. Nick had wanted to marry me when we were kids. At thirty-eight, he was still single. Tony was a few years older and married, with two young boys who were often with him in the kitchen after school sprinkling the pre-grated mozzarella cheese on large slabs of dough and then dropping dollops of thick red sauce on top of the cheese, before their father slid it onto a wooden pallet and into the flat ovens. It was Tony's special pizza recipe—he put the cheese on first so the sauce didn't "sog up" the dough. Father and sons worked in one smooth assembly line of duties: cheese, sauce, oven; cheese, sauce, oven. Tony would one day retire. His sons would become men and take over. Cheese, sauce, oven. Cheese, sauce, oven.

"Where are your *putana* friends?" Nick asked.

"My friends know what *putana* means. So cut the crap or I'm going to Domino's."

"Yeah, but you don't get the beer there, eh? We have the liquor."

Nick and Tony had gotten their Class B liquor license thanks to me, with a little help from Vince. It was damn hard to get a liquor license in Federal Hill because there were so many churches in the neighborhood. City ordinances forbade the sale of liquor within a two-hundred-foot radius of a school or place of worship.

"Your friends can hear me?" He made an exaggerated show of looking around the bar. "Eh? They can hear me now?"

"Just lose the machismo attitude fast. It's because of us you've got booze in here."

Nick said something to himself. I may have detected the word "alcoholics" in his mumbling, but then again, "alcoholics" was a pretty big word for him. He had probably just reiterated his belief that we were all a troupe of sluts, *especially* because of our drinking habits. Maybe he considered me salvageable because of my Italian heritage.

Nick was six foot two. With the right haircut and a Paul Stuart suit, Madison Avenue might have snatched him up in a New York minute and plastered him across the cover of GQ. But as far as Nick and Tony were concerned, short hair was for gay men and they'd never heard of Paul Stuart.

In Italian I ordered a beer from Nick. They got a real kick out of me speaking Italian to them. They were always accusing me of being too uppity.

"Zat all the Italian you know, for Chrissake? Let me teach you. Eh? I give you the private lessons."

"Eh!" Tony laughed from the kitchen. No matter where they were in the restaurant, they always picked up flawlessly on each other's sexual commentary.

He leaned toward me as I gulped my beer, refilling my glass from the tap as soon as the beer level declined an inch or so. "You alone tonight? We go for a ride later."

"My girlfriends will be here in about fifteen minutes, otherwise I'd jump at the chance. Do you have a cigarette?"

"Eh? Your father knows you smoke? Nice girls don't smoke."

He took one of his hands and slapped it against the other to suggest I needed a bit of male discipline. Reaching under the counter, he pulled out a pack of Marlboros, rapped the pack hard a few times against the heel of his hand until a cigarette popped up, and then held the pack out to me. "But you go outside, eh? No smoke inside or I get a ticket."

"Call the cops. By the time they get here, I'll be done."

He gave me a sour look and was probably ready to bitch-slap me with some macho retort, but a shriek of laughter distracted him. A group of young adults was on the far side of the bar, playing a pinball machine and drinking beer by the pitcher. "You see over there?" he continued. He nodded toward the pinball machine. "All young, they feel nothing except the minute it hurts, then" — he snapped his fingers — "nothing. You have too much emotion. You get older. Time to get married."

"Jesus, Nick. That's one depressing marriage proposal."

"You think I'm stupid because my English is not good and I make pizza all day. I take my money to the bank every day. I'm not so stupid. I make a good husband."

Nick continued his unorthodox proposal of marriage. "You need babies. Then you have no time to sit around in bars."

All the pinball players started screaming at once. Someone had won. I recognized Rod Lipton when he thrust his fist in the air like a kid from the hood.

"Hey!" Tony came out from the kitchen for a break. Sweat was pouring down his face. Unlike his brother, Tony's hair was thin and golden, balding at the forehead. He kept it shorter than Nick's but it was greasy and unkempt. "You keep it down, eh! I got other customers." Tony came from around the bar and took their empty beer pitcher away. Only when he was out of earshot did Tony swear at them under his breath.

Rod approached the bar to get Nick's attention. "We'll have another round, old chap."

Rod saw me, and his frown turned to a smile.

"Marianna, isn't it?"

Nick walked slowly away but stayed near the bar watching us.

"Hello, Mr. Lipton."

"Why not call me Rod? We're off campus."

"Okay. And you can still call me Miss Melone."

He reared his head back and smiled. Lipton in his own supercilious way was trying to be friendly. So what's a girl to do? I tried to be civil without fraternizing and risking the chance that we'd be seen drinking together in a bar.

"Sure, *Miss Melone*, if that makes you more comfortable."

He sat on the bar stool next to me. I found myself involuntarily gritting my teeth. Nick was right, I couldn't hide my feelings well enough for the smooth crew at Holton. I was hopelessly animated, emotional, and thus, transparent. I sat up straighter and tilted my chin toward my chest while stubbing out my half-smoked cigarette and trying to act like I was real happy he was there.

"I'm expecting some friends," I said.

Was I apologizing for being a single woman alone at a bar?

"You shouldn't smoke," he said. "I hate to see a beautiful woman smoking."

"How about we just talk about you."

"Ooh, you're so feisty."

"Feisty?"

"Yeah, spunky."

"Rod, really, we shouldn't be seen together at a bar, and I really am meeting some friends here shortly."

He glanced at the front door, signifying that he barely believed me, then moved to the edge of his bar stool and whispered in my ear, "I'll just sit here and wait with you. I want to talk to you about something kind of private anyway."

I remained silent. Nick was staring at us from the cash register.

"Emily Barton," he whispered again. "You know all about that, right? She was at one of our parties the other night."

I focused on the *Budweiser On Tap* handle in front of me as I readied to hear his justification of rape. Maybe Shannon would bolt through the doors on cue with her six-guns loaded. Not that I was a distressed damsel, but at the AG's, if a defendant got rough, I'd call in one of the cops and he'd twirl the bum around a few times until he got dizzy and fell over. While he was down, I'd dig a six-inch stiletto heel into his back and ask him if I could help him up. Muscle was the only thing I lacked to be an excellent thug. Shannon at least had the size if not the bulk.

But Rod Lipton wasn't some gang-rape defendant (yet), so I summoned the ghost of Grace Kelly to cool me down. I smiled graciously and said, "Yes, I've heard about those parties. They sound like quite a good time."

He drew his head back again. A demure smile, slightly raised eyebrows. "You *are* a surprise. I like it."

"I believe it's important for administrators to stay involved with students on their level. Be approachable."

He nodded slowly, not quite sure of me. "Cory and I were housemates at Reese, then we found this great place at Riverside Park. I know Barton's claiming it happened at our place."

I moseyed closer to him.

"But there were a lot of guys there that night. Most of the students at Holton were in or out that night. And the girls at Holton have been around the block a few times, you know. And they can drink, too."

There it was. The Emily-as-drunken-slut defense. I took a deep breath, remembering Nick's comment about my innate inability to control my emotions. I had a bad temper and was dangerously close to pushing Rod off the bar stool and shoving a broken beer bottle down his throat. Instead I offered a bit of sympathy for what he was suggesting was a trumped-up charge by a sloshed, oversexed coed.

"Why would Emily make this up?"

Rod moved back on the stool and broke our stares. "Who knows? It got a little too rough maybe? She drank too much?" Then he quickly added, "You know who Cory's uncle is, right?"

"Movie producer?"

Rod nodded, briskly this time. "Is she blaming Cory for this?"

"Confidentiality, Rod. I can't say."

"Yeah, I guess so. But you have to understand a guy like Cory. He's not going to admit anything. I mean, he wouldn't even dignify these allegations with a defense. But I know how rumors can get out of hand. Cory's a little naive."

"Sherman's uncle is a Hollywood movie producer, and Sherman's *naive?* That's a stretch. And don't forget, I met him, and he seemed about as naive as—"

"Okay then, *cocky.* Cory's too cocky for his own good. What I'm saying, Miss Melone, is that a lot of people are out to get him because he's from a famous, rich family. Do you understand what I'm saying?"

"Goodness gracious," I said in my best Scarlett O'Hara impersonation. "Are you suggestin' that a young woman would yell rape to blackmail someone who is famous and has scads and scads of money?"

He moved back to the middle of his bar stool and smiled. Rod was smart and slick—unlike me. He always waited a few cool seconds before he sallied.

"Good show, but don't put words in my mouth, huh?"

Rod Lipton, Cory Sherman, Ken Carlyle—they all could have taught me a thing or two about Jeff Kendall— if only I'd met them first. But then, Jeff Kendall had taught me some things too.

"Rod, why don't you say *exactly* what you mean and stop buttering up your words."

Rod either took my statement as a compliment or he was reacting to the sexually charged word "butter," because he smiled slickly before he answered. In a cool, matter-of-fact drone he said, "I'm simply saying that if Emily stays clear of us, we'll do the same. Okay? You won't hear another word about her. She should find the guy who did it, but it isn't one of us."

"Did Cory know Lisa Cummings?"

He shrugged. "Um . . . Yeah, a little. They were friends . . . I guess."

"Good friends? Like in boyfriend-girlfriend?"

He snickered. "How quaint."

"Were they?"

"I don't know what they did behind closed doors."

"Did she come to your parties?"

"It wasn't her style. She was too snobby to mingle with nouveau riche Hollywood money."

"But she and Cory knew each other?"

"Everyone knows everyone else at Holton. Small school."

"Sure, of course." I lifted my empty beer glass and gave him a mock toast. "Well, thanks for talking to me about Emily."

"Anytime, ma'am."

" 'Ma'am'?"

"Well, maybe you should let me call you Marianna."

At my tacit acquiescence Rod leaned calmly back on his bar stool and smiled. I could see his brain sizzling away while he quickly weighed the consequences of his next sentence. I smiled to help him make up his mind.

"I swear there's nothing going on at our place that you need to worry about. It's just a good time had by all."

"Maybe I should come by one night then?"

"Yeah . . . I guess that would be all right with Cory. Why not?"

I assumed Rod Lipton paid half the rent, so why wasn't he confident enough to extend a unilateral invitation? But I didn't need an engraved one. If I managed to get a five-minute lay of the land—or wolf's den as Mike called it—that was fine with me.

"Robbing the cradle again, Mari?" Shannon's voice boomed from the front door. She, Laurie, and Beth cascaded into the pizza joint like a tsunami that had just rolled over Tiffany's and the perfume counter at Saks.

Shannon gave Rod the once-over. "Go home and play with your trucks, son, we have adult business to discuss here."

Rod scoffed and slid off the bar stool. I gave him a friendly goodbye smile and a tortured wink as the girls herded me off to an empty booth. Rod remained at the counter by himself, sipping his beer and giving me the occasional glance and smirk as he watched us order.

We huddled for shoptalk. Shannon went first. "So we've got GHB in Hastings and Cummings, and now this Barton girl is coming forward?"

"And the Hastings blanket was from Health Services," I added. "Emily Barton had been to see Becker there. Lisa was having weekly sessions and so was Melinda—"

"Yup, yup," Laurie said, impatient for her own input. "We found out through subpoena that both the dead girls were seen there, but Holton's claiming no records of the visits, and the parents have hired lawyers to keep it that way. Did the Barton girl give you any names yet?"

"No, so I can't prove any connection with the drugs and Sherman's parties."

"Might not be one," Laurie said. "Barton may have been raped but she isn't dead."

I quickly answered. "Hastings and Cummings were tortured while they were still alive. And the autopsies would have shown that they died from drug OD, which they didn't—"

"So whoever did it wanted them dead. No accidental drug overdose," Shannon said. "Emily Barton, so far, is a separate incident. Agreed?"

Nick delivered our pizzas and beers to the bar, where he made me get up and bring them to the table. Nick was intimidated by women who weren't intimidated by him. He wouldn't come near us en masse.

Shannon ripped a slice of pepperoni-laced triple-cheese off the tray before it hit the table and we all chewed pizza and our thoughts for a few silent minutes, until Beth spoke up, and in her quiet, self-effacing manner said, "I have an idea."

I grabbed a piece of dry crust abandoned on Beth's plate, and, since we were all busy chewing anyway, we gave her our undivided attention. Poor Beth usually never got a chance to get a word in edgewise without a million interruptions.

"Why not have Lucky do some specialized testing on the GHB in Hastings and Cummings? Maybe the chemist at forensics can determine if it's coming from the same source. I mean, let's face it, GHB isn't Bayer aspirin. It's illegal, so this guy is either making it in his kitchen or it's coming from the same illegal source. Too much of a coincidence that they both have it in them and they're both Holton students."

"Jesus, Beth," I said. "You've never spoken this much in the entire five years I've known you."

"And," Shannon just had to add, "I've never known you to make this much sense."

"Maybe that's because I never get to finish a sentence," she struck back.

"Beth is right," Laurie said. "It won't tell us who's doing it, but it'll tell us if the girls were drinking at the same watering hole."

"And just maybe the trough is at Riverside Park." With that I looked at my watch. "I've got to go. You guys call Lucky about the GHB tests. He can't take orders from me anymore. I've got to make a call to an ex-cop with a warm gun in his holster."

All mouths stopped chewing and turned to me. Murder is one thing. Our love lives commanded absolute attention.

"He's head of security at Holton," I explained. "But he's not all haughty and uptight like the rest of them over there. We meet to talk over the newest cases."

"And by that little flush on your face, I bet he's already unholstered that warm gun of his and given you a few shots with it," said Shannon with her eyebrows raised halfway to her hairline.

Beth added her own sweet euphemism to Shannon's tart mix. "You've *smoked a cigarette* with him already? That was fast. Even for you, Mari."

"Watch it, Beth," I said. "And no, I haven't slept with him yet. But I'll tell you one thing, if he shoots his gun off the way he kisses, I'm becoming a lobbyist for Philip Morris."

CHAPTER TWENTY-SIX

An Invitation to a Party

NEXT MORNING AT THE office, I found Rita behind my desk swooning on the phone. She was panting when she hit the hold button and handed me the receiver. "The medical examiner's office," she said. "Ooh la la! What a voice."

It could only be Lucky's deep, molasses-smooth drawl that was sending Rita into a pre-orgasmic state.

"Have him come here for a meeting. I must see what he looks like," she begged.

"Morgan Freeman," I said as I took the receiver from her hand.

She rearranged her breasts in their uplift bra and walked back to her office.

"Hi, Lucky," I said.

"Miz Melone, I'm sorry to bother you, but can I trouble you for an address on that Cummings girl? I got some documents to send off to her family and we have her dormitory as her legal address."

"Why don't you send the stuff to me and I'll forward it?"

Lucky laughed, deep and low. Rita was right; his voice *was* sexy. "Now, Miz M, you don't think I'm stupid, do ya, or are you askin' me to do something not quite *kosher*?"

"All right, but do they say anything I don't already know?"

"Nope. Just prelim death certificate for insurance purposes and whatnot."

I quickly pulled up Lisa's data sheet, surprisingly not yet purged from our system, and read off her home address to him. "And what's the official cause of death?"

"Well, I shouldn't be telling you that either."

"Oh, come on, Lucky. How many bottles of champagne did the girls and I bring you? Autopsy tables set with extra-large gauze pads. Chilled lobsters. We toasted Moët in sterilized beakers! Suddenly you can't trust me?"

He sighed heavily over the phone to let me know he was telling me reluctantly. It was a warning sigh: *Don't make me regret this or it'll be the last time I tell you anything.*

"Drugged but not dead yet, then raped, then he cut her face up. In that order. She ends up bleeding to death. And that drug of course . . ."

"GHB?"

"Sure . . ."

His voice kept trailing off. The girls must have already gotten to him with their request for further testing on the GHB.

"Lucky, I already know about the tests. Can it be done?"

"We can try, but you know we're not testing from

a pure sample. Not that easy when it's from different people."

"What do you think the odds are of finding anything probative?"

"I'm not thinking nothing. *Thinking* is not my job here."

"I know you, Lucky. If there's something there, you'll find it. You're the best investigator in the state."

"Don't you go polishing me up. That's beneath you to use them tactics."

"But it's true, Lucky. You're the best because you love it."

"Are you prosecuting this case? 'Cuz I'm not sure I can tell you so much without getting my wings clipped over here."

"You know I'm not an AAG anymore. But I'll just get Shannon or Laurie to tell me. What's the difference?"

"Better that way 'cuz I get to keep my job."

"Okay. I understand."

"No problem, Miz Melone. And hey, we're still having them tailgate parties out back. Cold lobsters and beer straight from the chiller. No champagne since you girls ain't been coming around."

"We'll have a visit soon."

THE HOURS TICKED by until early afternoon, when Elliot appeared at my door, two feet imbedded at the threshold like steel fence posts. When I finally noticed him he looked as if he'd been staring at me for a few seconds at least.

"Your secretary isn't at her desk," he said. Without further invitation, he walked in and sat in front of my desk. "I have that story for you."

He laid the proposed newspaper article he had written on my desk as he spoke. "Emily Barton. I heard she's leaving school at the end of this semester and not coming back."

Once again I was out of the loop. I hadn't heard even the whisper of that rumor. Did my little friend Elliot have any other scoop to offer?

"Elliot, were you tutoring either Lisa or Emily?"

He shook his head. "Like most of the socialites in this place, they borrow my notes and pass them around like contraband sex magazines and eventually I get them back. But lately a lot of these kids don't even care about passing their courses anymore."

"Emily Barton told me she and Lisa had been studying together the night Lisa was killed. I think that's messing up Emily's mind. She might be the last person to have seen Lisa alive."

Elliot nodded, noncommittal.

Okay, nothing additional there.

"She said she left, and they were supposed to meet up later at a party but Lisa never showed. Was the party at Sherman's?"

He shrugged. "I wasn't there."

"And what about Cory Sherman? I just don't see him cutting up faces, especially while his victims are alive."

He shrugged again as if that were the least important element of the murders. "What makes this guy tick? That's what you have to ask yourself. Figure out where he gets pleasure and then predict his next move."

"Pleasure? I never understood that. Pleasure from killing."

"Cops always put so much importance on modus operandi. I think they just want to impress people with Latin phraseology."

"MO fits on a microscope slide easier than motive."

Elliot was in some realm of higher thinking and was barely listening to me. He was staring at the wall over my head as if he was already mentally composing the newspaper article. "It's like giving someone an aspirin for a brain tumor. The way a killer kills is a symptom of the disease. Figuring out the *reason* he kills is the cure. That's when the killing stops."

"Forget about the journalist career. How about a career in forensic psychiatry?"

"Whatever. I never even open a book because I can almost predict what the texts say. And I've been tortured with a photographic memory. I see things once and they're forever embedded in my brain. School is boring."

"Oh, right. You scored, what, second in the country on the SATs?"

"I got one question wrong. And they ended up discounting it because it had two possible answers."

"I have a sister who can't manage to budge from 1200."

"I can help her. That's what I do best." Elliot spoke with such an audible shrug that I wasn't sure what drove him. He seemed not to care if I gave him a hot tip for a news story, analyzed the murders with him all day, or hired him to tutor Cassie in her SATs.

"Why did you come to Holton instead of a big gun like Harvard?"

"Money. Holton offered a full scholarship."

"Do you get paid for the tutoring?"

"Sometimes. But I don't do it for the money. I told you I'm bored—and it's a great way to meet girls, since I can't impress them with my convertible sports car the way Cory and most of the others do. Except Rod. I don't think his family's in the same league with the rest of them either. But he looks the part better than I do. You know, that windblown, I-just-got-off-my-yacht look."

"I always liked the nerdy type in college—um . . . not that you're nerdy . . ."

"That's okay. I know who I am. But the problem is, the girls here don't like the nerdy types. They're more impressed with money and social status. Ergo, Sherman et al.'s popularity. I guess that's why I like hanging around you. You appreciate the cerebral type."

For the briefest second I thought of Mike McCoy. If Elliot was right about me, I wondered how Mike McCoy had managed to infiltrate my brain trust of "cerebral-type" boyfriends.

"Hey, can you get my sister's SAT scores up before her next try?"

"Pretty sure I can. I've done it before. A lot of it's just teaching someone the tricks in the questions. You don't have to know much to score high on SATs."

"Can I trust you?"

"What do you mean by that?"

"People are getting killed on this campus. Not the safest place in the world to be right now—which of course is what has Dean Carlyle so frantic. I can't imagine that more of the female students aren't taking the semester off."

"A couple have already transferred out permanently. But your sister will be quite safe with me. Especially if she's anything like you."

"Meaning?"

"Out in the open, readable, authentic."

"I'm that one-dimensional, huh?"

"No, you're like a fine piece of cut crystal. Sharp-edged and multifaceted but as lucid as a Zeiss lens."

"I'm not sure that's a compliment, but this conversation is making me uncomfortable, so let's drop it."

"I will make sure no one even gets *near* your sister on this campus. Satisfied?"

"Nonetheless, all tutoring shall take place in public areas. Is that clear?"

"Of course."

I gave Elliot Cassie's home and cell phone numbers and told him to call her. "I'll let her know to expect your call. She won't be thrilled, I assure you."

I thought I espied a new jauntiness in his demeanor as he popped out of his chair to leave. I had given him another job and he was happy.

"Figure out the *motive*, Miss Melone." He turned to leave. "And I'll call your sister."

After he disappeared down the hall, I read the highlights of his proposed story on Emily's date rape. Perfect in its sparseness and lack of emotion, the article calmly demanded attention. Elliot's writing was a cold performance in linear conviction. *Holton student to leave school before she identifies her legacied Holton stalker.* Elliot had been a little careless in pointing his finger in the direction of legacied students, but I forgave him that. He, like me, wasn't particularly fond of spoiled brats either.

At four-thirty I was ready to leave for the day. (Of course, the promise of dinner with Mike made me want four-thirty to be six.) I jingled my car keys in my right pocket as I walked briskly out of my office.

Trotting down the steps of Langley, I saw Cory Sherman and Rod Lipton approaching with an entourage of other similarly clad prepsters. As they got closer Rod recognized me first and whispered something to Cory. The group of six kids surrounded me. I felt as if I were in the middle of a rumble between rival gangs. And I was the sole member of my own gang.

"Miss Melone," Rod said. "How are you?"

I stopped. "Good evening, Mr. Lipton."

Cory then moved easily to the front of the group and took my hand from my side to shake it when I had no intention of offering it to him. I looked into eyes so pale blue that they seemed like amorphous pools melting into the whites of his eyes. In the harsh daylight his skin was without color, pale and thin; blue veins like ink lines were visible on his temples where his straight blond hair was casually whisked to the side. When Cory Sherman was an old man I imagined he would be hunched over and walk with a cane; long, sparse strands of grayish blond hair would be stuck to his balding head; his temples would be sunken in; and his teeth, now white and capped to twice their size, would be the only remnant of his youth, and would protrude from his thin lips like the scowl of a growling dog. In youth, he had an ethereal translucency, but with age he would begin to melt away into a hoary old ghost.

I quickly withdrew my hand from his.

Cory's veneered teeth broke through his thin lips. "Winona Ryder—that's who you look like, except for your height. She's tiny. Barely came up to my chin when I was talking to her at the Oscars last year."

"Hey, that reminds me," one of the other cohorts said to him. "Your uncle promised Carlyle a whole row of tickets. You working on that? Or we'll be in the soup with him."

"A whole row?" I said.

"He gives them to the bigger Holton donors along with season tickets to the Patriots games," his friend bragged. "Hey, Rod tells us he invited you to one of Cory's shindigs. You were just toying with him though, right? You wouldn't really come."

"Sure I would. I get to talk to students only after they're in some kind of trouble. I like to talk to the students before that. Get to know them better."

Rod's face was a blank canvas. Cory smiled. "This weekend then, come on by." He looked at Rod. "Friday, Saturday. Right, Rod, old boy?"

"Sounds good," I said. "I'll take it under consideration."

"Stop by. You have no idea how much fun we can be."

Rod pulled Cory by the sleeve. "Let's go, buddy. We'll see you later then, Miss Melone."

The other boys all rallied around them with assorted smirks and supportive laughter as Cory and Rod sauntered away. It was difficult to gauge their sincerity, but little old skeptic me figured there was a good chance Cory would go straight to Carlyle to complain about me and I'd hear about this encounter before the day was out. Give me a good old-fashioned bank robber any day rather than this crew of privileged misfits.

And speaking of misfits, Mike McCoy awaited. . . .

CHAPTER TWENTY-SEVEN

Baby, Baby, Baby

CHEZ PASCAL'S WAS AN out-of-the-way French restaurant on Hope Street, owned by a smart Italian chef from Boston who knew there were some uppity East Siders damn tired of spaghetti and meatballs. I had told Mike to meet me at the bar, and there he sat with a glass of red wine in his hand, watching the silent movie of a college basketball game to the accompaniment of Edith Piaf.

From the back, Mike was square. If I hadn't seen his taut muscles at the gym, I wouldn't know what was underneath his loose-fitting clothes. His navy blue blazer was tossed over the bar stool next to him. The cuffs of his blue shirt were rolled up beyond his wrists, where the dark hairs were sparsely suggesting what lay beyond, and his olive green wide-wale corduroy pants were cuffed and baggy. I couldn't see his feet, but I imagined his navy and gray argyle socks under rubber-soled loafers.

"Hello," I said softly.

"Babe!" He spun around on his bar stool. Every time

he smiled at me his smile seemed to grow. I couldn't take my eyes off his mouth. I would sit in my office and try to conjure his face in some silly daydream, and I could never recall it. I wanted to memorize at least one part of his face so I could remember it when the urge arose.

He grabbed his jacket from the stool. "Quite a fancy place," he said. "Should we get a table?" He walked behind me and slid the camel-hair coat off my shoulders.

Kristen, the owner's wife, seated us at a table in the adjoining, more private, room, and Mike placed both his hands on the table between us as if ready to use them in a flash. The pinky ring I had noticed the day he came bounding through the conference room doors was catching the chandelier sparkle in its square green stone.

I lowered my head and stared at his large, powerful-looking hands.

"Is that a class ring?"

"My partner's from when I was a street cop." His index finger tickled my hand as if asking for permission to come closer.

"Let me guess. You were going steady and your partner broke it off, so you kept the ring."

"I thought you worked with cops at the AG's."

"So?"

"And you don't know about cops who wear their partners' rings? Shame on you. 'Cause you're gonna feel like an earth slug when I tell you."

The waiter came to take our order and turned to me. "Hey there, Mari," he said. "Haven't seen you in a while."

I explained to Mike, "I've been here on a few dates." Then to the waiter I said, "I'll have what he's having," and I nodded toward the wineglass in Mike's hand.

"So you want to know why I'm wearing my partner's ring, or not?" Mike said.

"I can guess now. He got shot in the line of duty and you were with him. Right? And you feel guilty because you should have been able to protect him."

Mike tried to smile, but it was more of a grimace. Absent the sparkle, his smile was introspective. "Oh, he's dead all right, but not while 'in the line.' He was my best friend and my partner. And I was a young asshole. His wife shot him right in front of me."

I sat there like an idiot with my mouth open. "Dead?"

"I thought I could talk the gun out of her hand. Thank Christ they had no kids."

"Why did she shoot him?"

He shrugged. "Because it was more emotionally satisfying than divorce. I went to their house in the middle of a brutal fight. She came at us with his gun. I should have pushed him out of the way, confused her or something. But no, I think I'm gonna charm her with my sweet talk. She started shooting at him and then aimed at me."

Two fresh glasses and Mike's bottle of wine appeared on our table. I was surprised he'd ordered a special vintage. Had he done it just for me? Mike wasted no time clicking his glass to mine and taking a good hefty swig like it was a bottle of cold beer.

"And you got away, so you feel guilty?"

He looked past me, focusing on the memory. "I ran to wrestle the gun out of her hand as she was shooting at him like he was the target at a firing range. Fucking bitch!"

Swearing seemed to wake him from his trance.

"Sorry . . . I always get angry when I think of it. Anyway, I guess I should have stayed with him and kept talking to her, instead of running toward her to get the gun away, but I wasn't thinking clear. I did what I thought was right at the time. But I don't do guilt. It's a wimps-ass waste of time that doesn't change a thing."

I glanced outside to the park across the street and suddenly my mind transported me back to my old desk at the AG's office, typing with one hand and smoking a cigarette with the other, while "Beetle" Mulroy explained to me how he and his accomplice jacked up cars at two in the morning and shoved blocks under them to remove wheels and tire rims while the owners slept upstairs with open windows. This cops-and-robbers shoptalk with Mike was making me miss the girls. I craved one of Shannon's Camel cigarettes. Or maybe it was the female company I was craving, and the dank stench of the Fez, or one of our other, even raunchier hangouts.

In one clean, self-destructive sweep, I pushed my un-touched wine away. "I need a Grey Goose martini, dry."

"You sure?"

I nodded.

Mike motioned for the waiter and emptied my wine into his glass. I ordered the drink and sucked it down like lemonade at a church picnic. "Another one."

Mike raised his eyebrows.

"Don't start counting my drinks, damn it."

"Hey, no, not me!" He put his hands up in surrender. "I'm usually the one trying to get the girls drunk. It's just that . . . I don't want you blaming me—"

"How freaking lame. Would I do such a dippy thing? I'm starting to relax for the first time in weeks."

"You're lucky you're with me and not with some big

ugly brute who'll take advantage of you." He huffed the-
atrically, then paused. "My place or yours?"

About an hour later, three green swizzle sticks, covered in my fingerprints, still pierced my uneaten olives.
They lay on the table in front of me like prosecution ex-
hibits A through C, proving beyond a reasonable doubt
that I had downed three vodka martinis at a rate of approximately one every twenty minutes. Corroborating
evidence were the three red pimentos that flanked my
bread dish like dead goldfish. My cold halibut and white
beet salad were pushed to the side of the table next to
Mike's neatly half-eaten skirt steak. He was hunched
over the table, holding one of my hands with both of his.
When had his hands made that final journey to mine?
Our foreheads were almost touching. He was mumbling
all sorts of silly nonsense to me and I was slobbering over
his mushy words like a giddy teenager.

"You're different," he was saying. "Special . . . like I
told you that first day. You've got something about you—"

"If you say 'class' I'm walking out the door."

"*Engaging.* That's what I'd call it. Like the minute you
walk in a room you *engage* people. They just automati-
cally want to know who you are and what you're all about.
And it's not just me. I see it happen with other people
too." Mike's deep blue eyes were starting to sparkle again.
"And you always leave me wanting more."

I took a sip of Mike's wine. "I have to go to the bathroom," I said.

"You want some coffee?" he asked as I slid off my
chair.

I shook my head. "I'll be back in a minute." I felt him
watching me walk away.

The bathrooms were in the back of the restaurant

down a carpeted corridor. After I flushed the toilet, I
heard the outer door open, then bang closed. I came out
of the stall and saw Mike standing with his back to the
door, blocking the entrance. His eyebrows were furrowed
as if he were getting ready to break bad news.

"Come here," he whispered.

I stood by the stall, not moving, assessing his expression. No smile, no softness—almost a grimace of pain.
Like he was going to tell me about another dead student.

"Come here," he repeated.

I shook my head.

"Enough fooling around, babe."

I shook my head again, slower this time, and he came
bounding toward me, grabbed me and twirled me around,
backing me up against the door to keep it closed.

"McCoy, what—"

Before I could finish, he covered my mouth with his
large palm. The green ring sparkled beneath my eyes.
With his hand still covering my mouth, he brought his
sweaty face to mine and rubbed it along my forehead.
One by one he lifted his fingers away from my lips, and
as each finger rose, he kissed underneath, then took my
top lip in his mouth where he sucked it gently and rolled
his tongue under it. "Baby . . . baby," he whispered as he
mouthed my lips.

I tried to squeeze out of his grip, duck under his arms.
I tugged hard on his hair, pulling his head back, away
from me.

"Ow! Goddamn it!" He grabbed my hands by the
wrists and twisted them until I let go of his hair. "What
the hell is wrong with you?"

"You scared me. I thought you came in to tell me
about another murder or something."

He backed away. His lips spread slowly into a smile. "Geez, and all I wanted was a kiss." He lowered his head and waited for my response. "Not even a little one?"

He inched closer. Then closer. He kept his eyes on mine as he lowered his lips to my neck.

I let his mouth burrow into my collar as I laced my fingers back into his hair. But this time I pulled him closer, kneading my fingers through the thick shiny tangle of his head while his fingers snuck under my bra to my nipples.

He pressed his palms down the length of my body to my thighs, and then reached around to my ass and pulled me toward him. From his chest to his groin to his knees, he was hard against me. Harder he pushed into me, pressed me into the door as if he were trying to squeeze me through to the other side.

"I crave you," he whispered. "You want me to stop? I'll stop if you want," he breathed.

I reached into his jacket and under his shirt to wrap my arms around his thick firm waist and back. I felt his shoulder muscles tense as he pushed against me and I pulled myself into him. He forced his hand between us and unzipped my trousers, and then his own, and we instinctively worked against all reason and gravity to weld ourselves inseparably together.

"Hello? Anybody in there?" a woman called from outside the door.

"Out of order," I moaned. "Use the men's room."

CHAPTER TWENTY-EIGHT

Edith Made Me Do It

CALL IT A MISTAKE, but I let Mike come home with me to my brownstone floor-through on Benefit Street. He was duly impressed with the twelve-foot ceilings and marble floors of the old building—at least for the five seconds he saw them before spending the rest of the evening under the covers with me. . . .

Okay, so I knew I shouldn't be bedding coworkers—blame it on Edith Piaf and a gaggle of Grey Goose.

Of course that was a pretty damn lame excuse for an ex-prosecutor. Any brain-dead defense lawyer would have pummeled me in court if I'd tried to use it there, but I had this tendency toward overemotional screwups and, well, there you have it.

IT WAS SNOWING the next morning when we awoke. Mike tried to convince me I needed more bed rest, but I sent him home to shower and pulled myself out of my warm, albeit sticky, bed.

I walked through falling snow from my car to Langley. In New England the worst snows come in February and March, when twelve-hour blizzards are commonplace, followed the next day by a tenacious spring. But for me the sun was shining bright that morning.

"She cannot find a nice American boy?" Rita said in lieu of "Good morning."

My attention was riveted to the envelope Rita had dropped on my desk. Unfortunately, she wanted a few minutes of my time for some good old-fashioned schmoozing.

"My daughter goes to Belize on vacation and comes home engaged to a native. From the pictures she has shown me, this is a beautiful man, but how will she live in Belize?"

"What is this?" I held up the envelope.

"From Mike." Rita was straightening her hair in my mirror again. "And I will not be able to attend the wedding of my own daughter because I have to work. My vacation time is gone. I hope he has the money to support her, because I will not do it. I am finished paying. I have been working here twenty-eight years!"

"It'll probably blow over, Rita. These island romances usually do. When did Mike leave this?" I said, still fingering the sun-kissed envelope.

What I wanted was a quick answer and her quicker exit from my office so I could read the little love lyric in my hand. There were times I liked nothing better than sitting around with Rita, sharing one of her exotic teas and hearing her Holton stories, gossiping, trading secrets. But I was premenstrual; my hormones were raging, and all I could think of was the wet tongue that had licked the gummed flap closed.

"I did not see Mike come in," she said. "Perhaps he

dropped it off before I got here. Do you think you can help me get extra vacation if I must go?"

I gave up on the envelope and looked at her seriously. This was the first time Rita had asked me for help on anything. I was flattered. We had finally begun to reverse roles into the proper order.

"Rita, I'll do everything I can, including covering for you if you want to sneak off for a long weekend. Just say the word. I'll even talk to Carlyle if that's the problem."

She smiled. "I will let you know if this saga continues."

Rita graciously walked out. And as soon as she left, I ripped open the thing in my sweaty hands. It read, and I quote:

Hey babe, we're not done. Important matters to discuss — like when can we run away together? "O, Wilt thou leave me so unsatisfied?" Mike

First French, now Shakespeare. Hopefully Mike was in fact Romeo and not a Lothario. But in either case, I was so hot for him I didn't even care if he pulled an Othello on me.

My phone rang and I stuffed the note into my pocket. Let Rita pick up, I thought. Take a message.

The empty white envelope was sitting ripped open on my desk. I tore it in two, and then fourths and eighths, and threw it in my trash, and then picked it back out again because ripping an envelope into pieces, in and of itself, might look suspicious.

Suspicious of what?

I made a mental note to requisition a shredder.

"Knock, knock," Rita pushed my door open. "It is me again."

I stuffed the pieces of envelope into my other pocket.

"Yes, Rita, come in."

"Miss Barton called and wishes for you to call her back. She says she cannot reach Dr. Becker. And two messages from your friend Beth. She would like you to call her."

I located Emily Barton's data sheet on my desktop and scrolled to her campus telephone number. I hadn't heard from her since our last meeting, and I realized I'd been remiss in not contacting her after Elliot had told me of her "decision" to take the semester off.

I dialed her dorm room and several rings later a soft broken voice said the last syllable of hello as if she had begun talking before she picked up.

"Emily? It's Marianna Melone."

"I'm on the phone."

"Can I hold?"

"No."

"Call me back."

Silence.

I gave her both the extension to my direct number and my cell number. "Please call me back, Emily. I just want to talk to you, I promise."

"Thank you, Miss Melone. Bye."

I had about as much chance of hearing from her as . . .

The phone rang on my private line. I grabbed it after a half ring. "Hello."

"Mari? It's me—"

"Laurie, can't talk now."

"That GHB? Same chemical composition in both girls."

My other line was blinking. "Exact?"

"From the same batch."

"Okay, so that means we know the same guy killed both girls. So what?"

"Didn't you tell us the guys use it on campus over there?"

"Yeah."

"Then get a sample of what they're using and we'll match it up."

"Yeah, Laurie, sure. No sweat. How the frig am I going to do that?"

"Well . . . I don't know, Mari. But you're more creative with those things than I am. And from what you say, it shouldn't be too hard for you to get raped over there. Just *pretend* you don't want to get laid by one of those preteens and see if he tries to spike your Red Bull."

"Bye, call you later." I pushed the private line button. "Hello?"

"Miss Melone?" Emily was crying now, choking sobs.

"Emily? What's the matter?"

She may have been trying to talk but I heard nothing but sobbing.

"Lippitt House? I'll be there in a minute."

I ran the six blocks to Lippitt and up the front steps. I buzzed Emily's intercom, ready to call one of the security guards to open the doors if Emily was feeling antisocial — or was already neck-deep in a gas oven.

Someone buzzed me up. I ran up the four flights to Emily's room and banged on the closed door. It was unlocked and I bolted in to find her on her couch crying in her hands.

I sat next to her. "Emily?"

She didn't answer me but didn't have to — the *Veritas*

newspaper article with her name splashed across the front page was sitting on the coffee table.

She finally cracked out some words. "I can't face anyone after this."

"Tell me about Sherman's parties."

"Rod and Cory live together in a large apartment off campus." She looked at me.

"I know the ones. Overlooking the water."

She nodded. "These parties are not just students. Sometimes they have Cory's Hollywood friends there. Famous, rich, powerful. And he was so nice at first. Sweet, and—oh, but you already know all this."

I assumed she meant Cory, though "sweet" was certainly not a description I would use. "And you slept with him voluntarily at first?"

She nodded. "Only a few times and then I wanted to stop. He scared me—got real ugly."

"Explain."

She buried her face in her hands again. "He got rough. Like crazy rough."

"Like in hitting you?"

She shook her head violently. "I can't talk about it. It's too embarrassing."

Since she had no visible bruises, I could only guess what she meant by "rough."

"I tried to avoid him—*both* of them. I missed classes to avoid him. He was calling me all the time. Sometimes sweet, but after a while mean and nasty, making fun of me because I was avoiding him. At first he seemed weak, very needy, as if he needed a mother rather than a girlfriend. But then he wanted me to pretend to hurt him, hit him. And he would want the same from me. It got really sick."

"Yeah, well, what you think of as *rough* and *sick* some men consider fun and games. The only thing I'm interested in is that when you said *stop*, the fun and games didn't end immediately."

I'd heard enough and it all seemed to fit. But why she would initially be interested in a guy like Cory Sherman in the first place was a bit less obvious. Sure, he was handsome (if you were an impressionable college-age female and didn't know a snake when you saw one), and, yes, he was very rich. But pumped up like a Macy's parade float by his money and Hollywood hobnobbing, Cory was downright obnoxious. But I could see it so easily, the initial draw of him and then his turning on the girl when he got what he wanted from her; another conquest easily tossed aside. And here was a beauty like Emily Barton. What a prize she must have been. He probably took pride in the acquisition, and then joy in the abuse.

"Emily. What about drugs?"

"Drugs. I guess they were all over the place. But I never did any—voluntarily, anyway. They were making 'sex cocktails' one night. I left early."

Sex cocktails. Vodka on the rocks with a twist of GHB? I was about to ask her what a sex cocktail was when a loud banging on Emily's door made us both jump.

Emily looked at me and froze.

I got up and swung open the door, expecting to see Cory Sherman's pale face. I was quite taken aback, or I should say taken down, when Byron's ugly mug greeted me with a surprised look.

"Why, Byron, what an unpleasant surprise," I said.

"Yeah . . . yeah," she stuttered. "Dean Carlyle sent me over." She walked around me. "Emily, how are you doing?" she asked.

Emily looked at me and then back at Byron. "What is this? I haven't had this much attention from the administration the entire time I've been here. You're all worried about Rod and Cory, aren't you? You too, Miss Melone. This isn't about me at all."

Byron plodded forward with her nose in the air as if she were trying to make herself a few inches taller. "I don't know why *she's* here," Byron said. "But I came on Dean Carlyle's orders. He's worried about you, Emily."

Why was Byron Eckert there and not the school psychologist, Mitsy Becker?

Shielding poor Emily from Byron's bull-snorting nostrils, I stepped between them. "Tell me again what it is that you do at Holton, Byron. Fundraising, isn't it? Something to do with money, right? I'm wondering why Dean Carlyle sent you here and not Dr. Becker?"

"I can answer that," Emily said to me. "Because they're afraid I'll accuse the *boy wonders* over at Riverside Park Apartments of some bad deeds and their daddies will stop donating the monthly interest on their stock portfolios." Then Emily looked at me. "And *you* sure had me fooled there for a minute. I thought someone actually cared about me in this place."

I shook my head at her, but I knew there was no way I'd convince her I wasn't part of the protect-the-big-money-donors conspiracy.

I took a step toward her, "Look, Emily—"

"Just go. Both of you. Get out."

Byron left first and then I staggered after. I left Emily sitting forlornly, but at least securely alive, in her room.

BACK AT MY office, Elliot's call had been blinking on hold for ten minutes. He had petulantly insisted that Rita not hang up until I got there, so the line had been flashing away like a Morse code signal. Maybe Elliot was emotionally retarded because he was so damn intellectually advanced. Maybe you had to give up a little of one for more of the other. Funny how it worked that way. My father always used to say that about me: *Smart kid, that Marianna, but she doesn't know how to cross a damn street.*

"What do you want, Elliot?"

"Hey, you told me to protect her. But if you don't care, I'll just hang up."

"Care about what?"

"Your sister. She's at a pizza joint in Federal Hill drinking with the Cory Sherman/Rod Lipton entourage."

I bolted up from my chair. "Wait there. I'll be there in five minutes."

———— ∞∞∞ ————

CHAPTER TWENTY-NINE

Underage Drinking

ELLIOT WAS STANDING OUT on Atwells Avenue as I parked my car in a bus stop.

"How did she get hooked up with them?" I said, walking past Elliot toward Nick and Tony's. No matter how fast I walked, Elliot and I remained at a constant distance from each other like two perfectly tuned magnets.

"We were in the Holton cafeteria—Cassie and I—having our first tutoring session. They came over and convinced her to leave campus with them. I told them to lay off her but she got pissed at me for butting in."

"Why didn't you call me immediately?"

"I did, Miss Melone. You weren't in and I don't have your cell number. I made your secretary keep me on hold."

"You should have told Rita what it was about. She would have found me."

"I'm a student. She won't take orders from me. And I didn't think you'd want the administration to know."

I stopped walking.

Elliot sauntered up to me but kept his eyes straight ahead. "Did you want me to tell your secretary that your underage sister was drinking in a bar with Holton students?"

"Oh, yeah . . . right," I said. "Thanks."

Elliot began walking ahead as he spoke. "Anyway," he said, "your sister's a thickhead. Kids these days aspire to be pop singers or pro basketball players. They only tolerate academics as a fallback on their way to the instant millions of overnight superstars. And she's lazy academically. Just like the students here, spoiled by overindulgent parents, allowed to drink beer when they're teenagers, then the next logical step is college, drugs, and—"

"Stop!"

Although Elliot had just done a sterling job of analyzing Cassie, I still didn't like his presumption of familiarity, either with me or my sister. Of course it was my fault for inviting him so intimately into my personal affairs. But Elliot was so bright and so much my equal, it was difficult to realize that he was still only an impressionable student.

It was time to back away, to withdraw, for Elliot's sake, if not mine. "Cassie's parents—my parents—are not *overindulgent*. If they knew she was drinking right now, she'd be grounded until her wedding night."

He didn't answer me because by then we were entering Nick and Tony's.

Elliot remained at the door as I surged through a crowd of lunch-eating kids and headed for Cassie.

"Let me through," I said to a young man who was blocking me. "Let me through. Now!"

"Really, Miss *Meloni?* What if I don't? Will you put

a contract out on my life? Or make me an offer I can't refuse?"

Cory Sherman's blond hair was slicked back with the help of some antigravity styling gel. His chiseled face smirked from behind a large glass beer stein as he took a gulp. Even indoors his skin still had the sheen of translucent porcelain. He ended his *Godfather* references with a good laugh, and I felt like the downstairs maid who'd been slapped in the face by the master of the house. I clutched thin air for one of my usual snappy comebacks but came up empty-handed. Sadly, at the sound of my Italian name from his lips, I had been reduced to minced calamari. That old familiar feeling in the pit of my stomach flashed me a reminder of Jeff Kendall and his patrician attitude toward me, and even toward his boss, Vince Piganno, for whom, it seemed, Jeff only deigned to work until his corner office, next to Dad's, was ready.

"Let me through," I said softly.

He blocked me with his ear-to-ear grin for a second longer and then stepped aside.

Cassie was at a table with Rod Lipton and a couple of their other whitewashed preppy friends. Elliot had reached the group and was hovering off to the side.

"Hey, Orenstein. You come back to reclaim your goods?"

Elliot stuck his face into Sherman's. "You're a fucking jerk, Sherman," Elliot whispered. "I told you to leave her alone."

It was an odd sight, a clip snatched out of context from a longer sequence. Anyone walking in now would see Elliot as the aggressor, while handsome and debonair Rod Lipton, the closest to Cassie, gently and protectively stood by her.

I walked briskly to the table.

"Mari," Cassie twittered. "Hi there."

When she stood, Rod faced me. And then, as if he hadn't recognized me at first, he bowed a hello and feigned surprise with a slight furrow of his eyebrows. "Cassie is your sister? Well, yes, of course," he said, looking from her to me and then back again. "She's a beauty in progress."

"Beauty in progress," Cassie repeated as she smiled glowingly at him.

Elliot looked at me and walked away, knowing I would handle it from there. Or perhaps simply not interested in a public confrontation.

By now, Cory was standing at the bar a few feet away. He shook his head, smiled, and ordered another beer from Nick, who was scowling at me from the beer taps. "That your baby sister? How old's she now? Eh?"

"Did you card her, Nick, before you served her beer?"

"You keep watch over her, not me. She looks like the rest of these spoiled brats."

"Yeah," I shot back. "Probably half of them underage."

I took Cassie by the shoulder. "Let's go have some lunch, Cassie dear." While keeping a smile pasted on my lips, I led Cassie away and whispered angry warnings into her "progressively beautiful" ear.

"Are you out of your insipid little mind? I'm a prosecutor and you're in here breaking the friggin' law. . . ."

We approached my car, where I found Elliot had suddenly materialized.

"Everything okay?" he asked.

Cassie ducked into the car without a word.

He lowered his head into the open car door. "Cassie, I'll see you next week?"

Cassie gave Elliot a sour look and rolled up her window.

"She's mad as hell I turned her in. But she doesn't get it. These girls always fall for the flash . . . they just don't understand how guys like Sherman and Lipton operate."

"Maybe we should hold off on the tutoring for now, Elliot. Until all of this stuff at Holton settles down anyway."

Elliot's mouth fell open. I had never seen him so animated. "Are you blaming *me* for *them*?" He nodded toward Nick and Tony's Pizza, from which Rod and Sherman had not yet emerged. "I *did* try to stop her, but she's—"

"Yes. Okay. You're right, Cassie . . . can be a bit stubborn. . . . Anyway," I said, changing the subject, "do you need a ride back to school?" I hoped he would refuse.

"I'll walk," he said, turning away without looking at me.

During the drive home I had a motherly chat with Cassie. Our own mother was too naive to deal with Cassie on any meaningful level, so sometimes I took the reins, not that my jockeying was any more successful.

"I just hope you and your little friends aren't drinking and driving with your fake IDs again. Is that how you got the beer at Nick's?"

"They didn't even ask for ID with Cory Sherman there. They treated him like a king when he started flashing hundred-dollar bills."

"Cassie, honey, you can't be doing these things. One of these days you're going to get in trouble and I'm not going to be able to get you out of it."

"I'm sorry, Mari. Not about me, about you. I mean, you won't get fired again over this, will you?"

"Don't worry about me. I'll survive. You, on the other

hand, have your whole life ahead of you. And your choice of friends scares me. You're a lousy judge of character. Can't you see through people like Cory and Rod? They're bad guys."

"I know that, Mari. I know more than you think I know. I may not be as smart as you are but I'm not that stupid either. But just because people aren't nice doesn't mean they're not fun."

I shook my head. Some kids have to skin their knees before they learn where the potholes are. "Do you know what GHB is? It's a date-rape drug. I shouldn't be telling you this, and it's not to be repeated, but Sherman and Lipton, *just possibly*, might be using it on girls and then raping them. You *do not* want to be drinking anything with them, even a harmless can of Coke. Do you understand?"

I interpreted her silence as a yes, and then foolishly decided to throw one more log in the fire. "Some people you can trust, and some you can't. Those two you cannot trus—"

"*I get it, Mari! I get it.* Cool it."

"All right. All right. So how's your tutoring going with Elliot? He's a good kid, Cassie."

"I don't like him. Why can't a *hot* student help me?"

"Like Rod and Cory? Sure, they'll teach you a lot but it won't be on the SATs."

"Yeah, well, Elliot is like a nerdy scientist. His hair sticks up and he smells like the periodic table of elements."

"That's disgusting, but I like your metaphors. They're maturing. And just for your information, Albert Einstein needed a beauty salon too."

"Well, then I'm not letting him tutor me either."

I DROPPED MY sweet but ignorant sister at my parents' house, had dinner with my parents, and then headed home around eight o'clock via the Riverside Park apartment complex, looking for the ne'er-do-wells, Sherman and Lipton. I was itching to give them a few pieces of advice about drinking with my sister. Or maybe I went there because something about the two libertines was compelling me toward them. And then again, maybe I wanted an up-close-and-personal visit with them because everything else about the Holton murders was turning up dead ends.

Screaming and laughter on the third-floor balcony caught my attention and I looked up in time to see a man pummel a woman in the shoulder until she fell out of sight. I got out of my car and walked down the grassy slope toward the river. The apartment was lit up like a storefront window at Christmas. Maybe the guy up there had shoved her, or maybe he was giving her a love tap, but remembering my sister with a beer in her hand gave me the incentive to want to blow some guy's head off with Shannon's .44 Magnum. I marched to the front door and rang all ten third-floor bells. I was buzzed in immediately and elevated up to three, where I found kids lighting in and out of an open door like bees at a hive.

Rod Lipton was inside the living room adjusting buttons on the stereo with a beer bottle in his hand. The eye-popping beat of Jimi Hendrix pulsated through the apartment.

. . . and the wind cries Mary . . .

I hollered over the music, "Hey, Rod, how about some Motown as long as you're playing oldies?"

At my entrance, the empty space around me in the room widened as students moved away until it caught Rod's attention and he recognized me too. He lowered the volume a notch and with a cautious smile he said, "Miss Melone. What a pleasant surprise. Welcome to our humble abode."

I shook his outstretched hand.

"We really didn't know your sister was underage."

"She looks mature for her age," I offered.

"Can I get you something? Coke?"

"Liquid or powder?" I smiled sweetly.

He looked at his peers for approval of my humor. No one laughed. And some abandoned their bottles and glasses on the nearest flat surface and smartly slithered out the door.

Rod watched me walk to the couch where I saw Elliot sitting in front of a 56-inch flat-screen TV that was mounted on the wall.

"What the hell are you doing here?" I said.

Without looking at me he answered, "Watching a James Bond movie. Did you get your sister home all right?"

I ignored his question and glanced up at the screen, trying to identify which Bond film had so engrossed him. Nothing and no one looked familiar and I thought I'd seen them all. "When did this one come out?"

"Next month," Elliot said dryly. "Sherman's uncle sends them hot off the editing table."

Elliot finally looked up at me. His eyes were blood-shot and swollen.

I sat next to him. "You're stoned."

"Am I? Hmm, that must be why this movie seems so

complex." He looked at me and laughed. "I'm not stoned, just tired from lack of sleep. Cory's outside on the balcony," he said without skipping a beat. "You'll want to check out the table."

"What are you doing here? You don't even like these characters."

"I'm keeping tabs on the profanity and wantonness at Holton College—and seeing if I can pick up some spillover."

"Don't start turning into a jerk on me, Elliot."

"Well, won't you be chastened when I find out where all that GHB is coming from and give you the scoop?"

I cleared my throat and stood, surveying the room for Rod, who was nowhere in sight. He'd undoubtedly abandoned his interest in me once he was satisfied that I was safely entrenched on the couch with James Bond and Elliot Orenstein.

Straight ahead was a hallway off which, I assumed, was the bathroom, a handy excuse in case I was caught snooping. I advanced down the hall. The first door was securely closed, so I walked past it to a second, also shut but not as tightly. With my foot I teased the door open a crack and peered through to a rumpled bed on which a girl lay sleeping. Her hair, a cascade of reddish blonde curls, fanned out on a pillow. Her face was turned away.

I drew my head back as the door was abruptly slammed shut from the inside.

Back in the living room Elliot was still on the couch mesmerized by the big screen. I walked to the balcony, where Cory Sherman was sniffing a line of cocaine from a glass-top table.

He looked up at me. "What the fuck?"

"Hey, calm down, Cory, no problem," I said.

An ugly grimace. "What are you talking about?"

"You invited me here. Remember? It's cool."

Sherman tried to laugh it off. Two other students who apparently were sharing whatever he was inhaling moved quickly toward the door and hustled back inside the apartment. Sherman's expression lightened up. "Miss Melone, did we get you a refreshment yet?"

Rod was in the doorway.

Cory spoke to him like his private valet. "Why don't you get *Miss Melone* a drink? What will you have?" he asked me.

"I'll have what you're having." I nodded toward the glass table.

"Sure," Cory said as he brought me his half-empty beer bottle. "You want my beer? I can share."

"Thanks, but I meant the cocaine. It is cocaine, isn't it?"

Sherman's face crunched into another scowl. Pumped up on coke, he was switching emotional gears like channels on a rotary dial. He dismissively plopped into a patio chair.

"Can I talk to you inside a minute?" Rod said to me.

Rod was being too civil, so I ignored him. The best information is gotten from someone who's pissed off and ready to blow, so I stayed with Cory. I needed to make a quick decision about how much information I would share in order to secure their trust.

I sat opposite Cory on another chair, and knowing that Cory was too smart to be duped, I went right for the gold. "Can you tell me anything about Lisa and Melinda? I know they were friends of yours."

He shook his head. "Slicing up those pretty faces

and then letting them bleed to death. Fucking brutal stuff, huh?"

I hated to let him swear in my presence but I was on his turf now and had to play by his rules. "I didn't think that was common knowledge. How'd you know?"

"Talk," he said. "There are very few secrets in this place."

Rod came out with an opened bottle for me. I sat back and pretended to take a swig as a peace offering. The last thing I needed was to get slogged at a student party by beer—and their house specialty, GHB.

"What are you doing here anyway? You think I'm going to break down and tell you I killed two girls?" Cory laughed. "I'm stoned, not stupid. That's not my idea of fun anyway."

"Maybe the fun got out of hand and it was your way of keeping things quiet."

"Good theory, but what's your proof that anything got out of hand?"

"Emily Barton—"

"I don't even know that girl."

"Ah, but she seems to know you . . . intimately. And not just once."

Cory Sherman chilled fast. He didn't flinch. Coked up and all, he barely even reacted to my accusation.

"You got a pencil, Miss Melone? Let's make a list of the girls I've fucked on this campus. Two end up dead. Why them and not the others?"

"Who was that girl on the balcony before I got here? The one you hit?"

Rod had been standing in the doorway. He inched closer to us.

"Miss Melone?" Rod suddenly said. "About Mila. Believe me, no one hit her. I don't know what you think you saw from the street, but she wasn't injured in any way. She actually started the fight."

"Shut up, Rod," Sherman said.

Rod came closer to me and at over six feet tall he bowed his head to my eye level. "We're just regular college students having some fun. Believe me. If we knew anything about Lisa's death—or Melinda's—we'd be the first to help the police. They were our friends but they were never here at our parties."

Cory had lit up a cigarette. "Don't bother lying to her, Rod." He looked at me. "So they were here. Maybe we even screwed them. But we didn't kill them."

"What about Barton? Rape might not be murder, but it's in really bad taste."

Cory rose from his chair. "The only bad taste I worry about is a turned bottle of '61 Chateau Margaux."

"And are you lacing that Margaux with a sprinkle of GHB?"

Rod was watching us from a distance as if he were judging a crucial audition. But Sherman had apparently forgotten his lines. He stood speechless, looking out into the dark river over the balcony railing.

I looked from one to the other. "All righty then, this party's over for me. If either of you so much as blows on the hair of another student, I'll force Emily Barton to go to the police. So even if you're both innocent of murder, one of you, at least, will be doing time for rape, a.k.a. first-degree sexual assault."

Rod stiffened. Cory, however, laughed at me.

"No one raped that Barton girl," he said. "And if *she* says anything about my parties, she's got to admit she was here imbibing all the booze and illegal drugs!" He laughed again.

"Where are you getting the GHB, Sherman? Are you cooking it up here?"

He laughed out loud. "Yeah, I'm a real Emeril Lagasse. Can't you just see me in a white chef's coat?"

"And stay away from my sister." I walked out as Hendrix was belting out "Purple Haze," but I was seeing only red. Elliot was gone.

On the way to my car I dialed the police at the private number I always used from the AG's office. A young detective answered the phone. I gave him Cory's address and told him I'd just left a party where cocaine was snowing like a Bing Crosby Christmas. The putz cop was in his twenties and didn't know who Bing Crosby was, and consequently assumed I was a crank caller. Not that it mattered. Whatever cocaine was in Sherman's apartment, I'm sure, was long gone minutes after I walked out the door. But I'd get him sooner or later. Maybe not that night, but I was going to get the hoodlum princes if it was the last thing I did.

I slammed my shift into drive and heard the sudden whirl of a high-pitched engine. From out of nowhere appeared a red sports car of such elite origin that I myself was ignorant of its pedigree. The car slowed to a screeching halt next to mine and Mila Nazir emerged from the driver's side door. With the car's engine still screaming, she shouted something at me. Her black hair billowed in the wind behind her, and her eyes were dark and wild. Red lipstick was smeared across her lips as if she had been eating pomegranates with abandon. I exited my car to approach her. Her eyes followed mine until I was close enough that she could spit at me.

"Does Dean Carlyle know you're bothering us?" she said. "If you continue to harass me, I will have you sued. I will have you fired."

What drugs she was operating under I didn't know, but I backed away, realizing that she was out of control and at least temporarily out of her mind.

As if the demon had been exorcised, she became still and quiet. Blinking a few times, she slowly reentered her car and sat still behind the wheel. I waited for a safe second or two of silence and then walked to her.

"You shouldn't be driving," I said. "Pull over and park the car."

She looked at me and studied my face before she spoke. "Dean Carlyle made a mistake with you. A mistake."

She shook her head slowly, pulled her door closed, and drove away.

Back in my car, I revved up my engine as two people exited Rod and Cory's building. Walking in my direction was a man with a woman hanging tightly on his side. Her face was nuzzled into his neck, but her hair tumbled down his chest in strawberry blonde waves. They stopped and he steadied her against his body, began whispering to her, then turned her around to face him. I wouldn't have continued to watch, but the closer they got, the more the male resembled not a student but someone older, and, at even closer range, began to resemble an older man I recognized as—Mike McCoy.

Had the bedroom door in Lipton and Sherman's apartment been slammed in my face by Mike? Was a redheaded coed his perk for protecting Cory and Rod—a sacrificial coed under the influence of alcohol, or worse, GHB?

He's the one who always bails them out, Elliot had

warned me. *Mike McCoy is a puppet*. And what was it Emily had said? *He likes the students to call him Mike*.

I geared into reverse and parked, hidden, behind another car. I watched as they walked a short distance to Mike's car. He helped the girl into the passenger side, gently touching the top of her head to protect it from hitting the door, and then closing her in. As soon as he sat behind the wheel, she lunged toward him and fell against him where they became a solid mass of body and her head slid down his chest out of view. He immediately started the engine and sped off. For a more secluded venue perhaps? Maybe this was Mike's modus operandi with women: Pump them full of alcohol, take them for a test drive along the river, and then scurry off to complete the Indy 500 at his place. I suddenly felt like a dipstick in a string of Mike's regularly scheduled oil changes.

But, hey, I wasn't going to cry over Mike McCoy. Some guys you cry over—the one with whom you'd already picked out a name for the baby you were carrying, or the guy who'd made you pool your assets in a joint account shortly after *he* got the big bonus, and maybe the one you'd been doing Sunday crossword puzzles with for the last two consecutive years. These were the ones you pined after, the ones who were taking a little of your heart with them on their way out of town.

But Mike McCoy? Nah. He probably couldn't even *do* a crossword puzzle unless it was in the back of the *NASCAR Winston Cup Illustrated*.

My heart would heal soon enough. But my ego was a more fragile thing. If Mike was steeped in the nasty business of Cory and Rod's enterprises, how could I ever trust my judgement again? I dared not even consider the possibility that he was capable of rape. Murder. How could I not have seen the rough in the diamonds—his sparkling eyes and the danger behind them?

I drove straight home, shivering and feeling like death. I needed a good night's sleep to prepare me for another day at Holton, where I hoped in the morning the body count held steady at two.

THIRTY

Camp Cassie

I ARRIVED IN MY office early the next morning, deciding it was time to throw caution, and quite possibly my job, to the wind. Mitsy Becker's name had come up one too many times for me to keep ignoring it. I found her name in my online Rolodex and dialed her up.

"Hi, Dr. Becker, this is Marianna Melone."

There was a pause in which I sensed, if not wariness, at least a healthy dollop of caution, and then, "Yes. Hello, Marianna. Please call me Mitsy. You're in quite early this morning."

"Yes, and I hope I'm not disturbing you, but I'd like to look through some of your closed files. Some of what you and I do here at Holton seems to overlap. Emily Barton, for instance—"

"Why would you want closed files?"

"Just as a reference point. You know, to see how you were handling things, to shorten my learning curve here."

"Yes, of course. But then there is the confidentiality problem . . ."

"With the closed files of the dead girls also? And don't forget, I'm sworn to confidentiality too."

"Well . . . to tell you the truth, there are no closed files. When and if I ever open a file on a student, it's destroyed as soon as the student's *problem* is resolved—or when they stop coming. For routine things such as colds and flu—but those aren't the ones you're interested in, are they?"

"No. I'm interested in drug dependencies."

I heard a chuckle at the other end of the phone. "Files can be discovered by good attorneys, so shredding is the smartest course of action—or not opening them to begin with. We only keep records of dates and times. Scheduling records, if you will."

"Sounds a bit legally precarious to me. If I were a doctor treating a patient, I would want a record of it for my own protection."

"This is a small school, Marianna. I have chats now and then with some of the students. We don't have to keep a record of a simple discussion when there's no real treatment involved. And I assure you, no one will sue us for *keeping* their privacy."

"All right, then. Give it to me straight up, Mitsy. What happened with Lisa? The drugs. You don't think we had the last clear chance to help her? You don't think we failed her at all?"

Mitsy answered quickly, as if she had thought about this question already. Her genes were programmed for guilt, as mine were, but she'd already worked through it, as I supposed I might have done if I stayed at Holton long enough.

Or maybe not.

Mitsy answered, "Lisa was never caught with drugs on her. The most we could have done is sent her home. But amazingly, she was passing all her courses. You can't expel someone for being a threat to herself. Her family failed her, not this school."

There it was, Mitsy's absolution. It was Lisa's family's fault, not Holton's—or hers. Was Mitsy Becker in denial because she was a bad therapist, or was she denying things because she was worried too?

"Dr. Becker, failing courses shouldn't be the only reason we take a troubled kid under our wings. You know as well as I do that there are plenty of ways to pass classes that don't involve studying. A lot of brilliant kids end up in trouble, and their grades never suffer."

"Are you indicting *me*, Marianna? Do you think Lisa is my fault?"

"I think Lisa's death was a cumulative effort by Holton to protect its reputation at the expense of some of the students. Oddly enough, in an effort to protect Lisa, we let her down by looking the other way while she was falling deeper into trouble."

"Marianna, just a word of caution to the wise, if you wish to accept it. This isn't the attorney general's office and these kids aren't hardened criminals, so go easy on them, or it won't be easy for you."

"I'm not sure what that means."

"I'd like to see you do well here. We need someone like you—a breath of fresh air in this musty place. So try to listen to what Ken says with both ears open. He'll tell you how he wants to move these cases forward, but you have to listen very carefully."

"And when a matter is *resolved* in my office, I just throw the file away?"

"Rita will give the incident reports to Ken."

"And he keeps them?"

"We don't have to know everything. We just have to do our jobs and let Ken do his."

I let it go. I wasn't going to put Mitsy on the spot just because *I* was willing to buck authority and lose my job.

Mitsy and I hung up. I felt a little pang, as if I had given in too easily, but I understood Mitsy's healthy fear of fraternizing—with me or any of the employees. She was protecting everyone, herself included. Mitsy was like Switzerland. She was where you could hide secrets with no questions asked and a gracious smile. But if my secrets were safe with her, so were everyone else's.

The last few seconds Mitsy and I were on the phone, my light was blinking away. Rita had picked up the call and taken a message which she now relayed to me word for word, leaving out what I knew were my mother's histrionic exclamations.

Hand-picked by her school to attend, Cassie had been in chaotic preparation for a weeklong soccer camp on Cape Cod in Massachusetts. (Her SATs may have been Dumpster material, but at soccer she was tenure-track to pro. I, at her age, couldn't even kick a basketball.) Cassie was threatening not to attend because my mother had forbidden her to pack any clothes not sports-related. This would be my little sister's first time so far away from—in her words—her "overprotective, stifling parents," and rumor had it, said my mother, that there were off-campus parties planned for which Cassie had packed a number of provocative outfits.

I told Rita I'd be back shortly and then drove to my parents' place to find the militarily spit-polished house in a turmoil: Cassie's clothes were strewn over every available piece of furniture. Toiletries covered her bathroom floor as she made the excruciating decisions about which eye shadows to pack and which to leave forlornly behind, how many dozen pairs of soccer cleats she needed, and whether she would need a strapless bra. My mother wrung her hands in anticipatory terror. Her tragically bent reasoning was that even if Cassie managed to survive the bus ride to the Cape, she would surely be raped or butchered if she forayed into big bad Provincetown after dark. I made the mistake of warning Cassie about her previous use of fake IDs in bars and her recent underage drinking spree at Nick and Tony's, and my audio-acute mother overheard me. The three demons of hell were unleashed as Cassie, my mother, and I screamed at each other in seemingly foreign tongues. My presence proved useless, and after a final bellow at Cassie for making me leave work, I slammed out the door and felt guilty about it as soon as my front tires left the driveway. My short temper with Cassie always came back to haunt me in the form of guilt. I considered myself more like her mother than her sister, and I should have known better than to let her go off on a sleep-away trip with my parting words to her *You're going to end up in a ditch if you don't lose that cocky little attitude.*

I calmed down and sped back to work, swearing under my breath because now I was late and I'd undoubtedly lost my usual parking spot on George Street.

I was still looking for a substitute space when a police car drove past me and through the front gates. I discontinued my search and frantically followed the black-and-white. I pulled into a visitor parking spot and shrugged my shoulders at the potential Holton parking violation that would soon be added to the liability column of my deteriorating employment record.

In my office, O'Rourke had already made himself comfortable behind my desk. He was using his coffee cup as an ashtray while Rita danced around him spraying canned Lysol through his smoke rings and trying to interest him in a tasty chiclet of nicotine gum.

"*Fräulein!*" Rita noticed me first. "It is the police. I've been keeping him company." Her dark eyes dazzled as she held the Lysol can to her breast.

"Rita, you're an ace. I'll take it from here."

Like a proud mare at the finish line, Rita shook her chin-length mane and pixie bangs. "The pleasure was all mine." She backed out of my doorway.

It felt like home with O'Rourke in my office. Like the old days when we'd be playing cat and mouse with defendants' lives, and not thinking a lick about the consequences. And if I had been back at the AG's under this same scenario, I *would* be smiling. But something about being at Holton made me feel defensive. Like I was the robber and O'Rourke was coming for *me*.

He lumbered up from my chair when I walked in, slowly abdicating his superior position in my office. He walked to my door and closed it, which for him was a giant step toward independence. Wanting to keep me in suspense, he slowly slid a cigarette out of a pack of Marlboro Reds as I watched him. He forgot I was an ex-AG and I knew an old cop trick or two. They methodically light cigarettes, go into the bathroom with a newspaper, or make an urgent telephone call to their barber to make people wait a little bit longer for the bad news.

"What is it, O'Rourke? And you have to put that out. It's making me nauseous."

"Oh, sure. Sorry. No smoking in this building, right?"

"Not supposed to smoke in here, but—it's just that I get sick when I smell it first thing in the morning."

He dropped the cigarette in his full coffee cup. "You have any coffee made?"

I buzzed Rita to bring O'Rourke coffee, and then once again asked him what he wanted.

He leaned close, whispering. "Last night, a girl was brought to the emergency room at Miriam Hospital. Claims rape and wants to press charges. But sometimes these girls just have broken hearts. You know what I mean?"

"No, I really don't. Does she have red curly hair?"

"Um . . . nope, straight—dark—brunette. Quite a looker—"

I collapsed into my chair and closed my eyes for a silent moment of Hail Marys.

"O'Rourke, have you wholly discounted the possibility that she *was* raped?"

"Nah, she's a college girl. This was just a date gone bad."

I may have been in a bigger office with air-conditioning, but I sat up in my chair and took a good long look at the male detective sitting in front of me. Like old times at the AG's office, I was ready for what I knew was coming—talking about forcible rape to a male cop with a matching ego. Other than that, nothing had changed; rape was still a fiction created by women who'd changed their minds midway. And didn't everyone know that once a guy got an erection it was medically dangerous to stop the flow? Vasocongestion of the testicles or something.

"Oh balls, O'Rourke! Innocent until proven guilty

notwithstanding, you treat this as a rape until proven otherwise."

"Well, she won't talk to anyone from the station. So maybe you go see her. Tell her to let some time go by and see how she feels. Time makes people come to their senses."

"Are you saying she's lost her senses, therefore she is unaware of her complicity in the sexual encounter, or is she merely without sensibility to the consequences of her accusations?"

O'Rourke looked at me blankly, trying to get his hands around my question (and possibly strangle it).

"What's her name?" I asked.

"Emily Barton."

"Shit!"

Rita came in with coffee and O'Rourke stood. "Thank you kindly, ma'am." Rita curtsied and left. O'Rourke shimmied into his seat to keep the coffee from spilling.

"Listen," he said. "Mike told me to come to you this morning. I listen to Mike. We go way back from when he was on the beat."

Opportunity rings, I thought. Here was a chance to get the skinny from O'Rourke on Mike—his early retirement (and his arrested sexual development)—but I suspected trying to get information from one cop on another was like trying to separate conjoined twins. And then there was the problem of O'Rourke telling Mike I was trying to pump him for information. There's nothing worse than a nosy broad, and no quicker way to cut off the flow of good gossip by appearing anxious to get it.

So I kept my nosy mouth shut and let O'Rourke prattle on.

"Yeah, Mikey and I weren't real close, but you know

we're still brothers and all, and I do him a few favors now and then. So you just tell me what you want done here. Mikey says you're cool with it."

"How about following the law, O'Rourke? If Miss Barton gives us a name, how about you arrest the punk like a good cop should. Sound good? Keep up the exemplary work and I'll be in touch."

At my brazen sarcasm, O'Rourke gave me one of his sour looks. And I guess as a favor to *Mikey*, he didn't tell me to go pound sand, as he would have in the old days.

After O'Rourke left I allowed a few thoughts to bounce around in my head. When did Mike tell O'Rourke to come see me? And why did he still have so much clout with the Providence police? It was safer for me to confront Mike with my questions rather than ask O'Rourke and take the chance of jump-starting his brain.

I called Mike at every available number I had for him. Rita's attempts at locating him failed as well. Maybe he was still making nice with the wavy-haired student whom I assumed was still alive and kicking—hopefully—McCoy out of her bed.

I donned my Lone Ranger mask and went to visit Emily by myself.

EMILY WAS LYING in her hospital bed curled up on her side in a fetal position when I walked in. The lights in her private room were off. I left them that way as I stood by her bed. Other than blinking her eyes slowly open, she had no reaction to my entry.

"Hi, Emily."

She winced as she turned carefully onto her back as if every move hurt. Safely flat on her back she said, "Don't bother asking me. I don't know who did it this time."

"Why not?"

"Because I was drugged first. My mother spoke to a lawyer. I can sue the school, but how will that affect my life? Is anyone going to believe me? Rape victims who can get up and walk away are never really victims, are they?"

"Where were you when it happened?"

"I'd just had dinner in the cafeteria. I got woozy on the walk home. I passed out in the park, I think." Then she grimaced as if even the memory of it hurt.

"Patterson Park?"

She nodded.

"What were you doing in the park?"

"It's on my way home."

"Are you sure you weren't at Sherman's place and maybe someone slipped something in your drink?"

She shook her head in a smooth, measured movement. "I didn't drink last night. Check the hospital records for my blood alcohol level. I told you I was in the school cafeteria."

"Alone?"

"There were others around. We were all watching the news. It was a story about the murders here."

I nodded, at a loss for what else to say.

"The hospital tests. They found some weird drug in my system. It's my word against theirs that I took it voluntarily, isn't it? I've been to Cory's parties. If you lie down with dogs, you pick up fleas. Isn't that the old saying?"

"Did you talk to anyone in the cafeteria?"

She shook her head. "Look, when you don't have a date or a clique of friends, you end up alone in the cafeteria for dinner watching CNN. And ever since that story in the school paper, I'm a pariah around here."

"The rape kit was positive for semen?"

"He used a condom."

"Think of all the people you were around last night and don't discount anyone as being complicit. A real bad thing was done to you. Don't be afraid to point fingers if you can."

"What difference does it make who did it? I know I can't bring charges. It's my reputation that'll be trashed, not his."

"What if you just got lucky, Emily? Maybe whoever did this to you meant to kill you and got interrupted or something."

"Why me?"

"Why not you?"

I gave her my cell and office number again and walked out of her room.

I was waiting for the elevator when I saw Mike walking down the long white corridor toward Emily's room. He didn't see me, so I stepped out into the corridor. "Where are you going?"

"Hey." He looked past me to see if I was alone, then came on strong with his killer charm. "Babe, I miss you already," he whispered into my ear, then gave it a nibble.

I pulled away. "Stop it! Mike, why are Providence cops taking orders from you?"

"They don't. I ask for a favor now and then. Something wrong with people doing each other favors?"

"Yeah, if you're trying to strong-arm victims into recanting allegations."

He stepped back to the side of the corridor and pulled me with him by the elbow. "I'm just investigating here, honey. That's what I do."

" 'Honey'? And what about Carlyle? Does he know

about this? Or does he want it cleaned up before it even gets to his office?"

"Jesus! Calm down." Mike ran his fingers through his hair. "You always gotta make a drama out of everything. If there's a problem that leaks to the cops, I ask a couple of my buddies there for a hand, see if I can nip it in the bud. Is that so hard to understand? Tell me you and your AG girlfriends don't do the same thing sometimes. Go ahead. Tell me you gals never did something wrong that the cops covered up for you?"

"Oh my, Officer McCoy, are you referring to something specific?"

"You don't need my references. You're a pretty smart girl from what I hear."

"What's gotten into *you*, hard-ass?"

He backed away. "What the hell is wrong with *you*?"

I walked right back up in his face. "Don't you go in that hospital room and try to scare her. She can't even sit up yet. Was it Sherman and his cohorts?"

"That girl in there was at one of Sherman's parties. Into the den with wolves. She went at her own risk."

"I went to one of their parties too. That doesn't mean someone can put a drug in my drink and rape me. Or does it?"

"When did that start?"

"I told you I was going to befriend them to see what I could uncover—"

"You didn't *mention* you were gonna become *drinking* buddies!" Two nurses passed us in the hall and slowed their walk as Mike hammered away at me. "When? When were you there?"

"Are you jealous, Mike? Or just scared?"

"You bet I'm scared. I don't want to find out at this

point that you're stupid, because stupid women can't be trusted."

"You want to talk trust? Let's talk about the redhead. The girl from last night. The one in Sherman's bed when you slammed the door in my face."

His eyes were dark and cold. I couldn't read them.

"Look, forget it, Mike. One *fuck* doesn't make us committed or anything, right? But I want to know what you intend to do about these kids and their drug parties, because as a recently inducted chick into your apparent flock, I don't think you're the best one to be guarding the henhouse."

Mike unfroze and tried to take me by my shoulders, but I backed away. "Babe—Mari, I'm on top of this. Do not go near those parties. Leave it to me. You just handle the other things—"

"What other things? You keep protecting their asses. Who's going to complain about them if they have the head of security on their side?"

He stared at me with that same stunned look as if he'd run out of ammunition in the middle of gunfire.

I backed away from him. "You're Carlyle's stooge, aren't you? *The fixer.* And whatever Sherman and Lipton are up to, you're deep in it. How could I have been so wrong?"

He was shaking his head slowly when I left him there, and fifteen minutes later I was back in my office, where a dozen pink and white tulips were sitting on my desk in a vase. I hastily opened the card, ready to toss it in the trash, when I saw the word "Babe" written on the first line.

I can't get enough of you. Meet me after work at Kartabar, 5:30. Mike.

Then I did throw the note in the trash as Rita flounced through my open threshold. "Pretty, yes? They are just in time for spring. Tulips." While pretending to rearrange them, she asked me who sent them.

"Anonymous," I said. "Get them out of here."

"No, they are from Mike! He had me order them early this morning. They arrived just after you left."

"That figures. He couldn't pick crabgrass by himself."

"Ah, so they are sent because of a quarrel." She was laughing gaily. "Come, I will buy you some tea at the Bistro. You can tell me what the love letter says."

The phone rang and we both lunged for it, but I got to it first. "Hello?"

I recognized Byron Eckert's husky voice immediately.

"Rita," I said. "Would you mind getting me that tea? Next one's on me."

"But of course, my dear." She waved her hand good-naturedly and closed the door after herself.

Into the receiver, I said, "What do you want?"

"Meet me."

"Come to my office."

"No. This is not about you or me. A little Mexican place on Hope Street past Hope High School. Tortilla Flats."

CHAPTER THIRTY-ONE

Falling from the Catbird Seat

I ARRIVED AT TORTILLA FLATS a little after twelve. Byron was waiting at a small table in the bar area. A can of plain Schweppes club soda was sitting on the table as she fidgeted with what looked to be a Mirado Black Warrior pencil (my favorite). When she saw me she dropped the pencil to the table. "Melone," she said with a nod. "Glad you could make it."

"What's this about?"

"You want something to drink?"

"No."

"Good."

"Have you been employed at Holton since the day you graduated, Byron, if you don't mind my asking?"

"I do mind, and it's none of your business. But now that you ask, yes, and I'm an alum and I graduated with honors."

"Yes, I remember Ken mentioning it as if it were a meaningful part of your job description or something."

"It is. It means that I'll be at Holton long after you're gone."

Great, I thought to myself, enjoy it. Because in the end you'll rot and die like the rest of us. I chuckled lightly at my black humor, and Byron shifted uncomfortably in her seat. I felt abandoned and alone. Even impenetrable Byron appeared chipped to me—a cracked vase to be handled with care. Her eyes were weary; she looked almost sick of her own bitter personality, like it was eating at her from the inside out. Maybe I should try geniality, solicitousness . . . Hey, maybe I could even get Byron to become my friend?

Or, more likely, maybe I could get her to blow her helium-filled cool and shoot around the room like a deflating balloon.

"Byron, I'm not in the mood for a blood sport today. What do you want?"

She snorted through her nose like a pig. "What's the word on the street re the latest brouhaha?"

" 'Brouhaha'? Would that be your characterization of a brutal rape and murder?"

"Emily Barton isn't dead. And I hope you aren't sharing *inside* information *outside* Holton. Let Ken handle it. He's *super* at damage control."

Had I detected a note of sarcasm in her tone?

"Ken can't control the AG's office."

"But you can, can't you? Isn't that why you were hired, after all?"

"You tell me why, Byron. I bet you know why Ken hired me, since you and he seem to be as close as two bullets in a chamber."

"I'll answer that when you tell me why your *godfather*, Vince Piganno, fired you."

"Sure, Byron. When you tell me why *your* godfather, Ken Carlyle, keeps you on here when you're such a freaking liability. You've got the personality of an amoebic cyst. Anything else I can help you with before I go?"

"I hope you're enjoying yourself, because the ride's going to get real bumpy."

Maybe Byron expected me to break down and bare my soul to her, accompanied by a few tears. But Butch-Byron Eckert would be dressing in croc stilettos and silk taffeta before I exposed my fears to her.

"Why did your parents name you after a crippled male poet?" I asked her.

"George Gordon Byron was my mother's favorite Romantic writer, and I guess for a girl, Byron sounded better than George or Gordon. But I like the name. It fits my personality."

"I see what you mean." I leaned back and shoved my hands into the pockets of my Armani trousers. "We grow into our names, I think. How about Arianna Huffington? Can you imagine someone named Arianna, for instance, being unfeminine? I mean the name just makes you want to wrap a wreath of flowers around your head."

"Who the hell is Arianna Huffington, anyway?" Byron said. "Some kind of poseur. Has an accent, doesn't she? Greek? Italian? She's certainly no Huffington by *blood*."

"She's Greek by birth. And it's her husband who was gay, not her. So I guess she still qualifies as a female with a feminine name. Unlike you, *Byron*."

I figured that had a chance of making her blow a leak. But she hadn't even been listening to me. She looked at me as if I'd said something in Sanskrit.

"Listen, Melone, I'm not stooping to your level today—"

"Byron, you'd have to get on a ladder to stoop to my level—"

"Okay, stop!" She eased back into her chair. "I'm telling you, this is important."

She looked pale, whiter than usual.

"These parties over at Riverside Park. They call them 'Bollywood' parties . . ." She leaned closer. "Now, Melone, I need to know that this is just between you and me. I don't like you, and I know the feeling's mutual. But this is different. It's important."

"Maybe. Truce. For the sake of the students. What's on your mind?"

"They're using drugs that knock the girls out senseless so they don't know what's happening to them, and when they wake up, they've been raped. Sherman's got connections very few others have around here. Hollywood's celebrity elite is becoming more powerful than the presidency in this country. His old man's sowing the seeds for governor of California. Emily's the latest victim and maybe I don't want to see her dead like the others."

"Emily was in the cafeteria. She claims she never went near Sherman's last night."

"She's lying."

"Why would she lie?"

With raised eyebrows she shook her head at me, probably already having come to the same conclusion I had: Emily was too embarrassed to admit she was there.

"What's with the 'Bollywood'?"

"Mila Nazir. She's Pakistani. Did the ME check Melinda's and Lisa's blood for drugs? Cocaine? GHB?"

"Why are you telling me all this now?"

Byron stalled, running her hand through her bobbed blonde hair.

My cell phone rang, and when I leaned over to retrieve my bag from the chair next to me, I saw her foot tapping the floor. I looked up at her. She began chewing the inside of her cheek.

I decided to let the phone ring and placed my bag next to me again. "What's really on your mind? You're not telling me all this for my own edification."

"Cory Sherman. He needs this degree like he needs another pair of ostrich boots. If he doesn't graduate, he'll still be a filthy rich kid from Hollywood whose father will set him up in anything he wants to do. Or his old man will donate another wing to the school and he'll be back again in the fall. You see what I'm saying? Maybe—just maybe—Ken's making the wrong decisions this time, and it's going to come back and bite us all in the ass."

"You mean like losing your job?"

"No, I mean like losing my freedom. Look, Sherman and Lipton are getting out of hand and I don't want to be doing time with them. This is going beyond 'look the other way.' I'm no lawyer, but I'm seeing some trouble brewing. Especially if one of these girls decides to sue the school."

My cell rang again. This time I answered it.

"Hello?"

"Miss Melone? It's Emily."

"Yes, Emily?" I said into the phone.

"You said it was okay to call your cell—"

"Yes, it's fine. What's up?"

"Someone called me here in the hospital," she said. "Threatened me. I'm afraid of him. Afraid he'll come here."

"When are you getting released?"

"They want to keep me for another night, I think, but I want to leave. My mom will be here tomorrow."

"You're safer there than out, so stay put. Tomorrow, as soon as they release you, come straight to my office. Don't go back to your dorm room first. Understand? We're going to Carlyle together. No one should be threatening you."

As soon as I hung up, Byron resumed her conversation as if she had never stopped.

"See what I'm saying? This is going to blow up in our faces."

"What do you want from me?"

"If Ken hired you to keep the AG off our backs, I think he made a crucial error, because I know you still talk to your AG friends. Holton is a sitting duck for a full-blown investigation and I don't want to be the decoy."

"Why aren't you talking to Carlyle instead of me?"

"Ken's not the listening type, in case you haven't noticed. If he gets one whiff that I'm not on his side one hundred percent, I'm gone. We work too close for it to be any other way."

"And is Jeff Kendall your snitch?"

Almost imperceptibly, Byron swallowed. "Who?"

"Aw, you know who he is. The Holton alum who told you I was lousy lay. Remember? He's an AAG. Have you been frisking him for information?"

"I haven't seen Kendall since—"

"I have no idea what you're up to, Byron, but I'm not sharing my toys with you."

Byron kicked her chair back and stood. "You're wrong, Melone. I think Ken's making a mistake this time. I think he should throw Sherman out on his pampered ass. Just for the record. I'm not part of it."

"Part of what?"

"That's what I was trying to find out from you." She

breathed an honest sigh, pushed her chair back under the table, and trudged off.

ON MY WAY home, I took another detour by Riverside Park Apartments. Knowing it was unlikely I would see anything, I did it anyway, fantasizing that I'd catch Cory Sherman dropping a gum wrapper over the balcony so I could march up to his apartment and shove the litter down his throat.

Unfortunately, the balcony was dark. I slowed the car down and parked it so I could walk along the river and get closer to the apartments.

Well . . . all right . . . I'll be honest. When I was driving by, I spotted Mike's car parked on the road. Because of our not-so-minor spat outside Emily's hospital room, I had never answered his love missive about meeting him at Kartabar. Maybe (without sounding as if I was accusing him again) I could nonchalantly bump into him and find out why he was staked out in a secluded area outside Sherman and Lipton's apartment. Maybe I could nonchalantly ask him if he was there to rendezvous with his redheaded damsel in his mag-wheeled, rear-spoilered 1985 Mustang.

He was alone in the front seat, drinking coffee and reading the paper to pass the time as if he was on a stakeout. Funny how when I was liking Mike, his testosterone-powered car was almost endearing and cute. But now the sight of such an obviously greasy phallic symbol was making me wince. And having watched him scoop the coed into it the night before, the car was starting to sprout some real sinuous muscles.

Like the good cop he used to be, Mike spotted me in his rearview mirror and threw the newspaper down when I got out of my Jeep and started walking toward him. Whipping open the door, he lifted his legs out of the car and sat sideways half out of the front seat, waiting for me to walk by.

"Hey, babe. Want to kiss and make up?"

"What are you staking out in your Batmobile? Waiting for some Sherman spillover? Or are you his private bodyguard?"

So much for nonchalance.

"I called you when you didn't show up at the restaurant. Rita told me you were out."

"She's your little cupid, isn't she? Telling you that I'm at my desk with one hand on the phone, waiting for you to call, and that I'm just playing hard to get?"

He looked down at his lap and laughed to himself. "You're tough. Tougher than I thought."

"Shy and retiring isn't my shade, especially after I start to see red."

"Red? I don't get why you're so angry, babe."

"Drop the 'babe' routine." I looked up at Sherman's balcony. "Looks pretty quiet up there, Mike, so what are you doing here? Why are you *always* here, staking their place out?"

He paused. Grinding his jaw.

But I wasn't in a patient mood. "Answer me!"

"I'm counting to ten so I don't get out of this car and slug you."

"Go ahead, Mike, *make my day*. I'll have you arrested so fast you won't even hear the sirens coming—"

"I come here to make sure everything stays under control up there. And if it doesn't, I clean up the mess. Okay? That's my *job*. And who's staking who out? I'm a little tired of finding you on my tail."

"And I bet you didn't like me finding your tail in bed with the redhead last night, did you? In Sherman's apartment—in the bedroom."

"By Jove, I think you're jealous." He was actually nodding with a smile plastered across his face. "Yeah, my ex-wife was like that too. She thought I was screwing every skirt on the beat. It must be a woman thing."

"You probably *were* cheating on her. But I thought your wife dumped you for her high school sweetheart."

He crinkled his eyes. "Well, yeah, but the two things aren't exactly mutually exclusive. Are they?"

"Oh fuck you, Mike. What were you doing in Sherman's apartment last night?"

He raised his hands in surrender. "One of the kids from the party called me. Wouldn't give his name. He said there was a girl passed out up there and he was afraid she OD'd on something. I went up, got her, and brought her home. She was just drunk."

Perfect. There was no way I could check that story out.

"What else, Mike? You know more. Much more than you're telling me. How deep in this are you?"

"All right!" he snapped. "Mila Nazir. There's a Federal drug bust going down involving Mila Nazir and those bozos up there." He nodded toward Sherman and Lipton's balcony. "And that's why I've been parked here almost every night."

"*Really?* The Feds? And when exactly were you going to tell me this? Or am I some crazy broad who's good enough to bed but not smart enough to share info with?"

Mike looked at me straight on. "Funny thing, sweetheart, I been wondering the same thing myself. You've got more connections to this inside information than I do. I was a little miffed *you* haven't been talking to *me*."

"No, I don't think so. You're the one with secrets I've got to pry out of you. And who knows if even now you're telling me the truth. You're turning out to be a real disappointment, you know that, Mike?"

"Frankly, I'd like to know where you get off being so self-righteous. Obstruction of justice is a crime, isn't it, *Counselor*?"

He shot me a look that made me shiver. Who the hell was I to be spouting off about behavior above the law when the girls and I had walked away from the scene of a brutal murder without even calling the cops?

"I assume you're referring to the night Hastings was murdered." His silence was my answer. "Who told you?"

"What difference does it make who told me? The point is that you have a feminist chip on your shoulder that's bigger than your bra size. Calm down and stop acting like a stupid broad and I won't treat you like one."

Rather than answer him and expose any more fleshy female emotions, I left him sitting in his collagen-injected Batmobile, where suddenly he looked like sun-damaged cleavage in a push-up bra.

CHAPTER THIRTY-TWO

A Hole in the Bucket

MONDAY MORNING I WAS still in my AG rumble mode. I called Shannon and told her to get Laurie and meet me at the ME's before work. Surprisingly without argument, she agreed. So bright and early, I drove to the medical examiner's office and pulled directly to the back of the building, where the bodies were unloaded. I walked up in time to see one of the drivers jack open the rear door of a truck that had just rolled in with the early morning catch. Two cadavers in gray metallic bags were being unloaded like ponderous silverfish onto waiting gurneys. I followed them through a set of double doors into a wide hallway. Lucky spotted me from a few feet away and broke into a smile so broad that a gold-capped wisdom tooth shone in the back of his mouth.

"Oh, Miz M, be still my heart." He put his hand to his chest and made a fluttering motion.

Lucky reigned supreme in this place. He had seniority

over every other technician. The only deference he ever paid was to the doctors, and even then it was halfhearted.

"Come on with me. I got a live guest waiting for you."

I assumed it was Shannon who had come alone without Laurie. "Lead the way, old pal."

I followed him to a refrigerated room where stretchers holding bodies covered in plastic sheeting were lined up against the walls. Some had feet exposed or a few toes. Another was bloodred where the head should have been. It was missing.

"Lucky?" I said, still mesmerized by the headless body.

"See those buckets lined up in a row on them shelves? The head's up there. It'll go out with the body to the funeral home for burial. But, hey, I got a baby in another pail. They tell me I got to throw the baby away. They claim it's just a bunch of cells, but man, I can't get myself to toss it."

"A whole baby?"

He nodded slowly. "Well, long story short, the girl is raped by her father and she comes in dead and real pregnant. The baby inside . . . well . . . it sure does look like a real baby. But it wasn't born yet so we put it in a bucket during autopsy, and now the old man's lawyer goes to court and they say we got to toss the baby with the garbage. *Viability* or some legal talk. I tell the lawyer, Hey, you come take this bucket to the judge and put it on the bench under his nose while he's making his ruling. You'd have a funeral and a rightful burial faster than you can say 'bullshit.' Excuse me, Miz Melone, but it gets me riled when people start judging life and death from a golf cart."

There was something he wanted me to say. I was a lawyer; he wanted the opposing legal argument as to why the baby in the bucket should be buried instead of tossed with this morning's stale donuts and coffee. I couldn't give it to him. "Viability" had a legal meaning measured in time, and unfortunately, the thing in the bucket had missed it by a few weeks.

"The baby must not have been viable, Lucky. The parents are the girl's legal guardians. Nothing you can do."

"Yeah, that's what Mr. Kendall said too."

"Jeff?"

He led me into Examining Room 2, specially outfitted for bodies that needed to be quarantined either because of contagious illness like HIV, or because the body was so decomposed it harbored dangerous parasites and bacteria. There at the foot of an empty stainless steel table stood noxious Jeff Kendall with his head proudly erect like an unwavering sail in a brisk wind. My traitorous girlfriends were nowhere in sight.

"Raping the dead ones now?" I said.

"I hear you've got forensics doing specialized testing on the blood samples. They found something interesting and what I want to know is how you knew they would."

"Where are Shannon and Laurie?"

"At work where they belong."

"They told you I'd be here?"

Jeff in his typically succinct fashion shot an arrow through my chest. "Melone, their first allegiance is to Vince and their jobs, not you. Don't ever forget that."

I was too busy trying to stanch the flow of blood from my heart to answer him.

Lucky shook his head. "Ah . . . excuse me, folks. Am I done here?"

"Go," Jeff said with a nod, and Lucky quietly padded out the door.

And then I realized I wasn't an AG anymore and Jeff Kendall wasn't my colleague. What were we doing together swapping theories at the morgue? Why wasn't I spitting at him and walking out the door with Lucky?

"Why are you here, Jeff? Where are the girls? What's going on?"

Jeff leaned against the autopsy table and reached deeper into his front pockets. He looked up at the ventilation system and said, "You heard of a student at Holton named Mila Nazir?"

"Go ahead."

"She's Pakistani. She's bringing drugs into the school. Does that ring any chimes with you?"

"Maybe. What do you know about her? And how?"

"Mari, *dear*, from the grapevine. I'm an alum, remember."

"And does Vince know how close you are to your alumni brethren over there? And speaking of alumni *brothers*, you mean Byron Eckert?"

"Vince Piganno isn't stupid. He'll take information from any source willing to give it."

"Okay, then this is for Vince. Tell him Cory Sherman was fighting real rough with Mila Nazir the night I went to one of their parties—"

"You're going to student parties? You're a hothead, Melone. You're screwing up this job too."

"I went to keep tabs on what's going on there. No other reason. But I'm sure you'll rat me out to Carlyle before the clock strikes three. Just like you did with Vince."

"You're lucky all Vince did was fire you. You should be in jail for obstruction."

"Why are you suddenly talking to me? And who told you I'd be here? What's the matter, Jeff? You got me fired and it bit you in the ass because I aced a great job at your old alma mater and now I might know more about these murders than you do."

"What do you know?"

"I know you're scared, Jeff. I can tell by the wet spot between your legs."

He glanced at his crotch and when his head rose to me he looked like a snake ready to lunge.

"You bitch. You'll never know more than I do. That's going to be your final downfall, Melone. You think you're smarter than you actually are."

He walked out without waiting for an argument he knew I didn't have. Because, after all, if I thought I was smart but actually wasn't, then I'd be too cocky, and not smart enough, to realize just how off-track I was.

BACK IN MY office, I called Shannon to find out why she'd left me high and dry with Jeff Kendall at the morgue, and because I wanted to give her the heads-up on the off-chance I could persuade Emily Barton to go public against Sherman and file a criminal complaint.

And I missed the girls desperately. It just didn't feel the same without them by my side. Could women cut from such colorfast cloth as ours ever lose our diehard loyalty to each other? Maybe we could all have lunch. Breathe a little. Blow the afternoon breeze at a nail salon. Knock down a few beers at the Fez.

I got Beth on the line, who told me Shannon was on trial prosecuting a sixteen-year-old as an adult. The boy was accused of pushing his friend off a boat and watching him drown.

"Pretty heartless, huh, Mari?"

"Cold-blooded, I'd say. Must be a distant relative of

Jeff Kendall's, who, by the way, knew I was supposed to meet Shannon and Laurie at the ME's. How did he know, Beth?"

"Mari, I don't know."

"Well, if you ask me, which you shouldn't because I'm horribly biased, I think Jeff Kendall is playing both sides of the Carlyle/Vince fence. He's a true-to-form, honest-to-goodness, dyed-in-the-wool, hypocritical Holton alumnus. As is Byron Eckert. They must grow them that way in this place."

"But Jeff's probably guilty of nothing more than hating you, Mari. He heard Shannon talking to you, and he told Vince. Vince stopped them from coming to meet you."

"Damn. Did Shannon and Laurie get the third degree from Vince?"

"Not that I know of. But I know they want to talk to you. Something about the GHB . . . They got the blood work back from Lucky on the Barton girl. The GHB was pharmaceutical-grade. The pH in the dead girls was adjusted with store-bought vinegar—Heinz Distilled White to be exact."

I took a long, deep breath and felt my strength returning. "They can trace it to a brand?"

"All vinegar has slightly different pH and different ingredients. And pharmaceutical GHB isn't adjusted with vinegar. Ergo the GHB used on Barton as a date-rape drug was not the same GHB that was used on the dead girls. . . . But, Mari, I hope you're not messing up your job there . . . I mean, until Laurie and Shannon can get you back here, maybe you should just stick with the program and *not* try to do the AG's work. Let us take care of it from here."

I hung up with Beth, feeling like some guy had just

penned me a Dear John. My heart was hollowed out, like I'd missed some subliminal message in our conversation. Did the girls not meet me at the morgue because they were worried I was jeopardizing my job at Holton? Were they afraid I'd get fired from this job because they knew Vince was never letting me back? What if the girls were having a delayed reaction to the Hastings fiasco and had finally realized that I was a legal liability? Maybe they'd heard something and they were backing away from our vow of coconspirator solidarity.

When people started thinking they knew what was best for me, my reaction was to do the opposite. Not much different from a ten-year-old on the verge of puberty.

After leaving strict instructions with Rita not to let Emily off the line if she called, I headed to the courthouse in downtown Providence to surprise Shannon at trial and beg her to have lunch with me. After knocking heads with her a few times, she'd eventually tell it like it was—be brutally honest and then swagger away to let me drown in my tears. Shannon's lack of empathy wasn't selfishness. Her way of dealing with emotional distress was nondiscriminatory. Have a problem? Struggling with a difficult ethical issue? Shannon would generously gift you a bottle of Wite-Out or a big felt eraser. With great purpose she ignored the deeper meanings in almost everything except the middle of a turkey club sandwich.

MURDER CASES WERE tried in only a few courtrooms on the fourth floor. Shannon would be easy to find with the army of reporters convening for a juvenile murder trial.

Walking through the front doors, I felt immediately safe, smiling with the guards at the door who greeted me by name. As an unnecessary but courteous gesture,

I flashed my ID card at them and, in turn, they directed me around the metal detectors without even glancing at the card. I rode the elevator up and walked out onto the fourth floor as a familiar boxy male shape exited the elevator car next to me. Mike was headed toward my intended destination, so I followed him. His unmistakable gait was wide and determined and a half step speedier than usual. Today, Mike had somewhere important to go. I kept my head low, not wanting anyone to recognize me and call out my name. If Mike found me "spying" on him again, I'd never be able to dig myself out of it. He turned left and again I followed. He stood at the entrance to Courtroom 4C, a large, cavernous tomb of honey-colored veined oak, hundred-year-old built-in pews, worn marble floors, and floor-to-ceiling overhung windows still fitted with the marbled glass panes of a fun house. I stalled until Mike went in. He walked straight to the front and into the pew directly behind the railings separating the viewers from the lawyers and defendant's tables. I found a seat at the back of the courtroom while Shannon's strong voice soared across the room like a sharp arrow. Crystal clear and elegant, her diction was smoothed of the tough Boston twang that roughed up her speech when she was in her street-savvy mode. Shannon, like me, wore sedate suits to court, knee-grazing skirts and cropped jackets. She wouldn't give up her spikes, though. She said she kept the jury's rapt attention by prancing back and forth on stilted heels like a purebred Clydesdale. This was the role Shannon played only in courtrooms.

Mike sat in the front row and leaned forward with his arms resting on the wood partition, listening to Shannon give her closing argument and watching her body strut back and forth from the defendant to the jury box.

"Fifteen minutes," she said to them. "You heard the medical examiner say it. It took at least fifteen minutes for Bobby to drown. You heard him describe the way Bobby probably died. You also heard a state witness tell you what drowning feels like. Do you know the pain of drowning?" Shannon moved closer to the jury box, this time walking on the balls of her feet to keep her heels from distracting the jury as they thought about her question. "Do you know what it feels like to drown?" she asked them again when she was in their faces at the box.

"It *burns*," she told them. She drew out the final *s* until you could actually hear it sizzle on her tongue. "Our witness said water burns when it's in your lungs. Have you ever gotten water in your nose at the pool? A thousand times worse when you are drowning. When your lungs fill up with water, it feels like a fire inside your chest. You gulp for air but there is none. Eventually water is all around you and the urge to breathe is gone. An elephant is standing on your back, crushing it straight through to your chest. The pain is unbearable. And the terror. But you bear it because you have no choice. Peaceful unconsciousness isn't yours yet. You beg to die soon so the pain will let up. But your heart wants you alive, so it beats slower. Your body tries to stay alive as long as it can, hoping for a reprieve. Hoping that the defendant" — Shannon turned and pointed to him sitting stone-faced and cocky next to his lawyer — "will take pity and haul you back up to the boat. But he doesn't. He waits and watches you sink underwater, deeper and deeper, until the pain finally does ebb, and peaceful death is on its way. But you don't mind anymore because death is preferable to the choking, and burning, and thoughts of those you're leaving behind. . . ."

When Shannon was finished, the judge excused the jury for lunch and Mike stood, staring only at her, waiting for her to pack her briefcase and come through the wooden gates. When she reached him, he put his arm around her shoulder and rubbed her back as they left the courtroom together, Shannon with her arm resting lightly around his waist.

A few weeks ago Mike didn't know Shannon from a Roget's thesaurus. Now they were massaging each other's body parts.

I waited for the courtroom to empty, then stood on wobbly legs. But like a soldier left behind during combat, I rallied my defenses and dodged the gunfire of debilitating rejection by Shannon and Mike, who, both individually and jointly, were knocking the life out of me. I wasn't too surprised about Mike. He was the type of guy who was genetically coded to disappoint women. But Shannon? She was the real heartbreak.

CHAPTER THIRTY-THREE

—◦◦◦—

Poker Chip Blue

BY THE SIMPLE EXERCISE of placing one foot in front of the other, I left the courthouse and reached my car, turned the key in the ignition, and alternately pressed the accelerator and brakes by rote, until I reached my office and walked straight to Rita, knowing there was something I wanted to ask her but not being able to remember what it was.

Without looking up from her computer screen she said, "Miss Barton has not come by or called. I have a message from Mr. Orenstein and a cell phone number at which he says you must return his call."

"Right. Thanks, Rita."

As I walked to my office, life came slowly back into focus. I dialed Elliot. He answered on the second ring.

"Yes?" I said.

"Cory and Mila."

Elliot was breathless as if he'd been jogging or his brain had run a four-minute mile. Elliot was usually slumped over in ennui. That day he was zooming faster than a speeding bullet.

I told him to slow down and start again.

"Sorry." He coughed hard a few times and began again. "Cory and Mila Nazir are dealing drugs from school. Cory thinks he's James-fucking-double-07."

"Stop swearing, Elliot. You're still a student—and I'm not."

"But you're the first person I've met who is both willing and capable of blowing this place apart. I'm sick of this capitalist microcosm, the rewards doled out from the higher-ups for illegal behavior because of its profit margin. You got me started on this. Don't quit on me now."

I assumed by "higher-ups" he meant Carlyle and the administration. But I wasn't going to let him expound on a Carlyle-as-drug-lord dissertation. So far, despite Byron's fears, I still hadn't seen any evidence of rewards granted by Carlyle other than his usual tendency to look the other way when a rich and legacied student misbehaved. If Elliot had a philosophical axe to grind, I wasn't letting him point it on my gravestone. I prodded Elliot into a different direction, not necessarily a safer one, but one in which I was far more interested.

"Do you know if Lisa and Cory were together the night she died?"

"Why?"

"Because Emily told me something about Lisa meeting a guy that night before Sherman's party," I sort of lied. "She said Lisa was supposed to hook up with her later at Sherman's."

Okay, so why couldn't I lie a little to Elliot? It seemed the longer I was enrolled at this school of higher education, the easier it became to break the golden rules. And

I was getting the feeling that Elliot was enjoying himself looking down from a perch of intellectual superiority and that he was dropping crumbs of information for me like a path to grandma's house. Toying, perhaps, with what he considered my "naive gullibility."

He paused over the phone line. "You said Lisa and Emily were studying." He snorted. "And by studying, I mean cribbing off the notes Lisa had gotten from me in class. Of course, if Lisa and Emily were together, they'd been doing coke, so what was the point? They weren't going to learn anything whacked out on cocaine."

I was still feeling a pang of guilt over not doing more to help Lisa. I felt a need to defend myself. I wanted to tell him about Lisa's counseling with Mitsy and with her private MD in New York, but I was strapped to silence by damn confidentiality issues.

"Lisa was on top of her cocaine problem," I finally said.

"Oh sure, with Mitsy Becker, who puts Band-Aids on gaping wounds and then sends you back to the front. I warned you about Lisa the day I saw her in your office, and you didn't do anything either."

"It's the murderer's fault she's dead, Elliot, *not mine*."

"Okay, are you listening to me?" Elliot said. "That date-rape stuff—the GHB? That's the direction you should be heading. I found out the other night at the party that Cory and Rod are getting it from Mila—along with the cocaine they are making tons of cash from. I think there's a connection there."

"They're making money from the drugs?"

"That's what I hear from campus chatter."

"Does the name Jeff Kendall mean anything to you?"

"A student?"

"No, never mind. The GHB that Cory and Rod are getting, is it in pill form?"

"What's the difference?"

"It's homemade stuff on the dead girls, not pharmaceutical. It's not coming from LA or Pakistan. Someone's brewing it in his kitchen."

"Oh . . ." After a long pause, Elliot said, "That's a bump then. I don't think Sherman's got the brains for that."

Elliot wheezed a few more times—he sounded as if he were having an asthma attack. Why did nerdy people always have breathing problems? Did their brains work so fast that they simply forgot to inhale? Maybe asthma is an autoimmune disease responding to uncontrolled graymatter growth spurts. Maybe Elliot's body had begun to see his big brain as a foreign object growing out of proportion to his body: the runaway cerebrum; the brain as blob, snowballing out of control . . .

Or in Elliot's case it was probably just an allergic reaction to musty books.

I hung up with Elliot, sending him on his way while I chewed on his tidbits of new information and strutted into Rita's office, bumping into her on her way out. She gave me a verbal rundown of my calls, none of which was Emily Barton. Rita asked me if she could go to Miko to do some shopping. Miko was Rhode Island's homegrown answer to Victoria's Secret and Frederick's of Hollywood.

"Do you need anything?" she asked, holding a large envelope demurely over her breasts. "Because I just saw Monsieur McCoy and he left this package for you."

I sprinted back to my office and closed the door. Like a torrid scene from a drugstore romance novel, I ripped open the envelope. I swear I could feel beads of sweat tickling the crevice between my breasts. Had Mike created a new type of love letter, discreetly hidden in a yellow bubble-wrap mailer? And in this covert letter would he offer proof beyond a reasonable doubt that his presence at Sherman's party was indeed only a search-and-rescue mission of a damsel in distress? And while promising to forsake all his coed cuties (and that still unresolved underground friendship with Shannon), would he then profess his abiding love for me, whereupon I would exhale a sigh of relief and we would run off to the Dial-up Modem Diner together to live happily ever after over corned beef hash and sunny-side-up eggs. . . .

But alas, no dashing love letter. Not even the smell of his cheap aftershave wafted from the sheet. The only thing belonging to Mike inside the envelope was his ratty signature on the bottom of a bland incident report about a Holton student who'd been stopped by the local cops and charged with driving under the influence of alcohol. The kid was released on his own recognizance after his promise to reappear for arraignment in a week. I read the file and imagined my disciplinary strategy. I'd begun to think of it as my "Mitsy Strategy." Read the file, talk to the student, determine what should be done, tell Ken what you think should be done, and then do whatever the hell Ken tells you to do. Piece of cake. Unless you had a conscience.

I was placing the file in the back burner of my bottom desk drawer when I heard Mike's walkie-talkie cackling away in Rita's office. I made out nothing except "coming down" and then heard Mike say he was on his way to see Carlyle as he walked out f Rita's office. He grunted as he came toward my door and poked his head in.

Our stare was brief. No smile on his face. Certainly

none on mine. I still had not committed his face to memory, because it struck me anew. The strong features, black hair with strands of gray at the temple, freshly cut but still unfashionably an inch over the collar of his button-down blue shirt. Poker chip blue eyes. The broad mouth and soft lips that I could only remember as a sensation over my skin and against my own mouth.

While we were staring at each other, my phone rang. I hit the line button.

"Hi, Shannon," I said.

Mike turned his head quickly away and was gone without so much as a wink.

Shannon's voice was chipper. "Hey. Why didn't you come by?"

"When?"

"This morning, you paranoid schizophrenic. Weren't you in court? The guards told me they saw you."

"Oh yeah."

"Hey, buddy, you haven't been drinking, have you?"

"No, but the day is young."

"So why didn't you say hello?"

"Shannon, you didn't tell me you knew Mike McCoy—"

"Christ, Mari, I've been so busy with this murder trial and this drug thing going down at Holton—"

" 'This drug thing'?"

"Is this line safe?"

So now both Mike *and the girls* had failed to fill me in on the drug sting as soon as they knew. I still didn't believe Mike thought I knew first and hadn't told him. And why hadn't the girls told me as soon as they found out? What about that die-hard loyalty I thought we had to each other? Was I still operating on some infantile notions of a blood-sisterhood? Had Vince and/or Jeff convinced everyone I was a traitor and couldn't be trusted? *Was* I getting paranoid again? Christ, now that I thought about it, the only person who trusted me implicitly was the braincase loser, Elliot Orenstein, and now I was even beginning to suspect *his* motives for currying favor with me. He'd latched on to me like a love-smitten kid to his first-grade teacher. It was probably one of the first times in Elliot's life that he'd gotten positive reinforcement from anything other than a numerical grade report.

Shannon was still talking when I came out of my self-induced, post-traumatic stress coma.

". . . so Mila Nazir and the Sherman/Lipton dynamic duo, you know, like Spider-Woman, Batman, and Robin, they're all importing drugs and selling them from their freaking apartment on campus. McCoy didn't tell you any of this?"

"Speaking of whom . . . *why didn't you tell me you knew McCoy?*"

"Mari, after what I just told you, all you can think of is me netting a dumb cop?"

Why was she sounding so incredulous? Shannon liked nothing better than collecting airhead men she could order around—and under, and up and down, and every which way. The dumber the better. At face value Mike McCoy seemed her perfect specimen for mounting.

"Mari, stop acting like a goddamn lightweight. I just haven't been free to talk to you. This morning, after you asked us to meet you at the chiller, shithead Jeff ratted us to Vince and he stopped us from coming. And McCoy's okay, but not hot enough to screw *you* over for. We were also ordered to stay zip-mouthed by the Feds on the drug thing, but you know that wouldn't have stopped me. I just assumed you and McCoy were discussing everything over pillow talk. I thought he was filling you in. I mean information-wise, of course. Hah!"

"Yeah, sure, okay. But when did you meet McCoy? I mean, how?"

"Yesterday morning, after that Barton girl ended up in the hospital. He was here at the office with us at a meeting on the drug bust. And then he met me in court this morning about fixing some DWI over there. That's it. I swear on my mother's breast implants!"

"I just got a DWI case from him. Are you saying he came to *you* with it before he even gave me the file?"

"Maybe that's because he doesn't need to bother you with the small stuff. Maybe Carlyle told him to fix something up before it even got to you. I mean, I don't know how things are done over there, sweetie, but I didn't go looking for him. He came here on his own."

"Okay, okay, you're right. The DWI thing is bullshit. But, Christ, I saw him rubbing your back when you walked out of the courtroom."

"Yeah, I'd just told him his zipper was open and to save it until we got into the backseat."

When I didn't laugh, Shannon continued her defense, such as it was.

"I'm kidding, Mari. I'm kidding. Hey, look, I like giving guys a hard thing—I mean a hard time—and McCoy's a tough nut to crack. I like that."

"Don't let him fool you with that hard-nut routine. If you do put him in the backseat of your car he'll roll over for you faster than a golden retriever puppy."

"Well, if you ever see us together again, don't go thinking it's love. I'll just be cracking his nuts. You know what

I mean, buddy? I'm not getting any closer to his stinger than that lousy breath of his."

While Shannon was snorting one of her laughs I decided to keep my own counsel regarding my latest theories. Apparently no one except me suspected a connection between the Sherman "drug thing" and the murders. It's been my experience in life that when bad things start to happen in clusters, it's no coincidence; the bad things are connected. But I needed more than a gut feeling to go on or my case wouldn't get any closer to a courtroom than an honest criminal defense lawyer.

"Okay, Shannon, I have another one. Did you tell McCoy about us and the Hastings night?"

"It's Jeff. He's all over the place. Even Vince warned him to shut his trap from now on, or he'd fire him too. They were talking about Carlyle and how he came up with the idea to hire you. I'm betting Jeff and Carlyle were in cahoots. But I can't get a word out of Vince."

Shannon and I agreed to keep our party lines open and then signed off as Rita walked into my doorway. "Must I stay later or may I go shopping now?"

I knew what she had said, but wasn't processing it. Too many things on my mind made it difficult for me to focus on technicalities and social niceties. I expected Rita to merely deliver her message and then be gone, but she remained in my doorway expecting conversation and an early dismissal to get to her sex shop before closing time. I looked at her blankly.

"Did you forget to eat today?" she asked. "You are pale."

I got up and walked to my mirror. Rita stood behind me a few inches shorter. We studied my face, waiting for fangs to emerge or horns to sprout from my head.

"You are—how they say—gaunt, a bit withered. I think I must start feeding you."

Mike was back in my doorway. He walked in and put his arm around Rita's shoulder, giving her a kiss on the cheek. "Go wait in your office, huh, sweetie?"

Finally beaten, Rita huffed, and trotted dejectedly back to her office. Miko would have to wait another day.

"We need to talk." He stood with both hands on the door jambs, his arms spanning the entrance as if he were blocking my exit. But I had no intention of leaving. It was him I intended to throw out.

"Mike, I don't care who you're screwing. I just hope you're not screwing around with me. And I can't do this with you right now. I'm busy."

"Yeah?" He pushed himself through the doorway and into my office, where he pulled out a chair and flopped himself in it. "I'll just sit here until you're done. It's getting near closing time anyway."

"The fuck you will! I told you I'm busy right now."

His head snapped back in mock fear. "Whoa! And I'm afraid to swear around you?" He got up and bashed my door shut like it could have been the side of my head.

I glared back at him. When my adrenaline was pumping at peak anger levels (or after two shots of Patrón Silver), I had no fear. I could rant with a loaded gun in my face if I had the right energy flowing through me. Blame it on my Italian genes, but once I got emotional about something, the safest thing to do was to get behind a steel barrier and hope *my* gun wasn't loaded.

"Mike," I said in a low fervid growl like I was revving up a meat grinder for the gristly parts. "You're not afraid of me. You simply gauge your behavior based on what you think will be the most impressive for your immediate audience. You assume I want to be treated like a little princess because I made the mistake of being a little too starry-eyed with you. You think I merely tolerate words like 'fuck' and 'shithead' but that I don't use them myself because they make me shiver and quake. Well, I don't care *whom* you're *fucking* because I think you're a *shithead*. And no, you cannot sit in my office and wait for me to finish my work, because even if I were twiddling my thumbs in here, I don't want to talk to you right now unless it's related to drug stings and the occasional murder."

When I finished he nodded slowly, looking surprisingly sullen after my tirade. With his arrogant, devil-may-care attitude, I thought he might even laugh at me.

But he didn't.

"If you had a gun right now, you'd shoot me between the legs. It's something more than me keeping that drug sting info from you. So tell me what you're thinking, *Prosecutor* Melone. Tell me what's on your mind."

He looked me in the eyes. And then I knew I would never forget at least his eyes. He had stared at me too many times now for me to ever forget how they glittered at the edge like stars in a blue-black night sky. While I floated through his molten navy eyes, his bloated chromed Mustang started to shrink back into a cute little Tonka Toy.

But I resolved that he could stand there until he turned to stone. I would never tell him my real fear of him—the one I couldn't admit, even to myself. My fear of unknowable things. Those fears I had in court when I was looking at a murderer face to face and wondering what he was thinking as he pulled the trigger, or slit the throat, or tightened his grip on a soft white neck. I couldn't tell Mike that despite those fears, I still got jealous when I saw his arm on Shannon's back or his fingers laced through the red tresses of a twenty-year-old. I would never admit that despite his secrets I was falling hard for him and that love always scared me and made me stupid.

Rita's rigid voice came over the intercom and announced that Emily's mother had arrived by plane that morning and had been to the hospital to pick up her daughter but Emily was gone.

Mike interrupted our conversation. "Docs released her last night. You know, babe, you have my head spinning."

"Last night?"

"She trumped up some nonsense about pestering calls and got the hospital to discharge her early. They spirited her back to the dorm in an ambulance. She was good to go, so they said."

" 'Good to go' because the hospital doesn't want any liability if the Holton murderer performs his gruesome magic under their roof. And what makes you so sure the 'pestering calls' were 'trumped up'?"

Mike glared at me with stormy eyes while his words forced their way through gritted teeth: "I'm not a detective anymore. If the cops thought they should have done something about the calls, they would have."

With great deliberation I picked up the phone and buzzed Rita. I told her to go home. She could still make Miko if she hurried. I gently placed the receiver back into its cradle. I was taking my time so I could think first, before the real words on the tip of my tongue came tumbling out like rocks from a dump truck. The emotional part of me wanted to strangle Mike and kick his body out my door, but the prosecutor's blood still flowing through my veins stopped me. Why shoot the messenger when he might still have information to impart? Learn as much as you can, and *then* shoot. Or better yet, hand him back to Shannon for the final kill. Let her screw him to a wall with the electric drill of her sharp tongue.

"Okay, McCoy, what's really going on here? I'm not a soldier like you, and Carlyle doesn't seem to care about anything but bad press and the concomitant dwindling of annual donations. Emily was getting threatening calls in the hospital and now she's *missing*. And every time I turn around, I find you standing right in the middle of the pooled blood. Are we going to find Emily's body in the morning?"

Mike clenched his jaw and then slammed the flat of his hand on the desk in front of me like some kind of warning that I was next. Suddenly those liquid azure eyes lit up like a flame at the end of a candle. "Are you out of your fucking mind! *You're accusing me of murder.* Do you understand that? And do you also understand that you are making me very goddamn angry? Now, you tell me what *you're* keeping from *me.*"

I backed up a few emotional steps because Mike had tripped me up with an outburst that frankly I didn't think he was capable of. At least not with me. In a normal relationship I would have been glad we were getting it over with early. I mean, how often do women marry sweet guys only to find out, only after they're married, that these same "cuddlemuffins" consider breaking their wife's nose appropriate foreplay?

Had I just contemplated the "M" word in reference to Mike McCoy? I reminded myself that his actions in the past few days had elevated my suspicions to a capital "S."

"Okay, Mike, let's stand down a few feet."

I took a nice deep breath and adjusted the bass on my voice equalizer to a calming smooth-jazz level, and while mentally humming the tune to "The Girl from Ipanema," I said, "It seems that Emily is *kind of* missing and I'm starting to get a little bit concerned. *Why aren't you?*"

Mike breathed, then ran his fingers through his glossy hair. He flopped back in his chair. "We are getting so mucked up with all this shit, you and me. I wish we'd met at a different time—under different circumstances—before all this . . ."

"Oh Christ, Mike, don't play the star-crossed-lover routine now. We're both too old for that. The truth of the matter is neither of us belongs here. I'm a prosecutor, and you're a cop. You shouldn't be able to stomach this place either. We both sold out. I'm just trying to figure out how far you've gone. How much of your humanity you've traded for whatever it is you're getting in return."

He looked at me with a dark face, the light ebbing from his sparkling eyes. "There's a lot of water under both our bridges, Marianna, and we've both crossed over. I'm not a soul-searching kind of guy anymore."

"Maybe you never had a soul."

"A soul?"

"Yeah, you know, that impalpable thing that makes us human, separates us from the animals? A conscience, a second thought about anything other than the aggrandizement of your dick. *A soul.*"

"If you're looking for souls, go to a church. Other than that, go talk to Vince Piganno."

"Those are my choices? God or Vince Piganno?"

"I saw him at the AG's office the other day when I met your friend Shannon—"

"Ah, Shannon again—"

"I'd like to know why you're not an AAG anymore.

Something's not right with this whole scenario. What are you doing here?"

"You already know. Vince fired me because I was downtown when Melinda Hastings was murdered—saw her body flying across the street—and then I ran home and told no one. Vince fired me. Carlyle hired me. And here I am."

Mike guffawed like I'd just tripped over my own foot. "Either you think I'm stupid, or you definitely are."

I began my chronic teeth-clenching, because accepting IQ evaluations from someone like Mike McCoy was like swallowing a prickly pear whole.

He leaned over my desk close enough that I could smell that sickly aftershave. "How do I know you're not a plant here? An enticing but poisonous plant? From the little I know of Vince Piganno, he'd sooner put a hit on your tail than let you work here. So give me the truth. You and Piganno have your own little sting going on, don't you? You've been playing my strings like a fine-tuned violin." He plopped back into the chair and began shaking his head as if he'd just solved the black hole paradox. "Am I a fucking dope or what?"

"You're a dope and I'm not a plant."

"But you hate this job," he said. "And you don't even belong here. You're a prosecutor *through and through*."

He spoke his last sentence with the disdain of an ex-convict who'd been trammeled by the legal system once too often.

"I agree with you, but apparently Vince doesn't because he fired me right into his past. But let's get back to the *tense* present." I eased myself back in my chair and very calmly asked him, "Are the drugs connected to the murders?"

Mike's expression remained hard and sour. "Sherman, Lipton, and Mila Nazir have no interest in murder. And you're going to *fuck* everything up if you *do* get involved."

"But—"

He rose from his chair and glared down at me, threatening me with his height. "Unless someone invites you in, stay out of it!"

But I rose too. On my four-inch heels, eye to eye, I said, "Staying out of it would be about as hard for me as you staying out of Shannon's panties."

"Shannon doesn't wear panties."

Mike tornadoed out my door as I was lifting my desk chair for a home-run pitch.

CHAPTER THIRTY-FOUR

Last Call for the Carousel

RITA WAITED FOR MIKE to disappear down the hall, then popped her head into my office. "Perhaps this is not a good time . . . but your mother has called. She would like you to call her at home."

"Why haven't you left yet?" I asked her.

"To hear you and Mike fighting is so much more fun than a silly sex store! But now I will go. Good night," she sang as she floated down the hall after Mike.

I dialed home. My mother was worried because the coach of the soccer program had called her and told her that Cassie hadn't shown up for the six a.m. practice that morning, that she had gone off with a friend the night before and had not been back. Cassie hadn't been answering her cell phone either. Now, added to my list of other problematic issues, I had to play nursemaid to my negligent sister and overprotective mother. I screamed my frustration at my mother.

"Give me the number at the camp. And stay off the phone in case she calls you."

Terror muddles the brain. My mother had to repeat the camp number three times before she got it right. I dialed and waited an eternity of ten minutes for someone to locate the counselor, or coach, or whatever the hell the person allegedly in charge was called.

"Mrs. Melone?" A young man's voice came over the receiver.

"*Mari* Melone. I'm Cassie's sister."

"I'm so sorry over this confusion. We were thinking of calling her school but didn't want to get her in trouble—"

"Get her in trouble? She's missing!"

"Well, we assume it's just a teenage prank and she's arranged with her boyfriend to drive up here and spend the night off campus. Worrying everyone like this is not acceptable behav—"

"You *assume* this is a prank, so you don't alert her family? Are you out of your minds? For liability purposes alone you should have called her family as well as the local police. She's a minor in your care. If anything happens to her—"

"Well now, hold on a minute. She told her bunkmate that she was going for a ride with a friend from home. It isn't as if she disappeared from her bed in the middle of the night. This is not exactly an abduction we're dealing with here."

"Did it ever occur to you that some people go willingly with their kidnappers because there is a gun in their back, whether literally or figuratively? Have you called the police yet? Or are you going to wait *a few more days*?"

"Well, I'm not sure we should wait *days*—"

"Well, *sir*, my sarcasm is obviously too sophisticated for you. Maybe you've been hit by too many soccer balls. I am *not* suggesting we wait days. I am suggesting that you should have contacted the police *yesterday*. So I think, with all due respect to your authority in this matter, that you should call the police *now!*"

I gave him every telephone number at which I could be reached, and then called my friends in the AG's office. I struggled over telling Mike, and finally decided that in the interest of finding my sister at any cost, I should alert him; he was head of Holton security, after all. I found him by cell phone and the connection was bad, but he didn't sound overly concerned. "It hasn't been that long," he said. "But I'll spread the word anyway."

When I finally went home, I found my mother leaning over the sink, seeking therapeutic counseling from her parsley plant on the windowsill.

"If I don't cut it young, it becomes old and tasteless, even on the root," she said as she snipped off the tops.

She may have been talking to me, but the chances are good she was merely apologizing to the elderly parsley for mercy killing. She often discussed things with her plants.

My eyes watered at the sharp vinegar and garlic aroma coming from the pickled vegetables she had laid on the table in a bowl. Shades of bright green broccoli, white cauliflower, and orange carrot sticks had been floating for weeks in a vacuum jar at the back of the refrigerator, preserved by cider vinegar and whole garlic cloves.

My mother focused out the window toward the neighbors' yard as she spoke. "She promised to call as soon as she got there. And, of course . . . nothing yet. I call her and get no answer from her cell phone and they tell me they are giving her messages, but . . . nothing back. And now this. She is gone overnight. She will kill me yet."

"Cassie's a teenager. They torment you so you won't miss them when they go off to college. Nature has it all planned."

"You weren't like that." She turned to face me and dried her hands on her apron. "You were always with a soft heart. Clearheaded. Never a worry. Not like Cassie."

"I was a nerd, Mom. What can I say?"

"Nerd?"

"A loner. I studied, got As, didn't do what all the other kids were doing"—I thought of Elliot and how alike we probably were—"I only had one close girlfriend. Remember Annie? Our big night out was shopping at the mall."

"Yes, yes, Annabel."

I went to the sink and wet a paper towel, wiping cold clean water across my forehead. I had bumped into Annie in court during her last divorce. The life had drained out of her. She seemed dead to me, as if I'd somehow ascended into some higher life and she'd stayed behind in a domestic hell of her own making.

"I'm sure Cassie's fine, Mom. She's a drama queen. Remember the time she ran away for twenty-four hours and we found her in the front bushes in a sleeping bag?"

My father walked through the door and stopped for a minute to look at me. "Ooh! You visit with us *again* so soon? Something must be wrong."

I shook my head. "Come sit down."

"Oh no. I wash the dirty feet off my hands first." He went immediately up the back stairs, not wanting to contaminate our kitchen sink. I sat silently waiting for him to return while watching my mother go through her nightly

routine. I thought of Annie again. She was my age with
two husbands and three kids tugging on her shirt. Why
was the alarm on my biological clock set at a later date
than hers? Why hadn't I found my soul mate yet—the
person I could *settle down* with—when Annie had already downed two and was prowling for the third? Or was
I simply not ready to give up my own life and take responsibility for someone else's? And if I was simply resisting
marriage and children in an effort to remain independent
as long as I could, why were Shannon, Beth, and Laurie
afflicted as well? There seemed to be a restlessness in the
four of us, a need to find something more to life while we
were still young enough to hold our bellies and laugh out
loud. None of us wanted to be mixing pancake batter or
changing diapers when the circus master hollered out the
last call for the carousel.

My father came back down the stairs. He sat at the
table with me and picked a carrot from the bowl. He
crunched his teeth into it, releasing a pungent vinegar
and garlic smell into the warm room. "So, you like this
new job? Or you want to change again?"

"Holton pays better than the AG's, but the job is actually harder than I thought it would be. It's kind of like an
emotional juggling act."

My mother continued her ritual of washing lettuce in
a large colander, then transferring it to a pot and returning it to the colander for another rinse. She would do this
at least three times for lettuce and ten times if it was sandy
spinach or arugula.

"As a prosecutor, I didn't treat one person different from
another. Same cases. Same crimes. Same punishment. I'd
try them or plead them out. Even the defendants were the
same after a while. Names may have been different, but

they were all the same. Shortly before I left the AG's, I put a guy named Whittaker behind bars. He was a millionaire banker but a habitual drunk driver. Do you think the judge pulled me aside and said, 'Miss Melone, this is a volatile case. We have to treat it discreetly. Let's just let him go free and see what happens'? At Holton, we have 'special students,' who are rich, and the male students are treated differently from the female students, and blacks, whites, ethnics. . . . It's a whole caste system over there."

My father watched me and chewed. My mother turned from the sink again. It was too quiet in the house without Cassie.

"I don't like to hear this," my father said. "Maybe we don't want Cassie to go to a school like that."

As the seeds of worry began to germinate in each of our minds, our apprehension and fear overheated the kitchen and made the food smells almost nauseating.

"Cassie has not called from this camp yet?" my father asked.

We both looked at him and shook our heads no.

My mother joined my father and me at the kitchen table and we updated my father on the latest developments in Cassie's most recent malfeasance. Then the two of them, my parents, sat quietly, looking at me, waiting for my superhuman plan to make it all right again. Unfortunately, I had none. I was usually so full of ideas for them, telling them in my strong American way that everything was doable, all things fixable. Anything was possible. This was the first time in my adult life I had to help my parents and was failing them. There was nothing any of us could do except wait.

"The police have started a search," I finally said. "I spoke with the coach."

My mother crossed herself.

"I'm going up there," I said.

My father looked at his hands folded atop the table. "We need you here. You can do nothing more than what the police are doing. They are doing their job."

I looked at my mother for a response. She was numb with worry. My father was finished with the niceties of conversation. "We wait together. Cassie will call here first."

I swear she heard it before my father and I. My mother heard the phone before it even rang. Wondering where she was going, I watched her rising from her chair seconds before the ring pierced the slow, heavy silence of our small kitchen. "Who is this please? . . . Yes, she is here. Who is this please?"

My mother held the receiver to her chest. "It is for you," she said to me. "Please, Marianna, don't tell me anything bad. Please."

I took the phone from her. "Hello?"

"Miz Melone? That you now?"

I froze at the sound of Lucky's voice. I had never heard it in my kitchen before. Lucky's voice was something from another realm. Disjointed. Disembodied. From work, where everything involves someone else, not me, not my family. Morgues and medical examiners and death did not belong in my parents' kitchen. Lucky should not be calling here.

Should not.

"Yes," I said weakly.

"Miz M, I'm so sorry to bother you, but Miz Lynch is on her way here. She told me to call you. You got another student missing from Holton College and—"

"This is about work? You're calling me about work *here*?" He had never heard me screech.

"Well . . . as I said, Miz Lynch told me to call you. When you didn't answer your cell phone, she told me to try this number. I'm sorry to bother you, ma'am."

"No, no. Lucky, I'm sorry. Just that my sister . . . never mind . . . what is it, Lucky?" I looked at my parents and realized they were watching me with white faces and open mouths.

I shook my head to relieve their anxiety that the call was about Cassie, even though I suspected that it was.

"We got a body down here—"

The air caught in the lump of my throat.

"—young girl, hard to tell her age due to the fact that . . . hmm . . . well, ma'am, she's got no face."

I walked into the corner of the kitchen, as far away from my parents as the cord would allow. "How young, Lucky? What do you mean by 'young'?"

"Could be twenty, could be fifteen. Hard to tell—"

Fifteen?

"—and when I was preparing the body, I found a paper in the pocket of her jeans and it's got your name and cell phone number on it."

"Oh yes, yes. Of course." I tried to remain calm, for the sake of my parents, and in fact I appeared so calm, I looked half dead. It was one of my better defense mechanisms. I turned stone cold and all emotion drained out of me when I was sure catastrophe had finally arrived at my doorstep. I expected catastrophe, so when it was imminent, I hung my head and waited for the axe to sever my emotions from my body like a swift guillotine.

I hung up the phone. I couldn't remember if I'd told Lucky I was coming down or not. But I knew that was my intention. I would go to the morgue to see a dead young girl, and pray, as I've never prayed for anything before, that it wasn't my little sister Cassie.

"Mom? Dad? I have to go back to the office for a minute. Problem with some paperwork. I'll be back in half an hour. Promise," I lied cheerily.

"You are lying." My father always knew. I could lie to my mother, but never to my father. He always knew. I now wondered for the first time whether my mother always knew when I was lying too. She was just smart enough not to confront me; she knew that if, and when, I lied, it was for a good reason. My mother had a mother's instinct. She knew when lying was selfish, and when it was necessary.

"Let her go," my mother said. "She'll be back, and we will be here waiting." My mother was calm like me. Maybe she saw her own guillotine.

CHAPTER THIRTY-FIVE

Morgue 102

I TOOK THE FRONT DOOR to the ME's office and walked directly past the front desk with a nod. From the front of the building, visitors had to descend into the basement of the building, where the processing of bodies took place. In the past, I had always entered from the back, which was built into the ground so the bodies could be unloaded directly into the basement.

My business there had suddenly turned personal; the morgue was quiet, dark, and gloomy, just as it appeared to others who had walked before me to identify bodies of their loved ones. In the past the morgue had meant parties of laughs and black humor, of chilled lobster in Styrofoam coolers and Dom Perignon kept in eight-foot-long unoccupied refrigerated drawers. Now as I entered to view the body of a young girl who might possibly be my sister, the thought of eating dead lobsters made me sick.

Sitting in the windowless and airless reception area,

a man and woman held hands. They looked numb and paralytic, like the parents I had left at home. They could be here for no other reason than body identification. Another woman sat alone in a corner, shivering. I waited for someone to answer the buzzer next to the windowed door leading into the holding area. The blinds were closed tight but within seconds their slats flipped opened and Lucky's face appeared through the glass. He nodded at me and unbolted the door.

"Your girlfriends are already here," he said. "This something new? Why are you all coming to ID a body? And it's a bad one."

"Bad?"

"Well . . . those people, out there in the waitin' room, are missing their daughters. Now, usually I can tell if it's a match, you know? I been at this so long, I can look at the faces out there"—he nodded toward the waiting room—"and know if it's the ones connected to what's in here. But hell if I ain't stumped when the face in here is practically filleted from the bone."

Trying hard not to visualize it, I let that information find its way into my brain. As Lucky and I walked, I explained that my sister was missing from her soccer camp on the Cape. That she hadn't been seen since yesterday. Lucky said nothing, not even nodding in his usual respectful fashion. He was as dumbstruck as I was.

"Well, no, then I don't think it's your sister. This sweet thing was found here in Providence in the woods."

I heard his voice as an echo from far away. My vision began to blur. Nothing clear, everything stained white. I breathed deeper, as if the air would clear the smog I was looking through. But my rapid heavy breathing made me dizzy, and my head fell back into darkness until the next thing I saw was Shannon, Laurie, and Lucky staring over me as I lay on a cold steel table.

"How many times you been here, Miz M? You ain't never fainted before."

"Get the bourbon," Shannon ordered. "The Knob Creek from our private stash."

Lucky leaned closer into my face, worried, but he was talking to the girls as if I had left the room and wasn't coming back. "Is she okay? Maybe we should call 911."

"She'll be fine after a few slugs," Laurie said. "I'll get it."

Underneath me the table to which Lucky had lifted me was hard and unforgiving. Up in the ceiling was a hooded and domed light fixture, the bulb shrouded in glass for easy disinfecting of spattered blood and other body secretions. Shannon's face appeared next to Lucky's, and I spoke to both of them. "If Cassie is in that drawer just kill me and put me next to her. I can't go back home and face my parents."

"I know," Shannon said. "I know."

"I don't know *nothing* like that." Lucky shook his head briskly. He was getting to that point where he usually distanced himself from our shenanigans. I interpreted his shaking head to mean that he had no intention of packing me up in a metal drawer, no matter who we found in the adjoining one.

Laurie returned with a paper cup. Like a nurse, she pursed her lips to guide me as she lifted my head and brought the cup to my mouth. "Take a nice big one," she said.

A burning stream of liquid slid smoothly down my throat. "Help me up, Laur. I've got to find out."

Lucky wound his large strong arms around me and

lifted me to a sitting position. While he fed me another sip and then lifted me by the waist off the table, Laurie and Shannon each took her own hefty swig from the bottle. Shannon and Laurie led the way and we walked to the room where the refrigerated drawers were kept. Lucky never let go of my elbow.

We stopped in front of a breast-height steel drawer. As Lucky grasped the latch to pull it open, I put my hand over his, stalling him. The Cape was only two hours away. The killer could have brought Cassie back to Providence and done it here.

Lucky blew air up to the ceiling. Still looking up there, he said, "Well then, you sure you want to do this? We can get some tests first. Do it that way."

"Let's get it over with," Laurie said. "My tribe isn't keen on cadavers."

Lucky depressed the silver latch, jerked it hard until it released, then pulled the heavy stainless sarcophagus from its airtight seal. A white-draped mass spread slowly before us.

When I was twelve, our next-door neighbors had a dog. My mother believed animals belonged outside. She discouraged our attention to the huge German shepherd that weighed as much as we did. I found the dog one day, sick. She had fallen on a shallow step that she once could easily stride. She lay there, unable to get up, her legs splayed into the air, saliva dripping from her mouth; diarrhea caked her hind legs. The next day I went back to see if she was better. I found her dead on that same step.

It was winter and the ground was covered in dirty sheets of ice. Our neighbors, her owners, were not rich. They couldn't afford vets or even the cost of vet-assisted disposal, so for months until spring, the animal lay there covered by a plastic shower curtain, freezing peacefully at rest through the winter.

The mound spread before Lucky and me was only slightly larger than the frozen German shepherd in our neighbor's backyard. Lucky rested his hand at the corner of the sheet. "You know any marks on the body? Maybe we do it that way and keep the head covered."

Cassie's body was a mystery to me. My mother might recognize every mark on her, but from me, Cassie had hidden her nakedness with the modesty of a young girl whose body changes daily, hair by hair, rounding in small increments, turning from a dry, straight stem to a moist, curved flower almost overnight. But I would know Cassie by her hands. Like my father's, they were fleshy and short-fingered. I was jealous of Cassie's hands, knowing they would age better than mine, whose fingers were bony and long, showing every blood vessel through translucent, thin skin. Cassie's hands would always look young.

As Lucky pulled the sheet back, I stiffened in expectation, avoiding as well as I could the bloody mass contained by a plastic bag fastened at the neck. I followed the thin arms down to her hands.

And I fainted again.

This time I recovered quickly. Lucky had wrapped me in his large arms. He smelled of disinfectant and rubber. The room was cold. Lucky was warm. I looked into his face above me.

"Her hands?"

Laurie answered for him. "It's the same sicko, Mari. Except this time he cut up the hands too."

Laurie, unlike me, hated morgues and dead bodies. But this girl could have been Cassie, and I knew Laurie was doing this for me—painstakingly examining the mangled fingers with rubber-gloved hands. "He used some kind of hunting knife, looks like—jagged edges. You know, I bet he was trying to cut off the fingertips to make the ID harder. He probably gave up. It's damn hard to saw through bone."

"Oh shit, oh shit." I cried into Lucky's chest and he held me hard to him.

"I'm sorry, so sorry, Miz M. This is no good. I'm taking you out." He pushed the drawer closed with one hand and I watched the white mound disappear slowly like the foam at the end of a wave going back to sea. "You girls take her back to the room. I got to let those people sitting outside come on in here."

Shannon and Laurie walked me back to the autopsy room, where the three of us sat silently on the edge of the stainless steel table, sipping whiskey from paper cups. Within minutes, we heard a woman's loud scream, followed by a man moaning.

"It's not your sister," Laurie breathed.

Lucky returned a minute or two later.

"Good news," he said with a smile. "Tattoo on her back. The Bartons just ID'd their daughter Emily."

SHANNON AND LAURIE came back with me to my parents' house. They were still sitting at the kitchen table where I'd left them. I had no news for them, nor they for me, but I assured them, in one of my best theatrical performances, that everything was going to be just fine. Their silence continued unbroken.

The girls and I went upstairs to Cassie's room. Her computer screen was sitting dark on her desk; several practice SAT exam books lay sprawled next to it.

We all stood over the screen as I booted it up to check

for e-mail on the off chance that whichever "friend" had picked her up from camp had made plans with her to do so before Cassie left for the Cape. I combed through each and every message. None of them seemed pertinent to her disappearance. I hoped that wherever she was she was having the time of her life so we could all scream at her in the morning for worrying all of us so needlessly. She apparently had learned nothing from my warnings after her little drinking spree with Sherman and Lipton. Elliot was right. Cassie was thickheaded and stubborn. And she'd just fallen into a pothole.

THE THREE OF us huddled together in the street in front of my parents' house. Hands in pockets, blowing into our collars, stomping the ground to keep our feet warm, it was too cold for even Shannon to bare her hands for a quick smoke.

"Tomorrow, if you haven't heard from her," Laurie said, "we'll get the cops in on this and everyone else we can think of in this one-horse town. Forget Holton. Forget Vince. We've got to find your sister."

I nodded wordlessly and watched as Laurie and Shannon hopped into Shannon's Suburban and drove off. I should have gone back into the house, where I saw my father's face peering out at me from the front hall window. Instead I shot him a cowardly wave and escaped into the safety of my own car for a solitary ride home.

My brownstone had a small lot with assigned spaces for three cars in the back of the house. I pulled into my space, walked into the front foyer, and began my climb to the second floor when the doorbell rang. Mike, I assumed, had returned for another round in the ring with me. Or another one of his let's-kiss-and-make-up speeches.

I glanced down at the sidelight windows, where knowing friends usually stood to give me a view before I opened the door to them, but there was no one in sight. As angry as I was with him, I walked back down to the foyer, growing excited that maybe Mike *had* come to beg for forgiveness; to console me and tell me his cop friends had given Cassie top priority and he had it all under control in his big powerful (kiss my ring finger) hands. So I didn't bother peering through the peephole. My heart fluttered an extra beat as I pulled the heavy front door open expecting to fall into Mike's strong arms as he gave me the good news that Cassie had been found safe . . . was home in bed . . . alive . . . well . . .

Rod Lipton bolted through the entry. "Shit, it's cold out there."

"You," I said, disappointed. "You shouldn't be here."

"I heard your sister's missing. McCoy asked Cory and me about it. As soon as I heard, I knew what you'd think. Because of that day at the pizza place. But it isn't us. I don't know where she is."

"I didn't ask you."

"Can I come up for a minute?"

"No."

He shivered and looked behind him at the door still ajar, wincing as frigid air blew a part through his hair. "I should have worn a hat." He pushed the door closed.

I backed up a few steps. "Go home, Rod. What do you want here?"

"I want to talk to you about Emily too. I tried at the party the other night. Can we talk? Right here if you want." He looked up the stairs. "But upstairs is better. Put your cell on speed dial and hold it in your hand. If I wanted to hurt you, Miss Melone, I could have done it any number of nights I've seen you walking to your car after dark on George Street."

"And then followed me home?"

He shrugged. "I saw you unlocking the front door once."

I stepped aside and let him go up, as if not granting him verbal authority made my decision less stupid.

He began his climb to the second-floor landing and then stepped aside to let me unlock the door. Once inside, I took a book from the hall table and wedged it in the door to keep it from locking closed while he waited for me to give him further orders.

"Go sit in the living room."

He walked through the lead-paned pocket doors, looked around, but in the end refused a seat. I took a chair closest to the doors and flipped open my cell phone, dialing 911 but holding off on the "send" button. He looked down at me; I stared up at him; each of us waiting for the other to speak.

Sometimes when I'm in a plane, I play out the scenario for a crash. I listen to the engines rumble and I tell myself they're failing, struggling to keep the plane aloft. I was playing out the scenario of Rod rushing me, pushing me down, pulling a knife from his jacket . . .

He was standing silently in front of the window. Uncomfortable with him looking down at me, I rose from the chair. He sensed my unease and began talking.

"I know you're trying to unseal the Health Services records. But you can just ask Becker about Emily. I told her everything, but she's got no loyalty to anyone but the last guy who signed her paycheck."

"You went to Dr. Becker about Emily?"

"I had to. If I didn't go on the offensive—claim Emily was stalking *me*—she would have turned me in and I would have been expelled. So I had a few sessions with Becker, saying how pissed I was over the horrible rumors Emily was spreading about me."

He continued to present his defense: she was asking for it. It was a defense I knew well and was ready for. A defense that men like O'Rourke accepted as totally rational and vindicating. Unfortunately, even some women were all too ready to accept the feeble excuse. Like maybe Mitsy Becker, whose job security required her to sweep blame under the rug and then smooth out the nap of negative press. Sure, she'd sent Emily to me in the first place, but when I couldn't fix it and make it go away, Mitsy climbed off her limb and back to the safety of her Holton nest.

Rod shook his head. "Look, Emily was hot. Freaking gorgeous. And the sex? She played docile at first, submissive, and then I'd make her get rough with me. It was fun. That's all it was. She wanted it as much as I did. She started wearing those garter belts with no panties. You tell me what that was for—"

Rod. Not Cory. "Did you kill her?"

"No, and I didn't rape her either." He looked up at the ceiling. "Rape. Such a stupid word for it. I didn't hit her or anything. She wigged out and I left her alone after that."

"What do you want from me, Rod?"

"Emily's missing. I just wanted you to know. It wasn't me."

"Her body was just ID'd. Emily's dead."

I began to notice Rod's gray eyes turning silver, glazing over. He was high on something.

I started backpedaling into the foyer. "And what about Cassie? My sister. You're sure you know nothing about where she might be?"

His mouth fell open and he blinked slowly a few times, looking around my apartment as if he were trying to remember where he was and what he was doing there.

"You're stoned, aren't you?" I said.

"Fuck. I don't know anything about your sister."

"Liar."

Rod suddenly jumped in front of me and I backed up against the wall. He was so close I could feel the warmth of his body in the unheated foyer.

He looked down at me. A few strands of my hair tickled my face as he breathed. "You'd never believe a word I say anyway. Never. I'll always be a liar to you. You fucking think it's in my blood or something—that I'm incapable of telling the truth. It's in your eyes all the time. I could slit my wrists in front of you right now and you'd still think I was doing it for effect. How much you hate me. It's in your eyes."

Each of his exclamations had brought him closer to me. So close that I had turned my head to the side to keep my face from touching his jacket. I was facing the front door, the book still wedged in place. His anger seemed out of proportion to our past encounters. Was it paranoia from the drugs coursing through his veins? Or because he was a sociopath who thought all women were expendable, and just plain fun to rape and kill?

He suddenly bolted away from me, kicked the book into the hallway, and jogged down the stairs. I double-locked the door and turned the thermostat up to seventy-five degrees.

CHAPTER THIRTY-SIX

The Man in the Moon

ON MONDAY MORNING I rose from my bed at five-thirty. Cassie was still missing. I showered and, without thinking, pulled on jeans and a navy blazer. Still in my walk-in closet, I reached to the top shelf where several shoeboxes held about half a dozen designer shoes for special occasions, kept in their boxes safe from sunlight and dust. To the far right, behind the shoeboxes, was another box with a special lock, in which I kept an unloaded Walther .380 automatic. In my line of work, a gun was as necessary as a fresh pair of pantyhose. I took the gun from the shelf and loaded it with bullets taken from a separate hiding place on the shelf, checked that the safety was locked, and placed it in the inside zipper section of my Tod's backpack.

All night long I had done the math, adding up what I had from Holton with what I had from the AG's office, and the sum kept coming up odd. I was thinking maybe there was a point or two I was missing from 150 South Main that required a personal visit, and my encounter with Rod Lipton had left me with a chill I couldn't seem to shake, so I called Rita and left a message on her voice-mail that I might be in a few minutes late.

I walked into the reception area of my old offices at the AG's. No one was in yet. It was like walking into my mother's kitchen as a teenager after a late night out, stinking of cigarettes and alcohol—guilty, but safe. At the empty front reception desk, I heard the elevator doors open from the hall outside. The heavy cough was unmistakably Vince's.

"What the hell are you doing here?" He walked past me and into his office. I followed, as he knew I would.

Vince wouldn't look at me. He lit a cigarette. "What do you want?"

"I want to know about this drug sting I've been hearing about, what you have on the murders, and whether any of it involves my sister."

Vince coughed heavily as the smoke caught in his wet lungs. I waited for the cough to clear. He was stalling. Trying to figure out, in a few seconds of a pre-emphysemic fit, how much I knew.

"Run this by me again?" he said. "Your sister?"

"Stop stalling, Vince. Tell me what you know."

"Wait a friggin' minute before you start ordering me around."

He plopped into his thickly stuffed black leather chair, his head thudding back into the dented cushioning. He eyed me as he slowly lifted his legs up onto his desk. Crossing one ankle over the other and resting his Ferragamo tassel loafers on a mass of file folders, he used his desk as a footrest.

"Cassie was with Rod Lipton and Cory Sherman—I assume you recognize their names—shortly before she disappeared from soccer camp. I need to know if there's a connection. I'm not playing games anymore."

He twirled the smoke around in his mouth as he thought, then deftly blew a smoke ring from his Merit Ultra Light.

"Jesus, Vince, stop with the smoke signals! There are too many dead bodies turning up."

He lowered his feet to the floor and frowned, poking around with his butt for a clear spot in the soot-laden crystal ashtray on his desk in which to stub out his cigarette. With deliberate methodology, he smashed the butt into the glass until the filter split and tobacco burst out. "Your sister. I don't get it. What's she got to do with Holton?"

"It may have nothing to do with what's going on at Holton—the murders, the drugs—but I can't ignore the possibility. So this isn't about my job anymore, or Carlyle, or you. It's my family we're talking about."

Vince sat up straighter and leaned over his desk. "Have a seat, Meloni."

I pulled out a chair in front of his desk and sat. He passed me a cigarette, then sat back in his chair as well, and hefted his feet back on top of the desk. I took a puff of the cigarette, thinking how I hated working at Holton. In the few short weeks I'd been there, I'd learned that I'd never fit the mold.

Vince spoke. "You work at Holton because Jeff Kendall hates your guts."

"Jeff wanted me at Holton?"

"Carlyle wanted you, and I think he got Jeff to fill him in on your particulars so he could court you for the job. I guess Carlyle thought he'd be holding me hostage by hiring you. As if my loyalty to you would make me bend under pressure or something. He doesn't know us very well, does he? He doesn't know about our loyalties and how I can spin straw into gold."

Of course by "loyalty" he was referring to the lapse of *mine* over Hastings. "I'm really sorry about the Hastings murder, Vince. I started to tell you . . . but Jeff beat me to it and turned me in."

He shrugged and pulled another cigarette from his pack.

"So what'd you mean about spinning straw into gold?"

He looked over at his phone, where I could see a light flashing on his ten-line system. Someone was trying to reach him. "Forget that now. Go back to work. We'll talk another time—after this is over and your sister is back home."

"No, Vince. I need to know it all. Did you mean something, or was it just one of your flippancies?"

He took another drag of the newly lit cigarette and then stubbed that one out too. "These cigarettes are your fault," he said into the ashtray. "Because I'm worried."

Vince had begun a confession in his usual way: by blaming someone else. I knew he'd keep talking if I kept my mouth shut.

"At first I was mad as hell at you. I mean how could you even *think* of working for a pissant like Carlyle? But then I got to thinking . . . Well, the truth is, Meloni, I been trying to bust Carlyle for years on one damn thing or another. Sure I hate his guts. But now I really got something to sink my teeth into. This drug shit. It's real and it's illegal. But I could never get near that place. Get to the inside . . . where you are, now that you work there." He finally looked up at me. "And you work there because I fired you. Or maybe I should say I fired you—so you'd work there."

I let my jaw hang open for a few seconds. Before Cassie went missing, this news would have brought tears of joy to my eyes: Vince hadn't really fired me. I was just *positioned* at Holton College so Vince could get the information he needed to bust Carlyle. But now the tears welling up in my eyes were the sad kind, the kind that mean worry, fear, and premature grief if we didn't find Cassie alive.

I responded calmly. "You should have told me your plan, Vince. I would have done things differently. Especially with my sister. I wouldn't have let her near the place from the beginning had I known I was a plant for a drug bust."

He was grinding his thick square jaw, nodding, and still stubbing out cold butts in the ashtray. "I took a shot in the dark, Meloni. I didn't tell *anyone* what I was doing. How the hell was I supposed to know these murders would continue, and that you'd drag your sister into it? Never mind that now. You go back to work and finish your job, and I'll do mine here. Then we'll talk." He stood and came around to the front of his desk. "And the cops are looking for your sister, but between you and me, are you sure she didn't just run off with her boyfriend?"

"Is there anything else you're keeping from me that could involve her?"

He threw his hands up in the air. "Nothing. Absolutely nothing. You pretty much know everything I know now. So get out of here before Jeff sees you and tells Carlyle you were here, because I can only trust Jeff when he's in my sight."

I left it at that, because Vince was done talking. And I knew he'd never jeopardize my sister's life.

"One question before I leave."

Vince had his hand on the phone ready to lift the receiver where the lines had been flashing continuously. He shook his head. "Not now. I've got to get Carlyle in my grips first. We'll talk about your job when this whole thing is over."

"I don't care about my job anymore."

Vince was no neophyte to a certain monkish self-control. He would never show the weakness of surprise. Maybe knowing he was no longer the man in my moon or the sun in my sky made Vince a bit sad. But he wouldn't show sorrow either. He simply looked up at me and shook his head. "What do you want? I've got a lot of work here."

"Mike McCoy. Any dirt on him?"

He shrugged. "Other than the dirt that's rubbed off on him from rubbing shoulders with Carlyle?" Then Vince furrowed his brow. "You went from Jeff Kendall to Mike McCoy? You're one of those broads who likes to be abused, huh?"

"My sister's missing, Vince. I've got to know who I can trust."

"If I were you, Meloni, I wouldn't count *him* in."

CHAPTER THIRTY-SEVEN

≈≈≈

Black, White, and Blood

I ARRIVED AT HOLTON by eight-thirty. Elliot was shivering outside Langley as I marched up to the front gates.

"Why didn't you wait in my office?"

"I shouldn't be hanging around your office too much. I'm not supposed to *get you fired*, remember?"

I couldn't argue with him. He was right. But that was the problem with Elliot, he was so often annoyingly right.

"There's some kind of pot party going on in Patterson Park tonight. Sherman will be there."

"I can't really worry about Sherman anymore. My sister's missing. She went to soccer camp out on the Cape and now she's disappeared. Two days. No word."

"Wow. So you think it has something to do with Sherman or Lipton?"

At the foot of the stairs, I stopped and looked at him. "Why would you make that leap?"

"What's the only thing on your mind right now? Do you even care about busting them for drugs anymore?"

No, I thought. Cassie had become my prime concern.

"And," he said, "you're wondering if your sister is dead like the others—"

"Stop it!" I bolted away from him, up the stairs, and lunged at the massive front door.

He followed at my heels. "You think maybe the Holton killer has struck again." He mocked me in a low whispering voice. "Your head is spinning, wondering. Has she been raped? Murdered? Or did someone just pick her up from camp and take her partying for a couple of days to throw you off track? And if it was Sherman and Lipton, their plan is working. You don't care about their drug parties anymore. And what's worse, Miss Melone, is that you're blaming yourself. *You* put your sister in harm's way."

I was too sick to my stomach to admit to him he was right. But damn him. The little dweeb was right.

I got rid of Elliot by agreeing to meet him at six-thirty on a dead-end street that backed up to the woods at Patterson Park. Whether I'd go or not, I hadn't yet decided. Frankly, I was hoping that by then, I would have found Cassie.

I spent the day on the phone with police, the camp counselors, Cassie's address book contacts, and, naturally, the girls, but everything was coming up to that same dead end in the park by the river. Despite my panic that Cassie's disappearance was tied to the Holton murders, as Elliot had perceived, the most likely scenario, I kept telling myself, was that Cassie had simply gotten bored at the camp, gone off for the weekend with a high school friend, and was partying somewhere in the Cape. Meanwhile,

Cassie probably thought she'd gotten away with the innocent subterfuge, and had no idea that she was now officially a missing minor and that her family had already succumbed to the paralysis of grief.

But by six o'clock, there was still no word, so I left Langley and headed for my car. Darkness was in full dress black. Streetlights sputtered on, then off, and my imagination provided the London mist and dense fog that whirled in dizzy spirals around the smoke from a cigarette whose trail I could see from yards away. A silhouetted body was leaning against the hood of my parked Jeep. He was smoking. I stopped walking until he noticed me and stepped out into the streetlight.

"Hey there," Mike said. "Did I scare you?"

I let out the breath I'd been holding. "You smoke?"

"Only when I get involved with women."

"Chain smoker, huh? What are you doing here?"

"Seeing if you're okay. This thing with your sister must be rough for you."

Yes, I thought, rough as hell. If anything happened to Cassie, I would be losing my entire family in one clean sweep. As religious as they were, my parents would still never make it through the ordeal of burying Cassie. An incorporeal God could never replace their living, breathing child.

"We'll get through it."

"Stop playing so tough."

"What are you really doing here, Mike?"

"There's a questionably legal student party going down in the park off Grotto. It's student affairs and within our purview, so you won't get in trouble with Carlyle."

"*Purview.* Big word. You sure you're up to it?"

Muttering, he threw his butt down and smashed it with the heel of his shoe. "This is why I smoke."

"So you and Elliot Orenstein must be reading the same blogs. I'm supposed to meet him there in about twenty minutes."

"I don't swap spit with the students and you shouldn't either. Let's go."

I'd always thought "swapping spit" meant kissing, but I didn't correct him, because for all I knew that's exactly what he'd meant. And I didn't feel like getting into an argument with him over my playing kissy-face with Elliot Orenstein, nor did I think it wise to tell him that I'd let Rod Lipton into my apartment the night before. In fact, I was getting real shy about telling Mike anything anymore.

I followed him wordlessly up the street to his car parked next to a fire hydrant. He went directly to the drivers side and got in, not bothering to open my door for me, and we drove in silence to Patterson Park, where he pulled over to a wooded area overlooking a cliff and the Providence River, and then cut the engine. A few blocks away down the same river, Sherman's apartment was dark.

Mike threw open his door. "Smell that," he said, and jumped out of the car. I got out and we both inhaled. The air was thick with the smell of marijuana. We began our walk through the inky woods. The frozen grass crunched underfoot. For all I knew, Mike was a ruthless murderer and he had lured me into the secluded forest to kill me before I discovered that he had raped and butchered Melinda Hastings, Lisa Cummings, and Emily Barton. He knew enough about my personal life to lure Cassie too. And she would have gone willingly with an ex-cop who worked with me at Holton. As best I could, I chased these thoughts from my conscious mind, but apparently Mike and I were sharing brain waves.

"There aren't too many women who would do this," he said as we walked. "And as far as I can tell lately, I was just a one-night stand for you."

I stopped dead in my tracks. Behind a flock of trees, we saw flickering lights and breathed the blatant smoke of marijuana. "What is that?" I whispered.

"Spoiled Episcopalian offspring on drugs."

I stopped in the stalky weeds. "Don't go any closer. There's no place to hide."

"You don't think I'm afraid of these little punks, do ya?"

Mike surged through the trees and I followed cautiously behind him. He hollered into the air: "Swallow the pot or dump it, kiddies, cause I'm rescinding your drug privileges."

Like a pile of leaves in the wind, the circle of a dozen figures flew into a frenzy of activity and all lights went out. By the time Mike and I were upon them, complete darkness had obscured my vision. I slowed up and stopped. "McCoy?"

"Stay here," he said.

Cautiously I hung back in the trees as Mike left my side and walked into the thicket.

"All right, what's going on here?" I heard him say in the distance. "I want some answers."

I lost sight of him in the darkness and began to inch forward toward the voices, when one of them shouted "Now!" as a rapid succession of several 120-lumen blinding Mag-Lites stunned my reflexes and I clamped my eyes shut in total blindness. Instinctively I raised my arms in front of me to protect myself and then to feel my way ahead. After a few baby steps, I heard a hoarse whisper from behind me.

"Mari. *Marianna*," the voice repeated threateningly.

Right, and then left, and then from behind, my name was repeated in my ear as the breathy voice taunted my blindness. "*Can you feel me?*"

I ran back in the direction from which I thought Mike and I had come, and with each step I took farther back into the swell of trees, my feet caught in dead sticks and low-lying branches as I stumbled through them. A branch slapped my face, stinging it, catching my hair, pulling me back. And then a hard thud into my chest. Sudden-onset blindness makes you stupid. Was it a bullet? Had I run into a tree? Two hands on my chest pushed me down to the ground, onto my back, my unblinking eyes staring into a sky I couldn't see. The same hands flipped me over onto my stomach and pushed my face into the coarse ground, where stones and acorns, prickly leaves and mummified branches embedded themselves into my cheek. Down came a warm breath to my exposed ear. My lips, freezing into the icy ground, had no space to open. I moaned softly, trying to talk. Talk seemed to always be my only salvation.

"Mmmm . . . Mmmmm . . ." The only sound that would emerge from my mouth into the ground.

"I'm going to kill *you* next."

I shook my head under the pressure of the hands still holding my head down, the palm pressed firmly against my head, its fingers weaving into my hair. Then both hands were gone and I heard footsteps crunching away from me.

"Mari? Where the hell are you? Goddamn you. Marianna?"

I spat the dirt from my mouth. "Mike?" I whispered.

"Those little bastards," Mike growled.

Weighing the safety of the move, I considered sitting up. But I was still too scared and instead lay motionless on the ground.

Mike's voice again, inches from me, as he still hollered into the woods: "I'll find every last one of you—"

And then there was a hard thump . . . a gasp and a groan . . . and all was quiet again. Like a wounded animal in a herd of slaughtered deer, Mike fell heavily beside me—another trophy whose head would be mounted on a hunter's wall next to mine. I played dead right along with him and remained curled on the ground like an earthworm, waiting paralyzed, until my sight slowly returned and I recognized the outline of a fallen branch in front of me. The blessed night sky had reappeared, and with it my other senses came back to life in the smell of burnt wood and ashes.

"Mike?" I whispered.

"Shh," he whispered back. "Don't move yet."

"I'm blinded."

"High-intensity flashlights. Temporarily blind you. One of them knocked me down and side-kicked me in the gut. You alright?"

I felt his movements next to me. His shoulder against mine turning around and then his hands on my face, pushing hair out of my eyes.

"Are they gone?" I asked.

"I think so. Get up."

He stood on wobbly feet and pulled a pocket light from his coat.

"Why didn't you use that before?" I said.

"They caught me by surprise. I'm a little blind myself." He turned the flashlight on me and then on himself. Mike's jacket was covered in blood.

"You're bleeding."

He looked down at his chest. "I'm okay. Get up," he said.

"But you're covered in blood."

"Come on! Let's go."

I sat upright and felt a dampness on my cheek that my curious hands followed around the side of my head and into my hair. Sticky. My face and the back of my head were wet with blood too.

Mike knelt down and pulled me up by the arms. "Now. Run!"

I bolted up and ran again. This time with sight, I was able to find a connecting path and finally the clearing a few yards ahead of me. From behind me I heard Mike's heavy thudding steps run toward me and then stop. I continued running to the clearing where I saw his red steed still parked at the curb. I stopped, negotiating my next move. Should I run to the car or wait for Mike? Before I could move, I heard a woman's scream, loud and ear shattering. And then frantic panting as the voice came closer—hysterical—still the woman's voice.

"*Huh! Huh! Huh! Help meee . . .*"

I should have run, but something in me, my curiosity unhurt and still intact, rooted me in place. The plaintive voice was begging for help. A woman's voice pleading for help—I couldn't resist.

"*Ahhhh. Nooooo! Help meeee . . .*"

There, from the same clearing I had just exited, stumbled a woman about five eight, thin and dark. She raised her arms in front of her like a ghost in a fairy tale, sleepwalking through the darkness. She stumbled a few more steps and fell to her knees. I crept closer, and out to me she held her bleeding wrists from which one hand dangled.

Mike, his hands and chest covered in blood, lumbered out of the woods after her. I looked up at him in horror. His eyes were wild.

"You did this," I said.

"Are you fucking crazy?" he growled.

I looked down at the girl who had fallen at my feet. "It's Mila Nazir with her wrists slit open, you sick bastard!"

"Shut up, Marianna. I dropped my cell phone. Do you have one on you?"

I stood away from Mila's body and backed into the street, feeling in my pocket for my cell. "I'm calling the police," I said.

"Pithy idea," he answered. "Why didn't you think of it sooner?"

I ran farther into the street and dialed 911. I then dialed the Providence police thinking I could get help sooner by dialing direct.

O'Rourke answered. "Bernie's Meat Market. What's your beef?"

"O'Rourke, it's Mari Melone. Is that how you answer a police line?"

"Hey, this is a private line. Not for public emergencies. What's the problem?"

"Get an ambulance and some black-and-whites to Fox Point woods over by Patterson Park. A girl's been hurt. Maybe dead."

I flipped my phone closed. Mike was kneeling at Mila's body.

"Who recognized you in there? I heard someone call your name." Mike looked up at me.

Silent and stubborn, I remained on the street side of Mike's car, waiting for help. Within minutes, several uniforms emerged from three cars as the ambulance pulled up behind. One cop walked by me and went directly to Mike. Safe now in the growing crowd, I crept closer to Mike to hear his explanation for this evening's horrific events—and the blood that covered him.

He knelt back from Mila's body. "I tried to stop the bleeding," he explained. Makeshift tourniquets fashioned from Mike's leather belt were tied around Mila's wrists. "But she's gone. Nothing I could do."

The cop nodded as the ambulance techs did a pulse check.

"You had blood all over you before that, Mike," I said. "Tell them." I nodded toward the cops, then spoke directly to them. "He came out of the woods covered in blood. *After* Mila."

"Jesus, Marianna, you have blood on you too," Mike shot back. "Maybe you cut this girl up."

"You put the blood on me when you touched my face and hair with your bloody hands."

Mike stood and shook his head. "Some guy knocked me around in there. It must be blood transfer. This is crazy. I'm getting cleaned up."

"There's alcohol in the truck," a cop announced. "Come with me while we wait for the ME's office to get here."

"What?" I screeched. "That blood on him is evidence. You can't just wipe it away."

The cop walked up to me and stuck his nose in my face. "Hey, the blood is going to be this dead girl's. And it's on both of you, so any which way you slice it, if he killed her or not, finding her blood on him isn't going to prove anything. Like Mikey said, you're almost as bloody as he is."

My panting was subsiding and cold sweat was dripping down my back. I felt as if I were coming down from a drug-induced high, the ringing in my ears quieting. I had been alone in the woods with a cold-blooded killer. But thinking it could be Mike had begun to seem absurd. Good old *Mikey* could never inflict the injuries I'd seen. Like his excuse for being with the red-headed student, this explanation of his blood-soaked clothes was tidy and clean. And simply inarguable.

Another officer put his hand on my elbow. "Come on, let one of the cars drive you to the station, where we can get a statement. Mike's going to have to come too."

I zeroed in on Mike's indigo eyes, their color even deeper in the darkness, before I turned away and got into the assigned police car while Mike strutted off to his.

Mike and I had been temporarily separated in the woods so our stories wove in and out on minor details, but on the main events our narratives meshed and overlapped like two cars zigzagging to the same goal line. Neither one of us was a suspect because our motives were wholly lacking and the MO of Mila's murder was obviously similar to Hastings's, Cummings's, and Emily Barton's. It was deduced that the Holton killer had struck again, and the frequency of his attacks was escalating.

It was midnight when I reluctantly agreed to let Mike drive me back to my Jeep. There was an eerie silence between us during the ride, and when I opened the door of his car to leave, he sullenly watched and waited while I got into my car and pulled away. On my drive home I worked to understand Mike's and my inability to find words between us during our ride together from the station. Maybe it was nothing more than the physical and emotional exhaustion of the evening; my fear combined with his guilt for dragging us into danger. But my sleepless imagination worried that his silence was anger at me for accusing him of murder. As much as Mike and I had been through together—the silly bantering fights, the provocative repartee, even the lovemaking—we still didn't trust each other, and the chance of our reaching that place seemed to be moving farther away from us.

Despite numbing fatigue, I wasn't sleepy, and I was sure my parents were wide awake too, waiting for any word from me about their missing daughter. But I had no words of comfort and I didn't want to face them, so instead of going home to bed, I headed my Jeep to downtown Providence.

CHAPTER THIRTY-EIGHT

⸺⸺

Sunday School

SEVEN DAYS A WEEK, every two hours throughout the day and night, bells rang through downtown Providence, calling people to the doors of St. Francis Chapel on Weybosset Street, where services were held for anyone who needed them, regardless of denomination, faith, or the lack thereof. A short sidewalk away from speeding cars and high-rise buildings, homeless people sometimes set up camp outside with their newspaper tents and shopping-cart trailers. I felt welcomed even as a nonbeliever there. St. Francis was so unlike the ornate and heavily incensed Roman Catholic church my parents attended every Sunday near our house on Federal Hill, where a cultish blind faith was required for admission.

The monks who lived in the attached church house prayed or meditated between services and were always available for anyone in need of soul-searching, confessions, or a 911 call for an ambulance to the nearest emergency room. The Franciscan monks, who floated over the stained marble floors in full-length robes the color of mud, were as much a part of the church as the candles that burned continuously, the smell of the city streets, the damp, and the darkness. They performed an arcane ritual of slow rounds beginning at the altar, moving on to the candles, then to the back of the church, and returning to the altar to pray.

I'm not sure how I first found the place. My cloudy memory suggests that one night after a big-case-win celebratory dinner and too much wine (without the girls), I stumbled in from the Pot Au Feu restaurant around the corner. I was a responsible drunk. Knowing when I was too sloshed to see straight, I never got behind the wheel of a car.

The first time I'd wandered into the cathedral, I'd collapsed in a back pew near the door, ready for instant escape. The altar in front had seemed miles away from the entrance, so far, in fact, that I felt removed in the back, afraid that if I'd sat any closer—some pew in the middle for instance—I would be crossing the line from being a mere spectator to a needy participant. But after a while the soft chanting of the monks at the altar became music. Row by row I moved forward until I reached the front of the cathedral and eventually fell asleep in a front pew—or more likely passed out—until I heard the soft voice of one of the monks shaking me awake.

"Sister, sister? Although God welcomes you to his house, you are not allowed by city ordinance to sleep in this church. Sister? You must either sit up and pray, or sleep outside."

I opened my eyes to a hooded face with soft brown eyes.

"Too much to drink. Can't drive yet," I said.

"No need to explain. Even I have taken more than my share of wine. Stay until you're ready." He spoke to me awhile as I sobered up. He explained to me that the monks were the collective ear and voice of God, each one a stream, and together, the ocean. But I knew that before the church, each monk had been a boy in another life, and that they had probably begun life like me, with two parents, siblings, and a toy box, and that ultimately they had reached the same road I did with dashed beliefs in Santa Claus and the Tooth Fairy. But for some reason, these men retained a belief in God, a concept that to me was as preposterous as the Easter Bunny. I relegated religion to the likes of mah-jongg and bingo—it was for other people, those who had too much time on their hands, didn't like being alone, or old people afraid of dying. I, like Dr. Gannon at the morgue, held on to science as the explanation of life and death.

The night Mila was killed I drove to St. Francis Chapel. It had been years since I'd been back. I walked through the heavily paneled doors and immediately filled my lungs with the smell of frankincense and wax, a smell that spirited me back to my childhood when my parents still had the power to force me to attend Sunday services with them.

This time I walked directly to the front of the church and knelt before the altar. One of the brothers was kneeling there too, saying nothing, in that odd way they had of speaking to God in silence. I too spoke without voice, moving only my lips, as if without some show of effort, I wouldn't be heard. "Please, God," I prayed, "give me Cassie back safely. I'm sorry for my selfishness, my self-righteous crap, my lack of convictions, my constant questioning, my absence of gratitude. I'm sorry for my excuses and finger-pointing." At this point I started to cry, I think. My hands sparkled with tears though I hadn't felt them fall. "Please, God, give us Cassie back, if not for me, then for my parents, who, unlike me, have never doubted you, have always taken full responsibility for their actions, have never overestimated their importance, and have never been arrogant with the life they were given. Please, God, give us Cassie back."

When I felt the hand on my head, I turned to see that the brother who had been praying beside me had stood and was facing me. "I'll pray for all of you," he said.

CHAPTER THIRTY-NINE

Without Passport

I MAY NOT HAVE been ready for ordainment the next morning, but, as if anointed and discipled by the Holy Ghost, I spirited straight to Carlyle's office, bounding through his closed door as his secretary, the pigeon lady, squawked.

"Mila Nazir is dead," I said by way of introduction to Carlyle, who was standing behind his desk staring into space like an Alzheimer's victim. He turned his head slowly toward me, knowing something was wrong with my abrupt entrance, but not sure what.

"I'm sorry, sir," Joan said before closing the door again behind her.

"Marianna."

"She's dead, Ken. Emily Barton and now Mila Nazir were murdered like the others. Four Holton students are dead, so stop pretending this school isn't involved."

Ken tapped his desk with the fingers of his right hand. "Marianna, let's be sensible. We can still keep this under control."

He watched me, gauging my reaction, wondering in those split seconds how far he could let me in. Was my definition of "sensible" the same as his?

He gambled on my poker face and lifted a newspaper from his desk. "A friend of mine at the *Journal* sent me this copy. The article will be in the evening edition unless we give them some contradictory information more favorable to Holton. Are you with me here or not?"

I walked to him (because he would never come to me) and took the paper from his hand.

The Providence Journal Bulletin
More Holton Students Found Dead

> *The mutilated body of a Holton coed, who allegedly was asked to take a leave of absence from the school because of sexual harassment by another student, was found two nights ago in Fox Point. An unnamed source from the Holton administration has identified the body as that of Emily Barton. The same source has provided information that Miss Barton was poised to name and bring charges against her alleged harasser, another Holton student. No charges have been filed in connection with Miss Barton's death.*
>
> *In addition, a fourth Holton murder was reported, again in the Patterson Park area. Mila Nazir exited the area of the woods at about 7 p.m. last night and was pronounced dead shortly thereafter.*
>
> *A fifth young woman is missing in connection with this spate of incidents. Cassie Melone, the sister of a Holton administrator, was reported*

missing from a Cape Cod soccer camp on Friday.
Police from Massachusetts and Rhode Island are
continuing their search for her.

I looked up at Carlyle. "Who wrote this?"

"Is this true? About your sister?"

"She's missing, yes."

"The police have been calling me all morning trying
to determine where the *Journal* got this information."

"Cassie was with Sherman and Lipton before she
went away. They got her drunk to punish me. She went
off to camp the next day and we haven't heard from her
since."

"You will not go near Sherman, or any of the students,
until we have more proof." Ken swiped his fingers over
his mouth in a nervous gesture. His hands were shaking.

"Proof of what? I only want to ask him questions. Just
talk to him. I need to find my sister. The police will go
even if I don't."

"The police know nothing of this drinking incident or that she even knows those two students. Leave
Sherman alone. If you so much as go near that apartment
again, I will have to have you forcibly removed from the
campus."

My head was processing information at megahertz
speed. Had Cory Sherman told Carlyle that I'd gone to
his apartment? He'd gone to complain about me, and
Carlyle was actually taking his side. Or was the informant
Jeff Kendall again?

"Does Jeff Kendall report directly to you, Ken? Or is
it Mike McCoy? You know all about the drugs and Mila
Nazir, don't you?"

If he'd heard me, and simply wasn't answering, I had

no way of knowing. His eyes were a million miles away, looking off to a potted plant that sentried his doorway and was in dire need of water. It would be dead within a week and Carlyle would never deign to water it.

Sometimes naiveté escapes suddenly like a butterfly that you thought you held firmly by its delicate wings. Very late one night at the Fez, Beth—the Newport debutante, lifelong Dunes Club member, *Mayflower* descendant—told Laurie, Shannon, and me, after several pitchers of beer and a Patriots' loss, about her coming-out party on her sixteenth birthday, when an uninvited guest showed up who turned out to be the daughter her mother had given birth to months before she married Beth's father. Beth's butterfly flew away on her sixteenth birthday—and returned as her illegitimate half-sister.

My realization that Dean Kenneth Oberlin Carlyle had the moral fiber of a garden-variety street thug was nothing even remotely akin to Beth's sweet-sixteen discovery of another sibling, but it was pretty damn close. My butterfly was fluttering desperately up there on Carlyle's twelve-foot ceiling. So I quickly grounded myself and began ringing the bells that were going off in my brain in rapid succession as questions paired with answers in luminous harmony.

With dire, heavily loaded words, I shattered the glassy symphony. "I do not intend to find my sister *slaughtered* like a fucking cow so your little drug enterprise can continue unimpeded. This mayhem stops now."

Carlyle turned white as a sheet. "Don't be absurd. These murders have nothing to do with Sherman or his petty drug use. You must believe me and drop that angle completely. I cannot have him and this entire college dragged through the mire over your sister's disappearance. It's a coincidence for which there must be another explanation."

"Why do you continue to protect him? For donations? Another wing on the library?"

"Please, Marianna, please. You have no idea what you're doing. It has taken decades for Holton's reputation to mature from a small men's college to a distinguished center of secondary education in a very competitive market. But Holton is not Harvard yet. We can't survive this kind of negative publicity. I've given my life for this school. . . . Even if you hate me, let's save Holton. You're a part of our family now."

I almost felt sorry for him. Sorry that all around him Ken was so drowning in trouble that he had sunk to the level of polishing *me* up with fatuous concepts of our close-knit little Holton brood—drivel that probably made him sick to his stomach. He no more believed I could be part of Holton's family than he believed in affirmative action.

I placed the newspaper back on Carlyle's wraparound desk. It was clean and uncluttered and paperless, so unlike the way one would expect a professor's desk to look. But then Ken Carlyle wasn't a real professor. He didn't teach and grade exams and write on blackboards or use laser pointers on projected images. He had been elevated to an administrative position—he no longer got closer to the students than their data sheets, or "rap sheets" as Rita called them. His main function was fund-raising, damage control, and more fund-raising.

"Just tell me why you hired me, Ken. What the hell were you thinking by bringing me in?"

"Why aren't you angry at Piganno? He fired you without an ounce of mercy, yet you stay loyal to him. I thought . . . I thought you could keep things under control here. I assumed the Melinda Hastings murder would eventually lose its steam. An isolated incident, I thought. Catastrophic publicity, yes, but you . . . I thought you could temper the waters until it passed. Yes, you were a cheap publicity stunt. I admit it. But your loyalty is still to him, not me, not this school."

"What you see isn't loyalty to Vince Piganno or disloyalty to Holton. It's an innate sense of morality that I can't shake. I'm not like you, Ken. And I never will be."

As I walked away from him and out his door for the last time, he made his final appeal. "Marianna, please stay away from Cory Sherman. His father will sue the school if we make any unfounded allegations against him. And against a *civil* suit, we have no—"

"Connections," I finished the sentence for him. "If I were you I wouldn't be worrying about civil suits. I'd call a criminal lawyer. And fast."

I WALKED BACK to my office for the last time, pondering its absence of heartwarming snapshots, bouncing dog heads, or personalized leather desk sets. If I never set foot at Holton again, there was nothing to pack up and send me. I had never really moved in.

From nervous energy, I scrolled through my online Rolodex for numbers I might want to take along with me. But when I picked up my phone, I dialed a number never stored in my Holton database—a number I'd committed to heart and memory years ago.

When Beth got on the line her voice was like a songbird waking me up on a new spring day. It was a soothing voice I hadn't missed until I heard it again.

"Marianna? Are you all right? They won't let me leave here. I want to see you."

My voice answered weak and tremulous. "Cassie is missing from camp. I had a horrible fight with her before she left. My parents will literally die if anything's happened to her. I'm stuck with this one, Beth. I'm really scared and I don't know what to do."

"You don't sound right," she said.

"I'm sick. My parents are sick. They're depending on me to bring their baby home, and I should be able to figure this out, but I can't."

Beth was silent for a minute, but she remained on the line with me. I didn't know why I'd called her. Maybe because I was confused. Too much had happened too fast. Carlyle was wrong, there are no coincidences. Somewhere in this mess was the answer to Cassie's whereabouts, but the connections were blocked; I couldn't get the clues in the right order. I called Beth because she was methodical in everything she did. Her mind worked that way, from step one to step two. And she was clearheaded, never letting emotions cloud her thinking. Beth had a talent for serving things straight up and unadulterated. She would take a million puzzle pieces and arrange them on a table—colors with like colors, shapes she instinctively knew belonged together—predicting the completed picture without ever having seen it. Where I would race into it headlong, stumbling through a trial-and-error process guided only by gut feelings, Beth could reshuffle my pieces into a different order—the right order—and make sense, because she always stood back, looking at the apparent clutter from a cool distance. Like knowing the ingredients of a recipe she'd never tasted, I was hoping she could sip slowly now for the first time and identify the flavor I was failing to discern.

"Mari?" she said softly.

"Yes, Beth."

"Has Cassie ever been to Holton? It sounds as if it's become personal now. Could it be that the Holton murderer is coming after you—by taking Cassie?"

I felt like throwing up. Rita knocked on my door. "Miss Melone, that reporter, Elliot Orenstein, is on the phone for you."

"Tell him I can't talk to him right now."

"I love you," I said to Beth. "I've got to go." And I hung up.

On my way past her desk, I thanked Rita, knowing that when I left the office that day, I would probably never see her again, and I walked out of the front doors of Langley for the last time.

CHAPTER FORTY

Keeping Your Head on Straight

CARLYLE BEGAN CALLING MY cell phone at regular intervals as I triumphantly disobeyed him and drove directly to the Riverside Park Apartments and buzzed Sherman's apartment. The voice over the intercom asked who it was.

"Is Cassie Melone up there with you?" I said.

"Who is this?" he asked again.

"Do you have Cassie?"

Whoever it was hung up on me. I buzzed all the others to no avail, then waited patiently on a stone bench outside for another tenant to come home and open the front door. It always worked. It was just a matter of how long it would take. While I waited, my phone rang again with a number I didn't recognize.

"Hello?" I said. "Hello?"

Silence.

"It's me, Rod Lipton."

"Let me up. We need to talk."

No answer.

"Lipton, where is she? Help me here or I'm going straight to the cops."

"With what?"

"I recognized you both at that little pot party last night in the park," I lied. "Who sliced up Mila? You or your roommate?"

"I'm not in the apartment. Meet me. We'll go to the police together. You bring what you have and I'll fill in the blanks."

I still didn't believe a word he said. Except that he was scared. He had been scared the night he came to my apartment. I could see fear and I could hear it. And I was just as scared as he was.

"We aren't going to the police. First you tell me where Cassie is."

"Look, Carlyle doesn't want us talking to you. This has to be private."

"He told you that? Not to talk to me?"

"He told both of us not to talk to you. Cory and me. But that's what I'm going to tell you. Carlyle and Cory and Mila. I'm not involved in it. Can you meet me?"

Now he was making some sense, maybe even telling the truth this time, except of course for his involvement with Sherman's little candy store. If you live with wolves you either join the pack or get eaten. And once you've lain with them, you sense their desperation when afraid; you know their danger and appreciate their ability to turn their hunger on you when the prey gets scarce. Maybe Rod was hungry for protection. "Okay, Rod. Where do you want to meet?"

"Patterson Park. Down by the river."

"You're crazy or you think *I* am. Everyone who goes

into that park comes out dead. I'll meet you in a public place or nowhere."

I thought I heard him mumble "cocksucker," but I couldn't be sure.

"What's your answer, Rod?"

"Down by the river is the only secluded place in Providence. I can't let Cory—or Carlyle—see me with you."

"Calm down. Carlyle isn't going to send a hit man after you. Pull yourself together and meet me at Tortilla Flats. That's safe enough."

He hung up on me. I took that as a no, so I flipped the phone closed and threw it into my bag, looking up as Cory Sherman exited his building and strutted to the street. It was Cory who'd answered his intercom but he was so cocksure of himself he didn't even look around for me when he left the building.

"Sherman, wait up." I began walking toward him.

Without looking up, he did a sudden about-face and began walking toward me. Like two gunfighters in a duel to the death, we approached each other swiftly. I intended to walk right up to his snotty little nose and wipe it for him with the back of my hand, but when he finally raised his steely eyes to mine, they were as intransigent as the muzzle of a loaded gun, and I stopped dead.

"Lady, you are in big trouble. Add stalking to your list of offenses. My old man's got his lawyer working on it now."

"Where is my sister?"

He shook his head and laughed at me, then turned and walked away as I continued to scream.

"Where's my sister? Where's Cassie?"

Sherman turned around to me but continued walking

backwards to his car while he bared his teeth and held an imaginary knife at his wrist, miming a sawing motion so realistic I could almost hear metal against bone.

I ran at him screaming, but he kept laughing at me as I got nearer, then he turned and ran to a silver Porsche parked in the street and peeled away. I dialed the police and got O'Rourke again. "Send a car to Riverside Park Apartments and get into Cory Sherman's place. He might have my sister there."

"Do we have a warrant?"

"O'Rourke, just knock on the door for now. If you can't get in, call Shannon or Laurie at the AG's. They'll get the warrant for you. Please, do it now!"

"Sure thing, Miss Melone."

Good old O'Rourke. To each other, cops were brethren. Prosecutors were awarded the status of poor second cousins, because we were still lawyers after all, but I could torture O'Rourke to within an inch of his pathetic life and he still always came through when I needed him.

Desperate for a better plan, I drove to Patterson Park hoping Rod would show up there. I had nowhere else to go except home to face grieving parents who, though they hadn't yet admitted it to each other, were probably already making funeral arrangements in the privacy of their own minds. I sat in the car by the river where Emily had first been raped, Mila had fallen dead, and Emily's mutilated body had been found. My phone rang again.

"I'm here, Rod," I said without saying hello.

"Miss Melone? It's Elliot. Is everything all right? I called your office, but no one knows where you are."

"Elliot, did you plant that *Journal* story about Cassie?"

"Of course. It was a shot in the dark to stir things up. Did it work? Have you heard from anyone?"

"I think he has her."

"Sherman? If he's hurt your sister—"

"Stop it, Elliot! Don't even *suggest* that."

Elliot's cold intellectual forecast of probable events was like a stab to my chest. His inference that Cassie could be the next victim, and mutilated like the others, was a logical progression of events, but one I had refused to verbally acknowledge. It seemed heartless for him to give it breath in my presence.

"What are you going to do now?" he asked.

"Where can I reach you, Elliot? Your cell?"

"Yeah, but hear the beeps? It's losing juice fast. I haven't charged it in a couple of days."

"Call me back, then. Call me every half hour. I'm scared. Lipton wants to meet me at a secluded area in Patterson Park. He says he knows where Cassie is. I don't believe the little rat, but he knows more than he's saying."

"Have you told the police?"

"They're getting a warrant for the Sherman/Lipton lair even as we speak. And Carlyle knows what I suspect. Whoever the killer is, he's run out of options. He's at the end, Elliot. I can feel it. It's almost over."

Elliot heard the call-waiting beep on my phone. "Who's calling you? Is that Rod?"

"I don't know. I've got to go." I hit the send button on my cell.

"Mari. It's me. Laurie. Listen to this. Emily Barton was drugged with homemade GHB this time. Same as in the first two murders and different from the first time she was tested in the hospital after the rape. Heinz Distilled White, and this time she ended up dead."

"Nazir too?"

"Nah, she didn't get the benefit of drugs. He just

lopped at her wrists for a quick kill. She had a gash to her carotid too. Poor girl had it the worst."

"Laur, my phone's beeping again. Keep in touch."

I hung up and Rod was on the line.

"Where are you?" I said.

"Drive down into Patterson Park by the dirt road to the river. There's a picnic area with tables. I'm here waiting. Get here, now, if you want to see your sister again."

"You little fuck! Where is she!"

"Get here." He hung up on me. I hit received calls and then the send button to the last call, but of course there was no answer. He knew I would meet him now if there was even the slimmest chance he knew anything about Cassie.

I took the dirt road turnoff toward a picnic area by the water, behind overgrown pines and weed bushes. Directly beyond the long wooden tables, down a deep slope, was the water's edge. I drove down the ravine as far as I could before braking and then cutting the engine to the quiet of the lapping shoreline.

At another time, the scene would have been soothing, a step into a romantic past, the cold ground thawing, an early spring picnic by the lake. But Rod Lipton sullied the dream as he sat on one of the tables with a canned beer in his fist, his muddy sneakers on the bench. Directly over his head a mammoth weeping willow tree was sprouting tiny lime green shoots.

One can was missing from a six-pack sitting on the seat beside his feet. He was bending down for a second beer as I approached. He snapped the flip-top open for me and placed the can on the table. Without looking at me said, "Join me for a beer?"

"I have a gun in my bag. Start talking. I'll give you one minute before I start shooting. Where is my sister?"

Rod and I both jumped when my cell phone rang. He looked at me. I looked at my phone. It was Mike. Keeping a peripheral view of Rod, I turned partially away to take the call privately.

"Where the hell are you?" Mike growled. "Ken called me. He said you're stalking Sherman and I'm supposed to stop you. But we both know if I tell you not to do something, you'll do it *twice* just for spite."

"Three times, *babe*, maybe four." Mike always seemed to challenge me like I was some silly girl who needed looking after. He had a tendency to talk to me the way I talked to Cassie—like a parent. And like Cassie, I acted like a headstrong child and lashed out at him in a blind white heat—while taking my eyes off Rod. "Go to hell! I'm with Rod Lipton down by the river and—"

Rod's cold, clammy fingers ripped the phone from my hand. His hair, usually slicked back and clean, was overdue for a wash. Greasy clumps hung over his forehead as he stared down at my phone in his hand.

"Who keeps calling you?" He looked up at me. His eyes crinkled like they were staring into direct sun. "Who were you talking to?"

"You're stoned again," I said. "What's going on? Just lay it out for me and I'll help you get through it."

His jaws ground together. "What's going on? The whole fucking world is falling apart," he shouted. "I'm hanging out with Cory Sherman, that's what's the matter. And I'm going to fall flat on my face in his shit while Cory gets fished out of the sewer by his father and his uncle. They'll swoop down in the family jet to hoist him up. And on his way up and out, Cory's not going to be thinking about saving my ass."

"Rod, listen to me. I no longer care about Carlyle, or Cory, or drugs, or even the murders for that matter. I just want my sister."

I walked closer to him, slowly, calmly, barely breathing. He was an ignited bomb ready to explode at the slightest tremor. His hands still held my phone in a death grip.

"Did you tell anyone else you were coming here?" he asked.

"Of course I did."

"You told McCoy, didn't you?"

"Yes," I said. "And the Feds are on to your little drug enterprise with Sherman. Now tell me about Cassie so we can both get away from this in one piece and let Sherman take the hit."

"You bitch." He hurled my phone in to the bushes. "You think I'm a moron, don't you? Cory's not going to make me take the rap for murder. I don't give a shit who his father is. I had some fun with Emily and some of the others, but I didn't kill her, or Lisa or Melinda."

I heard his teeth grinding into each other. Rod's eyes were turning burnished silver again, glossing over.

"Some of these girls . . . they love being abused," he said. "It's their pathetic attempt to punish their overindulgent parents. Every time they spread their legs they're daring their old men to look between them. These fucking sex parties of Cory's. Who do you think gets the most thrill out of them? Not Cory. He can have any piece of ass he wants anytime. The girls love it, because they love being dirty. In their minds they're fucking their rich fathers."

"Emily said she was raped in the park, not at your parties."

He laughed. "Which time? She was so drugged, she doesn't remember shit anyway. She probably walked out confused and then passed out in the park on her way home." His head snapped to the sound of my phone ringing from where it rested in the bushes. "Who's calling you?"

"I don't know." I was getting tired of chatting with him. His time was up. I took a chance and moved toward the high weeds. "If you don't know anything about my sister, I'm done with you. I'm going for my phone."

He pulled my hair from behind and dragged me down to the ground. I twisted around trying to face him, thinking I needed to look him in the eyes as he killed me. Thinking maybe I could stop him with my eyes.

He looked at me and seemed to hiccup, like a child's strangled spasm of tears. "Cory got the roofies but he never needed to use them. I told you. Girls screw Cory for nothing. He didn't have to drug them. He's fucking famous. But me? I got the leftovers."

I lay on the ground, completely drenched in sweat, while my body shivered. "It was all you, wasn't it? It was never Cory with any of the girls because he didn't need to use drugs to have sex with them. You needed the GHB. You drugged them first and then raped them. And it wasn't just Emily."

He rubbed his eyes like a child waking from sleep. "I'm so scared. I haven't slept in days," he said. "I didn't kill anyone."

I believed him. Or at least I believed he *thought* he hadn't killed anyone. When a mind is askew with drugs and fear, memories are deceitful counselors, like vivid dreams you awake from convinced they were real.

"These *roofies* you got from Cory. They were pills, like from a pharmacy?"

"Yeah, pills. Cory must have done it," he said again.

"Why would Cory kill Emily? Or the others? Why?"

"He's afraid because of the drugs. His cover getting blown. Lisa, Melinda, and Mila were loose cannons. And they loved their coke. Ask McCoy. He was always around picking up the pieces."

"Pieces of what?"

"Ass. I don't know! He knows more about Cory than I do." He studied the ground as if he were trying to count the blades of grass or find something hidden there. "It was Cory doing it all. It must have been, but I swear I didn't know that part."

"Maybe it was you trying to cover things up. Because you're right about one thing. Cory's father will save him. And McCoy will probably vouch for him too. You, on the other hand, will take all the heat. So you tried to cover up the loose ends by killing the witnesses to the drugs—especially the GHB you were using on the girls to rape them. Am I right, Rod?"

Rod clamped his eyes shut and then brought his hands up to cover his face, cloaking himself from the violence that seemed to be splitting his conscience open. He was breathing heavily, his hands still covering his face, and while he struggled with what I assumed was an imminent admission of guilt, I jumped away from him and ran to the woods to get my phone.

I heard his feet crunching on the leaves behind me. Within seconds he was at my heels, his vinegary breath washing over the back of my neck like dirty steam from a city subway grate.

"I didn't kill anyone!" he said, yanking me back by my shoulder. Like shards of glass, pain shot through my chest and arm as he pulled on me. I dug my heels into the ground fighting against his pull, but he kicked me from behind and my legs buckled at the knee. I was back on the ground, kneeling, my head bent forward from the pain. He rushed in front of me and fell to his knees, and shoving his face into mine, he gripped my chin with an icy hand and dug his fingers into my skin. "What did you do? Tell people I killed Emily just because I fucked her?"

I fought against his pull, afraid to look the devil in the eyes and let Rod's thoughts corrupt mine. Killing is no simple thing. It is screaming. It's a struggle. It is the protruding bloodshot eyes of a strangled victim. It is pain. It is blood. But with each successive kill, the act becomes commonplace, and as necessary to the killer as eating or sleep. I had to stay calm long enough to figure out how to get away from Rod before he made his decision to kill me.

His forehead was covered in sweat and his eyes were wide with panic, filling with tears. He let go of my face. "No," he whined. "You got it all wrong. Maybe it was Cory. Maybe you're right. I didn't think so, but if you're sure the killings had something to do with the drugs then maybe you're right, it was Cory, because I didn't do it. I swear. I swear it wasn't me."

I felt my body relaxing at the lament of his pleas. His face was a mask of terror at the realization that I was so logically accusing him of the murder of fellow students. He pushed his face into mine again, inches from mine, beer on his breath. "Listen to me," he said. "Cory and Mila were bringing the drugs in and selling them from campus. Carlyle found out, and instead of expelling them he gave them a half-ass warning. Carlyle only cares about the money. You should know that by now if you're working for him."

"Carlyle allowed the drug dealing? Absurd. You're a goddamn liar," I said.

Stunned at my reply, he grabbed for me as I bolted up and tried to run to my car. This time he pushed me forward to the ground and then flipped me over like a rag doll. Facing me, his hands tightened around my neck, his teeth clenched in struggle, I choked until my eyes began to bulge.

Unable to avert my eyes, I looked deep into his, trying to understand what he was thinking, or if he was thinking at all. They had emptied of their fear and their hate. They were empty of anything I recognized as emotion. What I saw in Rod's eyes was merely the effort of a difficult act. The calling forth of the strength needed to break the bones of my neck and crush the air out of me. He was lost in a stupor of brute strength. And when he was finished, exhausted, he would pant for air and look down at the inert body at his feet—my lifeless body, as the girls would see it, crumpled in a heap on the ground.

As Rod tightened his hold on my neck, I lifted my hand, weak and shaking, and reached for his sweating forehead to stroke it with a soothing grace and try to awaken him from this horrid nightmare we were sharing—when behind him, just over his head, Elliot appeared, holding a seven-inch hunting knife high in the air.

CHAPTER FORTY-ONE

Wet Dreams

ROD LET GO OF my neck and turned toward Elliot, whose face was masked in resolute calm. His eyelids were heavy and half closed, as if he might fall asleep at any second. My throat was throbbing in pain. When I tried to talk, my voice was stuck and strangled, so I watched wordlessly and without protest as Elliot slammed the point of the knife into Rod's neck, pushing it in with such force that Rod's whole body bent backward, his gaping mouth gurgling blood, trying to scream. Backwards Rod fell, but Elliot still wouldn't let up. He pushed the knife harder until Rod buckled over on his back into the grass, and still Elliot forced the knife deeper through Rod's throat until the blade and Rod's neck became impaled in the ground. Elliot finally released his hand from the knife and sat back on his haunches, and thus relaxed, with his head tilted, he surveyed his achievement: Rod's neck nailed to the ground by the embedded knife. Like a fountain from his carotid artery, the blood from Rod's neck was spouting in a heavy flow down toward the river.

I leaned over to Rod's body and felt for a wrist pulse, one . . . two . . . and then nothing. I stared at Rod but spoke to Elliot.

"Why did you do that? The two of us could have subdued him. I have a gun and you had a knife."

Elliot stood and looked up into the heavens, not quite asking for forgiveness, but supplicant, perhaps sorry at this turn of events? Rod's eyes were still open, staring up into the sky as well, but he was beyond questions. The trees were making a clean rustling sound in the breeze. Rod was dead. Elliot was eerily silent. Only the branches and an occasional bird disturbed the lull. I needed to hear some sane words. Any pre-Holton voice would do. I craved a voice from a time before Melinda Hastings's body flew through the air in front of me, causing this whirlwind of events that was ending with five dead Holton students and my baby sister missing and possibly dead.

The girls. I needed to call my friends.

"I'm going to find my phone. Rod threw it up there in the trees. We've got to call an ambulance. I've got to get the phone and call for help."

"He's dead," Elliot said softly. "No point. I *told* you to be careful, Miss Melone. Sherman and Lipton are stupid, ugly-minded people."

Elliot marched purposefully back to the picnic table and found my bag on the ground. He had a plan, so I watched and waited. He was the outsider with no emotional stake in any of this. Maybe he had some clear-headed, rational idea of what to do next and how to find Cassie.

I watched him and waited, still trusting his superior

intellect and assuming that he knew better what to do next.

"Can you get into Sherman's place?" he asked while he fished through my bag. "Will the guards let you in?"

"Those apartments are private property. Not part of the campus. Why?"

"Let's go. We'll find a way to get in."

Was he so naive to think we could just leave Rod lying dead on the ground with a knife in this throat? Was it only because of my legal background that I knew, self-defense or not, the police had to be called? I could keep overzealous Elliot out of trouble by attesting to the fact that he killed Rod to save my life, even though, in concert, we might have stopped Rod without killing him. I was willing to tweak Elliot's fate, protect him for saving me, but the police still had to be called.

"I'm getting my phone. We can't leave him here like this."

Elliot dumped the contents of my bag on the ground. "Where is it? You told Rod you had it in here."

"The phone isn't in there, Elliot. I told you, it's up in the grass."

A gleam appeared in Elliot's hand. He was holding my gun, fiddling with the trigger, as he barked orders at me. "Get the knife. Pull it out of him. We need it. Then go up to your car." I heard the click of the gun's cocking mechanism. "Did I ever tell you that Melinda Hastings called me a fat dirty loser?"

"Melinda?"

"She called me a toad, a lizard who should adapt to procreation without sex to spare females from having to mate with me. Pretty big words for a dumb drugged socialite, huh?"

There was a Holton student on the ground, dead by Elliot's hand and possibly my complicity. My sister had been missing for days, and if the past murders suggested a pattern, she was already dead. My mind felt like mud.

Think fast, Melone. Think fast.

But my brain was on hold because of the live gun twinkling in Elliot's hand.

"Elliot, do not play with the gun. It's loaded. We've got to call the police and find my sister."

"Your precious sister." He looked at me with the same piercing eyes I'd seen that first day he walked into my office. "After what you saw Sherman and Lipton do—take her away and get her drunk—you told *me* I wasn't allowed near her anymore—"

"I didn't say that—"

"But not Rod and Cory, the golden boys. She preferred their filthy company. And you started pushing me away, ignoring my calls, lying to me, treating me like a contagious leper."

"Elliot?"

"Like Lisa Cummings. She's another spoiled little shit."

"*Another?* Elliot what are you telling me?"

He trudged back to Rod's body. "I told you to get the knife and go up to your car!" He leaned over Rod, and as swiftly and stealthily as a bolt of lightning, he yanked the dripping knife out of Rod's neck. The lifeless body bounced twice on the ground under Elliot's wrenching force. Elliot remained stoic and unmoved by Rod's blood that had splattered all over the front of his shirt.

I watched the scene in horror. "Oh my god."

He looked down at his blood-splattered shirt and grimaced. "Fuck," he said. "I don't have a clean one."

"A clean one?" I repeated his words, buying time for the punch line, hoping he'd look up at me and laugh.

"Elliot?"

Then suddenly he seemed to have remembered me — that I was still there with him and he needed to answer me. To respond to my presence.

"You've made this very difficult, Miss Melone."

"Tell me what you mean. Tell me this is not what I think. Tell me it's a joke!" I screamed.

"It's not a fucking joke!" he screamed back. "Why didn't you stay away from me? Stay out of it."

"*It* . . . as in *murders*?"

He looked at me coldly, perhaps calculating his next move. But I'd never been able to read Elliot very well, and that fact was never more obvious to me than it was then, as he stood before me, the murderer who had been beside me all the time.

"Oh, Elliot . . . no . . ." And then what else could I say? The bridge between us had collapsed, and as if he had fallen into a bottomless gulf, the person I thought I'd known was lost to me.

"Elliot," I said again softly, trying to bring him back to familiar turf. "Let's talk this through. Like we have in the past."

"Don't patronize me. I'm sick of it."

"Okay, but think about this. What are your options now? What are you going to do without my help?"

"I don't need your help," he said calmly. "Because everyone thinks Sherman is the one. They'll think he killed Rod too. Especially after we plant the knife in his apartment."

"No! You're pissing me off now. We aren't *framing* anyone for anything. I'm calling the police. Put the goddamn gun down, tell me where Cassie is, and then just get out of here. I'll take care of the rest."

But what I knew then was that Elliot had no respect for me, or my ability to "take care" of anything. I was never Carlyle's cover, as Elliot had once suggested. Elliot had used me as his *own* cover. Had my presence at Holton actually extended his killing spree? Would he have been caught sooner if I'd not been hired and then used by him as a pawn? He had always been in control. Even when I unwittingly sought him out for help, Elliot allowed me to believe he was honored by my attention. He let me believe we were partners sharing a common goal, when all along he was using me for his own ends. And still, I had no good plan to deal with him, except to find out what he'd done with Cassie, and then get my family as far away from him as I could.

Elliot looked at me with a cocky expression. He was still clearly in control and in a world of his own as, I should have seen before now, he always had been. "You aren't getting any of this, are you?" he said.

I shivered in utter exhaustion. Fighting Rod suddenly seemed easy. Rod was driven by the fear and self-preservation of the innocent. But this person standing before me—I had no idea what provoked him—or what it would take to stop him.

As I stared at him, his chest began undulating in waves, each one deeper than the one before until each breath turned into an audible gasp. His intake of air became a high-pitched shriek, and then a long low growl of its exhalation, until he was gasping for air that suddenly stopped flowing in. His eyes widened. In seconds he would faint without breath. He dropped his head to his chest, not breathing at all, and held it there, and when he lifted his face to me, his lips had turned a grayish blue, and his eyes were rolling in their sockets.

"You can't breathe," I whispered.

I would have been terrified by an inability to breathe, but Elliot's face showed only anger, as if his body was disappointing him. He tried to answer me, but like the skipping of a scratched CD, only spurts of broken sounds came from his lips. He needed to talk, and he tried to force his throat open to speak, but between every word he pursed his lips and sucked in strangled streams of air.

"In the beginning . . . you're the one person . . . who . . . respected me. You listened to me. And I hoped Cassie . . . would too."

"Cassie's just a kid, Elliot. Like all these college girls, she was attracted to the glamour of someone like Sherman. You need someone older, more mature, who appreciates—"

Elliot was fiercely shaking his head, trying to stop me from talking so he could continue. He wasn't buying my babble. He had discounted my words for the obvious ruse they were.

"But she treated me like the others. That day . . . in the cafeteria. They came over and your bratty little sister . . . just walked away with them. I wasn't worth . . . a wave goodbye."

I stepped closer to him.

"Get away from me!"

The anger seemed to help him. He took a deep breath, but then began choking again. He lifted the loaded gun in his hand, threatening me to stay back.

I hugged my sides and began to shake. "Okay. Okay, Elliot. Calm down."

"Move back!" he hollered again.

Backing away, I lifted my hands in surrender. "But I thought you were worried about Lisa. You warned me about her cocaine addiction—tried to help her. Why?"

"She called me that night. Commanded me, like a servant, to bring my notes to Emily's room. I agreed to meet her at Sherman's party. But she wouldn't be seen with me there. She insisted on meeting outside. In the park." He smiled. "So, yeah, I agreed. I met her outside— in the park. She never made it to the party."

I felt a wave of nausea at the thrill he seemed to get in recounting his bloody revenge against Lisa. Sure, she was a bitch, but did she deserve to die over it? The law said she didn't.

"So you pretended to be worried about her. Just like with Cassie. You pretended to be concerned about her going off with Rod and Cory—but you were just obsessively jealous. But you can't *own* people, Elliot. You can't *control* everything."

Elliot was breathing loudly, watching my lips move but no longer listening to me. "You have to help me . . . get into Sherman's apartment so we can hide this knife there . . . okay, Miss Melone?" He was choking for air again.

"You can call me *Marianna* now," I whispered. "And you don't need to point the gun at me. Find your inhaler. You need it."

But Elliot, as always, was ahead of me. Instead of lowering the gun, he dropped the bloody knife to the ground, and with his free hand, he struggled to get into a side pocket of his jacket while he held the gun still aimed at me. It was loaded, cocked, and I was no hero, so I watched quietly as he found his inhaler and shot it twice into his mouth.

The color in Elliot's face was returning to normal, his lips were regaining color. He stood stone-faced as he held my gun in one hand and picked up the bloody knife with the other.

"Elliot, where is Cassie?" I asked carefully. I was afraid of him now as I realized all I'd missed when he'd acted as my ally. He planted seeds and culled information from me by day, while at night, he stalked and mutilated his prey. And now he had Cassie . . . "She's not one of them, Elliot. Cassie's just a middle-class kid who's had the same iPod since they first came out."

He nodded. "Emily wasn't like them either. Emily didn't throw her privileged background around like crisp hundred-dollar bills. But she knew I was the last person to see Lisa alive. I couldn't let her go." He looked down and grimaced, as if the thought of killing Emily made him sick, or sad. "I had to make it look like the others, but I tried to be gentle—"

"Stop it! I can't listen to this."

His head rose slowly to mine. His eyes were slit and questioning, as if he was trying to make me understand the necessity of his brutal acts—as if there were some logic to the murders that he could explain, and that I would understand. "Killing the others though," he said, "that was the pleasure I never got from them while they were alive because they thought they were too good for me."

"Okay, okay. I understand," I lied. "So now do you see what I'm saying? Cassie's a good girl like Emily. The others were drug-addicted ignorant bitches. And of course you're right, framing Sherman for the murders is brilliant.

Sherman will bring Carlyle down with him. It's ineluctable perfection."

He looked down at the gun in his hand and it glimmered as if the sun had given him a cue. "But you. What I do about you? You and Emily shouldn't have been hurt." He shook his head, still lowered. "I hate making mistakes."

I whipped away from him and stumbled up the slope toward my car, looking back to talk to him, to see if the gun was still aimed. I needed to keep Elliot talking and his finger on the trigger at rest. So I crawled and climbed and talked as he began to follow me like an obedient pet—with a gun in his hand, pointed at my back.

"Is Cassie all right?" I asked.

But Elliot had tuned me out. "We'll get the knife into Sherman's apartment."

"Okay. We can do that now," I said lightly, as if we had just agreed to share a cone of rocky road ice cream. "We'll get the knife into Sherman's place and then go get Cassie. Okay, Elliot? . . . okay?"

He jumped in front of me. "Stop talking to me like I'm a dumb kid. Forget Cassie. She's in my dorm room, but you won't see her again."

"Why won't I see her? What did you do?"

He stabbed the gun at me like an accusing finger, jabbing it toward my forehead with each emphatic statement. "*You* aren't as bright as I thought you were. I'm not letting *you* go. So it doesn't really matter where Cassie is because you're never going to see her again *anyway*."

"She's alive. Cassie's okay? Because if she's all right, I don't care what you want from me. You're wrong in thinking you have to hurt me—"

"Just go to the car and shut up."

I continued to talk as I faced forward and began climbing up the slope again. "Why can't we talk like we've done in the past? We always got along. We've always talked."

I felt the butt of the gun slam into the back of my head. I tripped and rolled on my back to watch his next move. He seemed so much farther away from me than the few feet he actually was. His eyes seemed clouded by a cataract film, as if he'd gone into a trance that I was just now beginning to realize might be the killer's haven. He was en route to that place where conscience is suspended.

"Get up," he said. "Don't talk anymore. Go to the car."

When we reached my car, he walked in front of me, opened the driver's door, and directed me in with the muzzle of the gun. I sat behind the wheel and I fumbled for the key in the ignition.

"Cory's apartment?" I asked.

"No. Give me the keys." His eyes were focused on some distant place. He would no longer look at me, and if the eyes are the bridge to the soul, he had tumbled into an abyss. I had the sense just then that one of us—or both—would never see another dawn.

"Listen, Elliot, I'll give you the keys. You take the car, and let me and Cassie go. There's no evidence linking you with the deaths and I won't say anything. Rod was self-defense. It's over. I quit my job at Holton. I'm never going back—"

"Too much has happened. Melinda, Lisa, Mila, Emily, and—" He glanced down the hill at Rod who was still drenching the ground with his last blood. "I hate mistakes."

He threw the bloody knife into the backseat and kicked me over to the passenger side. I surrendered the keys to him, knowing that if he drove, I would have some control. He turned the key in the ignition and started the engine. Pushing the gun into my temple, he ordered, "Sit up."

I had no sooner sat up than he slammed my forehead against the dashboard and I heard the painless crunch of the gun on my skull. When my eyesight returned, Elliot was out of the car. He leaned back into the driver's side and I grabbed his arm, not caring if the gun went off, only knowing I had run out of time. He tried to yank his arm from me, but I held the sleeve of his bloody shirt and I wouldn't let go. I needed to stay with him until I found my sister. I couldn't let him go until I knew she was safe.

He used my grip to drag me back across the front seat to the driver's side, and then he twisted my hand until it was bent against my forearm. I let go before my wrist snapped, and he slammed my head into the steering wheel. I was dizzy, nauseous. I closed my eyes and gasped for air, and somewhere in the din of my pounding head I felt him reach over me and release the parking brake and move the shift into drive. The door slammed closed, and the car began to roll forward, crackling over dried branches and dead leaves. I looked up at the river ahead as the car picked up speed and bounced forward. Another wave of nausea, and then I remembered the smell of vomit and I must have passed out, because when I awoke (or was I dreaming?), my Jeep was speeding down the embankment. River reeds raced by the windows as I struggled to unbuckle my seat belt, but too soon I felt the earth give way, and I looked up at the water surrounding me. And then from somewhere far away I heard a woman screaming. Screaming my sister's name. Screaming for her mother. Her father. Screaming, as water rose above the windows and the car made its bubbling descent to the bottom of the river.

CHAPTER FORTY-TWO

—∞∞∞—

Gone Fishing

SOMETHING JOLTED ME, THE car hitting bottom, and I awoke—a fish in a bowl. My ears were plugged in a watery silence. I heard a muffled hissing as the car engine gurgled to a halt. My fingers pushed through heavy water for the window control, but the engine had sputtered dead and the control was useless. I needed a breath. Just one more breath and I could try to push open the door. I felt my lungs burning and my vision going dark. I passed out again and was dreaming of Mike. Underwater, his black hair billowed around his face through the window. Air bubbled from his mouth. Those fierce deep-blue eyes came toward me and then away and back again as he pounded his fists against the glass, trying to hit me. He was angry, screaming something at me.

Maybe he had come with Elliot and was trying to kill me. But I wasn't afraid. Let him kill me fast so the tight burning in my chest would subside. I wanted to let Mike in, to hold him, wrap my legs around his body, take a deep breath from his mouth. I just wanted air. I tried to open the car door for him, let him in, but I couldn't budge it. Mike was slamming something against the window. A car jack? Muscles contorted his angry face, but as hard and fast as he tried to bang against the glass, his movements under dense water were slow and awkward. He seemed to be striking at me. When I reached up to guard my face, shattered glass floated at me. Mike lunged in, pulled me out, and dragged me farther underwater.

My vision went in and out of focus, dark then light, then a total blackout, until I awoke in the pool I swam in as a child. Almost drowning once, I'd been terrified of water ever since. Mike dragged me to the deepest end, where my feet couldn't touch the ground. I rubbed my mouth against his lips and watched my hair swirl around his face. Taking the air from his mouth—his lips over mine—he gave me his breath. He pulled away from me, swimming up, and the world went dark again as I knew it would if he ever stopped kissing me.

Then the water was gone, and we were on dry land, but I still couldn't breathe. And Mike was still angry. Why? Why, Mike? What did I do? His fist came at me again, slamming the flat of his hand against my face. Slapping me again and again.

"Goddamn you!" he screamed. "Fuck you! Fuck you!"

He punched his fist into my chest, over and over, and I felt nothing but sadness.

He was on top of me now, coming down at me, angrier than before. He was tired, and dripping, and the look on his face told me he didn't want to do it anymore. He wanted to stop hitting me. One more time, his face told me, and he would finish. With one more hard blow, I would stop breathing forever and finally sleep.

MY EYES BLINKED open to a paramedic in a white uniform who was holding an ammonia tab under my nose. His face was looming above me. I raised my hand to touch his face, to see if he was real, but my arm was too heavy to lift. He was so far away, and beyond him, farther in the distance, were branches of a weeping willow tree and then a darkening sky. The wind had picked up.

"You guys have a blanket in the truck?"

I turned my head toward the gruff voice. Mike was tearing off his wet clothes. "Can't you see she's shivering like a live wire?"

Mike was shirtless and dripping, yelling into a cell phone for backup.

The paramedic brought a blanket and dropped it at Mike's feet, then backed away from me, letting Mike take his place at my side. Mike knelt and savagely ripped off my wet jacket as if he were doing it for himself and not me, like I was a child who didn't know better and had to be roughly disciplined. He pulled at the buttons of my blouse until they broke away all at once. Bending me over his forearm, he slid my blouse off from behind. With only a bra on, I felt instantly warmer. He grabbed the ambulance-issue blanket from the ground and covered me, tucking the sides underneath me.

Each shallow breath burned deep inside my chest. I tried to speak but every word was a cough. I tried again and again until I felt a soft stream of painless air come through my throat. I formed the air into a soft whisper.

"Kiss me again, Mike."

"Later, babe. You just threw up."

He stood at the sound of approaching sirens. Another patrol car had driven down the embankment. Vince got out with the driver and was standing with uniformed police. Behind them, Laurie and Shannon emerged from Shannon's white Suburban and were running toward me.

Shannon bowed by my side. "What happened here, sweetie?"

"My car," I coughed. "In the water."

"Oh shit."

"Cassie?" I whispered again through my burning throat.

"There's a dragnet in Massachusetts. All of Cape Cod is out searching with dogs."

"Not at the Cape . . . Here . . . in Providence."

"We got that warrant for Sherman's place. She isn't there. No sign of her around here either. You know something we don't?"

I nodded. "No car. Only mine . . . in the water. He might be walking."

"Who?"

"Elliot Orenstein. Hastings. Mila. Emily. All. Has Cassie too."

Laurie, who had been standing behind Shannon, quickly started screaming to the cops: "Wait a minute! There's another guy involved." Then she looked back to me. "You didn't kill Lipton?"

I shook my head weakly at the absurdity of their assumption that I, even in self-defense, could so viciously slam a knife into someone's neck. "He could be on foot."

"Who is it?" Vince Piganno's face was pudgy as he leaned over me. Gravity was unkind to him. But it was a warm face, soft and concerned, eyebrows furrowed, the kind of face you want on your side.

"Vince," Shannon said. "Elliot Orenstein. Is he a student at Holton? He has Cassie too."

"Christ almighty. We weren't even warm on this one." He lifted his head and screamed to one of the cops. "She doesn't look good. White as a Lutheran. Someone get her to the hospital. And I want more uniforms here. We're looking for another guy."

"Vince," I said.

"Shut up. You're going to the ER."

"Piganno?" Carlyle's thin voice came from somewhere behind me. "You and I have to talk," he said firmly but weakly.

Vince barked his response. "Who the hell called you here? I'll talk to you downtown, Carlyle, when your face is in stripes for being the biggest drug trafficker since the Boston crime family. You're a freakin' kingpin. Go back to your private den and wait for the cuffs."

"Jeff Kendall gave him the heads-up you were on your way, Vince," Mike said quietly. "Kendall's been telling him our every move."

Vince looked back at Carlyle. "You're as guilty as the day is long. You knew about those kids—rich little punks—and their drug-importing business. And, McCoy, it was right under your nose too. So if you don't behave I'll put you in the cell next to him."

Carlyle stepped forward. "I did not know the extent of Nazir's involvement with Sherman. I thought it was Sherman and Lipton and a few parties. You can't prove I knew anything else. And why would I get involved in such a dirty affair? Your reasoning is flawed, Vince."

"Tell it to the Feds. You were probably getting drug

money from students and calling it *donations* from their families. Alumni donations, my ass."

"That's absurd and you know it. We have to report the source of donations internally even if they remain anonymous to the public."

A paramedic shoved the sparring duo of Carlyle and Piganno out of the way and pushed an oxygen mask over my face. I swatted him away and pulled the mask away.

While Vince and Carlyle were busy taking verbal shots at each other, Mike returned stealthily to my side and helped me sit up. He held his hand on my forehead and lowered his lips to mine, kissing me lightly.

I put my lips to his ear and whispered, "Lippitt House. Elliot said Cassie's in his dorm room. Go—before the police. He might hurt her if he hears sirens or sees cops. He might trust you—alone."

Topless and now dry, I was beginning to shiver.

Mike took off and pushed Shannon to my side. She began removing her jacket.

"Shannon, we've got to go get Cassie."

"And where do you think you're going half-naked?" Shannon said. "Who do you think you are? Me?"

"It might be too late. We've got to get her *now*. Get me out of here."

"They'll stop us," she whispered. "You need a hospital. Maybe you just let me and Laurie go."

"Help me up. Pretend you're taking me to the ER."

Laurie and Shannon hoisted me up. While Laurie dressed me in Shannon's leather jacket, Shannon spoke in her tough voice loud enough for Vince and anyone else within a one-mile radius to hear her. "We're taking her to Rhode Island Hospital. If anyone needs to know."

Shannon and Laurie at my sides, I hobbled to

Shannon's Suburban, where they put me in the backseat and got in the front.

"Where to, boss?" Shannon asked over her broad shoulder.

"Lippitt House."

CHAPTER FORTY-THREE

———◦◦◦◦———

Going Home

ON MY DIRECTION, SHANNON drove to Elliot's dorm. We'd already had our argument in the car, both Shannon and Laurie telling me it was a really dumb idea. Elliot might have gone there, and we would be putting Cassie in worse danger by backing him up against a wall. Let the police go first. I argued my purely emotional position: There was no way he'd go there immediately after a double murder—Rod's and mine. He'd just take off. And I didn't care anyway. I was going wherever I thought Cassie was. My unspoken fear being that Elliot wouldn't go there because Cassie was already dead.

"Just go," I ordered. "I don't have the strength to explain."

In deference to my weakened physical and emotional state (under normal circumstances Shannon would have told me to go pound sand and then done whatever she wanted), Shannon followed my command and pulled her Suburban to the front doors of Lippitt House. She and

Laurie hopped out and held on to me as we walked slowly through the main doors and located Elliot's name next to the bell for Apartment 4F. We made a keyless entry by ringing every doorbell until someone buzzed us up.

Laurie was planning our break-in as we walked to the end of the hall to Elliot's room.

"He's not going to invite us in for tea and scones. Do you have any ideas on how to break a door down?"

"I'll get one of the guards to open it," I said, remembering Elliot's suggestion.

Laurie suggested straightforward guile. "Is he Jewish? I'll pretend I'm from the Jewish Defense League and we need signatures for something."

Shannon stopped walking and looked at Laurie as if she had just vomited all over herself. "And I always thought *you* were the smart one."

"Shut up then," Laurie quickly retorted. "What do *you* suggest?"

"Um . . . gee . . . let me think. How about breaking the fucking door down with our feet?"

"In your brand-new Giuseppe Zanottis? I don't think so. Unless you're planning to jimmy the lock with your metal heel tips."

I snapped at them with the little energy I had left. "Please stop fooling around. Cassie might be in there." Then I put my ear against the door.

While the girls stood back and waited, I listened to silence for half a minute. Shannon gave me her cell to dial the guard station and Laurie simply turned the knob. The door was unlocked.

Elliot's bed, apparently rarely slept in, was blanketed in books. Clothes and sneakers were strewn on the floor. The room had a familiar metallic odor.

Shannon lit a cigarette the way cops always did at the morgue to cover the smell of blood and corpses. "It friggin' smells like guts in here," she whispered.

Next to Elliot's computer on a white towel sat an opened bottle of Heinz white vinegar. Next to that were several beakers and eyedroppers—a veritable chem kit.

One glance around the room told us that Cassie wasn't there. What were Elliot's interests? Where else did he hang out? I cursed myself for having been in his company so often and knowing so little about him.

Cassie had dismissed him too—a nerdy scientist who smells, she'd called him. So why had she left camp with him? Had he lured her away with some story about an emergency involving me? A chill went through me as I thought that maybe he'd given her a glimpse into the future—that I was the Holton murderer's next intended victim.

And why hadn't Cassie called me to verify? But I already knew the answer. That little Band-Aid of advice—the words of wisdom I'd offered that day at Nick and Tony's. What had I said? "Don't trust Sherman and Lipton . . . They're drugging girls and raping them. . . . How's your tutoring going with Elliot? . . . Elliot's the kind of guy you can trust." Isn't that the message I'd inadvertently given her? I might as well have delivered Cassie to the murderer's front step.

An ear-splitting pop cracked the air.

Shannon, Laurie, and I screamed in unison. No stranger to the sound of guns, we knew the shot was close by.

"The bathroom," Laurie whispered, pointing to a door camouflaged in the wall behind us.

We ran in and found Mike staring at us with a puzzled look on his face. His confused expression was unfamiliar;

his bravado under pressure was second only to Vince's, and Mike was never at a loss for action, even if it was the wrong one. So I knew by his stillness, the sad look on his face, that something was wrong. Very wrong.

Laurie grabbed my elbow. I pushed away from her, reached Mike, and stopped. As if he were the curator of an art gallery and were proudly presenting his newest gala, he backed away from me slowly, hesitantly, waiting for my reaction to this abstract painting in broad splatters of scarlet red—the color still wet—that surrounded me on the walls and ceiling, and, as I watched, dripped down the front of Mike's white shirt.

I heard a cell phone click open, an odd softness in Laurie's voice, then a rare whisper and the word "ambulance."

Shannon was inching up behind me.

Mike reached out his hand to me and took me by the wrist, pulling me to him. I watched helplessly as his eyes flickered and his head fell forward to his chest as he crumpled slowly against the wall and slid to the floor. I looked up at the sound of the approaching sirens. And that's when I saw Elliot partially hidden behind shower curtains, standing in front of the bathtub with my Walther .380 in his hand. It was pointed at my head.

Shannon, standing next to me like a crossing guard, lifted her left arm slowly and held the flat of her hand toward Elliot. "Stop," she said softly. "Think about this. You don't really want to do that."

As she spoke softly to him, wooing him with a gentleness I'd never heard in her voice before, her right arm swung weightlessly up by her side, and the pop of her gun echoed through the air only after the red spot between

Elliot's eyes began to drip. He stared blankly at me, one, two seconds, then folded to the floor.

Shannon holstered her gun and went directly to the tub, sweeping the curtains aside in one swift motion. Cassie was in the bathtub, drenched in blood.

"No! Cassie!" I couldn't run to her. My legs were stone. My body finally failing me under this latest shock.

My little sister lay motionless, her eyes closed, her head tilted to the side facing us, her lips parted. She didn't look dead, but I knew she was. She couldn't have been in a bathtub in a dorm room for three days and still be alive. She was spunkier than that. Cassie would have gotten away—if she could have.

"Shannon . . . Laurie . . ." I had finally been taken down. I rolled into a cocoon on the floor, and wailed like a baby. "I can't . . . Help me."

Laurie left me and went to Shannon, who was bending down to Cassie.

On her knees, Laurie gently placed her hand on Cassie's forehead.

"It's okay, baby," Laurie said, wiping Cassie's wet hair from her face. "It's okay. It's over."

"*No, Laurie!*" I screamed. "*Noooo . . . ! Cassie!*"

Laurie turned to Shannon, who was already on her phone dialing 911 again.

My body was burning. Sweating. And then freezing cold.

And then darkness.

CHAPTER FORTY-FOUR

Do Not Disturb

WHEN I AWOKE, LAURIE was rifling through the metal drawers of my bedside table. My forehead had been bandaged and an intravenous drip stand was by my bed. The saline bag was empty and the needle had been removed from my hand while I slept.

"Look at this," Laurie said, lifting a black book from the drawer. "They put Bibles in the drawers here. What do they think this is? A Holiday Inn?"

"More like a YMCA flophouse if you ask me," Shannon quipped from a distance. "No wonder everyone gets sick in hospitals. This septic tank needs a Roto-Rooter house call."

I watched their comedy routine and listened patiently. I was afraid to interrupt them, to say my sister's name. I was afraid to ask the obvious. They would tell me in their own time and I would wait. They were making jokes and I was terrified, because I knew the longer they avoided the issue, the more jokes they told, the worse it would be when they finally told me.

Laurie, as if hearing my internal reasoning, or reading the fear in my eyes, quickly moved onto the bed with me. "She's in the next room. Orenstein drugged her senseless but nothing else. She'll be fine. Your parents are shuffling back and forth between your rooms. They're with her now." Laurie flipped the Bible open. "Now let us all join hands for the reading of a passage from Psalms."

I heard Shannon's guffaw from across the room. She walked over to me with an unlit cigarette hanging from her lip while Laurie slammed the book closed and threw it back into the drawer.

"Haven't you smoked that damn thing yet?" I asked.

"Oh yeah? Well, you look like something the cat dragged in."

I looked up at Shannon seriously now. "Elliot Orenstein?"

"On a slab. And let me tell you, he looks a hell of a lot better than you do right now."

Shannon and Laurie laughed, and somewhere in the distance I heard Beth's small voice.

"I don't know how you two can make jokes at a time like this."

Shannon pulled a chair to my bedside and joined Laurie. Beth walked over and I saw her sweet, liquid-blue eyes over me. God, how I missed them.

"How could I have trusted that sick bastard Elliot with Cassie? How could I have been so wrong about him? Crazy Lisa," I said. "And Melinda and poor innocent Emily. All of them killed by a psychotic nerd who was tired of being rejected. He just wanted a girl to take him seriously."

Then I remembered Mike, but his name caught in my throat and I went silent again, because I knew that when the girls thought it was time—when they thought I was ready—we'd talk about him too. Talk about how he'd charmed me, then frightened me into suspecting him; how he'd saved me from the river; how he'd found Cassie. And how he died.

"Don't be so naive," Laurie said quickly. "Elliot Orenstein didn't serial-mutilate and kill because of a broken heart. He had some serious head issues going on that we can't even hope to understand. And he was like the 'cunning spider to the fly.' Everyone trusted him. Including you, Mari. I've got to say, I'm a little surprised."

"Stop it," Beth said. "Leave her alone. No one even knew he existed, that's how close *we* were to *not* finding him. Mari got that serial nutcase all by herself."

"I'm not sure who got who. He was this brilliant kid pretending to help me solve a murder, and all the time, he wanted the information just to see how much I had on him. And he always looked so pathetic. I felt sorry for him without ever feeling his rage underneath."

Then Laurie again. "Forget about it. What did the Bard say? All's well that ends well. Orenstein is history. Now Vince is lusting after Sherman. He wants Carlyle too, but I think he's stumped again by the elusive dean. Vince claims Carlyle was taking a finder's fee on the dope and loading up Holton coffers with 'discreet private donations.' Imagine that? Dean Kenneth Oberlin Carlyle, the blue-blooded blackmailer."

"I think all Carlyle wanted was the presidency when Hatchett retired."

"If Vince has his way, Carlyle's retirement will be in

some cushy federal prison." Laurie pushed hair out of my sweaty face.

"Why is there never smoking in hospitals?" Shannon said. "I mean, not just now, with all these godforsaken no-smoking laws. They've never let you smoke in these joints."

"Oxygen, for one thing," Beth said. "And then there's always the fact that people are usually sick in here and don't want to add lung cancer to their medical records."

"Thanks, Bethster."

"And why do you always have to make up nicknames for people? It's just *Beth*."

"I bore easy," Shannon stated unapologetically. She threw her still-unlit soggy Camel in the trash.

Laurie relinquished her seat on my bed to Beth, but she kept talking as she walked to the window and pulled open the curtains. Laurie was still working the case. "We had Sherman in our sights for a drug operation from California. But through phone records and a tail, we found something even bigger."

"Mila Nazir," I said.

Laurie nodded. "That's when the Feds joined the party."

"But you knew all this, Mari. We kept you filled in on everything," Beth said. Then she glanced at her two other AG friends. "Didn't we?"

But Vince Piganno prevented Laurie and Shannon from answering. His voice boomed through the open doorway. "You got good instincts, Meloni, that's why I let you take that job at Holton. It's instincts that were telling you these murders were connected to the drugs. I always wanted to dig deeper and get inside Holton to Carlyle.

When he offered you that job, I got to thinking. If I didn't let you back from your suspension you'd accept his offer and be inside enemy territory without passing Go. It seemed like a stroke of genius at the time."

"You did what?" Shannon barked.

"Holton's a fortress," he said. "We could only pussy-foot around it. I needed an insider there and I knew Mari would rip the guts out of it. And she didn't disappoint me." He looked at me now like a coach at his prized fighter. "Even if Carlyle manages to slip through my fingers again, Holton will never be the same."

"You *let* her work there to go after Carlyle?" Laurie said. "After all the begging and plotting we were doing to get her back . . . why didn't you just friggin' say so?"

"Wait a minute. I didn't *put* her there. I suspended her to scare the crap out of her. Then Carlyle offers the job and I thought, Hey, great. We'll get dirt on that school that we could never get on the outside."

Vince could have saved us a lot of sleepless nights if he'd told us his plan from the start. Somewhere inside him, he had a big heart, but he was the kind of guy who forgot that other people had them too. Typical Vince Piganno. Play with people's lives like they're chess pieces because he believed his reasons were altruistic. He was a big egotistical kid with an underdeveloped conscience.

I wondered if Vince believed in God.

"And I told you that day in my office, Meloni, if I'd thought for a second I was putting your sister in danger, I wouldn't have done it. Who knew you'd drag her onto the campus?"

My silence allowed them all to collectively ponder Vince's question. Slowly but surely, all eyes in the suddenly stifling room turned to me.

Shannon, more calmly than I expected, said, "Wait a minute. You knew what he was up to and you didn't tell us?"

I took a deep breath and lay my head on the chopping block. "I hooked Cassie up with Elliot to tutor her for her SATs. But I *never* would have done that if I thought I was there as a plant. And by the time Vince told me his *plan*, Cassie was already missing. And I didn't think Vince wanted anyone else to know until the whole thing was over. . . ."

"That's what I like to hear," Vince said. "Your first loyalty should always be to me."

Though I was thinking it, I didn't have the heart to tell Vince that I *would* have told the girls if my head hadn't been so muddled with trying to find Cassie. I just never got the chance.

Shannon scoffed at Vince. "You should have told *me* what you were up to so I wouldn't have used your miserable mug as target practice every afternoon."

"All right. That's enough fun for one day, girlies." Vince had never walked through the doorway into my room and had already pivoted to leave. Over his shoulder he said, "Meloni, take a week off or whatever the docs say, and then *all of you* back to work as usual. I suspended Jeff this morning for insubordination—he was telling Carlyle every time I took a shit."

"Byron Eckert," I said. "Carlyle's right-hand man. That's why she was getting antsy."

"*She?*" Shannon said.

"Yeah, but a man in more ways than name only. She must have known Jeff was talking to Carlyle and she got scared that maybe she was out of the loop."

"Well, Jeff Kendall's out of my loop for the time

being," Vince said. "Of course his old man will make me an offer I can't refuse and I'll have to take him back eventually, but I still have your empty seat to fill, so, Meloni, you're back in." He raised his arm in the air for a wave goodbye, and then lumbered out and was gone without so much as a *sayonara*.

Shannon got up to leave. "I'm out of here too. Let's wrap this reunion up so I can grab a smoke. And they're not keeping you here long, Mari. Sending you home with some antibiotics or something. That river was pretty mucky. It's probably an illegal waste dump. They don't want you getting an infection and dying now that you're a big hero. Other than that, your lungs are probably cleaner than mine. Come on, we'll take you for a spin around this depressing joint before we leave. You can go visit your sister down the hall."

Laurie Nightingale and Nurse Beth loaded me into a wheelchair. Beth took the reins and we began an exciting trek down the hospital corridors. At the nurses' station Laurie detoured for a quick chat while Beth put my wheels on hold. Laurie walked back to us, nodded at Beth, and we were on our way again. Shannon excused herself at a bank of elevators so she could head outside for her smoke and an early escape. "See you all later. I'm going back to the office and then I need a drink. Laurie, Beth? About seven? The Fez? Mari, we'll get you a to-go bag. Vox rocks, right?"

Beth shook her head in disgust and Laurie filled Beth and me in on what she had learned at the nurses' station. "Cassie's down in the lab getting some blood work done. Your parents rode down with her."

Beth nodded at the information but continued pushing me down the corridor, away from my room. At the end of the hall we stopped and she rolled me through an open doorway where two beds lay side by side. One empty, the other—

"Hey, babe." His weak voice rose from the bed nearest the window.

My heart fluttered in my chest.

In Elliot's bathroom, after he'd been shot, Mike didn't fall. He let go, let his body slide along the wall to the floor. And that halcyon look in his eyes before they closed for the last time had screamed so loudly of peaceful surrender that I too had simply let him go without a fight. We had both surrendered him to death so quickly that not for one second did I believe he could still be alive.

Beth rolled my chair to the side of the bed where Mike lay flat, wrapped in gauze from neck to waist. His bare arms lay outstretched by his sides.

Cassie was fine. Mike was alive. I closed my eyes and said a silent prayer of thanks to a God I continued to hope would disprove my current agnostic beliefs and actually turn out to exist.

When my lids opened, the tears dripped down my face in a flood. Mike's devilish smile broke through the drugged pain of his face, and he winked.

I felt a fever coming on. I couldn't catch my breath. The room was spinning. I felt faint. I still had no immunity to Mike's infectious wink.

"Hi, slugger," he said. "You okay?"

Laurie and Beth were already backing out of the room.

"Hey, girls," I said. "Do me a favor on your way out? Close the door after you, and put the Do Not Disturb sign up."

"Hah!" Laurie laughed and pulled the door closed, leaving Mike and me alone.

I pulled myself out of my wheelchair, and sat softly on the side of his bed. I ran my hands lightly over his gauzed chest. "You rotten bastard," I said. "I was convinced you were dead."

"And that's my fault?"

"No. I'm just a pessimist."

He lifted his hand unsteadily and stroked my face. "We're quite the disabled pair, aren't we, babe?"

"That term of endearment is getting a little shopworn. Can't you come up with anything besides 'babe'?"

"You mean like one that's just for you?"

"Yes," I whispered, muzzling his mouth with my lips. "Mmm . . . Speak to me with that unbelievable kisser."

"I'm all lips, babe, but can't we save the talking for later?"

"Who said anything about talking?"

"Whatever you say. *Darlin'*."

About the Author

———◆◆◆———

Celeste Marsella received her B.A. and M.A. from NYU and her J.D. from New York Law School. She is a member of four state bars—New York, Pennsylvania, Rhode Island, and Florida—and has actively practiced in all except Florida. In Rhode Island, where her daughter was born, she worked in a gritty criminal law firm. Celeste now writes full time and is currently at work on her next novel in this series, *Perfectly Criminal*, coming from Dell in Spring 2009.

If you enjoyed *Defenseless*,
don't miss Shannon's story:

PERFECTLY CRIMINAL

A NOVEL BY
CELESTE MARSELLA

ON SALE APRIL 2009